# Chronicles of the White Rose

## Book One

## The Stradivarius Affair

By

Laurie J. Kendall

© 2003 by Laurie J. Kendall. All rights reserved.

No part of this book may be reproduced, stored in a retrieval system, or transmitted by any means, electronic, mechanical, photocopying, recording, or otherwise, without written permission from the author.

ISBN: 1-4107-3900-7 (e-book)
ISBN: 1-4107-3899-X (Paperback)

This book is printed on acid free paper.

1stBooks - rev. 04/21/03

*This book is dedicated to my soul mate and life companion Bobbie DeVoll. Without her love, faith, and support this history would have been impossible to tell.*

I would also like to thank Cheryl Dunye, who taught me that "sometimes you have to create your own history."

iv

# Prologue

# Gay Berlin
## 1927

John Carrington strolled along the Kunfurstendamn, anxiously glancing at his watch and then to the nearest street number. "Where the hell is it?" he muttered to himself.

In the 1920s, Berlin had the reputation of being the gayest city in Europe. The Kunfurstendamn district, with its carnivalesque atmosphere was a big money-making area that the growing tourist industry took full advantage of, offering tours that catered to wealthy homosexuals and the curious elite. Everything was for sale on the Kunfurstendamn. Excellent cuisine, local brew, voyeuristic delight, music and merriment, pleasure or pain, one had only to name their appetite. The district had over forty gay bars, a fine assortment of cafes, and a dozen or so smoky cabarets. It was also home to more than two thousand male prostitutes. Foreigners and tourists flocked to the district hoping to escape the sexual repression of their own cities, while enjoying the sensual freedom the Kunfurstendamn offered. Even the Berlin police understood the benefits generated in the Kunfurstendamn, and were happy to overlook Germany's homosexual law, Paragraph 175, for a share in the profits.

"Looking for someone, handsome?" John heard a soft falsetto voice whisper over his shoulder. Startled, he spun around to see a lipsticked and rouged young drag queen, wearing a red chiffon evening gown and gloves.

"Uh, oh, no!" John stammered, as a blush rose on his cheeks.

With an exaggerated pout on her lips, the young queen shrugged her shoulders and replied with a sigh, "Oh, so sad for you, and too bad for me." Then she grinned, turned on her heels, and started walking back to her corner.

"Wait!" John called. "Can you tell me where the National Cafe is?"

"Ah, so I was right after all," teased the soft falsetto voice. "The handsome stranger does belong to the tribe, but not to Berlin. Yes?"

"Yes," John answered. "I'm from England."

"Oh, I do so adore Englishmen. You are here for the opening of the film? Yes?"

"What film?"

The young queen slid closer to John, and gracefully caressed his cheek with a long gloved finger. "Why, *Laws of Love,* of course," she said with a wink, and an inviting smile. "It's the remake of the 1919 film, *Different From The Others,* staring that absolutely gorgeous man, Conrad Veidt. They also say that our godfather plays a small part toward the end."

"And just who might our 'godfather' be?" John asked with a tease in his voice.

"Have you not heard of our glorious godfather, Magnus Hirschfeld?" her falsetto voice quipped indignantly.

"Yes, of course I have heard of him," John answered flatly. "That's who I'm here to meet, Magnus Hirschfeld. In fact, I'm late for an appointment with him. So, can you direct me to the National Cafe or not?"

With a flip of her wrist the beautiful young queen pointed, "It's up the street, about three blocks on the right." And with another exaggerated pout on her lips she whined, "I will only forgive you for disappointing me so badly because your appointment is with our godfather. But you must promise to come back and escort me to the theater another night."

"You have my word, my lady," John grinned as he made a slight bow. Then he turned and raced up the street.

On his way, John took closer notice of his surroundings. It wasn't long before he found himself standing under the Grand Theater marquee. The bright lights spelled out *"Laws of Love, Staring Conrad Veidt and Magnus Hirschfeld."* A half dozen or so drag queens milled around one side of the entrance, expecting to be purchased and escorted inside, while a larger group of well dressed young men stood on the opposite side, expecting the same thing. Each of the queens toyed with John as he paused to read the marquee.

"Is the tall and handsome stranger in need of a date, perhaps?" they catcalled to him. John grinned and shook his head. Then he chuckled to himself. *Berlin is not that much different than Piccadilly, back home.*

One of the well dressed boys came over to John, trying to engage him. "Perhaps the gentleman prefers gentlemen?"

"Actually," John answered, "he does. But alas, not tonight, I'm afraid."

The young man pulled his shoulders up square, bowed slightly, and with a smile on his lips replied, "Another time perhaps. Good evening to you, Sir."

"Good evening to you," John answered with a quick nod. Then, turning to continue on his way, he nearly ran over a couple getting out of a taxi. "Excuse me, Sir!" he exclaimed.

Instantly he realized his mistake, for they were obviously a lesbian couple. The taller one was dressed in a black tuxedo, complete with tails, and the other wore an evening gown similar to those worn by the drag queens. "Pardon me. Excuse me," John sighed with embarrassment. The tux-clad dyke gave him an angry glare, and proceeded to escort her date to the ticket booth without dignifying his apology.

Flustered by all the distractions, John headed up the street again. As he walked he noticed every street corner had a news stand that displayed a variety of different gay or lesbian publications for sale. Some were obviously political papers while others were purely for entertainment. Many headlines spoke to the issue of repealing Paragraph 175, and what new strides were being taken in that direction. John already knew that Paragraph 175 was the German sodomy law, and thought of the lesbians he had nearly run over. *The law doesn't apply to them in any way. Lesbians are relatively immune where the law is concerned.* Currently, the Nazi party was arguing in the Reichstag to expand Paragraph 175 to include lesbian sex, but the women's movement had finally taken action on behalf of lesbian sisters and started a counter lobby against the Nazi proposal.

Magnus Hirschfeld's name was splattered all over the front pages of many newspapers. Since 1919, when he opened his *Institute for Sexual Science* in Berlin, Hirschfeld had dedicated his life to the abolition of Paragraph 175. Being a physician as well as a homosexual, Hirschfeld had a keen interest in sexology and the law. Over the years he had written several books and articles that included the *Yearbook for Sexual Intermediate Stages, Scientific Humanitarian,* and *Homosexuality.* He had come to the conclusion that homosexuality was a purely biological matter, and therefore should not be legislated by the government.

Hirschfeld's institute, housed in a luxurious Berlin mansion, was staffed with four physicians and their assistants. Along with its dedication to the study of homosexuality, the institute also provided a variety of other services. Medical treatment was made available to those who could not afford it otherwise, and who were suffering from venereal diseases or other potentially embarrassing afflictions. A staff psychiatrist provided therapy to those with mental disorders. Every class of people in Europe utilized the institute's programs for sex education, family planning, marriage and career counseling, as well as for coming to terms with their homosexuality. And for students, the mansion's grand library held the most extensive collection of books and manuscripts concerning homosexuality in the entire world. The institute also provided legal counseling for men who had been arrested and charged with violations of Paragraph 175. By and large, however, it was the mansion's museum that brought most visitors to the institute.

The curious came to see the museum's extensive collection of sadomasochistic devices; whips and chains designed to give pleasure and pain. They also came to see the portraits of famous couples such as Whitman and Doyal, Ludwig and Kainz, Wilde and Lord Douglas. The art gallery also housed paintings and photographs created by Hirschfeld's patients. From King Ludwig posing with his penis as his scepter, to scenes of bestiality, to an assortment of sordid bedroom photographs, these pictures represented every sexual activity and perversion known to humanity. However, it was the exhibition of fetish objects that made most visitors giggle. The museum displayed lacy ladies undergarments worn by Prussian Army officers under their uniforms, and high-heeled boots and open toed shoes for those with foot fetishes. Last, but not least, there were the garments of the exhibitionists. Trench coats and leggings, displayed on mannequins, flashed visitors as they passed the glass display cases.

Although fascinated, and anxious to see the institute for himself, it was Hirschfeld himself that John had come to see. John had been present at a lecture given by Hirschfeld in London several years earlier, and was eager to talk with him about his efforts at law reform, and what effect the Nazi party might have on those efforts.

With these thoughts running through his head, and again not paying attention to where he was walking, John ran squarely into a Brownshirt officer escorting a pretty young woman into a cafe. Before he could apologize, the Brownshirt grabbed John by his collar and spat in his face. "Watch where you are going, you filthy fagot!" he yelled. Then he shoved John down onto the sidewalk. "It's your kind who is degrading the purity of the Aryan race. If I were not with such a beautiful woman tonight, I would kill you where you lay. Now get out of my sight before I forget my lady is present."

John scrambled to his hands and knees and shook his head to regain his composure. Rising to his full height while adjusting his cuffs and collar, John stared at the officer. Then he reared back and let his fist fly. Instantly, the Brownshirt hit the cement and was out cold. John bowed deeply to the lady and said, "Pardon me, Fraulein, but your escort was very rude. Good manners are the mark of a gentleman. You would do well to remember that." Turning on his heels, John dashed away quickly, disappearing into the crowd. Up the street a few yards, he crossed to the other side, and there in front of him, stenciled in gold letters above the door were the words "National Cafe." *Finally,* John thought, *I could certainly use a cup of tea.*

Inside, he looked around to see if he could spot Magnus Hirschfeld. Instantly, John recognized the man in the back corner. Hirschfeld was a mature gentleman of about sixty years with light brown hair and prominent silver streaks running over his temples. But it was his thick spectacles and tailored black suit that John remembered most. He just stood there, momentarily transfixed, staring at the great man.

This was the man who had argued before the Reichstag for the abolition of Paragraph 175. This was the man the Brownshirts of Munich had beaten after a lecture and left for dead. This was the man who, when found by the police, was taken to a surgical clinic where he was diagnosed with

x

a skull fracture. The next morning the newspaper reported the attack had been fatal, and Hirschfeld read his own obituary. He was also the man who had been charged with, and found guilty of, disseminating obscene material to students when he had sent out his sexual survey to several Berlin schools. This was the man who had given such an impassioned speech in his own defense, saying:

*At the beginning of this week, a well-known homosexual student at the School of Technology poisoned himself because of his homosexuality. In my medical practice, I have at present a student in the same school who shot himself in the heart. Just a few weeks ago, in this very room, I attended a case against two blackmailers who had driven a homosexual gentleman - one of the most honorable men whom I knew - to suicide...I could present hundreds of cases like this, and others similar to it. I felt it was necessary to bring about this inquiry in order to free humanity of a blemish that it will some day think back on with the deepest sense of shame.*

Finally, John was about to meet the great man he had come to admire and respect so much.

If it hadn't been for Hirschfeld's work, the gay and lesbian people of Europe would never have enjoyed the freedoms they had in the twentieth century. Nor would they have had such a strong sense of identity. Neither John Carrington, nor Magnus Hirschfeld could ever have imagined how much that identity would mean when the Nazis came to power in 1933.

xii

# Chapter One

## Something In The Wind
## December, 1932

Night descended on the city of a thousand spires as Julius Barkowski and Leeza von Rauthenau made their way through the old city of Prague. Looking back from the Charles Bridge, the spires of Tynn Church began to fade into the darkness as the water of the Vltava River ran cold beneath their feet. Even the giant statues of the saints on the bridge began to fade. Only the lights of the votive candles illuminated their ghostly features.

When Julius spotted the first star of the evening, being as giddy as a schoolgirl, he stretched out his arms toward the heavens and twirled himself round and round, his violin case dangling at the end of one finger. "Star light, star bright, first star I see tonight. I wish I may, I wish I might, have the wish I wish tonight. And, I wish for a handsome prince in shinning armor to come to our concert tonight and fall madly in love with me!"

"Julius! You darling idiot!" Leeza chastised, gently punching him in the shoulder. "Have you not a brain in your head? That's a Stradivarius dangling on the end of your fingertip, not some silly rag doll. You simply must be more careful."

"Ouch! It is you who must be more careful, Leeza!" Julius pouted as he rubbed his shoulder. "What if you had bruised my playing arm? Remember, I am the star of the orchestra, you know!" Whining, Julius teased, "You're so butch! Such a brut!"

Julius Barkowski was a handsome young man of twenty-six. Tall and well proportioned, he carried himself with an air of sophistication and grace. His dark hair framed his noble features and his blue eyes sparkled in the candlelight. With his swarthy charm and good looks he could easily have been mistaken for Viennese royalty as he confidently ambled onto every stage, giving a slight bow to the audience, and taking the first violinist's chair.

Julius, however, was anything but royalty. Because he was a Jew, he had been raised in the Warsaw ghetto of Poland. His father, a cantor in the synagogue and tailor in a Warsaw department store, had encouraged Julius' musical talent from the time he could stand. At the age of five Julius began giving pantomime performances for his family. In the evenings, when the cantor would play a phonograph album of the symphony, Julius would jump to his feet and begin moving his fingers over an imaginary violin. It was then that cantor realized it was time for music lessons. Right from the start, it seemed Julius was a child protégé. He quickly surpassed teacher after teacher, and when he turned sixteen, the cantor sent him to study in Salzburg, at the Mozarteum.

Once there, music was not the only thing Julius learned. Free from the religious restrictions of a Jewish home, Julius quickly realized there was more to love than marrying an Orthodox woman, which he had never envisioned himself doing. Shortly after arriving in Salzburg, a handsome Viennese gentleman took notice of Julius and offered to show him around the city. Eventually, through this gentleman's strategic introduction Julius' talent was publicly recognized, and he was invited to join the Vienna orchestra at the Musikverein. The rest was, as they say, history.

Vienna had much to offer in the way of gay life. There were bars and coffeehouses, theaters and opera houses, and the city seemed to revolve around the love of music. Julius quickly became the darling of the gay community, having more fans than he ever could have imagined, and more prospective lovers than he knew what to do with. He constantly found himself surrounded by men of all ages, many of them wealthy and willing to shower him with gifts for the mere pleasure of being seen in his company. It wasn't long before Julius became accustomed to the finer things in life. Yes, Vienna was a cornucopia of delights for a young man with Julius' particular appetites, and he fully intended to sample each dish that was offered.

"How dare you call me such a name!" Leeza roared. "You know it isn't true. I'm just as feminine as you are!"

"Oh! Now who's not telling the truth? I don't have a feminine bone in my body!" Julius retorted. "I am a man of refinement, distinction, grace, and charm, who just happens to adore gentlemen of the same quality." Then, placing his hands on his hips, and grinning a devilish grin, he asked, "And, just how would you describe yourself, pray tell?"

Leeza leaned against the cold, stone railing of the Charles Bridge and thought for a moment. "I'm a strong, independent, self-reliant woman with more style than any one person has the right to possess," Leeza laughed. "And I just happen to adore ladies who are as charming and graceful as you are, dear Julius."

"Bravo, Leeza. Bravo!" Julius laughed as he gave her a friendly embrace.

In truth, Leeza was more feminine than Julius gave her credit for. Although she would never have described herself as a beautiful lady, in fact, she was. Leeza possessed a grace and elegance all her own, qualities that the public rarely glimpsed behind Julius' glory. Leeza was a remarkable woman. Possessing an extraordinary balance of strength and femininity, charm and passion, intellect and emotion. Although not the star that Julius was, she also had her fans. She was the orchestra's only lesbian violinist, and was quite the rage among the lesbian population of Europe. They appreciated her talent, but lusted after her absolutely perfect five foot six, trim figure. Her publicity photograph hung in almost every lesbian bar and cafe in Berlin. A photo of her in a black tuxedo with a white lace ascot, and her long black hair tied back with a white ribbon, almost became an object of worship for her adoring female fans.

Leeza was from one of Germany's oldest and noblest families. Her father, Wolfgang von Rauthenau, had built Rauthenau Steel with his younger brother Karl. Rauthenau Steel had been Germany's leading producer of steel for military armaments before the war. When Wolfgang was killed during the war, Leeza inherited his share of the company, and Karl became her surrogate father as well as the new president of Rauthenau Steel. Katrine, Leeza's mother, was a strikingly beautiful woman, but she had never quite recovered from the death of her beloved husband, and withdrew into her memories of Wolfgang and their life together. Her frail mental state had prevented her from being a real mother to Leeza. Karl, on the other hand, who had never married, fully enjoyed playing both mother and father to Leeza.

He made sure she wanted for nothing. When she showed an interest in music, he purchased lessons for her from the finest teachers in Berlin. Many nights he passed away the hours listening to Leeza play. By the time she was ten years old she had learned to play the piano, flute, and violin, but it was the violin that captured her heart. The small delicate instrument let her spirit sore above the mansion, beyond the city, to where dreams come true. Eventually, the teachers in Berlin told Karl that she should go to Vienna to study. There was nothing more they could teach her in Berlin. Karl had objected because Leeza was only sixteen years old at the time. Regardless of how she pleaded, he refused to let her go until she was eighteen.

"Bravo!" Julius sang out again. "That must be why you are absolutely mad about me, because of my charm and grace?"

"Oh, no!" Leeza giggled, "I love you for your rugged manliness."

4

As soon as she arrived in Vienna, Leeza fell passionately in love with her first female music teacher. Fortunately, the older Hanna Jaeger was wise to the doe eyed girl who stared at her with such longing. After their first week of practice together Hanna took Leeza out for coffee and pastry at the Sacher Hotel. Tenderly stroking Leeza's cheek, and taking her hand gently in her own, Hanna whispered, "Leeza, I am flattered by your affection." She dropped her head when she saw the glow of infatuation rise in Leeza's eyes. Pulling her hands away, she shook her head and sighed, "But, I am simply too old for you, child. You have your whole life in front of you, and mine is at the beginning of its end. Surely you know other young women who…"

Leeza was instantly crushed. Tears began flowing down her cheeks. She quickly excused herself from the table and ran to hail a taxi. Seconds later, Hanna was standing beside her as the cab pulled up. "I will see you home, Leeza," she whispered, gently taking Leeza's hand in her own.

As Hanna reached down to open the back door of the cab, Leeza exclaimed, "No, that's all right! I have made quite a fool of myself tonight. I think I would rather be alone."

"Nonsense. I won't hear of it," Hanna replied as she slid across the back seat of the cab. "Twenty-six Hegelgasse, bitte." Leeza stood outside the cab, dumbfounded. "Are you coming, Dear?" Hanna asked patiently. Just then it started to rain and Leeza reluctantly climbed in next to Hanna.

When they arrived in front of Leeza's building, Hanna said, "Bitte, please wait Driver." Then she followed Leeza through the glass doors into the lobby and up the first flight of stairs to her apartment. Leeza unlocked the door and stepped inside. When she turned to say good night, Hanna stepped inside, forcing Leeza to take a step back. Gently,

5

Hanna took Leeza's face in her hands and kissed her tenderly on the lips. Heat flooded Leeza's body and she parted her lips slightly. She felt Hanna's tongue, warm and sweet, enter her mouth. Hanna suddenly pulled away. The kiss was more than she had intended. "I could easily fall in love with you, Leeza. But it would not be fair to you." Then she turned and walked away.

Leeza's heart was broken, but she knew Hanna had been right. She knew she wasn't truly in love with Hanna, only that she had been in love with the possibility of love. The next day when she returned to the music school, the director told her that Hanna had come the night before with a message. She had been called away because of a family illness. He didn't know when Hanna would return, but Leeza knew she would never see her again, and ached with the knowledge.

A year later, after being invited to fill an open chair in the violin section at the Musikverein, Leeza met Julius. They had fallen deeply in love with each other from the first moment Leeza had entered the practice hall. It was platonic love of course, for they had each recognized a kindred spirit in the other. Through the years of working and traveling together they had become closer than siblings. Closer in fact, than many married couples. Traveling with the orchestra left them little time to develop serious outside love interests, so they quickly devoted themselves to each other.

"And, what is this about a prince in shinning armor?" Leeza quipped. "What about me?"

"Leeza, darling, you know I love you truly, but you simply don't have what I am in desperate need of."

"No. I don't suppose I do," Leeza sighed. "But, then again, you don't have what I am in desperate need of either. Would that you were truly a woman, Julius. I would love you all the more," she giggled.

"Look at us, will you! We're talented, beautiful, and ever so passionate, with no one to lavish ourselves on. What a pair!" Julius groaned as he gazed up into the sky. Then, excitedly he exclaimed, "But, there is still hope, dear Leeza. Look! Another star! Quick! Make a wish."

Leeza gazed in the direction Julius pointed and started to laugh. Stepping back from the railing, she stretched out her arms and twirled around as Julius had. "Star light, star bright, first star I see tonight. I wish I may, I wish I might, have the wish I wish tonight. Oh please God, bring a beautiful princess to our concert tonight. And let her fall hopelessly in love with me."

Julius stepped toward Leeza and swung his arm around her shoulder. "What else could she do, my darling? You are so beautiful. What woman wouldn't fall in love with you?"

Leeza pulled Julius closer, leaning her head on his shoulder with a sigh. "Oh, Jules, then why haven't I ever been truly in love before?"

"Because, my darling, you have this wonderful little notion that falling in love is all about romance. It's not, you know. You keep waiting for the perfect woman to come along and sweep you off your feet. You expect that your heart has to race and your knees have to quiver before you can make love to someone. Well, that's just nonsense. Sex has very little to do with love. So you might as well just jump in and get your feet wet. If you see something you like, buy it for heavens sake! At the rate you're going, you'll be a virgin until you are thirty."

Leeza pulled away from Julius and slapped his chest playfully. "I'm not a virgin," she exclaimed indignantly. Julius just grinned. "Well, not completely, anyway!" she frowned.

"Don't worry, my darling," Julius laughed. "When this holiday concert tour is over, I shall purchase you a beautiful princess for Christmas."

"I don't want you to purchase anyone for me, Jules. I want to fall in love naturally. When it happens, it happens."

"Whatever you want, my darling. But don't wait too long. Should my prince show up, I wouldn't want to leave you all alone."

Taking Julius' words to heart, Leeza glanced up at him and then back to the star. *Please bring a princess for me to love,* she thought. *I am so tired of being alone.*

Leeza had always been aware of her attraction to women, but she had never really allowed herself the pleasure of experiencing them. Over the last few years she had dated causally, but made sure that each date ended with nothing more than a kiss at the door. For Leeza, love and sex were one and the same. Making love was just that, creating love with someone whom you truly cared for. She could not imagine sharing such intimacy with someone who could never touch her soul.

*Making love should be a spiritual experience,* she thought, *not just a romp in the hay. But waiting for someone to touch my soul could take forever. Maybe Jules is right. Maybe love and sex are nothing more than a sport, and I should just learn to play the game. After all, isn't that how everyone else sees it? I just don't want to be alone for the rest of my life. Yet, in my heart I know there is someone out there for me. Someone who will love me as deeply and completely as I will love her. Be patient, Leeza. You'll find her,"* she told herself.

---

Karl von Rauthenau sat alone in his library reading the newspaper and sipping his morning coffee. His rich mahogany desk was stacked with business documents and memos waiting for his signature, but this morning he chose to ignore them. Rumors, whispered in his ear by business associates, suggested that Hitler was currently negotiating with President Hindenburg for control of the Reichstag. That thought disturbed Karl this morning. *It can never happen,* he thought. *The Nazis don't have enough seats in the Reichstag to take control.*

Even though Karl was the head of an old aristocratic family, he was a social democrat, and was sure that his party would never cater to the likes of Adolf Hitler. However, there on the front page of the newspaper was a picture of Hitler with his Brownshirts, parading in front of the Chancellery building in Berlin. The headline read: *"Hitler Declares Jews Backstabbers."*

Karl grumbled to himself, "Who does that upstart Bavarian corporal think he is? He's a funny little man, with a strange mustache. A charlatan, nothing more." Then he flipped through the rest of the paper for something more interesting to read. But still, the thought of Adolf Hitler in charge of the Reichstag sent a chill up his spine.

It was true that Germany suffered from economic hard times. With the guilt of the war laid squarely on its back, Germany found itself responsible for paying tremendous war reparations to the allied nations, which it could not afford. After all, six million of its citizens were unemployed. Inflation was at an all time high. The Deutsche Mark had dropped in value so much that at one point it took a wheelbarrow full just to buy a loaf of bread. Many people could not afford to feed their families because their Deutsche Marks were more valuable as toilet paper than as currency.

For fifteen years the Weimar Republic of Germany had struggled to pay the war reparations while still having enough to create a strong economy for itself. However, economic issues were not the only problems the Weimar government had to deal with. So many German men were killed during the war that most children were fatherless. Almost every household in Germany had lost a father, grandfather, son, grandson, brother, uncle, or nephew, which left the civilian population devastated. Still, as difficult as it was to rebuild the economy and the population, rebuilding moral and national pride was the real culprit. Neither civilians nor military men could understand why their strong nation had lost the war, nor could they understand why they had been blamed for it.

In their minds, Germany had simply gone to war to aid its ally, Austria. But Austria had not been blamed for the war, Germany had. Its people bore the entire guilt and they simply could not understand why. To them it had been a simple matter of aiding their neighbors. No one understood how such a strong and proud country could have been so completely overwhelmed at the end of the war, and they themselves were looking for someone to blame. These were the issues that Hitler spoke to directly. He promoted the "stab in the back theory," blaming the "communist Jews" for having betrayed Germany during the final months of the war. And his ideas were spreading.

Karl contemplated these issues as he half-heartedly scanned the newspaper. *We are so close to recovery,* he thought. *We are just beginning to turn the country around. It has taken some time, but the people are returning to work, and there is more food available now than there has been in the last fifteen years. Hell, the factory just got a new railroad contract for God's sake. That contract will provide three hundred more people with jobs. What more does Hitler think he can do?*

Karl von Rauthenau was a tall, distinguished looking man in his late fifties. With silver gray hair, clear blue eyes, and ramrod posture. He gave the immediate impression of power and authority. Karl had been a submarine captain in the German navy during the war, and was a decorated national hero. His boat had been one of the few that had made it home.

Karl had also been one of Kaiser Wilhelm's inner circle until the scandal of 1907, in which several of the Kaiser's entourage were tried on charges of homosexual conduct. Fortunately, Karl's nobility and reputation kept him from being charged. Rauthenau Steel had produced much of Germany's armaments, including the iron hull of his own submarine, and no one had been willing to sacrifice Karl for arms production. He was the genius behind the factory's production capabilities.

As the clock on the mantle struck nine o'clock there came a knock on the study door which pulled Karl from his thoughts. "Come," he commanded. A few moments later, Karl's butler entered the study carrying a silver tray with an envelope on it.

"This was just delivered for you, Sir."

Reaching across the desk, Karl took the envelope and said, "Thank you, Manfred."

"Will you be making a reply, Sir?"

Karl turned the envelope over and saw the seal of the Captain Wilhelm Schroeder. He frowned, quickly opening the envelope to read the card. "No, Manfred. It is just a note from Captain Schroeder informing me he will be attending the Christmas party here on Saturday night."

"Very good, Sir. Will that be all?"

"Yes," Karl replied. "You may go." Manfred spun on his heals and started for the door just as Karl had another thought. "Oh! Manfred," he called, "have we received a reply from Doctor Klaus Gessler yet?"

"Yes, Sir. Doctor Gessler's secretary called yesterday to confirm that he will be attending the party."

"Thank you, Manfred," Karl exclaimed with relief, "I was dreading the possibility that i might have to spend the entire evening with Wilhelm."

"No, Sir. That will not be likely," Manfred smiled. Manfred knew Karl's relationships intimately, and he much

11

preferred the gentle Dr. Klaus Gessler to the Nazi sympathizing Captain Wilhelm Schroeder.

Karl glanced up and frowned playfully at Manfred. Clearing his throat, he asked, "Have we heard from any others in the Gentlemen's Poetry Society of Berlin?"

"Yes, Sir." Reaching into his breast pocket, Manfred pulled out a list and declared smartly, "Along with Doctor Gessler and Captain Schroeder, Herr Adolf Brand, Doctor Magnus Hirschfeld, and Herr Kurt Hiller have all sent word that they will be attending."

"Very well, Manfred. That will be all." Karl knew Manfred had only his happiness in mind, but never the less he was still embarrassed that his butler had seen in Wilhelm what he, himself, had not. After years of being together, Karl was still amazed that their break-up came because of political differences. Wilhelm had agreed with Hitler's ranting about the Jews. He truly believed that the Jews were the reason Germany had lost the Great War, but Karl knew better. Germany had lost the war because they had aroused the sleeping American giant by using unfair, and unrestricted submarine warfare.

After Germany sunk the *Lusitania* off the coast of Ireland, America was forced to become an enemy. Karl sat, remembering the steel his factory had produced to make those damned U-boats, and how those boats had ultimately sunk his own country. Then he thought of Hitler and imagined Rauthenau Steel producing tons of steel for future U-boats, U-boats that Captain Wilhelm Schroeder might one day command. The thought made him shudder. *Remember the Lusitania, Wilhelm. I shall never forget it.*

Karl ran his hand through his hair and glanced over at the huge mahogany bookcases that lined the walls of his study. His eyes landed on a classic edition of Goethe's *Faust.* Slowly walking over to the book case he reached up and pulled down the small leather bound volume and flipped through it. *If old Hindenburg gives into Adolf Hitler he will be selling his soul to the devil, just as Faust did.*

Then Karl's eyes landed on the autographed play by Friedrich von Klinger, *Strum und Drang.* He laughed ironically to himself. Storm and Stress would be exactly what Hitler would bring. Until Hitler, *Strum und Drang* had spoken to the private passions within Karl, the secret desire to break with conventional norms. Karl had never been one to venture too far from socially acceptable standards, always putting duty, honor, and God above his own desires. Since the war, his thoughts on the meaning of duty and honor were troubled. Now *Strum und Drang* no longer represented youthful passions. *Storm and strife, that's what Herr Hitler will bring.* His thoughts then turned to Leeza.

Karl loved Germany, but he loved his niece more. Because there was really nothing he could do for Germany after the war, raising Leeza had become the focus of his life. Leeza was the center of his world. He was a doting uncle and an adoring fan. But now he feared for her. Should Hitler and the Nazis come to power, they would create a storm that would tear Germany apart. Karl knew he and Leeza would be pulled into the very depths of that storm. *What can I do to prevent it from happening?* he wondered. Then he thought of Leeza's concert in Prague that night. She would be home next weekend to enjoy the holidays with her family. He couldn't wait to see her. Berlin had been very lonely since his break up with Wilhelm and Leeza had left for Vienna. Such sad and depressing thoughts needed a remedy. Then Karl thought of Manfred's intimation and decided to call Dr. Klaus Gessler with an invitation to join him for dinner that evening.

The Christmas music from the string quartet swirled around Leeza and her mother as they emerged at the top of the grand stair case. Everyone gazed up at them in amazement. Leeza's green velvet gown seemed to glow in the light of the crystal chandelier, giving the illusion that she was gliding down the stairs. Everyone shouted greetings and gathered at the foot of the staircase to receive them.

Karl raced up several steps, extending his arms to them. "How lovely you both look this evening."

Katrine smiled at Karl. Under her breath she whispered, "I may still look lovely, but have you ever seen Leeza look so beautiful, or so grown up?"

Karl squeezed Leeza's arm and said with a wink in her direction, "Never have I seen two more exquisite women than the ones on my arms tonight."

Leeza returned her Uncle Karl's squeeze, which told him how much she appreciated how gentle and considerate he was with her mother. Katrine had been a striking woman in her day, and was still quite beautiful for all that she had been through. After Wolfgang's death, Karl had moved into the mansion with them to ensure that they were well taken care of. He and Katrine had always been friends, and was just as devoted to her as he was to Leeza.

"How beautiful the house looks tonight, Uncle Karl! I am so happy to be home, among all of our friends," she sighed.

"You have been terribly missed, my dear. You know that they will demand you play for them tonight," he replied as they reached the bottom of the staircase.

As the music slowly faded away, greetings of "Merry Christmas," came from all corners of the room. Leeza and Katrine mingled with their guests, returning holiday greetings and wishing all a gracious welcome to their home.

When the music began again Captain Schroeder approached Leeza, inviting her to dance. Wilhelm had been a loving fixture in her home when she was growing up. She accepted immediately. "I am so glad you will still dance with me, Leeza. I thought that maybe..."

"Not another word about it, Wilhelm," Leeza smiled. "What has happened between you and Uncle Karl has nothing to do with me. While he has been like a father to me, you have been like an uncle. So, I shall dance with you every time you ask, and I will enjoy your company."

Moments later Karl and Katrine began waltzing around the floor behind Wilhelm and Leeza. After allowing them a few turns around the dance floor, the other guests finally joined them. Men dance with women, women danced with women, and men danced with men. There was nothing quite like the annual von Rauthenau Christmas party. It was known as the best Christmas party in Germany. Karl had a flare for decorating with the most beautiful lights. The Christmas tree, and in fact, the whole house was gorgeous. The music was superb, as usual, and the food and Champagne were magnificent. Anyone who was anyone in the gay community was invited, and everyone came year after year.

When the next song began Karl moved through the crowd shaking hands and smiling as he searched for Klaus Gessler. Over the past week they had spent a significant amount of time together, and Karl had fallen hopelessly in love. "Klaus, come with me, bitte. I want you to meet Leeza!" They stood at the edge of the dance floor and a second later when Karl spotted Leeza dancing with Julius, he took Klaus in his arms and twirled him around the floor. Klaus smiled warmly, and Karl stared deep into his eyes. "You know," he whispered in Klaus' ear, "you have warmed an old man's heart. I didn't think that I would ever love or be loved, again."

Klaus was a shy, gentle man, who had fallen deeply in love with Karl as well. He softly whispered back, "You are loved, Karl. More than you know!"

From the corner of the room Wilhelm watched Karl and Klaus dancing. Their obvious happiness cause a bitter bile to rise in his throat. He crushed out his cigarette in disgust. *You're making a fool of yourself, Karl, and you don't even know it. Prancing around with a man half your age. Don't you know everyone is laughing at you behind your back? I'm the only man who has ever loved you, Karl. Don't be a fool!*

Wilhelm loved Karl deeply, but somehow they had lost their understanding of each other. Wilhelm believed that Karl had forgotten what it meant to be a proud soldier, fighting for his country. After the war Wilhelm had lost that sense of himself too. He had lost his career, his pride, and his self-worth. He had allowed himself to become a bitter, resentful, and angry man. He couldn't understand how Karl, a decorated war hero, could not be just as angry as he was about loosing the war. And furthermore, he could not understand why Karl could not see the pride Hitler was bringing back to Germany. *How can he not see it? Is he really so blind?*

When they finally caught up with Leeza and Julius on the dance floor, Karl quickly pulled them all aside and introduced them to each other. Julius, being his usual boisterous self, threw his arm around Klaus' shoulder and exclaimed, "So, you are the handsome devil that's put the fire back in old Karl here."

Leeza saw Karl blush, and quickly took Klaus' hand. "It is wonderful to meet you, Herr Doctor. You must be a very special man. Uncle Karl doesn't fall in love with just any pretty face. I'm looking forward to getting to know you."

Klaus smiled and offered Leeza his arm. Together they waltzed round and round, capturing every eye in the ballroom. Karl threw his arm around Julius' shoulder and whispered in his ear, "Come with me my boy. I want to talk to you about something, and I have a gift for you." No one noticed as Karl shut the study door behind them.

Later, they emerged just as Leeza was raising her violin to her chin. From the platform she noticed them entering the room and nodded with a smile. Slowly, she drew the bow across the strings of her violin and the sweet melody of *Silent Night* filled the room. The guests stood mesmerized as Leeza swayed with the music. After a few seconds she nodded to them, and they began to sing "Silent night, holy night. All is calm, all is bright."

Their voices echoed through the mansion and out into the street. Even those outside, rushing here and there, paused to listen. "Round yon virgin, mother and child. Holy infant so tender and mild." It seemed that for this one moment, all the world was caught in this one refrain, "Sleep in heavenly peace, sleep in heavenly peace." After she finished, Leeza stood perfectly still until the last note had completely faded away. The crowd stood perfectly still as well. Then, as if having to pry them from their hypnotized state, Leeza bowed deeply and they began to applaud. "Bravo! Bravo!" they shouted.

Leeza blushed and gave several more bows. Finally she nodded to the string quartet and they began a cheerful waltz that drew the guests' attention away long enough for her to escape. Quickly, she made her way over to Julius and Karl. Karl extended his arms and enveloped her warmly. "I am so proud of you, Leeza," he whispered. "I couldn't love you more if you were my own daughter." Leeza returned his hug, squeezing him ever so tight. When she pulled away their eyes locked. In that moment her eyes told Karl everything she was feeling. She loved him more than her own parents.

"Uh hum," Julius cleared his throat and shifted from one foot to another. "Uh hum! Wonderful performance, darling, but your third string could use a bit of tuning," he said with a grin, tapping his new violin case.

Leeza threw her hands on her hips and glared at him indignantly. Almost speechless she snapped, "Then your ears need to be tuned, Julius dear!" He laughed and continued tapping his new violin case until the tapping caught her attention. The case was made of rich burgundy leather. It was quite handsome. "What is that?" she chirped.

"A gift."

"From who?"

"My greatest fan!" Julius casually remarked, nodding toward Karl.

Leeza glanced at Karl and then back to Julius, and then back to Karl. "You gave this tone deaf, irresponsible child such a fine new case?"

"I did!" Karl nodded. "The poor boy's old case was in tatters. It was likely to burst open at any moment and dump the Stradivarius out on the ground! What could I do?" Then he winked at Julius and said, "Merry Christmas, my boy. And, happy Hanukkah!"

# Chapter Two

## The Clouds Gather

Berlin was growing tense. More tense than usual. The political mood of the city hung like a black mist over the people, grinding their holiday cheer into the mud soaked ground. "Heinrich, my boots need a shine," Roehm barked from behind his desk. "That idiot, Goering, is throwing one of his prissy holiday parties and Adolf wants to attend. It's disgusting."

"Yes, Sir!" Heinrich snapped. "Will I be attending also, Sir?"

"No. Not this time."

Heinrich was a tall, husky, thick-necked young man from a strict, hard working farming family near Trier. With sandy blond hair and blue eyes, he was the prefect model of a strong Aryan soldier. He had come to Berlin a few months earlier on holiday and never returned home. Home was the last place he wanted to be. Heinrich's parents expected him to marry and tend the farm as his brother had, but Heinrich found it increasingly difficult to conceal his true desires. He had never been interested in girls. Rather, he had always been fascinated with strong, domineering men. He had a large collection of body building magazines, and was constantly teased for it by his older brother. When his father caught him day dreaming over the magazines instead of doing his chores, he beat Heinrich. As Heinrich grew up, the beating only served to excite him more. In his late teens, after each beating he would find an excuse to go to the barn where he had the privacy to relieve himself of his excitement.

Once in Berlin, Heinrich found himself drawn to its infamous night life and cornucopia of sexual delights, all of

19

which he intended to sample. However, it wasn't until he stumbled into a bar off the Kunfurstendamn that he found exactly what he was looking for. Set back off the main street in an alley, the bar felt like a dungeon. The lighting was poor, with only a spotlight illuminating the main stage near the back. Immediately, Heinrich noticed there were no women in this bar. The room was filled only with men, soldiers from the looks of it. Each was dressed in one kind of uniform or another. Everyone sized him up the minute he walked in the door. After giving him a good looking over, each man returned his gaze to the back of the bar. Heinrich felt out of place, but couldn't bring himself to leave.

Following the gaze of the other men, Heinrich saw Ernst Roehm for the first time up on the stage. Roehm was dressed in a full Brownshirt uniform. His black leather boots were dripping with sweat that fell from his face. In front of Roehm, several men lined up with their backs to the audience. Each had their shirt off and their pants pulled down around their ankles. Roehm, with his long leather bullwhip, was 'disciplining' the boys under his command. Each one had long red stripes across his muscled back and buttocks. Roehm, his concentration unbroken by Heinrich's entrance, continued counting each stroke. Heinrich watched the scene in fascination.

Finally, a man at the bar noticed Heinrich's intense stare. "You want some of that, farm boy?" Heinrich ignored the man's comment and shoved his hands into his pockets. The man laughed and called out again. "You'd better run along home, farm boy. This is no place for a child like you."

Heinrich glared at the teasing man. Rage flared up in the pit of his stomach. He felt challenged and exhilarated all at the same time. "I can take more than any of those pussies up there!" he spat at the teasing man.

The teasing man just shrugged. "We'll see."

20

Heinrich looked back to the stage, fascinated with the exhibition. As he watched he felt his cock growing harder with each stroke of Roehm's whip. More excited than he had ever been before, and longing to be under Roehm's command, the novice made his way to the back for a closer look. With each stroke of Roehm's whip, Heinrich winced in ecstasy. Casually, he put his hand in his pocket and began rubbing his crotch. Suddenly, Roehm glanced over to the dark corner where Heinrich was standing. He instantly recognized the green farm boy for what he was and grinned.

"Twenty-four, and twenty-five," Roehm counted with the last cracks of the whip. Spent from the exertion, he just stood there, drenched in sweat. Several of the men fell to the floor when he finally walked away. Heinrich, who couldn't take his eyes off Roehm, noticed he had walked over to the teasing man and they were pointing in his direction and laughing. He felt the rage well up in his belly again. Suddenly, he rushed to the bar with every intention of knocking the teasing man off his stool, but Roehm grabbed him by the nap of the neck and shoved him to the floor instead.

"You liked the show, did you, farm boy? Well, no one watches for free." Then he dragged Heinrich to the stage and commanded, "Lick my boots clean, farm boy!"

Heinrich fell to his knees and took one of Roehm's boots in his hands. Caressing it with long even strokes, he dropped his head and opened his mouth. With one long stroke of his tongue, Heinrich worked his way from the toe to the heel of Roehm's sweaty boot. Then he looked up at Roehm and grinned.

Everyone in the bar started clapping and shouting for Roehm to initiate the big dumb farm kid. "Give it to him, Ernst!" they hooted. "Let's see what the boy's got."

Roehm reached down and grabbed Heinrich by the hair, jerking his head backward. Then he slowly unzipped his pants and pulled out his throbbing member and shoved it into Heinrich's mouth. "Suck it, boy! Suck it hard!" Roehm commanded as he began humping Heinrich's face.

Heinrich opened his throat, taking Roehm's immense dick all the way down. Then he pulled back, and glared up at Roehm in defiance. Roehm was surprised by the boy's willfulness, and reached down to pull Heinrich's shirt up over his head. Heinrich tore the shirt from his own lean body, and turned his back on Roehm.

Again Roehm was surprised by the boy's will, but he was excited by this novice at the same time. No one had ever challenged him this much. "Now you have done it, boy!" he barked. "Now you are really going to get it." Roehm reached around Heinrich's waist, unbuckled his belt, and unzipped his pants. Then he jerked them down around his knees and commanded, "Grab you ankles, boy!"

Heinrich complied as Roehm stepped back, tugging the bull whip from his belt. With the first stroke of Roehm's whip, Heinrich became Roehm's slave for life. Never had he felt such exquisite pain. With each following stroke, Heinrich felt himself growing more and more devoted to Roehm. Roehm, amazed at how much the boy could take, felt himself growing more and more infatuated with the farm boy under his control. By the time Roehm had counted to thirty-five strokes, a record for the bar, their relationship was sealed. Master and slave were bonded, and Heinrich was initiated into the Brownshirts the next day.

"Are you sure you won't need me at the party, Sir?" Heinrich asked. "Surely you will be bored to tears without me."

"Yes, yes, Heinrich, but it's not that kind of party! Tonight, Adolf Hitler will be there. It's no place for you. It's purely political. Nothing you would understand. I will not require your presence until I come home later tonight. Make sure you are ready for me!" But Heinrich understood more than Roehm gave him credit for.

The smell of stale cigarette smoke and ink permeated the office of Adolf Brand. As owner and editor in chief of *Der Eignen*, the leading gay men's magazine in Europe, Adolf was extremely outspoken when it came to politics. "Fuck Hitler," he yelled into the telephone, "and fuck Hindenburg if he gives into that arrogant little shit!" Adolf paused to listen and then screamed into the receiver, "No! I do not authorize any changes. I want the cover story to run just as I wrote it! *'Gay Party Needed In The Reichstag!'* Run it just like that!" He slammed the phone down and reached for another cigarette.

Adolf Brand was an impatient man in his late fifties, with thinning brown hair and dull brown eyes. His most notable feature was his paunch, which sagged over his belt in a bulbous manor. In his youth Adolf had been a fine figure of a man, but the years of sitting behind a desk had taken their toll on his physique. Known for his brash, tactless reporting style and flair for the sensational, Adolf had made many enemies in the gay and lesbian community. Over the years, in his struggle for gay rights, he had outted several prominent gay politicians in Germany, which had eventually destroyed their careers.

The most notable was Kaplan Dasbach, head of the Catholic Center Party which opposed the repeal of Paragraph 175. Adolf reported that Kaplan Dasbach was being blackmailed by a male prostitute. He felt completely justified in his actions, and was sure that Magnus Hirschfeld would support him. After all, Hirschfeld and others had been trying to get Paragraph 175 overturned for years, and the politicians Adolf targeted were doing nothing to help the cause. But Adolf had been wrong about Dr. Hirschfeld's position. Hirschfeld disagreed with the tactic. He denounced Adolf for having used it when he was called to testify in the liable suit brought by Dasbach. Adolf was sentenced to eighteen months in prison, and resented most of the aristocrats in the gay community because of it.

However, to a younger generation that demanded quick change, Adolf Brand was a hero. They considered him to be a hard hitting, no nonsense activist who might single handedly bring about the repeal of Paragraph 175 through his political commentary and activist magazine.

After lighting his cigarette Adolf pressed the intercom button on his desk. "Fritz, get Magnus Hirschfeld on the telephone!"

"Right away, Herr Brand," Fritz's voice crackled through the intercom.

Adolf leaned back in his chair, propping his feet up on his desk. *Surely Magnus will stand with me on this issue. After all, he's been calling for a gay political party for years. We have been struggling for the same thing, and now is the time to act if we're to stop Hitler's Nazi party from gaining control of the Reichstag. Surely we can put the past behind us.*

However, in spite of all his bluster, Adolf was not sure that Magnus Hirschfeld would really stand with him to form a gay political party. Hirschfeld had been the first to condemn him for outing the politicians. Since that time the two had been at odds with each other, and had failed to reconcile their different approaches to the political problem.

A few moments later Fritz's voice crackled over the intercom. "I'm sorry, Herr Brand. Doctor Hirschfeld is not at his institute. He is away on a lecture tour."

"Bull shit!" Adolf barked, "I just saw him at the von Rauthenau Christmas party Saturday night."

"Yes, Sir. But, his secretary said he took the morning train to Paris."

"How could he plan a lecture tour now, when Germany is about to revert back to the dark ages? When will he be back?"

"I don't know, Herr Brand."

"Well, fuck him then!" Adolf yelled. "We will run the article without his comments!"

Adolf knew the more polite members of the community had shunned him and he resented it. The only reason he had been invited to the von Rauthenau Christmas party was because he and Karl had been friends long before the Dasbach incident. They had met in college when both were still young men. In fact, Karl had helped Adolf come out.

*Der Eignen* had made Adolf a wealthy man, but that had not always been the case. As the son of a common chicken farmer, he had grown up without most comforts. Adolf watched his father struggle to make ends meet, and swore that one day he would be a man of great importance and wealth. Finally, at twenty-two, after his father's death, he left the farm to attend college in Berlin. There he met Karl, and they became fast friends. While Karl had studied engineering, Adolf had studied journalism. Karl read some of Adolf's poetry and encouraged him to study writing. He introduced Adolf to an older gentleman, a professor of literature, whom he thought might enjoy Adolf's company. Immediately, the professor took Adolf under his wing and into his bed. Adolf flourished under the professor's tutelage, and soon began working on the university newspaper. That was about the time Magnus Hirschfeld's case was brought to trial in a Berlin court.

Adolf followed the case with fascination, writing a series of articles for the school paper with great precision. Hirschfeld had sent a survey out to the Charlottenburger Technical High School which queried three thousand male students as to their sexual attractions. He also sent the same survey out to his friend's factory, Rauthenau Steel, where he had given a lecture on homosexuality to the workers

25

there. These surveys were Hirschfeld's attempt to take a census of how many gay people were living in Berlin. He needed to know if there were enough votes to form a gay political party. However, his plan backfired. A conservative newspaper got hold of one of the questionnaires and denounced Dr. Hirschfeld for trying to seduce students into the homosexual lifestyle. Eventually, he was found guilty and forced to pay a fine.

All of Adolf's articles were very well written, and reported the facts correctly as the trial progressed. However, after Dr. Hirschfeld was found guilty, Adolf wrote a piece that completely supported the survey and Dr. Hirschfeld. When Adolf's editor refused to publish the piece, saying he did not want such filth in the university newspaper, Adolf became enraged and stormed off the campus never to return.

For several months he roamed aimlessly around Berlin, often prostituting himself for a meal. He never got over his rage and dreamt of a way to finance his own paper. Finally, his chance came. One night while in the company of an older gentleman from England, who photographed handsome young men, Adolf picked up on the idea and bought himself a camera. Eventually, he sold enough pictures to body-building magazines to purchase his first printing press. From there Adolf began producing his own gay magazine. After several months of trial and error he figured out that the issues which contained the most smut and controversial political material were the ones that sold the most copies.

Within a year Adolf discovered the secret formula to successful magazine publishing. Sexual innuendo, controversy, and political unrest were the tools he would use to build his fame and fortune. But the price of his fortune had come at the cost of his social respectability. Adolf's own ego and unrelenting rage had excluded him from earning his place among the distinguished authors and publishers of Germany.

Punching the intercom button again, he barked, "Fritz! Did they say who Hirschfeld left in charge over at the institute?"

"A Doctor Klaus Gessler, Sir. Would you like me to get him on the telephone for you?"

"No! I'll go over there myself. I'll be gone most of the morning so don't let those damn idiots down in the press room change a word of my article!"

"Yes, Sir!"

---

Dr. Klaus Gessler had been an associate of Dr. Hirschfeld's for several years, working as the chief of staff for the *Institute for Sexual Science*. Klaus was a somewhat younger man, only thirty-eight, with a fine physique, sandy blond hair, and bright blue eyes. As a child he hadn't been interested in playing the games of other children. He was a gentle and compassionate boy who was fascinated with his father's ability to heal people when they were sick. The only thing Klaus ever wanted to be was a doctor like his father. While the other children played outdoors, he stayed inside studying anatomy charts and maps of the circulatory system.

The Gessler house had always been a well ordered Austrian home. Klaus' parents had never been overly affectionate with any of their children or each other. The only affection Klaus ever saw between his parents was when his father left for work in the morning. He would kiss his wife and daughters on their cheeks, and shake hands with his sons. This was the extent of the intimacy Klaus received, and he grew up believing it was all that was necessary between a husband and wife. Of course he

27

realized that sexual relations were a part of marriage, but in Klaus' mind sex was only a duty to be performed when the couple wanted to produce children. With this idea firmly planted in his mind, Klaus never felt the need to date or explore his own sexuality. He just assumed he would study medicine, graduate from medical school, find a wife, and settle into the same life he saw his parents lead.

For the most part, Klaus had assumed correctly. After graduating from medical school in Vienna, his father had arranged his marriage to the daughter of another prominent Austrian physician. Life was just as Klaus had expected it to be. He woke each morning, had breakfast with his wife, kissed her on the cheek as he left for work, and returned each night to sleep beside her. But his wife was much more affectionate than he had ever seen his mother be with his father. She was an attentive woman, always touching him and kissing him on the neck. Her overt affections made Klaus feel uncomfortable. He was not sexually aroused by her, and making love seemed like a chore. It wasn't long before he began spending many of his nights at the hospital. Uncomfortable at home, and confused by his lack of sexual interest in his wife, the hospital became his sanctuary. There he could think about medicine, which was what he truly loved.

Unfortunately, the hospital soon became a place of torment as well. Klaus' growing awareness of his sexual arousal when examining men frustrated him even further. During physical examinations his erection grew so hard and strong that he would have to relieve himself in the privacy of his office. Finally he went to the medical library and began a study on human sexuality. This was the first time he had come across the writings of Dr. Magnus Hirschfeld. Soon, Klaus realized he was a homosexual.

This revelation was agonizing. Klaus not only worried about himself, but also about his wife. He realized he could never be the affectionate husband she needed, and he grieved for her. He also worried about his medical practice. Should he be found out he might lose his license to practice at the hospital. But it was the thought of his father finding out that tormented Klaus the most. So he resolved to try even harder to live the life his father had modeled for him.

Month after month Klaus desperately tried to be a loving husband, devoted doctor, and upstanding member in his parish. He threw himself into his work, coming home so exhausted that he could barely stay awake through dinner. Night after night he fell asleep before his wife could manipulate her way into his arms. Finally, after a year of marriage when people started asking about children, Klaus knew he had to do something about the situation.

Luckily a medical symposium was being held in Berlin that year. This event gave Klaus the excuse he needed to get away. Once there he headed straight for the *Institute for Sexual Science*, where he met Dr. Hirschfeld for the first time. As the week passed, Klaus had several appointments with Dr. Hirschfeld and spent the rest of his time studying in the Institute's library and museum. Dr. Hirschfeld introduced Klaus to several other gay men who had come to Berlin for the same reasons. Many were married, held prominent positions, and were just discovering their own sexuality. And although Klaus did not allow himself to sample the sexual freedoms of Berlin, he did begin to feel more comfortable with the thought of it.

However, his thoughts always returned to his wife. Guilt and remorse plagued him. Ultimately, he knew there was no other option than divorce, so he returned home and released his wife from her vow. She deserved to have someone who could love her the way she needed to be loved. The way Klaus never could. After filing for divorce he packed up his office and returned to Berlin where he started a small practice in the Kunfurstendamn district. A couple of years later, after developing a professional relationship with Dr. Hirschfeld, Klaus was offered a staff position at the institute. Eventually he became its chief of staff, and took over the day to day operations while Dr. Hirschfeld lectured abroad.

Klaus sat with his legs propped up on his desk, thinking of Karl. Suddenly the phone rang, breaking him away from his day dream. Picking up the receiver he said, "Yes, Marta?"

"Doctor Gessler, Herr Adolf Brand is here to see you, without an appointment."

"That's all right Marta. Send him in."

A few seconds latter Adolf came strolling through the door. "Good day, Herr Doctor."

Klaus rose to his feet and extended his hand to Adolf. "Good day to you, Herr Brand. What can I do for you? Tell me that you don't need a penicillin shot!"

Adolf grinned. "No. Nothing like that. Although I wish I had done something that I might need a shot for!" he laughed.

Klaus laughed too. "Well, won't you take a seat? How can I be of service?"

"Actually," Adolf commented nonchalantly, "I was hoping to speak with Doctor Hirschfeld, but I am told he is out of the country on a lecture tour."

"That is correct."

"Do you know when he'll be back?"

"He's scheduled to be gone for several months, Herr Brand. Perhaps I can help you?"

"Perhaps," Adolf said as he rubbed his chin. "Over the years Doctor Hirschfeld has talked about forming a gay political party. I was wondering if he would still be interested in something like that."

Klaus paused for a moment to think. The last thing he wanted to do was speak for Dr. Hirschfeld, especially when it came to his political convictions. "I know that Doctor Hirschfeld still believes our community would benefit from having its own political party. As for his plans to form one,

I don't know of anything that he's working on at this particular moment."

"What would you say if I told you that in the next cover story of my magazine, I am calling for one to be formed?"

"The Weimar Constitution states that any group able to marshal sixty thousand votes can establish it's own political party and send a representative to the Reichstag. I would ask if you have that many votes?"

"Doctor Gessler, let me tell you that my magazine, *Der Eignen*, has one hundred thousand subscribers, and that *The Girlfriend,* has at least twenty-five thousand subscribers. Between all of the gay and lesbian publications, we have a circulation that's well over a million!"

"Yes, I am aware of that. But those subscribers are all over Europe. How many are actually here in Germany? And how many of those are 'out' enough to sign the registration forms?"

"That is what I don't know, and that's precisely why I am here," Adolf sighed. "I believe that if we don't organize a party now, it may soon be too late!"

"What do you mean?"

"You have heard the rumors about Hitler's meetings with Hindenburg?"

Klaus nodded. "Yes."

Adolf waved his hand widely. "Surely you know that if he gains control of the Reichstag things will change drastically!"

"Yes, I believe things would change dramatically. But, what does that have to do with the gay and lesbian community? Berlin will always be Berlin! Hitler can't stop us from forming a political party, now or ever. Not as long as we have the constitution."

"Constitutions can be changed, Doctor Gessler. They can even be abolished."

Klaus frowned. He didn't like the way the conversation was going. "You know, of course, that Roehm is Hitler's best friend and he is gay. I don't think Hitler has a problem with gay people."

"I am not saying he does, Herr Doctor, only that we never know what the future holds. I believe that it's best if we take precautions against unforeseen complications now, while we still can," Adolf urged. "Now, again, I ask you, would you support a gay political party?"

Klaus thought about it for a moment. "Yes, on first thought, I would support such a party. But, I would like to have a little more time to think about it before I make a public statement."

"What about Doctor Hirschfeld? Will he support it?"

"I can't speak for him, but as you know, this is something he has dreamed of for a long time. However, you will have to wait and talk to him when he returns."

"I hope we have that much time," Adolf growled. "As for your statement, when can I quote you?"

"Let me think about it for a few days. I'll get back to you."

"Doctor Gessler, surely you see that in order to organize, we must have the support and approval of all the leaders in the gay and lesbian community. Will you ask around for me?"

"I can do that. Informally, of course."

"What about Karl? What do you think he will say?"

"I know you and Karl go back a long way. Why don't you ask him yourself?

# Chapter Three

## The Storm Bursts
## January, 1933

Hanna Wagner furiously clanked out an invoice on the old typewriter at her desk. Her office was just outside of Karl's. She had been his personal secretary for years. Hanna loved working for him because with Karl von Rauthenau, she never had to worry about any office hanky-panky. Not that most women would have minded any advancements he cared to make, but Hanna was an old dyke from way back, and appreciated the fact that she and Karl understood each other. Hanna did her job very well and Karl gave her the freedom to do it. She practically ran Rauthenau Steel, at least the business end of it, and Karl compensated her generously.

"Hanna!" Karl called as he stuck his head through the doorway between their offices. "How much do we have in petty cash?"

"Ten thousand marks," Hanna answered promptly without looking up from her typewriter.

"And, in the business account?"

"Two hundred and ten million."

"And, in the payroll account?"

"Three hundred and fifty thousand."

"And, my personal account?"

"One hundred thousand."

"What is the balance of the accounts receivable?"

"After I finish this invoice it will be five hundred thousand, give or take."

"What about accounts payable?"

"Two hundred thousand carried over into the new year," Hanna answered as a matter of course, but then began to wonder what all the questions were about. She had never known Karl to be so concerned about the finances. "Why?" she asked with a cigarette dangling from the corner of her mouth. "What's going on? Is there something you haven't told me?" she barked.

"No, Hanna," Karl answered quickly. "I was just wondering."

"Ah huh! So, how much do you need?" she asked as if she were his parent.

"Honestly, Hanna! Sometimes I think you own this company and it is I who work for you!"

"Humph," she grunted in reply.

Hanna Wagner was a handsome woman in her mid fifties. She had graying blond hair and bright blue eyes. She and Karl went back a long way. Before the Great War they had met at the Eldorado Klub, where they often drank their lunches together. Hanna had worked near the bar, as a secretary to one of the leading bankers in Berlin. But after the war, when the bank closed, she found herself unemployed along with the rest of Germany.

When Karl's brother was killed, and he had taken over the family business, he immediately thought of Hanna. Calling her for help was the best business decision he had ever made. He was the genius behind the production line, but she was the one who kept the company afloat while other businesses were going bankrupt because of the economy. Hanna had moved into her office and gotten the account books in tip-top shape within her first month at Rauthenau Steel. Karl owed her a debt of gratitude, and never failed to show his appreciation when it came time to pass out the bonuses.

During the war Hanna had a lover, an army nurse, but she had been killed when she volunteered to go to the front lines. Since then Hanna had lived alone. Although she was still a good looking woman, she refused to let anyone into

34

her life. Over the years she began to think of Karl and Leeza as her family.

"Truly, Hanna! I haven't spent a dime. I was simply thinking of making an investment in Switzerland, and I wanted to know how much was available."

"Enough!" she grunted. "But, you shouldn't make any investments until I check them for you. You stick to engineering and let me handle the money."

"I think I can handle it just this once, Hanna. Honestly, you need to take a lover to keep your mind off how much I am spending!" Karl teased.

"Humph!" she grunted out a puff of smoke.

Karl's other right hand at the factory was his foreman, Albert Weisman. Albert took care of the crew and the maintenance of the equipment. Actually, he did a lot more than that, for which Karl was especially grateful. Although Albert was straight, and didn't fully understand Karl's peculiarity, they had developed a deep respect for one another. Karl trusted Albert immensely, and the trust was mutual."

Walking out to the loading platform, Karl called out, "Albert, bitte, may I see you for a moment?"

Albert waved from where he knelt, greasing the drive shaft of a conveyor belt, "Ja, Right away, Herr Karl."

When Albert came into Karl's office, Karl shut the door behind him. Then he walked around and sat behind his desk. "Albert," he said haltingly, "this is none of my business, and I would never presume to intrude on your private affairs, but with what is going on, I feel that it is my duty to ensure your welfare."

Albert looked at Karl questioningly. "What do you mean, Herr Karl. I have always tried to be extremely safe while working here in the factory. I follow all the safety rules, and I make sure that the men also…"

"No! No, Albert," Karl interrupted, "that's not what I mean."

35

"Then what, Sir?" Albert asked, as if he had done something wrong.

"I am concerned about Herr Hitler, Albert."

Albert sighed and wiped his forehead as if the very name made him break out in a sweat. "Ja. I think many people are concerned about Herr Hitler."

"Albert," Karl tried to put as much compassion in his voice as he could, "I just wanted to know if you had made any provisions for leaving the country, and if you hadn't, I wondered if I might be of assistance?"

"Oh no, Sir. I would never leave you, or my job, or my country. I could never do that. Besides, Herr Hitler is just a bag of hot air, I think. He sounds big and scary," Albert laughed, "but he just makes a lot of noise."

Karl leaned back in his chair and starred at the smile on Albert's face. Then he leaned forward with an intense look. "You know, if you ever need anything you can come to me, don't you?"

"Yes, Sir. I know you are my friend. And you know that I am your friend. You can count on me to stay and keep this factory in top running condition!"

Albert's words stung Karl. He wondered if the dear old man could comprehended anything of what he was trying to tell him. Then he smiled and said, "Just remember Albert, you can come to me any time you are in trouble or need help. Do you understand?"

Now Albert looked confused. "Yes, Sir. I know I can count on you for help if I need it, and you can count on me if you need help. Now, Sir, I should get back to work, Ja?"

"Ja, Albert."

---

On January 30, 1933, Goebbels, Goering, Roehm, and several Brownshirt officers stood at their windows in the

Kaiserhof hotel, just up Reichskanzlerplatz from the Chancellery. Each waited anxiously to see Hitler emerge triumphantly from his interview with President Hindenburg.

"We shall know by the look on his face," whispered Goebbels, "whether he has succeeded or not." No one responded.

Heinrich Mueller stood next to Roehm as he stared intently out the window. Heinrich noticed Roehm's breath becoming raspier with each passing moment. Soon beads of sweat began forming on his brow as his pelvis began making slight thrusting motions. Heinrich glanced down at the bulge in his master's pants and knew that he would soon need to release his excitement.

From the moment they met, Heinrich had devoted himself to Roehm, becoming a Brownshirt and Roehm's personal secretary, and slave. He went everywhere with Roehm, attending to his every need. Goering and Goebbels, and for that matter everyone else in the party knew just what the nature of their relationship was, but they overlooked it because Roehm was Hitler's closest friend. No one dared to speak a word against him, and Roehm knew it. Besides, everyone in the party had their own dark little secrets.

Roehm knew that Herman Goering, although of noble birth, was not the model of morality the party wanted to project. Goering had his secrets, all right. Having been wounded in the Great War the doctors prescribed morphine, which he quickly became addicted to. It wasn't long until he was using every drug he could lay his hands on. But this was not his only secret. His personal closet was filled with women's lingerie. It was whispered that he often forgot to remove his make-up after some of his private parties, and went out in public wearing rouge.

However, none of the secrets made any difference at this moment. As soon as the Nazi party took control of the Reichstag no one would be able to say anything against them. As they watched from the window Heinrich thought about the glorious victory celebration he would soon have with Roehm in their private room. Even he could not have imagined how soon that celebration would take place. The interview with Hindenburg did not take long. Just moments after Hitler had gone in, he emerged as the new Chancellor of Germany. Goering, Goebbels, and Roehm all stood transfixed at their windows as they watched Hitler's stone face approach the Kaiserhof.

Finally, the door opened, no one said a word. Each waited to see the expression on Hitler's face. Standing silently in the threshold, he said nothing. The only evidence of his victory was the tears streaming down his face. Overcome by the waiting, they ran to his side, congratulating him with handshakes and hugs of adoration. Soon after, Roehm motioned for Heinrich to go to their room and make himself ready.

Later that night thousands of S.A. Brownshirt troops marched by torch-light from Tiergarten to the Brandenburg Gate, and on down Wilhelmstrasse past the Chancellery. No one in Berlin could have imagined there were so many of them. They came from all over the country to attend their party's victory celebration. As they passed the Chancellery they saluted their familiar hail to the new Führer, who stood in an open window returning their salute. Of course Ernst Roehm and Heinrich Mueller led the procession.

Most German citizens were not Nazi party members and really did not understand what all the fuss was about. Germany was in the throws of a dying economy that the Weimar government was unable to heal quickly enough. Racked by war reparations, food shortages, and the death of so many men, the new democracy was in shambles before it had ever had a real chance to rebuild the country. Unemployment, lack of health care, and the horrors of modern warfare all served to depress the German people beyond their ability to cope. Political party after political party had promised reform and prosperity, but Hitler and the Nazi party were the only ones that offered a renewed sense of pride in being German. For this, many Germans were grateful, but they had no idea of how Hitler was going to put food on their tables.

Hour after hour the torch light parade passed the Chancellery building. The beating drums and blaring brass bands were deafening. Under the torch light thousands of uniformed men moved like a slithering serpent through the streets. Their swastika banners seemed to float high above the serpent's dark body. No one could possibly imagine how this serpent would wrap itself around the throat of Europe, and strike its venom into the very heart of the German people. No one, that is, except Adolf Hitler, the new Chancellor of Germany.

---

"I can't believe Hindenburg would just hand over the keys of the kingdom to that little tramp. Just like that!" Amy Trevor snapped her fingers.

"Is that how you'll report it, Trevor?" Jim Newman asked as he snuffed out his cigarette.

"That's the way it happened, so you can bet that's they way I'm gonna write it!"

"It sounds like someone's idea of a bad joke, Miss Trevor," laughed Marshall Turner, the BBC reporter. "But you Yanks get so emotional about everything. It's not good journalism, you know."

"Now wait a minute you limey prick," Jim spat as he poured himself another glass of scotch. "Bein' Yanks has nothin' to do with it. It's women. Women get emotional over everything. They have no business bein' reporters in a foreign country, or back home for that matter."

39

Amy Trevor was immediately irritated by Jim Newman's remark. "What do you know about women, you ass!"

"I know enough about 'em to know exactly what they're good for."

"You're such a bastard, Jim," Amy grumped. "You don't know anything about women, and you sure as hell couldn't please a woman if you had one in bed with you right now!"

Jim grinned and spat back, "Hey now Trevor, I know I'm not quite the lover you are, but I've had my share of women, and I ain't had a complaint yet!"

"That's because you never stick around long enough to hear them!"

"And do you know why I don't stick around afterwards? Cause women are too emotional. All they want is that lovey-dovey crap. I don't go in for all that."

"You are such a jerk! What does any of this have to do with being a good reporter?"

"Everything! You think you can be as good a reporter as me, just like you think you can be as good a lover as me. Well, you can't. I'll tell you one more time, Trevor, you can't send a woman to do a man's job, and that includes reportin' and screwin'."

"Just because you have a dick doesn't mean you can do either job well!"

Marshall Turner laughed as he lit a cigarette. "She's got you there, ol' chap. Now be a good sport and give the lady a break."

"Lady!" Jim choked on his scotch. "Trevor ain't no lady. She's a…a…well, ah…she's a…you know. One of those women who likes women."

Marshall chuckled and winked at Amy. "Would you like to borrow my thesaurus, ol' boy. You seem a bit tongue tied for a writer."

Amy smiled and winked at Marshall. "I believe the word he is groping for is 'lesbian.' He means to call me a lesbian," Amy laughed.

"Well, whatever ya call it," Jim grumbled, "it ain't the same as bein' a man. And you can't convince me you could please a woman better than I could. Let's face it, Trevor, you just don't have the right stuff for it. And you never will!"

Amy grinned. "He's just pissed off cause I get more than he does."

Slapping his knee, Marshall roared with laughter. "On that note I think I shall head off to bed. Good night, all."

"Good night, you traitor!" Jim slurred.

"Good night, Marshall. Sleep well," Amy grinned.

Amy Trevor was a beautiful blond with stunning green eyes. As an American journalist, working for the Universal News Service as a foreign correspondent, she had come to Berlin almost three years ago. Berlin was home now, and she especially enjoyed the Kunfurstendamn district where she found the exotic European women fascinating.

"Get out, Jim. I want to be alone."

"No you don't," Jim retorted as he plunked himself down on her bed. "Come on, Trevor, you know you want me. In fact you need me."

"Need you? What on God's green earth do I need you for?"

Jim grinned, "I'm exactly what you need, Trevor. A real man. Have you ever been with a real man before? It could change everything, you know."

"The only thing I know is that if I had a nickel for every time I heard that line I'd be a rich woman. Now get out, Newman, before I throw you out!"

Jim pulled himself off her bed, tucked in his shirt, and grabbed his bottle of scotch. "OK, but it's your loss, Trevor. I could have changed your life tonight."

41

Amy didn't bother to yell at him as he closed the door. However, he had been right about one thing. She didn't want to be alone. *With all the available women in Berlin, you'd think I wouldn't have to spend my nights alone.* Gazing out of the hotel window, she watched as a sexy woman strolled up the boulevard toward the hotel. *Hum! Tight skirt. Spiked heels. Gorgeous red hair.* "Probably straight as a pin," Amy said to herself in disgust. Then she grabbed her coat and headed for the Monocle Klub.

———————

Wilhelm slammed his fist down on Karl's desk. "Why can't you open your mind to the possibility that Hitler might just be right, Karl. You fought in the Great War! You know what it was like! How can you say that he'll lead us to destruction? He will lead us to freedom, I tell you. He's already said that he'll pay no more war reparations. And you know he will rebuild the military. That means a lot of money will be coming into your factory. Hitler wants you on his side, Karl! Think of what that could mean. Rearmament will be good for the economy for God's sake!"

"And what about war, Wilhelm? Will that be good for the people?" Karl asked impatiently.

"Who said anything about war, Karl? We are talking about the economy?"

"There is only one reason to rearm ourselves, and that is for war!" Karl demanded.

"The only war Hitler has declared is the one against the Jews, and they deserve it, Karl. You know they do!"

"I know no such thing, Wilhelm," Karl yelled as he slammed his own fist on his desk. "The only thing I know is that it has taken this country a long time to recover from the last war, and now, just as we are starting to get back on our feet, Hitler wants to do it all over again."

"Only to the Jews this time, Karl! Only to the Jews! Why can't you see that they are our real enemy?"

At this point Karl's face was almost purple with rage. Through clenched teeth he hissed, "The only enemy I see before me is a man who insists on spreading hatred and malice! Now, get out of my home, Wilhelm!"

Captain Wilhelm Schroeder pulled himself up to his full six feet and snapped to attention. "Is that what your new boy friend has told you, Karl. Isn't he a Jew?"

Karl clenched his hands into fists and shoved them in his pockets. "Wilhelm, I think you had better leave now before I can no longer control myself. It would be better to part now, before I can't remember why I loved you."

Wilhelm snapped a smart salute. "Yes, Sir!" Then he did an about face and marched out of Karl's study. On the way out the front door he ran squarely into Dr. Klaus Gessler, knocking him to the ground. When Wilhelm realized who he had run over he was filled with jealousy and shouted, "Get out of my way you filthy Jewish faggot!"

Klaus picked himself up with Manfred's help and called out meekly, "I'm not Jewish, I'm Austrian, Catholic."

# Chapter Four

# The Last St. Valentine's Day Drag Ball

December, January, and February were always the busiest months at the hospital. Anneliese often pulled double shifts to help out with incoming patients. Influenza ran rampant during the dark cold months of winter, and she nursed all those on her floor as best she could. Usually there was not much that she could do for them, accept to make sure they drank plenty of fluids and took enough aspirin to keep their fevers down. This year there were so many of them that Anneliese, and the other nurses ran themselves ragged trying to care for them all. How she longed for spring, and the relief it would bring. Most of all she looked forward to the Ladies of the White Rose St. Valentine's Day Drag Ball, even though she didn't have a date.

Anneliese Elster was a pretty young woman of twenty-two, with red hair and fiery brown eyes. She lived alone in the Kunfurstendamn. Each night on her way home she stopped to buy a copy of *The Girlfriend*, *Women's Love*, or one of the other lesbian magazines before she headed off to her lonely apartment.

Anneliese was shy. She always had been. It wasn't until her roommate in college introduced her to the lesbian community of Berlin that she found the courage to think about her own desires. After graduation, her girlfriend had been hired by a hospital in Munich and left Anneliese to suffer the loss her first love. Since then she had frequented the Monocle Klub in hopes of finding someone to share her life with, but she was always too shy to make the first move, and she always looked so tired that most women felt they would be imposing on her solitude if they asked her dance.

"Hey, Anneliese," Margo called from behind the bar, "it's almost two o'clock. I was just about to close up."

Anneliese glanced around the bar. There was no one else in the place accept Margo. "Do you have time to serve just one last drink?" she asked meekly.

"You pull another double shift at the hospital, kid?"

"Yes. This influenza has half of Berlin down." It was obvious Anneliese was exhausted.

"Sure, kid. Come on in and belly up to the bar. What'll ya have?" Margo asked in a kindly, but gruff voice.

"Gin and tonic, bitte."

As Margo mixed the drink and placed it on the bar in front of Anneliese, she asked, "So kid, goin' home alone again tonight?" Anneliese nodded her head and blushed. "That's a shame. You're a good lookin' dame. I mean, hell, if I was twenty years younger, you'd have to shoot me to get me away from your door."

Anneliese gazed up at Margo and blushed again. "That's the nicest thing anyone has said to me all week," she groaned.

Margo smiled a gentle smile. "Drink up. I'll fix you another one. On me this time."

"Thank you," Anneliese sighed. "I could use it. By the way, where's Gretchen? Doesn't she normally close up?"

"She's sick too. I'm just covering the night shifts until she gets better. But I gotta tell ya, it's just about killing me. I'm too old for all this night life anymore." Margo placed the drink on the bar and brushed her bobbed dark hair from her eyes. "I work over at the Austrian Embassy during the day and the lack of sleep the last couple of nights is taking its toll on these old bones."

Anneliese grinned as she began to feel the effects of the first drink. "I didn't know you were Austrian."

"Oh, yeah. I was born in the Tyrol. Just a little village outside of Salzburg, up near Hallstatt. Been here since

1920, when I got this civil service job at the embassy. Now I'm just biding my time until I retire, and boy am I ready."

Anneliese began to giggle. "You know, age has never mattered to me. I have always thought that older women make better lovers."

"Oh, you think so, do you?" Margo chuckled, knowing that the gin was getting to Anneliese.

"Well, I'm much too old to be your lover, sweetheart. I'm not up for raisin' no kids. And besides, you don't want an old dyke like me. Hell, look at you. You are beautiful! You could have any woman in the place if you would give yourself half a chance."

Anneliese seductively brushed her hand against Margo's as she reached to take the empty glass off the bar. "I am not a kid," she said coyly. "And I think you are a very handsome woman, Margo."

"Ah, that's just the booze talkin'. You go on home now, and get yourself some sleep."

Anneliese leaned over the bar and cupped Margo's face in her hands. Margo could not help but see Anneliese's full round breast bulging from the top of her low cut blouse. She took a long, slow breath and fought the desire to nuzzle her face between them. But her imagination took flight, and in her mind she saw herself reaching around and caressing Anneliese's firm little cheeks.

Anneliese seemed to read Margo's thoughts and pulled her face into her cleavage. Margo breathed in her sweet aroma. Reaching up, she filled her hands with Anneliese's voluptuous breasts. Anneliese was raising in Margo a passion she had not felt in years. "I want you," she whispered, as she smothered herself in Anneliese's essence.

"Take me," Anneliese whispered back.

Without thinking twice Margo swept her arm across the bar, clearing it of empty glasses. As they crashed to the floor, she hurdled over the bar and took Anneliese's into her arms. Anneliese kissed her with an intensity that signaled

46

her own passion. Responding to the fever of the kiss, Margo hoisted Anneliese's petite little body up onto the bar. Holding the kiss, she began unbuttoning Anneliese's blouse, and slid it off her shoulders. Sliding her hands around Anneliese's slender shoulders, she unhooked her bra and once again filled her hands with Anneliese's breasts. Gently, she squeezed them, letting the bra fall away. Pulling Anneliese closer, Margo moved her tongue slowly across Anneliese's lips and then down her neck, and on to her nipples.

Anneliese released a small cry of ecstasy as she grabbed the back of Margo's head and arched her back. Margo began sucking harder and faster until Anneliese could no longer contain herself her passion. She slid her hips forward on the bar. Margo knew what she wanted. Still sucking her tender nipples, Margo reached around Anneliese's waist and lifted her off the bar. With one hand she undid Anneliese's skirt and let it fall to the floor. Then she slid her hand under Anneliese's panties and squeezed her cheeks. Rubbing and caressing, Margo work the panties down and they also fell to the floor.

As soon as she was free of them, Anneliese wrapped her legs around Margo's waist while Margo continued kissing her throbbing nipples. Margo lifted Anneliese back onto the bar and gently slid her hand between Anneliese's thighs. Caressing her soft mound, Margo found Anneliese's moisture. Anneliese opened wide. Margo entered with a gentle thrust. Anneliese cried out in pleasure. Her moisture filled Margo's hand as she slid in and out of Anneliese.

Releasing Anneliese's breast with a swirl, Margo ran her tongue down Anneliese's bare body, over her stomach and navel, and down to her furry mound. Anneliese was sweet in Margo's mouth. She began probing Anneliese's crevasses with her tongue. Anneliese writhed under Margo's touch, and began arching her pelvis to meet

Margo's kisses. Margo began trusting more firmly, all the while sucking passionately on Anneliese's fiery clit.

Anneliese responded by wrapping her legs around Margo's neck, thrusting her wet mound deeper into Margo's mouth. In and out, Margo pumped harder and faster, and with each thrust, Anneliese rose to meet her. Her creamy essence gushed out as Margo brought Anneliese to her ecstasy. Margo felt her muscles tighten as she came, and gave her one last thrust to push her over the edge. Anneliese cried out in pure pleasure, and then collapsed, shuddering on the bar. Margo stayed inside Anneliese a few more seconds, feeling the orgasm pulse through her.

When Anneliese finally relaxed, Margo pulled out and smiled. Then she ran her tongue over Anneliese's moisture one more time, just to see her shudder again. "So, you were telling the truth after all. You're not a kid."

"No, I am not a kid," Anneliese whispered contentedly.

Margo laughed. "Come on, let me take you home."

---

For the last twelve years the White Rose Ladies Society had hosted their annual St. Valentine's Day Drag Ball at the Bristol Hotel, the finest hotel in the Kunfurstendamn. Every year, the entire gay community looked forward to this one special night, knowing that the ladies of the White Rose Society worked all year to make each ball more memorable and elegant that the year before. This year's ball was no exception. The room was decorated in black and white, with splashes of red. Each table was covered with a black linen tablecloth, and in the center stood a fluted cut crystal vase with a single long-stemmed white rose. At the base of the vase was a wreath of white roses with four red votive candles placed inside smaller cut crystal holders. Their flames reflected through the crystal and cast rays of red over the wreaths of white. Around the room, standing bouquets of long-stemmed white roses lined the walls and rose peddles were sprinkled around the polished dance floor. From the crystal chandelier hung boughs of greenery, white roses, and streams of red ribbon. The buffet table displayed a huge ice carving of a rose, around which cut crystal dishes and platters offered Beluga caviar, an assortment of cheese, crackers, meats and bread. The champagne, of course, was French. A garland of white roses and red ribbon lined the orchestra stage. The orchestra was brought in from Vienna, and was playing a soft Brahms as guests were arriving.

Helene Stocker and Lotte Hahm, prominent leaders in the lesbian community, and senior officers of the White Rose Ladies Society, stood at the head of the receiving line greeting their guests. By their side stood the prominent artist Gertrude Sandmann, novelists Maximiliane Ackers and Ruth Roelling, and lyricist Vera Lachmann.

The White Rose Ladies Society had been formed as a social group in the early days of the gay movement in Berlin. Long before Magnus Hirschfeld opened the *Institute for Sexual Science*, Helene Stocker was a leader in Germany's women's movement. When an effort was made by the government to include lesbians in Germany's Paragraph 175, Hirschfeld's *Scientific Humanitarian League* teamed up with Helene's *League for the Protection of Maternity and Sexual Reform*. Together, both groups successfully fought the legal change and Helene and Magnus became fast friends.

Now, the White Rose Ladies Society sponsored the St. Valentine's Day Drag Ball in celebration of the gay and lesbian community's freedom in Berlin. The money raised went to support the local women's center and several women's rights organizations. They also provided three university scholarships each year, and were very proud of their members who had become doctors, professors, and authors.

Everyone was welcome at the St. Valentine's Day Drag Ball, provided they could afford the price of the ticket. There were no class distinctions on this particular evening. Folks from all over Germany saved all year to attend this one event. This was the one night when aristocrat and commoner could rub shoulders and toast each other without feeling uncomfortable. The formal drag allowed for a certain amount of anonymity. Tuxedo clad men escorted their dates who wore long luxurious evening gowns. Tuxedo clad women, with mustaches and beards, escorted their dates, who also wore evening gowns. On this night everyone could be anything they wanted, and no one batted an eye as long as the dress was formal and elegant.

"Ah, Herr von Rauthenau!" Helene exclaimed as Karl entered the room with Klaus on his arm. "How handsome you look this evening! And you, Doctor Gessler, how handsome you are in your tuxedo! Welcome! Welcome!"

Karl smiled, giving a slight bow. "Thank you, Helene. And may I say how handsome you are this evening in your tuxedo."

"Yes," exclaimed Klaus, glancing at all of the women in the receiving line, "how lovely you all look!"

"Where is your beautiful niece, Herr von Rauthenau?" Lotte asked. "The ball simply wouldn't be the same without our musical White Rose."

Karl grinned. "She'll be along shortly. I'm afraid her date was having a bit of trouble with his wig!"

"Well, yes, those damn things can be rather troublesome," Helene grumbled. "Especially when one is not use to wearing them."

"I can only imagine. Oh, by the way," Karl said as he reached into his breast pocket and pulled out an envelope, "I have something for you." Helene looked at him quizzically. "It's just a little something I want the ladies to have in case of rain. One never knows what evil wind will blow next."

The smile fell from Helene's face as she stared at the envelope. "I understand," she said whispered, taking the envelope and placing it in her breast pocket. "Thank you, Karl. Let us hope that rainy day never comes, shall we?"

"Yes, of course. Now, if you would be kind enough to direct us to our table we would be most grateful."

Just then Leeza and Julius entered the ball room. Upon seeing them, the crowd paused and applauded. "Leeeeezzzza, Deeear," Helene cried! "How wonderful of you and Julius to come to our little party!"

Julius extended his evening gloved hand to Helene. "Julia, darling! It's Julia!"

Helene snapped her heals together and bowed as she took Julius' hand. "Of course Fraulein Julia! What a dummkopf I am. Please, accept my apology."

Julius smiled gaily and replied with a curtsy. "Naturally I forgive you. What lady wouldn't forgive such a handsome gentleman?"

Helene grinned up at him and then glanced over at Leeza, who stood musing at the exaggerated scene. "And, how are you this evening, my dear?"

"I'm sorry we are late, Helene. Julia here," Leeza jerked her thumb in Julius' direction, "couldn't get her hair on straight!"

Everyone around them laughed as Helene exclaimed, "I heard! I heard! Nasty business having to fuss with those things. That's why I prefer a tux. You only have to get the tie right and the rest falls into place. Now, let me pin a rose on your tux, and I'll show you to your table."

On her way to the table, Leeza glanced around the room and noticed the other members of the White Rose Ladies Society were all wearing white rose corsages or boutonnières as well. Then she notices that the room was filled with the scent of them, warm and sweet.

*The smell of love*, she thought. *Maybe she will be here tonight!* The thought of meeting the right woman made

Leeza's heart leap inside her chest as she shyly glanced around the room again. This time she saw her old friend Anneliese, dancing with someone she recognized from the Monocle Klub, but didn't personally know. *How beautiful Anneliese looks tonight. Better than she's looked in a long time. She must be getting more rest. And look, she and her girlfriend are wearing white roses!*

Leeza watched the couple dancing as she took her seat at the table next to Julius. "Look, Jules! Look how beautiful Anneliese looks tonight. She must be getting more rest lately, and she is wearing a white rose. They must have asked her to join the society! How wonderful for her!"

Glancing across the room to the dancing couple, Julius exclaimed, "That's not the look of rest, darling. That's the look of love. Or, at least satisfaction! You should try it sometime," he muttered under his breath.

Leeza was surprised by Julius' remark and quickly looked back toward her friend. *Love? Anneliese, in love? Could it be?* "Jules, be a dear and dance with me."

"So soon? I haven't even had a glass of Champagne yet!"

Leeza grabbed him by his gloved arm and hoisted him to his feet. "Come on, Uncle Karl and Klaus are dancing already."

"Well yes," he stumbled on his high heels, "of course they are. They're in love. We're not!"

"Oh, shut up and dance with me!" Leeza commanded. Dragging Julius out to the dance floor, she whispered, "When we get there, waltz toward them. I want to find out who Anneliese is with."

"Women!" Julius exclaimed. "Why don't you just walk up to her and ask?"

"Because!" Leeza whispered as she took Julius in her arms and began waltzing him around the floor, "it would be rude. I know I have seen that woman, but I can't remember her name!"

"Oy!" Julius exclaimed with an exasperated tone in his voice. "Let me show you how it's done." He took over the lead and waltzed Leeza right over to Margo and Anneliese. Then he let Leeza go and tapped Anneliese on the shoulder. "Excuse me," he said assertively, "May I cut in. It's not often that I have the opportunity to dance with such a handsome individual."

Stunned, Anneliese stepped aside. Margo bowed and took Julius into her arms. When Anneliese turned to leave the dance floor she saw Leeza standing behind her. Excited, she threw open her arms and squealed, "Leeeezza, I am so happy to see you. I was hoping you could come home for the ball!"

The two old friends wrapped their arms around each other and hugged affectionately. "You look wonderful, Anneliese!" Leeza whispered in her ear. "And, look! You have on a White Rose. When did this happen? And who is the handsome woman you're with?"

"Oh, Leeza! I'm so in love! Her name is Margo. She works at the Austrian Embassy. We met at the Monocle Klub. And, the best thing of all, she truly loves me!"

"How wonderful for you!"

"As for the White Rose, Margo was a member. She invited me to join a few weeks ago." Then Anneliese noticed Leeza's White Rose and she smiled. "Looks like we're in the same club!"

"Yes! Helene asked me to join at our Christmas party. I didn't think I could because I'm in Vienna the majority of the year, but she was so excited about it that I couldn't help but say yes. Anyway, enough about me." Leeza placed her hands on Anneliese's shoulders, holding her at arms length while staring into her eyes. "Tell me more about you and Margo." Anneliese just blushed. "Love? When did this happen? I tell you, I go away for a few years and geesh, you go and fall in love with someone else!"

"Oh, you!" Anneliese teased. "You know I love you, truly! But, let's face it, we are both femme. Regardless of how you are dressed tonight!"

"Ah! You are breaking my heart," Leeza teased back. Then she took Anneliese in her arms and waltzed her around the floor. "I had to wear this stupid tuxedo because I didn't have a date. Julius agreed to come with me only if he could wear one of my evening gowns! So here I am, butching it up while he's out there camping it up!"

They laughed uproariously as the music faded. Everyone applauded and Anneliese grabbed Leeza by the hand, dragging her off the dance floor. "Come on! I want you to meet Margo!" Like a couple of school girls, they ran over to where Margo and Julius were thanking each other for their dance. "Margo! Margo! I want you to meet one of my oldest and dearest friends! Leeza von Rauthenau this is Margo Wolff!"

Suspiciously, Margo looked Leeza up one side and down the other. Then she extended her hand and was instantly relieved when Leeza placed her delicate fingers gently in Margo's palm. *Femme*! *Thank God!* Margo smiled and bowed deeply. "I am pleased to meet you, Leeza! Anneliese has told me so much about you. I have seen your picture in every bar in town."

"And I am very pleased to meet you, Margo. Anyone who can make Anneliese look so radiant, and feel so happy, has my lasting gratitude."

"Believe me, loving Anneliese is the easiest thing in the world. She has brought such joy into my life."

Anneliese and Margo joined Leeza and Julius, and Karl and Klaus, at their table. "How lovely to see you again, Anneliese," Karl said as he rose to greet her. Taking her hand, he smiled sincerely and said, "We missed you at our Christmas party!"

"I was heartbroken when I couldn't come, Herr von Rauthenau, but things at the hospital were crazy."

"Yes, well at least you could make it this evening! And looking so lovely I might add! Would you care to dance?"

By now, Margo realized that everyone at the table meant a great deal to Anneliese, and that they were all genuinely nice people, for aristocrats. She quickly began to relaxed enough to thoroughly enjoy the rest of the evening.

Eventually, Julius deserted Leeza for a tall handsome stranger, and Margo and Anneliese returned to their own little world of love and romance. As for Karl and Klaus, well, they too were in their own fairy tale world. *As usual, I'm all alone in a room full of people*, Leeza thought.

After an evening of chit-chat with old friends and playing a few songs with the orchestra, Leeza was relieved when the orchestra director announced the last dance. Watching from the table, as those she loved held the ones they loved close, Leeza's heart grew heavy. *Everyone has someone and I have no one.* Suddenly, from behind her, Leeza heard a soft voice ask, "Would you like to dance?"

The voice had a strange accent, but it was rich and warm. Turning, Leeza looked up into the soft green eyes of Amy Trevor. Leeza's heart skipped a beat. *She's beautiful!* Amy was dressed in a dark blue satin formal that clung to her delicate body as if she had been poured into it. Her long golden hair flowed over her smooth shoulders and down to the middle of her back. Her eyes were glowing with anticipation, but her smile was hesitant, as if she were afraid Leeza would refuse her.

Leeza stood up and gazed deeply into Amy's eyes. "Yes," was all her halting breath could manage. Never had she imagined that such a beautiful woman would ask her to dance. They stood motionless, staring into each other's eyes, either wanting to break the spell of their gaze. A few seconds passed, and then Amy took Leeza's hand. *Soft, warm,* Leeaz thought. Silently they walked to the dance floor. Turning toward each other, they resumed their deep gaze. Leeza's body began to tremble as Amy slid her arm around her waist and led her into the dance. Resting her hand on Amy's shoulder, she hadn't imagined that her body could react so instinctively to the simple touch. As if they had been dancing together for years, their bodied began moving as one. Around the dance floor they glided, never taking their eyes from each others. Leeza felt a warmth rush through her body, something she hadn't felt since Hanna had kissed her at her apartment in Vienna so many years ago. *Her hands, her eyes, her touch, their all so inviting.* Leeza wanted to pull Amy closer, to touch her, to kiss her, to lose herself in the moment. *Beautiful lady, I could love you!*

When the music faded away and everyone began applauding the orchestra, Leeza and Amy held their pose, lost in their own romantic moment. Amy whispered, "Thank you."

"Thank you," Leeza whispered back. The applause broke the rapture of the moment, and they self-consciously released each other. Leeza looked toward the orchestra and began to applaud. A few seconds later she looked back toward Amy, but she was gone. Standing there, desperately searching for Amy in the crowd, Leeza looked bewildered. A moment later Anneliese and Margo caught her up in their joyous wake as they returned to their table.

Anneliese grabbed hold of Leeza's are and squealed, "Wasn't this the most marvelous ball? I could have danced all night!"

"Ja, me too!" Margo exclaimed as she threw her arm over Leeza's shoulders. "This was really fun." Neither noticed Leeza's lost expression.

"Yes," Leeza sighed as she glanced eagerly around the room. *Where did she go?* Then her heart sank when she realized Amy had gone. *I don't even know her name.*

The music had been wonderful. The decorations were gorgeous. The guests had had a wonderful time. Everyone looked stunning in their finest attire, and had danced as if in they hadn't a care in the world. Best of all, the White Rose Ladies Society had raised several thousand marks for their charities. Yet, no one suspected what the morning would bring.

---

"That son of a bitch!" Adolf Brand yelled as he slammed down the phone. "I knew it! I knew it! That son of a bitch has gone and done it!" Adolf was fuming when there came a quiet tap on his office door. "What!" he barked.

The door opened slightly, just enough for Fritz to poke his head in. "Herr Brand, are you all right?" he asked meekly.

"No, I am not all right!" Adolf roared. "Do I look like I am all right?"

"No, Sir! Your face is all red and puffy and…"

"Oh shut up, Fritz! You idiot!"

"Yes, Sir," Fritz answered haltingly. Then, at the risk of being yelled at again, he asked, "What has happened to upset you so, Herr Brand?"

"Hitler! That's what!"

"What has he done, Sir?"

"I'll tell you what he has done, Fritz," Adolf yelled as he rose from his chair shaking his fist in the air. "I'll tell you exactly what he has done. That little bastard has been in office for seventeen fucking days, and already he's outlawed all gay rights organization! That's what he's done, Fritz! He has outlawed all gay political organizations! So, there goes our chance to form a party, Fritz! Now, just what do you think of that?"

Fritz thought for a moment and said with a flip of his wrist, "I don't like his mustache. It looks funny."

"Get out," Adolf screamed, "before I strangle you right here and now! How can I write the most important article of my life with an idiot like you hanging around! Get out, I tell you! Get out!" Fritz quickly pulled his head back through the door and closed it. Just as he reached his desk he heard Adolf yell, "And, get me Karl von Rauthenau on the phone!"

---

The next evening Karl called for a meeting of the Gentlemen's Poetry Society of Berlin, and Klaus suggested they all come to the Institute for dinner. Klaus had been invited to join the group only recently, and was eager to entertain such a distinguished group of gentlemen. As per his instructions, the staff had set the table in the Institute's grand dining hall, making sure the table linens were crisply pressed, the silver shined, the crystal sparkled, and the china was spotless.

At the table that evening, Klaus sat at the head of the table, with Karl to his right. The other guests included General Franz Mann of the old Prussian Army, and the publisher Wolfgang Hadler, along with several other prominent Berlin professionals. There were bankers, lawyers, doctors, and even a member of the Reichstag. Each brought a unique perspective to the discussion. However, tonight their thoughts were not on poetry. Karl could not help but think of the play *Strum und Drang,* and casually brought it up for discussion as a way of breaking the ice. It was obvious everyone felt the need to discuss current political events which had traditionally been a taboo topic during their gatherings. It was felt that politics was a distracting subject which, if allowed, would fracture a purer discussion of literature and the arts. But tonight was different.

"The *Strum und Drang* movement represented major changes in our society's attitudes," General Mann interjected. "The storm and strife of unsettled passions motivated young artists to express these feelings through their work, not unlike what we are seeing today. Society is unsettled, fearful, and hungry for a new way. When a society is in such turmoil, it can't help but be reflected in its art."

"Yes," Karl agreed. "Undoubtedly, the strife we are presently experiencing is but the birth pangs of a new social order."

"Undoubtedly!" exclaimed Wolfgang Hadler. "And how will the people react to this new society? As Goethe described in *Faust*, Germany may well be selling its soul to the devil."

"Gentlemen, it is evident to all that we wish to discuss recent political events," Klaus said calmly. "Therefore, I motion that we adjourn our meeting, allowing ourselves the opportunity to discuss that which is truly of interest to us this evening."

Klaus' motion was carried by the entire membership, so they adjourned to the library for brandy and cigars. Wolfgang was anxious to discuss the most recent issue of *Der Eignen.* "What did you think of Adolf Brand's latest headline, Karl?"

"The one calling for the formation of a gay political party in Germany?"

"Yes! Yes! That's the one. An interesting idea, don't you think?"

Karl sighed. "Yes, I think it is an interesting idea. Although I don't know how effective it would be. Adolf is somewhat of an idealist."

"But, do you think it could be done?"

"I don't know," Karl answered. "I suppose the numbers are there, but it would be such a small party, I don't know that it could make a difference in the Reichstag."

"Well, God knows we need to do something to shut Corporal Hitler up," General Mann exclaimed as he exhaled his cigar smoke.

"Yes," interjected Klaus, "but as Magnus has always said, 'Except for a few minor cliques, homosexuals are in reality almost totally lacking in feelings of solidarity. In fact, it would be difficult to find another class of mankind which has proved so incapable of organizing to secure its basic rights.' Magnus would agree with Karl, and so do I. Whether we supported it or not, how effective could such a political party be when it has no solidarity among its members?"

Klaus' statement gave the group pause for thought. Then the banker, Herr Trotter, brought up another issue. "Political ideology aside, the Nazis are no threat to us. Why should we form a party to vote against them? After all, Hitler's second in command is Ernst Roehm, one of the most notorious queers in Berlin."

"Obviously, Herr Trotter, you have not heard the latest news," Karl said grimly. "Regardless of whether some of the top Nazis are as queer as we are, Hitler has outlawed all gay rights organizations!"

"What!" Herr Trotter exclaimed. "When did this happen?"

"Only this morning," Karl sighed.

After a couple of hours of discussing Hitler, and the ramifications of his new law, the gentlemen of the Society agreed they should all be very cautious, but could afford to hope for the best. Most still believed that Ernst Roehm's friendship with Hitler would prevent any widespread persecution of homosexuals.

Karl was not so sure. "The next few months will tell," he said as he stood up. "And, with that, I must bid you all a good evening."

On his way home, Karl's thoughts were drawn to Captain Wilhelm Schroeder. Early in the evening Karl realized Wilhelm was not going to attend as he usually did. Nor had he attended the St. Valentine's Day Drag Ball. *He must have known ahead of time that Hitler was going to make this move. Why didn't he warn us?* When he got home Karl sat in the study thinking about his last conversation with Wilhelm. *What was it he said? Something about Hitler wanting me on his side? Was that Wilhelm's way of telling me?*

---

That same night Heinrich Meuller sat at the bar in the Eldorado Klub talking with a boy from Amsterdam. "So, you are communist too," he grinned.

"Ja. I believe that the workers of the country should rise up and take control of what they have worked so hard to produce," the boy slurred. "The rich always get richer by the sweat of our brow, and we are left with a pittance."

"Ja! I couldn't agree with you more!" Heinrich smiled and nodded. "Let me buy you another beer, my friend." The boy nodded his appreciation. *He's perfect*, Heinrich thought. *Absolutely perfect! Everyone in the place has heard him say that he is a communist, and they all know he is a little faggot! All I have to do is take him to a bunch of straight bars over the next couple of weeks, and get him liquor up enough to start preaching about the glories of communism. That should give us enough witnesses.*

---

On the evening of February 27, 1933, the most powerful men in Germany were dining in two different locations. Vice-Chancellor von Papen entertained President von Hindenburg at the Herren Klub on Vosstrasse. Hitler dined in the country home of Joseph Goebbels. Both waited patiently for their telephones to ring.

When the calls finally came, von Paper immediately drove President von Hindenburg home, and then headed for the Reichstag. When he arrived, Goebbels and Hitler were already on their way, and Hermann Goering was at the scene, puffing and ranting how the fire had been set by communists plotting against the new government. "This is the beginning of the Communist revolution! We must not wait a minute. We will show no mercy. Every Communist official must be shot where he is found. I say we sting up every Communist deputy this very night!"

A few seconds later Marinus van der Lubbe, the gay Dutch boy Heinrich had seduced, came stumbling and choking out of the burning Reichstag building at the same moment Heinrich Mueller, and his squad of Brownshirts, emerged from the underground passage which ran between the Reichstag and Hermann Goering's home. Marinus van der Lubbe was arrested on the spot and executed a few days later. No one would listen to him when he said that he had been taken to the Reichstag by a big blond man named Heinrich, who had actually set the fire.

The following morning Hitler forced President Hindenburg to sign the "Decree for the Protection of the People and the State," which effectively suspended all individual and civil liberties. From that day forward, rights of privacy were no longer ensured by the postal service, or the telephone and telegraph services. Rights of free expression, assembly, and association were restricted. Homes could be searched without proper warrants, and property could be confiscated without a hearing.

Most importantly, less than a month later, on March 24, 1933, the Enabling Act was passed in the Reichstag. This new act suspended the Weimar Constitution and even the Reichstag itself. As their last official act, the Reichstag members voted Hitler as the absolute authority in Germany.

With the constitution suspended and marshal law declared, President Hindenburg no longer had any constitutional right to govern. All had gone according to plan. The Reichstag fire brought down the Weimar Republic, and Roehm congratulated Heinrich on his glorious service to the Führer.

# Chapter Five

## Warning From The Shadows

As Karl drove to the National Cafe he replayed the hurried telephone call over in his mind. *Wilhelm sounded worried. Or scared, maybe. What could be so terribly important that he must drag me out at this time of night? After all, we've already said everything there is to say.* There were no cars parked in front of the cafe so Karl didn't have far to walk. Even though it was dark he spotted Captain Schroeder right away, sitting by himself in the back corner. *How unlike Wilhelm to sit in the shadows*, Karl thought as he removed his gloves and overcoat.

Wilhelm had seen Karl come in, but made no move to attract his attention. When Karl sat down across from him, he said, "Thank you for coming."

"This had better be important, Wilhelm. It's freezing out tonight and I believe we have nothing more to say to each other." The waiter followed Karl over to the table and asked if he could get him anything. "Coffee, bitte."

"Very good, Sir."

"Now, what's this all about, Wilhelm?"

Wilhelm hunched over his cup of coffee and whispered as if he was afraid someone would overhear him. "A press release came across my desk today, Karl." He took a sip of his coffee. "I shouldn't be telling you this, but I thought you should know." Wilhelm glanced around the room suspiciously. Then he ran his fingers through his hair.

Karl grew impatient. He was just about to stand up and leave when the waiter returned with his coffee. "Spit it out, Wilhelm! If it is so damned important!"

Waiting for the waiter to retreat out of ear shot, Wilhelm hunched over again and asked, "Karl, have you ever heard of a place called Dachau?"

Karl thought for a moment. *Why does that name sound familiar?*

Not waiting for Karl to figure it out, Wilhelm proceeded. "It is a small town just outside of Munich. There's an old munitions factory there. It was very productive during the Great War. Now, Hitler has other plans for the place."

Karl's heart raced at this news. "He plans to reopen the factory?"

"No," Wilhelm whispered. "He is turning it into a concentration camp!"

Karl took a sip of his coffee and tried to understand what Wilhelm was telling him. "So, if Herr Hitler is not manufacturing munitions, what does this place have to do with me?"

"Karl, Hitler is setting up special courts. These courts will do nothing but judge cases of political dissidents. When they are found guilty, the prisoners will be automatically sent to Dachau! Do you understand what I am trying to tell you."

"No. "I'm not a political dissident. I am a loyal German citizen. So, what does this have to with me?" Karl hissed angrily.

"It has everything to do with you!" Wilhelm raised his voice and then quickly lowered it. "I tried to tell you a while ago, but you wouldn't listen. Hitler needs you, and your factory, in order to rearm Germany. I know how you feel about producing steel for the military. You have made that perfectly clear. But I tell you now that the time is quickly coming when the Führer will be calling on you to do just that!"

"Never!" shouted Karl. Then he lowered his voice. "I will never allow my factory to produce steel for weapons!"

"Then you will go to Dachau, Karl! And you will die there!"

Karl just stared at Wilhelm for a second. "Why? How will I end up in Dachau for refusing to produce weapons? Tell me that, Wilhelm! The last time I looked, I still owned Rauthenau Steel, and Germany is still a free country. I can do anything I want with the factory!"

"No, you can't Karl!" Wilhelm snapped. "Don't you see? Don't you understand? He will have you tried as a political dissident!"

"Why are you telling me this, Wilhelm? You know I am no dissident. Everyone knows that I love my country. I would never do anything to harm it. I'm not a communist. I'm not a political dissident."

"Yes, Karl, I know that. But you are a homosexual."

Karl was stunned. Suddenly the horrible trials of the early 1900s flooded into his mind. The trial of Oscar Wilde, the Eulenburg affair, and the rumors about the Kaiser. Many good men had lost their careers, their families, and their lives because of those trials. Then Karl imagined himself standing before this special court trying to defend himself against charges of homosexuality. "What can I do, Wilhelm? I can't change who I am?"

"You must oblige Hitler when he calls on you. You must agree to everything he demands. That's the only way you'll be safe."

Karl looked down into his cup of coffee and then back into Wilhelm's eyes. "How can you serve such a monster?"

"Karl, he's not a monster. I believe he truly loves Germany, and wants to restore her to her rightful place in the world. In order to do that sacrifices will have to be made. Everyone will have to cooperate if we are to rise again. And for those who don't cooperate, Dachau will be waiting for them."

"Why do you tell me this, Wilhelm?"

"Because you are a stubborn man, Karl. And because I still love you. I don't want to see you hurt yourself."

"Hurt myself?" Karl hissed. "Hurt myself? You claim that you love me, and yet you serve a man who would sentence me to prison for simply loving you in return. That makes no sense, Wilhelm, and you know it!"

"Hitler does not care who we love, Karl. He doesn't care about homosexuality. Hell, his second in command is Ernst Roehm, for God's sake. The only thing he cares about is who will help him make Germany strong again!"

"Well, obviously we disagree on how to accomplish that!" Karl spat. "We have had this discussion a thousand times, Wilhelm. Nothing has changed."

"Yes it has, Karl. Dachau has changed it! If you don't believe me, pick up a copy of the Munich newspaper in the morning."

---

The next morning, March 21, 1933, Karl read the following announcement made by Heinrich Himmler, Commissioner of Police for the city of Munich, in the *Munchner Neuesten Nackrichten*:

*On Wednesday, March 22, 1933, the first concentration camp will be opened in the vicinity of Dachau. It can accommodate 5,000 people. We have adopted this measure, undeterred by paltry scruples, in the conviction that our action will help to restore calm to our country and is in the best interests of our people.*

"The first concentration camp," Karl whispered to himself. "Accommodate 5,000 people. My God, how many political dissidents can there be?" Then he reached for the telephone. "Yes, operator, I would like to place a call to Vienna, bitte." After waiting several minutes for the call to be put through, he heard Julius' sleepy voice on the other end of the line. "Good morning, my boy! How is that new violin case working out?"

---

A few days later Karl was sitting at a conference table in the Chancellery building along with the other top industrialists in Germany. He had been summoned to this 'top secret' meeting by a man in a trench coat who had not identified himself. He assumed the others gathered around the table had been summoned in the same fashion. Karl recognized several of them on sight. There was Krupp von Bohlen of the Krupp Works, Bosch and Schnitzler of I.G. Farben, and Voegler, head of the United Steel Works. Also gathered around the table were Joseph Goebbels, Hermann Goering, Heinrich Himmler, Ernst Roehm, General Franz Halder, and Admiral Wilhelm Canaris. *Quite a distinguished group*, Karl thought.

Suddenly, the huge double doors of the conference room swung open and Adolf Hitler entered. Immediately all the Nazis in the room rose to their feet and saluted. Karl stood, shoving his hands into his pockets. The gesture didn't go unnoticed as Hitler marched to the head of the table. He stood there stone faced, keeping them all on their feet. Finally, he lifted his hand acknowledging the salute, and then nodded for them to sit down. Everyone took their seat while giving Hitler their full attention.

"Private enterprise, Gentlemen," Hitler began, "cannot be maintained in the age of democracy. It is conceivable only if the people have a sound idea of authority and personality. All the worldly goods we possess we owe to the struggle of the chosen. We must not forget that all the benefits of culture must be introduced more or less with an iron fist. Therefore, it is my solemn promise to you that the Nazi party will eliminate the Marxists among your workers, and restore to you the Wehrmacht, and a solid economy."

Krupp, and most of the other industrialists, immediately jumped to their feet applauding. Again, Karl rose slowly, but no sound came when he put his hands together. Hitler raised his hand and everyone sat down again. "Now, we stand before the last election. Regardless of the outcome, there will be no retreat. If necessary, I will stay in power by other means, with other weapons." Again, the industrialists rose to their feet cheering, and Hitler bowed his head in acknowledgment of their applause. Then he stood up suddenly and marched out the conference room.

Eventually, Goering spoke up. "Gentlemen, financial sacrifices will have to be made which surely would be much easier for industry to bear if it realized that the election will surely be the last one for the next ten years, probably even for the next hundred years. We are laying down the line for the fight against the Red Terror." Again, there was applause.

*So,* Karl thought, *this is what it is all about. Hitler is going to call for an election of confidence, and he needs our support to pull it off. He needs our contributions to launch his propaganda campaign. He's telling us that if we donate to the party he will get rid of the trade unions for us. No wonder Krupp and the others are so excited.*

Ernst Roehm rose to his feet when the applause died down. "Gentlemen, to show his good faith, the Führer has called for a national boycott of all Jewish shops on April 1. No longer will the money of hard working Germans line the pockets of thieving Jews. He also promises you that by May 1, you will no longer have to deal with the suffocating Marxist trade unions. For this favor the Führer asks for your support and willingness to help him rebuild Germany into the greatest nation on Earth!"

Krupp von Bohlen, the rich munitions baron, jumped to his feet and exclaimed, "We are extremely grateful to the Führer for having given us such a clear picture. I am quite sure that we all understand perfectly. And furthermore, I suggest that we pass the hat, here and now, as the first step toward showing the Führer that we totally support his actions." With that, Krupp grabbed up his hat and reached for his wallet.

When the hat was passed to Karl he smiled apologetically, and he patted his breast pocket. "I'm sorry, Herr Krupp, I did not realize when I left home this morning that I would be attending a fund raising meeting. I haven't a mark on me."

"Not to worry, Herr von Rauthenau. I will make your donation for you. You can pay me back later," Krupp grinned, knowing full well that Karl's wallet held a reasonable amount of cash.

*You sly bastard*, Karl thought. "That is very kind of you, Herr Krupp, but unnecessary. When I return to my office this afternoon I will have my secretary make out a note to the Führer. Will one hundred thousand marks be sufficient?"

"That will do nicely, Herr von Rauthenau. Very nicely, indeed." After he finished his trip around the table, Krupp counted up the donations and handed them to Goebbels. "With the addition of Herr von Rauthenau's contribution, I am happy to present the Führer with three million marks," he boasted as he shoved his thumbs into his vest pockets. "This should ensure his campaign goes well!"

*Yes*, Karl thought, *that much money pretty much seals our fate. Don't they see what they are doing? They had the chance to stop him right here, but they let their greed override their judgment. They just sold Germany to the devil for the sake of a few extra marks.*

Amy Trevor had been pretty down since the St. Valentine's Day Drag Ball. She hadn't been able to concentrate on much of anything except that night. Tonight, sitting in the hotel bar filled with reporters, Amy felt more alone than she had before she met Leeza. *Leeza von Rauthenau. Sounds so noble. God she's gorgeous. What an ass I was to run away. How stupid can I be? Why did I do that? Damn it, Trevor, you're an idiot!*

Amy had lied the night she told Jim Newman she got more than he did. The truth was that she had not been with anyone since she left the states three years ago. Her heart had been broken when her college sweetheart, and first real lover, had run off to marry a man. After that Amy had joined the Universal News Service, and left the country. She had simply been overwhelmed the night of the ball. She had not expected to feel the rush of emotion that Leeza released in her. Amy was scared of being hurt again, and never realized it until that night.

*You gotta stop thinkin' about her. She's long gone, you fool,* Amy thought to herself. *But, her eyes...they were like...There you go again, Trevor. Cut it out! You're not here to be romancing a beautiful woman. You're here to do a job.*

Amy reported the news of the planned national boycott against the Jews which was scheduled for April 1, 1933. When they read her article, American Jews became outraged. Rabbi Stephen S. Wise, leader of the American Jewish Congress and American Zionists, organized a mass demonstration for March 27, at Madison Square Garden in New York. But when the German Jews learned about the demonstration, they started sending telegrams to their brethren in the United States, and even appealed to the United States Embassy in Berlin to stop the rally at Madison Square Garden.

"Are they crazy?" Jim Newman barked. "Why would they want to stop the demonstration?"

"Because, Jim, they're scared to death! Can't you understand that their about to loose their businesses, their livelihoods!" Amy yelled. "They are simply scared to death! What do you think will happen to them if this rally goes off?"

"Well, by God, someone had better do something before they're all gone, and it might as well be Americans," Jim yelled back.

"I am afraid he is right, Miss Trevor," Marshall Turner interjected. "You Yanks have a way of getting things done."

Amy thought about that for a moment. As much as she hated to admit that Jim was right, she knew American protest might be the only way to stop what was happening. Grudgingly, she gave in. "Yeah, you might just be right about that, Marshall. After all, we convinced the King of England back in 1776, didn't we?

Marshall laughed out loud, "Indeed!"

"I think I'll go write an article in support of the rally," Amy grinned. *Too bad nobody will protest for the gays.*

A few days later, as most of the international news reporters and photographers gathered around the bar of the Adlon Hotel, their home away from home, to discuss the results of the Madison Square Garden rally, the phone behind the bar rang. The bartender answered it and then handed the receiver to Jim Newman.

"Yeah," he barked into the phone. After listening for a few seconds he said, "Yeah! Be right there." Hanging up the phone, Jim looked around for his photographer. Spotting him over in the corner talking to Amy, he walked up casually and said, "Hey, Miller, you wanna head on over to Schwarzes Cafe and grab a bite to eat?"

72

"Yeah, sure. Ya wanna come along Amy?"

"Naw," Jim interrupted before Amy could answer, "Dames don't like the place. They say the food's too greasy. Come on, Miller. Get a move on, will ya."

Amy knew very well that the food at Schwarzes Cafe was not greasy, and that Jim Newman was in too much of a hurry. He hadn't finished his drink at the bar. *He left almost a half a beer sitting there. That can only mean one thing. He's tryin' to scoop me.* Quickly, she picked up her brief case and followed Newman and Miller out of the hotel. They crossed the street and turned to the right, toward the Chancellery building. *Schwarzes Cafe is in the opposite direction, Jim. Try and scoop me, will ya. We'll see about that.* Amy followed them all the way down to the Chancellery and then pulled out her press pass and hung it around her neck.

The Chancellery foyer was packed with German reporters all waiting for Joseph Goebbels to appear at the top of the staircase. "Something about the Jewish boycott," she overheard one of them say to his photographer. *God, I hope they are going to stop it*, Amy thought. Just then, Goebbels appeared and the reporters quieted down.

"Today, the Führer wished to show his compassion. Instead of making the boycott against Jewish shops permanent, he has chosen to make it a one day boycott. The Führer is quite sure that even though the boycott is scheduled for Saturday, April 1, when most Jewish shops will be closed, his point will be made clear. Loyal Germans no longer wish to do business with Jews. That is all." Goebbels walked away without answering any of the questions shouted by the reporter, and Amy smiled to herself. *Chalk one more up for the Yanks!*

# Chapter Six

## The Loss Of Knowledge

In the early morning hours of April 1, 1933, a thick fog covered the streets of Berlin. Quietly, Heinrich led his squad into the Jewish section of the city. *This is perfect*, he thought. *The fog will give us all the cover we need.* Although his Brownshirts had been ordered to dress in civilian clothes, the weather was sure to give them even more anonymity. "You men, start here on this side of the street!" he ordered. "And you others, start over there!"

Heinrich's troops went to work immediately. Across the front of shop after shop the Brownshirts sloshed red paint. Soon, red swastikas and ugly slogans like *"Juden swine"* and *"Kill the Jews!"* covered windows, doors, and sidewalks. Heinrich's men were extremely efficient as they moved onto the next street. Eventually, every shop in the Jewish section of Berlin was covered in red paint. Then they waited.

As Berliners woke, and began their Saturday errands, most were completely unaware of what had happened in the early morning hours. Used to Jewish shops being closed on Saturdays, hardly anyone took notice of the Brownshirts' handiwork. Even the Jews themselves took little notice. They just shook their heads in disgust as they passed the wet paint on their way to the synagogue for Shabbat services. Heinrich and his men watched from the shadows. *What's going on? Don't they care? Don't the stupid swine understand the message?*

"Look at them!" one of Heinrich's men whispered in amazement. "It's as if they don't see it!"

"Well," Heinrich barked as he watched an old man come out of his clock shop, "we'll just have to make them see it. Come on!"

Springing into action, Heinrich ran over to the old man and grabbed him, shoving his face into the red paint splashed across his window. "Dirty, stinking Jew," he yelled as he pounded his fist into the old man's back. "Don't you see the message? Don't you understand? We don't want you here! Get out! Get out of Germany!"

From behind, Heinrich's men encouraged him with shouts of "Kill the Jew bastard! Kill him!"

Heinrich kept pounding the old man until he collapsed on the sidewalk. Enraged that the old Jew had fallen so quickly, he spun around, glassy eyed, in search of his next victim. "Come on boys, let's get 'em!" he screamed as he broke into a run. The Brownshirts followed enthusiastically, laying hands on everyone who came across their path. By midmorning three Jews had been murdered and fifty-six more had been beaten nearly to death.

Still, most Berliners hardly took notice of the boycott or the violence. They had gone about their business as if nothing unusual had happened. They completely failed to be inspired by the violence of the Brownshirts, and didn't seem to be too concerned about the terror of a few Jews. Neither was the newspaper impressed enough to even cover the story.

"That's not the way it was supposed to be!" Roehm shouted. "You were supposed to arouse their anger, you dummkopf!"

"I am sorry, Sir!" Heinrich snapped to attention.

"I am not pleased, Heinrich! Nor is the Führer!"

"Yes, Sir!"

"How can we move against the Jews if German citizens don't hate them? We expected much more from you, Heinrich! You know I will have to punish you for your failure in this matter."

"Yes, Sir!" Heinrich snapped to attention with a gleam in his eye.

"After that, we must turn the German people's hearts and minds toward hate."

"Yes, Sir!"

"When we have accomplished that, they will follow us blindly."

"Yes, Sir! But, how can we make them hate the Jews if they don't already?"

Roehm stroked his chin and thought about that for a few seconds. "Oh, they do, Heinrich. They just don't fear them. Fear is the key. Fear! Our Führer has written it. Have you not read *Mein Kampf*? The German people already hate the Jews. Now all we have to do is teach them to fear the Jews. Once they are afraid, they will turn on them willingly."

And fear was just what the Nazis instilled. On April 26, 1933, a special police force was created. The Gestapo. This elite police force, with Heinrich Himmler as its head, was authorized to act secretly on behalf of the state. Gestapo agents arrested anyone who seemed remotely threatening to the new government, and terrorized the rest of Germany at will.

In the middle of the night Gestapo agents burst into private homes, without benefit of a warrant, and spirited away individuals who would later be ransomed back to their families. While awaiting their ransom, these concentration camp prisoners would be sadistically beaten, sometimes even murdered. Homosexuals were the first to be arrested; then German Socialists and wealthy Jews. It didn't take long for the mere mention of the Gestapo's name to send chills down the spines of most German citizens.

One evening, as they dined together, Roehm casually mention to Heinrich, "We need to pay a visit to Hirschfeld's Institute." Heinrich glanced up in confusion. "Himmler and his Gestapo will eventually make their way to the Institute. I'm sure the good doctor has kept a file on me.

Every time I got the clap I paid him a little visit, and I don't want my file falling into the hands of those maggots Himmler's got working for him. My file would make perfect blackmail material. That's the last thing I need right now."

"I will take care of it right away, Sir!" Heinrich grinned.

"In the usual manor, if you please, Heinrich. We don't need anyone knowing our business, now do we?"

"No, Sir. Of course not. I think the boys at the university will do nicely, don't you?"

"Quite nicely, indeed!"

---

On the morning of May 6, 1933, a blaring brass band marched up Otto-Suhr-Allee and stopped in front of # 93, the palatial mansion of the *Institute for Sexual Science*. Seconds later several dozen college students jumped out of the backs of four trucks as they screeched to a halt behind the band. Heinrich yelled, "Run the faggots out, boys!"

The angry mob of students rushed the doors of the Institute yelling and screaming, "Clear out the queers! Death to faggots!" With clubs and knives they smashed everything in the Institute's foyer. Some slashed paintings, others overturned bottles of ink on carpets and tapestries, and the remainder smashed the furniture and sculptures to bits. Moments later, Heinrich shouted and pointed them in the direction of the Institute's museum. Off they went to pillage and destroy, howling like a pack of angry wolves as they went. Heinrich sneaked off in the opposite direction toward Dr. Hirschfeld's private office.

Forcing the door open, he quickly rummaged through the filing cabinet and found what he was looking for. Staring at it, he thought, *My master's most intimate secrets. Surely this will please him.* Shoving the file under his shirt, he glanced down at the remaining files in the cabinet. There were several names he recognized. He pulled them from the cabinet and quickly stuffed them under his shirt as well. *These may come in quite handy one day.* Suddenly he heard shouts of outrage coming from the foyer. He slammed the filing cabinet shut and pulled the door closed behind him.

"What in the hell is going on here?" Klaus Gessler shouted as he pulled on his suit coat. "Hey, you! Stop there!" he cried to a boy who was carrying out the painting of King Ludwig posing with his penis as his scepter. The college boy just laughed and headed straight for the door. Reaching the bottom of the stairs, Klaus yelled at him again, "Hey, you can't..." But, it was too late. Heinrich had picked up a broken chair leg and smashed it across Klaus' skull. The world suddenly went spinning into darkness as he fell unconsciousness.

"Yes, we can!" Heinrich hissed. "We can do anything we want!"

Eventually, the Berlin police showed up with the Gestapo on their heels, but Heinrich was long gone. He had gotten in and out quickly and efficiently, without anyone ever knowing he had been there. Even the college students didn't know his real name. When they were asked who had instigated this crusade, the only answer they could give was a shrug of their shoulders. "These queers are destroying the fabric of our good German culture!" they cried in their own defense. "We couldn't just stand by and do nothing while they spread their filth among us!" The college students had said exactly what Heinrich had told them to say, never realizing that they had been nothing more than pawns in his covert game.

Releasing the college students, and dismissing the Berlin police, the Gestapo took over the operation. They had been planning to raid the *Institute for Sexual Science*, but wanted to wait for Dr. Magnus Hirschfeld to return from his lecture tour abroad. They had wanted to arrest him during the raid. Instead, they had to satisfy themselves with Klaus. "Take him to Sachsenhausen," the lead agent yelled, "and I want every file and every book in the place taken to headquarters for inspection."

Box after box of files were carried out. Over seven thousand books, documenting one hundred and fifty years of gay and lesbian lives, were carelessly tossed in the back of the trucks. The Institute's entire library, along with what remained of the art and displays from the museum, were cast away like so much trash. These treasures of knowledge were never to be read again.

A few nights later, the Institute's books and manuscripts were set on fire in front of the Opera House in Berlin. Crowds of Berliners assembled to see the book burning, and cheered wildly as each was tossed onto the heaping bonfire.

"No more faggots," they yelled in a rhythmic chant, "no more Jews! No more faggots! No more Jews!" That night the gay and lesbian community of the world lost an irreplaceable bank of knowledge as the smoke rose above the flames. In prison, Klaus grieved the loss when his Gestapo interrogator sadistically informed him of what was going on at the Opera House that very minute.

---

"Those bastards!" raged Adolf Brand. "They had no right!"

After listening to Adolf rant and rave for an hour and a half, Fritz suggested, "Let's go get a beer, Herr Brand. I'll buy."

Adolf stopped in front of his window, staring out into the misty spring night. Then dropping his head he whispered, "How could they, Fritz? They had no right."

"Come, Herr Brand. You need a drink."

Adolf pulled himself from his grief long enough to pick up his overcoat. Then Fritz took him by the elbow, leading him down the stairs and out through the lobby doors. Together they walked quietly down Motzstrass. When they came to the corner of Kalckreuthstrasse they looked toward the Eldorado Klub. Suddenly, they heard a police wagon's siren coming up behind them. Fritz pulled Adolf into the shadow of the building. They waited as the police wagon came to a halt in front of the Eldorado. Several policemen piled out and charged into the bar. Moments later they began dragging gay men out, and tossing them in the back of the police wagon.

"What's going on?" Adolf barked. He still had not quite recovered from the shock of the book burning.

"It's a raid, Herr Brand."

"Obviously, you idiot! But, why? That bar hasn't been raided since 1919."

Fritz had no answers for Adolf, but they did overhear one of the police officers taking orders from a Gestapo agent who had pulled up just a few seconds after the police wagon had. "After you finish up with these queers, head over to the Kleist Casino and clean it out. These faggot bars are an unparalleled breeding ground of dirt and filth, and the Führer wants them cleaned out!"

"Yes, Sir! Right away!" the policeman snapped. "Whatever the Führer wants!"

"Did you hear that, Fritz?"

Fritz nodded his head and whispered in awe, "Ja, I heard that."

"Let's get back to the office. I have a story to write!" Both men shoved their hands in their pockets and quickly headed back to the office of *Der Eignen*. When he entered the office, Adolf threw his overcoat in the corner and shouted at Fritz, "Call all our reporters. Get them out of bed if you have to. Tell them I want them out in the streets. I want reports from every bar in the city by two o'clock. You got that?"

"I got it!" Fritz exclaimed. "By two o'clock. Reports from all bars."

An hour later the first reports started coming in. The National Cafe had been raided as well as the Magic Flute Dance Palace. As the hours ticked by reports trickled in that twenty more bars had been raided, and over a thousand gay men had been taken into custody.

*My God*, Adolf thought, *Where are they going to put them all?* "Fritz, I want a man over at police headquarters. I want to know what's going on over there. The jail has got to be packed by now! Oh, and find out how much bail is being set at."

As Adolf and Fritz waited for the call to come in from police headquarters they paced and grumbled to themselves. "Damn Nazis!" "Fucking Hitler!" "Cock sucking Roehm!"

Finally the phone rang. Adolf turned suddenly, almost running over Fritz as he scrambled to pick up the receiver. Snatching the phone from Fritz's hand, Adolf shouted, "Out of my way, you dummkopf! Brand here! Talk!" Adolf's face went white as a sheet as he listened to the report coming in. "Uh huh. Uh huh. Uh huh," he mumbled. "Where did they take them? Uh huh. Yes. Uh huh. Well get over there. I want to know what's going on!"

When Adolf hung up the telephone Fritz asked, "What is it, Herr Brand. You don't look too good."

"They are not at police headquarters," Adolf whispered.

"Who? The reporters?"

"No. The men who were arrested."

"What do you mean?"

"Just what I said, they're not there."

"Well, where are they?"

"Dieter thinks they have been taken directly to Sachsenhausen!"

"Why Sachsenhausen?"

81

"There's a rumor that it's been turned into a concentration camp."

"Dear God!" Fritz cried.

"If it's true, God is the only one who can save them."

"But, they haven't even had a trial. No one can be sentenced without a trial, Herr Brand. And even if they were found guilty, homosexuals serve their sentences in regular prisons, not concentration camps."

"Dieter said the regular jails and prisons are full. Everyone who is arrested from now on goes directly to a concentration camp."

Both men began pacing again. Finally, Adolf sat down at his typewriter and threaded in a piece of paper. As he began clanking away at the keys, Fritz interrupted him. "Excuse me, Herr Brand, but do you think it wise to write about the Nazis after what has happened tonight?"

"You may be right, Fritz, but I can't just sit here and do nothing. The readers count on us for information, and I'm not going to let them down now. They need to know what's going on."

---

With heavy dark bags under his eyes, Karl rubbed the three day old stubble on his cheek. He'd been at his desk for days waiting for some news. Totally exhausted, his eyes filled with tears as he replayed the scene in his mind. The Gestapo had dragged Klaus' lifeless body out of the Institute, and had thrown him into the back of a car. Karl had seen blood trickling from his head, but didn't know whether he was alive or dead.

Karl had been there because of a breakfast date with Klaus. When he arrived on the scene, the S.A. guards had sealed off the street and would not let him pass. He had to watch, helplessly, from the corner.

"Klaus, where are you?" Karl whispered. "Where have they taken you? Are you still among the living?" *Yes, you are alive. I would know if you were dead. I love you so much. I would know if you were...God please, watch over him wherever he is.*

Suddenly the phone rang, startling Karl out of his half daydream, half prayer. "Yes, Hello!" he stammered as he pounced on the receiver.

"Hello! Uncle Karl? Is that you?"

"Leeza?"

"Yes, Uncle, it's Leeza. What's wrong? You sound distraught?"

"I uh...I am just a little tired Leeza." Karl did not want to worry her.

"I know you better than that, Uncle Karl. Something is wrong! Is it Klaus?"

Karl paused in surprise. "How did you know?"

"Julius just brought over the latest edition of *Der Eignen*. There is an article about Doctor Hirschfeld's institute and the raids on the bars. Is Klaus all right, Uncle Karl?"

"I don't know, Leeza. I was there, at the Institute, when they took him away. His head was bleeding very badly. No one will tell me where they have taken him."

"Did they hurt you?" The fear in Leeza's voice was apparent. "Are you all right?"

"Yes, yes. I'm fine."

"Are you sure? Maybe I should come home!"

"No!" Karl commanded. "That is the last thing I want you to do, Leeza. Things are going crazy here in Berlin. No! I want you to stay in Vienna. You'll be safe there."

"What do you mean, 'safe there.' Are you in danger, Uncle Karl?"

"No! I'm fine, Leeza. It's just that I don't know where Klaus is, and I am worried."

"Have you called the hospitals?"

"Yes, and the police. No one has seen or heard from him. It was the Gestapo who took him, and no one in their headquarters will talk to me. It's just so damn frustrating not knowing."

Leeza didn't respond right away. Then she whispered, "Do you think he is…"

"No! I would know if he were dead. My heart, it would tell me," Karl sighed.

"Yes," Leeza hesitated. "I suppose it would."

Karl smiled. *How can she understand? She has never been in love before. She can't possibly know what it's like to be so connected to someone.* "You'll just have to trust me about that."

"I still think I should come home, Uncle. I can take a few days off. I'll call another musician to cover for me."

"No! No, Leeza, really. I need all of my energy concentrated on Klaus right now. It would be best for me if you stayed in Vienna. Honestly! And besides, your mother is here to watch over me. Really, I am all right. I just need to find out where Klaus is!"

"Have you called Uncle Wilhelm?"

"No!" Karl grunted. "And, I will not!"

"For heavens sake, why not!" Leeza cried. "Uncle Wilhelm can help! He has connections, you know!"

"Yes, I know he has connections! It's precisely those connections that took Klaus away in the first place! And stop calling him Uncle! He is no longer a member of this family and I will never ask him for help! Never!"

"Not even for Klaus," Leeza asked indignantly. Karl wouldn't answer, but just sighed in frustration. Then he hung up the phone.

About an hour later the phone rang again. It was Wilhelm. "Meet me at the train station in one hour. I know where your friend is. If you really want to know, you'll be there." That was all Wilhelm would say before he hung up.

84

At the train station, Karl was forty-five minutes early. He had left home as soon as the call had come from Wilhelm. Now, pacing around the rows of empty benches, he kept glancing at his watch to check the time. Impatiently, he picked up a newspaper and flipped through the pages looking for some interesting piece to distract him; something that would take his mind off Klaus.

A few seconds later he slammed the paper down on the bench next to him. *That bastard! Wilhelm was probably in on the whole thing, right from the start. He was so jealous of Klaus. He was probably the one who had him picked up in the first place.* Then Karl looked up just in time to see Wilhelm walk through the doors of Potsdamerbahnhof.

Quickly he stood up and walked toward him, but Wilhelm shook his head slightly and glanced toward the men's room. Karl looked confused, then glanced around to see who might be watching. In the corner stood a dark little man in a trench coat. Instinctively, Karl knew he was a Gestapo agent. Slowly, he walked past Wilhelm to the WC.

After placing his brief case on the bench, and flipping through the same paper Karl had, Wilhelm headed for the men's room too. When he came through the door, he said, "Good God, Karl! You look like shit! When was the last time you shaved or..."

Karl had been waiting for Wilhelm. He threw his forearm across Wilhelm's chest and shoved him up against the door. "Tell me where he is!" he hissed.

Wilhelm shoved back, throwing Karl off balance and sending him tumbling to the floor. "That's what I am here for, you fool, if you'll give me half a chance." Then Wilhelm adjusted his collar and cuffs before answering. "Sachsenhausen! Your precious boy is in Sachsenhausen!" he spat.

Karl looked confused. "Sachsenhausen?" he whispered. "Why Sachsenhausen?"

85

"Because he is a homosexual, Karl! I told you Hitler was going to clean up this country, and he's starting in Berlin, with the homosexual trash in the Kunfurstendamn. But there are so many of them that the jails could not hold them all, so after the raid on Hirschfeld's institute, Sachsenhausen was quickly converted into a concentration camp. I tried to warn you, but you wouldn't listen! Now your precious lover is in Sachsenhausen and it's your fault!"

The color drained from Karl's face. Tears welled up in his eyes as his last conversation with Wilhelm ran through his mind. "But, why him? Klaus is not political in the least. What has he done? What have I done?" he begged, trying to comprehend how this was his fault.

"You didn't make the cash donation at the meeting with the Führer, you idiot! I told you to make yourself available to him. Now, your dear lover is in a concentration camp, and you are being watched!"

Karl stood there in shock. Tears streamed down his face. Pleadingly he said, "But, I did make the donation! Wilhelm, I gave one hundred thousand marks."

"Not at the meeting, you didn't!"

"I sent a check that very afternoon! What else does he want?" Then suddenly, Karl remembered the arrogance he had shown at the meeting. The image of him patting himself on the chest flooded his mind. "Oh, my God!" he cried. "I have killed Klaus." His body began to quake from holding back his sobs.

Wilhelm stared at Karl with contempt. "I told you to be careful, Karl. Now look what's happened. You shouldn't have been so arrogant. The Führer needs you. More precisely, he needs your money and eventually your factory. I would suggest that from now on you follow the lead of the other industrialists or you'll find yourself in Sachsenhausen too." Again, Karl's body shook with grief filled tremors.

Seeing Karl's agony softened Wilhelm's anger. Tenderly, he reached out to take him in his arms. Karl began to sob uncontrollably. Wilhelm sighed, "It was not your fault. I'm sorry I said that. They've been planning the raid on the Institute for some time now. They were just waiting for Doctor Hirschfeld to return before they did it. Those college kids just sped up their time table, that's all. Doctor Gessler was caught in the wrong place at the wrong time. It wasn't your fault."

"Then you must help me," Karl pleaded. "Help me get him out! You can do it! I know you can! You have the right connections."

"No!" Wilhelm barked sternly. "I can't help him, Karl! I won't!"

Karl wrenched himself from Wilhelm's embrace and glared at him harshly. "You said you knew they were planning to raid the Institute. You could have warned me, but you didn't. You just let it happen. Hell, you wanted it to happen, didn't you, Wilhelm? You just stood back and let the Gestapo take Klaus because you were jealous of him. Did you think this would bring us back together, Wilhelm? Did you think this would make me love you again? Well it won't, Wilhelm!" Karl sobbed. "I will hate you for the rest of my life for this. Hate you! Do you hear me, Wilhelm? I will hate you forever for this!"

"Karl," Wilhelm said trying to placate him, "Doctor Gessler is fine. All they want him for is ransom. Surely he will call on you when the time comes. Just pay the ransom and he'll be released."

Karl glared at Wilhelm. "Is that why you came here, Wilhelm, to make sure I would pay the ransom to your precious Führer?"

Wilhelm shook his head. "No, Karl. I came here because Leeza asked me too!" Then he turned and opened the door saying, "I did this for Leeza."

# Chapter Seven

## Hope For The Holiday

The twenty-two mile drive up to Oranienburg was pleasant this time of year. All of the trees had filled out with their new leaves, and the flowers were in full bloom. The air smelled sweet and warm, filling Karl's senses with momentary pleasure as he drove through the countryside. *Klaus can smell these same flowers,* he told himself, trying to banish the nightmarish images that continually filled his mind since Wilhelm had spoken the name of Sachsenhausen. *Surely he feels the warm sun on his face, and breaths in the same sweet air of summer.*

It had been days since Karl learned that Klaus was in Sachsenhausen. He waited impatiently for the ransom call to come, but it never came. Trying to comfort himself, he thought, *Klaus has no family in Germany. Maybe they didn't know they could contact me. Maybe if I go to visit him the Gestapo will take the hint.* But in the back of his mind he knew that the Gestapo knew. After all, hadn't Wilhelm told him as much? *This is my fault, sweet Klaus, but I promise you I will make it right. I will pay whatever they demand, and then I will beg for your forgiveness.*

The little village of Oranienburg was a pretty little town with flower boxes on every window sill. As Karl passed a little bakery, he thought how nice it would be to take a fresh breakfast pastry to Klaus, and spun the car around.

"Good morning," chirped the baker as the little chime on the door rang, announcing Karl's entrance.

"Good Morning," Karl answered with a smile.

"Beautiful morning, Ja"

"Yes."

"The birds are singing. The flowers are sweet. And the coffee is hot," the baker grinned. "What can I get for mien Herr?"

Karl breathed in deeply and smiled. "Everything looks and smells so wonderful. Let's see, I'll take one of the gerwiirzkuchen and a dozen linzer cookies."

"Ah, a very good selection, mien Herr. The red raspberry jam in the linzer is especially good. My wife made it!"

"Then I shall relish every bite!" Karl grinned. While the baker boxed up the cake and cookies Karl asked, "How do I get to Sachsenhausen from here?"

The baker suddenly lost his jolly smile as the color drained from his face. "When you get to the middle of town, bear right and follow the road toward the East. It is only a few miles, but you don't want to go there, mien Herr," he whispered, giving Karl a quick glance. "That is a very bad place."

"I must," Karl groaned. "I uh…I have a friend…He is…uh…The pastries are for him."

The baker hung his head. "Then it is very bad for your friend, mien Herr."

"What do you mean?"

"I deliver bread to the officers there," sighed the baker without looking at Karl. "Sometimes I see the prisoners."

"And!"

"They are not treated very well, mien Herr."

"What do you mean?" Karl demanded.

"I mean, if my dog looked like most of those men I would shoot it, and put it out of its misery." Karl just stared at the baker in disbelief. A few seconds of silence passed before the baker spoke again. "If you are intent on visiting your friend, and if the guards let you see him, you should prepare yourself. He may not be the man you once knew."

"He hasn't been there that long," Karl said, more to himself than to the baker. "Surely, he has endured well enough after only a couple of weeks?"

"I have seen strong men go in there. Within a few days I barely recognize them."

Karl looked into the baker's eyes. "I have to see him," he seemed to beg.

"I don't know if the guards will let you in. Sometimes they are quite unreasonable."

"But, I have to get in. I have to see him!" Karl exclaimed, almost in a panic.

"There may be a way." The baker gave Karl a wry grin. "I happen to know that Sergeant Krebbs, the gate commander, is particularly fond of mandelbretzen, almond pretzels." Karl glanced at the baker anxiously. "Should you take him a few, I'm sure he will let you see your friend." The light returned to the bakers face as he quickly boxed up a couple of the pretzels. "My treat!"

"Danke, Herr…?"

"Grimes. Hans Grimes!"

"Danke, Herr Grimes! Danke! I shall not forget your kindness," Karl exclaimed as he paid for the other pastries.

"Good luck to you, mien Herr, and God be with your friend."

---

When Karl reached the center of town he bore right just as the baker had told him to. About a mile and a half outside of town he saw the glistening white walls that surrounded the camp. From a distance, Sachsenhausen looked clean and bright with its green slate roofs, crisp white buildings, and manicured lawn and garden that led up to the black iron gate. But, as he drove closer the sweet smell of flowers faded away. The closer Karl got to the camp the more rank the air smelled. After he parked the car outside the gate he drew out his handkerchief and held it to his nose. *What is that awful smell? There must be a dead cow out in that field somewhere.* Then taking his pastry boxes in hand, he determined to think of Klaus and not the dead cow.

As he approach the gate, Karl noticed that at the top, the iron formed the words *Arbeit macht frei.* "Work brings freedom," he muttered under his breath.

A guard quickly stepped out and ordered, "Halt! State your business!"

"I would like to see Sergeant Krebbs, bitte."

The guard gave Karl a good looking over and then went back into the small building to the left of the gate. A moment later a huge bulk of a man stepped out. "I am Sergeant Krebbs. What do you want?" he barked.

*He has obviously eaten too many pretzels.* "I am here to visit a friend of mine," Karl answered with a determined note in his voice. "Doctor Klaus Gessler, bitte."

"There is no visitation today," Krebbs grumbled, eyeing the pastry boxes, "Herr...?"

"Karl von Rauthenau. I am told that you have a fondness for mandelbretzen, Sergeant Krebbs. I know your duties must keep you very busy these days and I thought you might enjoy some. They're fresh from the bakery."

Sergeant Krebbs eyed the box and said, "From Herr Grimes' bakery?"

Karl thought he should not betray where his information came from and quickly answered, "No. From a bakery in Wedding. I stopped on the way out here this morning."

"The one on the corner of Muller and Amsterdamer?" Krebbs asked. His mouth was visibly watering.

"No. But if you prefer..." Karl nonchalantly started to tuck the box of pretzels back under his arm.

"That is quite all right, Herr von Rauthenau," Krebbs exclaimed. "But, should you come for another visit, I do prefer the mandelbretzen from Herr Wiechert's bakery. They are extraordinary. Now, who was it you wanted to see?" he asked as he took the pastry box from Karl.

Karl knew immediately that he and Krebbs had come to an understanding. Wiechert's mandelbretzen for one visit with Klaus. "Doctor Klaus Gessler."

"Well, let's see if I can locate him for you." Sergeant Krebbs shouted for his corporal to bring out the prisoner roster. Glancing up and down the pages, Krebbs finally exclaimed, "Ah yes, here he is. Gessler, Klaus, prisoner 2147. Corporal, go and fetch prisoner 2147. Bring him here to the gate."

"Yes, Sir!" the Corporal snapped and headed off through the gate, down the long drive way.

Karl looked over at Krebbs in confusion. "You are bringing him here to the gate? Isn't there a visitation room somewhere?"

"This is a work camp, Herr von Rauthenau, not a luxury hotel. The prisoners are here to work, not visit. You may speak to your friend through the gate, and only for a short time." Then he spun on his heels and made for the guard station, no doubt to eat his mandelbretzen immediately.

*This is not what I expected,* Karl thought as he began pacing back and forth in front of the huge iron gate. *And what is that noxious smell? Good God, why doesn't someone bury that cow?* Karl pulled out his handkerchief again. *At least they know that I am Klaus' friend. Now, surely someone will contact me for his ransom.*

Several minutes later the Corporal appeared at the end of the long drive way, escorting someone in what looked like black and white stripped pajamas. *That's not Klaus, you idiot,* Karl thought. But as he stared at the black and white stripped clad man coming closer, Karl's knees buckled, and he fell against the gate. *Klaus? My God, what have they done to you?*

Klaus' head hung as he staggered along the road in front of the Corporal. He had no idea where they were taking him now, but was so tired he didn't care. His head had been shaved, and he reeked with body odor. The blow Heinrich had given him left a huge gash on the side of his head. Flies buzzed around the caked on blood. Finally, as he stepped near the white line painted across the road, about ten feet behind the gate. The Corporal yelled, "Halt!" Klaus stumbled to a halt, but didn't look up as he waited for the Corporal's next order.

"Klaus?" Karl whispered. Klaus still did not lift his head. "Klaus," Karl called a little louder. When Klaus still did not lift his head, Karl yelled, "Klaus!"

Finally, Klaus raised his eyes slightly. Squinting, trying to focus on the voice that had spoken his name, he slowly began to recognize Karl, standing on the other side of the gate.

"Karl? Is that you, Karl?"

"Yes, Klaus," he answered anxiously. "It is me."

"Karl?" Klaus asked again, as if he were coming out of a foggy dream.

"Yes, Klaus. It is Karl. I am here."

"Karl?" Klaus whispered as if he still could not believe what he heard. "Where are you?"

"I am here, Klaus! Right here. Look up, Klaus. Look up at me. I am here." Karl stretched his arm through the bars of the gate.

Klaus squinted again, straining to see Karl as if he were miles away. "Karl? Karl, where am I?"

Karl burst out in tears. Helplessly, he reached out to Klaus through the bars. "You are in Sachsenhausen, Klaus. You have been here for almost two weeks. My God, what have they done to you?"

Just then Sergeant Krebbs emerged from the guard station and said gruffly, "Herr von Rauthenau, you must step away from the gate. And Prisoner 2147 must not cross that white line. Say what you have come to say, the prisoner has to return to work in a few minutes."

Karl glared at Krebbs. He wanted to go over and beat the pig senseless, but he couldn't risk loosing the chance to see Klaus. "Doctor Gessler needs medical attention, Sergeant Krebbs. Surely you can see that?"

"He saw a doctor before he arrived, Herr von Rauthenau. You see, his head has been shaved. Now, finish what you have to say before I have the Corporal take him back to work."

Again Karl glared at Krebbs. *If I had more time I would kill you right now, you son of a bitch.* Looking back through the gate, Karl called out. "Klaus, have they spoken to you about your ransom?"

"Ransom?" Klaus slurred. Then suddenly, Klaus seemed to come to full consciousness for just a few seconds. "Karl, help me!" he pleaded. "I will die in here!"

"Don't worry, Klaus. I will get you out of here, if its the last thing I do. Here, I have brought you some pastries."

"Time's up," Krebbs yelled from the guard station.

"But, he didn't get these cookies."

"Prisoners want cookies, Herr von Rauthenau, and I want to take my young Fraulein to the opera this weekend," Krebbs said suggestively.

Karl quickly understood what Krebbs was demanding. "Ah yes, let's see here," he said as he reached for his wallet. "I believe this will cover two tickets to the opera." Krebbs started to take the bills, but Karl pulled them back. "However, if I am to treat you to a night at the opera, surely you can do me the small courtesy of letting me see Doctor Gessler eat the cookies I brought for him."

Sergeant Krebbs motioned for the Corporal to give the box to the prisoner. When Klaus opened it he could hardly believe his eyes. He immediately devoured the cookies and then started on the cake. Karl watched Klaus gorged himself, and he began to cry. *Has he eaten anything in all the time he's been here?*

When Klaus had stuffed the last morsel into his mouth, Krebbs reached up and snatched the bills from Karl's fist. "It is good when gentlemen can do favors for one another, huh Herr von Rauthenau." Then glancing over at the Corporal he barked, "Take him away!"

"No!" Klaus cried. "Just a few more minutes, bitte"

"Your time is up, Herr von Rauthenau. Prisoner 2147 must return to work."

"His name is Doctor Klaus Gessler, not Prisoner 2147," Karl hissed as he watched Klaus stagger back down the long drive way and disappear through the inner camp wall.

*I must bring more than just cookies and cakes tomorrow*, Karl thought as he drove back to Berlin. *And, I should probably bring a fist full of theater tickets along with the mandelbretzen from Wiechert's bakery.*

Unfortunately, all the mandelbretzen in the world could not buy Karl another visit with Klaus. The S.A. camp commander ordered Sergeant Krebbs to refuse Karl every time he came to the Sachsenhausen gate that summer.

---

By September, 1933, the Reich Chamber of Culture introduced new Artistic laws in Germany. No Jewish artists were allowed to sell their art to Germans. No Jewish musicians were permitted to play their music publicly, nor were Jewish compositions allowed to be played before German audiences. Jewish authors were no longer permitted to publish their writing in Germany, and all radio programs, newspapers, and magazines were now under state censorship, which meant that all pornographic material was banned.

"But, they can't close us down, Herr Brand! The Weimar Constitution guarantees the right of free speech!"

"The Weimar Constitution is dead, Fritz, or hadn't you noticed?" Adolf barked as he tossed another book onto the stack that Fritz was packing into moving boxes.

"This is simply not fair!"

"Fritz, why don't you sachet right on over to Nazi headquarters and take the matter up with Herr Hitler! I'm sure he'll give your opinion due consideration."

"Well," Fritz huffed, "you don't have to be so bitchy about it. All I am saying is that it's not fair." Adolf's mouth dropped open. He stared at Fritz in astonishment. Fritz glanced up and said, "What?"

Adolf was almost speechless. "That's the first time you have ever said anything like that to me, Fritz! Usually it's 'yes, Sir,' 'no, Sir,' 'right away, Sir.' But now that I'm not your boss anymore, you call me a bitch?" Adolf burst out laughing.

Now it was Fritz' turn to be speechless. He hadn't realized he had been so candid with his former employer. But Adolf's laughter was contagious, and soon he too found himself laughing uncontrollably. "Yes, Sir!" he wailed.

After they exhausted themselves with laughter, the room became unusually quiet. "What are you going to do now, Fritz?" Adolf asked solemnly.

Plunking the last book on the top of last moving box, Fritz camped it up. "Oh, what's a boy to do these days? I thought I might visit Paris. Berlin just isn't fun any more, what with all the bars closed down, and half the men in the city off in prison somewhere." But this time neither of them laughed. More seriously, Fritz asked, "And what are you going to do, Herr Brand? *Der Eignen* has been your whole life for the last fifteen years."

Adolf looked down at Fritz with a wry grin. "Promise you won't laugh if I tell you?"

"On my honor!"

"What honor? You're a whore and everybody knows it!"

"Herr Brand," Fritz whined with a flip of his wrist, "how can you call me such a name? You break my heart!" Then he smiled, flung his hands on his hips, and demanded, "Now, tell me your secret."

Adolf laughed till his sides ached. "I had no idea you were such a queen, Fritz! But, if you must know, I'm getting married."

"What!" Fritz shrieked with excitement. "The great Adolf Brand is finally settling down and making a nest? He must be a handsome young thing! What's his name?"

Adolf laughed again, but this time it was sarcastic. "Her name is Gretchen. She's an old lesbian friend of mine. She's offered to marry me so the Gestapo will leave me alone."

Fritz burst into laughter again, but when Adolf didn't join in Fritz curbed it immediately. "You can't be serious," he groaned.

"Of course I'm serious," Adolf spat. "You want me to end up like Klaus Gessler, off rotting in a concentration camp somewhere? That's what they'll do to me, you know! You would be wise to follow my lead and find yourself a nice lesbian to marry."

Fritz shuddered at the thought. "I could never..."

"There are a lot of gay men marrying their lesbian friends these days. There's no shame in it! It's perfectly logical, you know!"

"Well, yes, but I could never make love to a..."

"You don't make love to them, you dummkopf! You just marry them. It's a platonic relationship."

"Oh! In name only? That sort of thing?"

"Exactly! In name only. After all, we are both homosexual. She has her girlfriend and I have my...well, I have my relationships."

Fritz thought about that for a while and then seemed to accept that it could work. "But what about the magazine, Herr Brand? Won't you miss *Der Eignen*?"

"Fritz," Adolf said slowly as the tears welled up in his eyes, "letting it die is the hardest thing I have ever done, but it's either *Der Eignen* or Adolf Brand. I think I would rather live to write again."

---

*It has been seven months since they took Klaus away,* Karl thought as he sat at his desk waiting for Manfred to bring in his morning coffee and paper. *How much longer can this madness go on?* Suddenly the telephone rang. "Yes?" Karl answered.

"Your package was delivered as usual, Herr von Rauthenau."

"Danke, Herr Grimes. How was he?"

"The same."

"Danke," Karl said as he hung up the telephone.

After being turned away from the gate of Sachsenhausen several times, Karl remembered that Hans Grimes had mentioned he sometimes made deliveries to the officers' mess in the camp, so he went to him for help. Together they worked out a scheme that kept Karl informed as to Klaus' condition.

Through Hans, Karl paid Sergeant Krebbs a regular salary. For his part, Krebbs always made sure that Klaus was assigned to the work detail which unloaded Hans' bakery truck. Because these men worked in the kitchen, they were better cared for than the rest of the prisoners. They took regular showers so they wouldn't offend the S.A. officers, and they received better uniforms, shoes, and food. Each time Hans made a delivery he managed to sneak a few extra rolls to Klaus, who ate them on the spot.

This was Karl's only way of getting information from inside the camp. Klaus told Hans that the awful smell around the camp was not from a dead cow, but from the dead bodies of prisoners. The S.A. could not transport them fast enough and many lay rotting until the camp crematorium had been built in July. Since then the smell had subsided somewhat. Shortly after Karl had seen Klaus the S.A. had taken him to the small hospital in Oranienburg. In essence, the Nazis were blackmailing Karl with Klaus' life. Klaus' health ensured that Karl would continue to cooperate with the Party.

*At least my visit accomplished that much, but why don't they just ransom him? Surely they know I'll continue to stuff their coffers because I would fear they would take him again.*

A few seconds after Karl hung up from talking to Hans, Manfred came in with the morning paper and coffee. "I think you will find this morning's headline particularly interesting, Sir," Manfred said as he poured the coffee.

Karl flipped open the paper and read the headline out loud. "*December 20, 1933. 'Führer Grants Christmas Eve Pardons to Many Concentration Camp Prisoners!'* Oh, my God! Manfred, do you know what this means?" Karl shouted with astonishment. "Klaus is going to be released! He will be home for the Holidays!"

"Yes, Sir," Manfred replied stoically. "I thought this news would please you."

"Please me?" Karl jumped up from the desk and ran around to give Manfred a huge bear hug. "Please me? This does more than please me, Manfred! This elates me!" Karl sang as he threw his arms in the air and began jumping around the room. "This...this...this news sets my soul on fire. I revel in this news. I glory in this news."

"Quite, Sir," Manfred huffed. "Will that be all, Sir?" he asked, knowing full well that it would not be, but relieved to see Karl so happy after all these months.

"Oh no, Manfred! We have so much to do before Christmas Eve! I must call Leeza at once. She simply must come home for Christmas. I know I told her not to, but she has been so worried about Klaus. Oh, and we must do some Christmas shopping. Klaus will need a whole new wardrobe. Oh, and the tree Manfred, I know I told you and the staff that we wouldn't be decorating this year, but now we must! We have to get a tree, and the lights and garland must go up."

Manfred waited patiently for Karl to finish rattling off his list of instructions. "Will that be all, Sir?"

Karl ran his fingers through his hair and then over his stubbled chin. "I'm forgetting something, Manfred."

"Dinner, Sir."

"Dinner!" Karl laughed through gleaming eyes. "Yes, that's right! We have to do something for Christmas dinner! My God, I almost forgot! Tell Cook to prepare the biggest goose she can find, and that wonderful sweet potato dish she makes every year. And don't forget the Black Forest Cake!" Karl said, shaking his finger over his head as he charged up the stairs to shower and shave. "Make that two. And, eggnog. Plenty of eggnog! There are a million things to do, Manfred, and so little time."

Manfred smiled as he watched Karl disappear down the hall talking to himself a mile a minute. Then he went to the desk and sipped the cup of coffee Karl left, while finishing the news article Karl had failed to read.

The article told how Germany's lawyers and judges were upset by the special courts of the Nazis, and how they had sentenced so many to concentration camps without the benefit of a lawful trial. *"It is a travesty of justice,"* one judge was quoted. *"It is completely illegal,"* said a Munich lawyer. *"Dachau is overflowing with presumably innocent people, and still they are building more barracks. They are completely overriding our authority,"* said another judge from Hamburg. The article went on to say, *"Because of the*

100

*outrage of Germany's legal experts, the Führer has agreed to show his compassion on Christmas Eve by granting pardons to several thousand political prisoners."*

"Compassion, my ass," Manfred grumbled. "Hitler can't afford to piss off every judge and lawyer in Germany. He still needs their support. But at least Herr Karl is happy. Yes, there just might be hope for this holiday after all."

# Chapter Eight

## The Night Of The Long Knives
## 1934

As usual Manfred brought coffee and the paper into the study where Karl waited for his morning telephone call from Hans. The long months of waiting had warn heavy on him and Manfred worried for his health. Christmas had come and gone, along with New Years Day, St. Valentine's Day, Easter, and May Day. Still Klaus had not been released. Even though Hitler had granted thousands of pardons, Himmler and Roehm had found ways to keep most prisoners in the concentration camps. Only a few hundred had been released, mostly women. Hans usually called three or four times a week to update Karl on Klaus' situation, but after so many months Karl was beginning to loose hope. As usual when the phone rang it startled him, but he no longer pounced on it with eager anticipation.

"Yes," Karl said flatly as he picked up the receiver. Manfred watched him carefully as he took these calls. After the let down of Christmas Eve, Karl had withdrawn from everyone. With each day that passed he grew thinner and thinner, and more and more depressed.

"Why wasn't he there?" Karl groaned. Manfred watched as Karl leaned forward in his chair. "How bad is it?" Karl began to show more concern than he had in months. "Has he been seen by the camp physician?" Manfred's heart began to race. "What do you mean you don't know?" Karl shouted. Then he paused and settled back in his chair. "Yes. Yes, I understand. I know there's nothing you can do. Danke, Hans. I truly appreciate all that you are doing for him, and for me. Yes. Goodbye."

"Something is wrong, Sir?" Manfred asked calmly.

"Klaus is very ill. He was not at work when Hans made his delivery. One of the other prisoners told him that Klaus has an extremely high fever. He thinks it's Typhus."

"Has Doctor Gessler been seen by a physician, Sir?"

"Hans didn't know."

"That is unfortunate," Manfred replied solemnly. Karl leaned back in his chair and stared off into space. Manfred watched as he seemed to drift farther away in his depression. "Sir," Manfred called, but Karl didn't seem to hear him. "Sir!" Manfred tried again. Still there was no response. Finally Manfred decided he had to take matters into his own hands. He walked around the desk and leaned over Karl, pulling him up by his collar. "Sir!" At last there was a response. Manfred had startled Karl out of his stupor.

"What!" he shouted.

"Forgive me, Sir, but this is not like you!" Manfred shouted back sternly. Then he released Karl's collar and stood up straight. Keeping the same stern edge in his voice, he said, "You are a man of action. You always have been. I have watched you time and again, dealing quickly and efficiently with business crises, family problems, and national emergencies. Why have you let this one grind you into the ground? I'll tell you why. Because you feel guilty! Well, so what! Whether you are guilty or not, Doctor Gessler needs your help." Manfred reached over and picked up the phone and handed it to Karl. "You know what you need to do, Sir! Now kindly get off your ass and do it!" With that said, Manfred gave the bottom of his suit coat a tug, did an about face, and marched out of the room.

Karl sat there dumfounded, totally shocked by Manfred's behavior. *I've never seen him act like that.* Then he glanced at the phone in his hand. *I know what to do? Just who does he want me to call, the Führer?*

A second later Manfred stuck his head through the study door and said calmly, "Captain Schroeder's telephone number is in your private book, Sir." Then he disappeared again behind the door.

*Wilhelm? He wants me to call Wilhelm? What good will that do?* Then Karl paused and thought about what Manfred had said. *He's right. If this had been a business crisis or something with the family, I would have moved heaven and earth to solve the problem. I have let my own feelings of guilt paralyze me.*

A few seconds later Karl dialed the telephone. "Captain Schroeder, bitte."

---

Karl was surprised by Wilhelm's eagerness to see him after the harshness of their last meeting. Now, there he sat in Karl's office at the factory, all pressed and crisp looking in his naval uniform. "You look like hell, Karl. When was the last time you shaved?"

"That's what you asked me the last time we met," Karl replied softly as he ran his hand over his chin and smiled. "It has been a few days." Karl decided to take the gentle approach with Wilhelm this time. "I haven't been doing so well, as you can see."

"Are you ill?" Wilhelm asked with a certain compassion in his voice.

*He still cares for me.* "No. I...I have been extremely worried lately."

Wilhelm sat back in the chair and grinned. "Worried about Doctor Gessler no doubt."

*Be easy, Karl. Don't push him.* "About many things," Karl sighed. "And, yes, also about Klaus. He is very ill you know. Probably Typhus."

"Typhus is rampant in most of the camps now."

"So I have heard."

"And you called to ask for my help?"

Karl sighed again and then spoke very gently. "I was hoping that for old time's sake you might be able to…"

"You really love him don't you, Karl?" Wilhelm asked with even more compassion.

Karl thought about that for a moment. "Yes, I suppose I do."

"You used to love me." Now there was pain in Wilhelm's voice.

"I still do," Karl said softly, "nothing can ever change what I feel for you."

"Obviously something changed, Karl. Or we wouldn't be having this conversation."

"Wilhelm, I have loved you since we served in the navy together. But circumstances have changed the way we live our lives. You needed your military pride back. I did not. You needed something I couldn't give you, something you found in Herr Hitler. I just hope he deserves your loyalty. I only want your happiness. In any case, circumstances changed our situations, but not our love for each other. We both know that."

"Do you love him as much as you loved me?" Wilhelm asked sadly.

"Yes," Karl said flatly, "but it is a different kind of love. I don't have with Klaus what I had with you. You were passion. He is…peace."

Wilhelm hung his head for a moment. "I'll do what I can, but not for him. For you, Karl. I want you to find the peace you deserve."

---

The camp commander of Sachsenhausen was not used to German naval officers requesting tours of his facility. Everyone knew how the military and the S.A. felt about each other. The Brownshirts were a bunch of undisciplined thugs who had been given too much power. They were an embarrassment to the military. The military, on the other hand, was legitimate and loved by the people. The Brownshirts resented that fact.

"What brings you to our little camp, Captain...uh...?"

"Captain Tannen!" Wilhelm grumbled, having thought up the name on the drive out to Oranienburg. "You are producing munitions here, yes?"

"Yes."

"I have been ordered to inspect your facility for the possibility of converting it to naval munitions manufacturing."

"But mein Captain, I see by your insignia that you are with naval intelligence. Why were you chosen to make a manufacturing inspection?"

Wilhelm glared at the arrogant Brownshirt. He leaned over his desk, almost coming nose to nose with the commander. "Because this will be a secret conversion," Wilhelm hissed. "The Führer has plans for rearming our fleet and this is to be kept top secret. I was never here. You never gave me this little tour! Do I make myself clear, Commander?"

The commander nodded his head in awe. "Perfectly, Captain." Then haltingly he said, "I hope...the Führer...will be informed that I cooperated fully!"

"Of course Commander!" Wilhelm smiled. "Of course. I am to brief the Führer personally, of everything I find here. Shall we be going?"

"Yes, Sir! Right away, Sir!" the Commander puffed.

Wilhelm had heard the horror stories about the concentration camps, but was overwhelmed with the reality he now saw in front of him. From the outside no one would have ever known what abhorrence lay within. Hundreds of men, sick and frail, worked hunched over tables loading green powder into small shell casings in the camp's munitions factory.

As he walked, Wilhelm took notes on everything he saw. The prisoners looked like skeletons with black and white stripped material draped over their bones. They were dirty and they stunk from not having proper hygiene facilities. Their eyes were lifeless and sunken. Their skin was shriveled and pale. They worked steadily, never taking their eyes from the shells, but the S.A. guards constantly harassed them to work faster.

"How many shells do you produce a day?" Wilhelm asked as he continued taking notes.

"Ten thousand," replied the camp Commander nervously.

"I see. And if we were to convert this facility to larger shells, instead of these small arms rounds?"

"I don't know, Sir. We would need all new equipment, and..."

"Better workers!" Wilhelm snapped indignantly. "This is atrocious!"

"They are all political prisoners and Jews, Sir," the Commander whined defensively, "what can you expect from the likes of them?"

"I can expect better care for the Führer's slaves, Commander!" Wilhelm spat. Then he calmed his voice and casually remarked, "New equipment will not be a problem. I can have it delivered in a few days. But if we don't have healthy slaves to work the machines, how will the Führer arm his fleet? Now you will show me their barracks, the mess hall, and their shower facilities, bitte."

The Commander nodded and quickly escorted Wilhelm back through a small gate in the camp wall, into the barracks area. "This is a very old camp, Captain," the Commander explained, as if he were embarrassed. "We don't have fine new barracks and showers like Dachau."

"That can be arranged, Commander," Wilhelm remarked as he stepped inside the first barrack. Walking up and down the rows of bunks he searched for Klaus among

107

the sick and dying men. In building after building they lay coughing and choking, many in their own vomit and feces. Finally, in the ninth barrack Wilhelm saw Klaus. He was obviously delirious with fever. *He's dying*, Wilhelm thought.

Pausing in front of Klaus, Wilhelm reached into his pocket for a handkerchief. "This is disgusting, Commander!" he barked. "In every building I have been in there are ill prisoners. How is the Führer going to win a war if his slaves can't produce the ammunition?" The Commander couldn't think of anything to say. He just shrugged his shoulders. "Look at this man for instance. He is not old! He should be up working, but instead he lays here dying. I want him taken to the camp hospital before I leave! Do you understand? I want all of them in the hospital right now!"

"Captain!" the Commander cried, "we don't have a camp hospital."

Wilhelm knew very well there was no hospital at Sachsenhausen, but looked disgusted anyway. "Well, what would you suggest, Commander?"

"I don't know, Sir. I don't know what to do with them."

"I would suggest you start by finding a doctor!" Wilhelm shouted in Klaus' direction.

Klaus had been listening to every word the officers spoke from the moment they entered the barrack, but he was afraid to open his eyes. He feared they would drag him out to stand in formation if they thought he was conscious. As he listened he was sure there was something familiar about one of those voices. *It's the fever. It's making me hear things.*

"I want a Doc-tor!" Wilhelm shouted. Then he lowered his voice, "I want a Doc-tor to see these men."

*Doctor*, Klaus thought. *Yes, need to see a doctor.* He let his eyes part slightly, just enough to take a quick peek.

*Who is that? Looks familiar.* Then Klaus let his eyes close. *It's the fever. Seeing things.*

"And after the Doc-tor" Wilhelm kicked the bunk, "has seen these men, I want a report from that Doc-tor!" he yelled as he kicked the bunk again and glared down at Klaus.

*Something in the way he says doc-tor.* Klaus opened his eyes again and tried to focus on the officer staring at him. *Who is that? Have seen him before?* Then slowly recognition took hold. *Wilhelm? Wilhelm, is that you?*

Wilhelm could see Klaus' eyes through the slits of his lids and hoped he understood. "I want a Doc-tor right now!" Wilhelm said with a wink that only Klaus could have seen.

"I am a doctor," Klaus choked. "I am a doctor."

Wilhelm smiled down at Klaus and winked again as he turned to face the Brownshirt. "There, you see, Commander. You do have a camp doctor! All you have to do is get him to a hospital and then he will serve the Führer very well, don't you think?"

The Commander was stunned. "Uh...Yes, Captain Tannen. He will serve the Führer very well indeed. But I have no authority to transfer a prisoner to a hospital, Sir."

Wilhelm didn't have to work at looking impatient with the Commander. "I have been ordered to assess the fitness of this facility for the Führer's enterprises. If I fail in my task I can assure you, Commander, the Führer will know why! If you don't have the authority to transfer your own prisoner to the hospital maybe you are not the right man for this job," Wilhelm spat.

"Uh...yes, Sir! Uh...I mean no, Sir! I have the authority." The Commander twitched nervously. "It's just that I have never..."

"Well you will now, won't you?"

"Yes, Sir. Right away."

"Very good. And after that is taken care of, I want all the sick to be moved to a separate barrack. We can't have them infecting the rest of the prisoners. Then I want all prisoners showered and properly fed. I want all of their clothes, blankets, and mattresses burned. Then I want them replaced with clean ones. You do have enough clean ones, don't you Commander?"

"Yes, Sir, in the camp's warehouse."

"How many times a day are the prisoners fed?" Wilhelm asked calmly.

"Once! In the evenings."

"I want them fed twice a day!"

"Yes, Sir!"

"We can't have the Führer's slaves falling down on the job from hunger now can we, Commander?"

"No, Sir!"

"And one more thing," Wilhelm stared hard at the Commander.

"Yes, Sir?"

"Remember, I was never here! Do you understand, Commander? I was never here!"

"Yes, Sir!" the Commander snapped to attention. "You were never here. I understand!" After he relaxed the Commander leaned toward Wilhelm and whispered, "After all, we can't let the Führer's top secret plan get out."

"Very good, Commander. Your diligence in this matter will be rewarded, I'm sure. Now have a couple of your guards drag this wretch out. I will follow them to the hospital to ensure that there are no problems."

"That will not be necessary, Commander. I will see to the matter personally."

"Very well, Commander," Wilhelm smiled.

It wasn't five minutes after Wilhelm parked his car at a market in Oranienburg that he saw the truck from the camp pass by. After taking the time to light a cigarette he put the car in gear and followed the truck from a discreet distance.

110

It took them almost an hour to reach the hospital in Berlin, and Wilhelm followed it all the way just to make sure it got there. When he saw the guards drag Klaus into the emergency room he looked around for a public telephone.

When Karl answered, Wilhelm simply said, "He's at St. Augustine's. In the emergency ward."

"Thank God," Karl cried. "And thank you, Wilhelm!"

Wilhelm laughed, "Don't thank me. Thank Captain Tannen."

"Who is Captain Tannen?" Karl queried nervously.

"A stunningly handsome man. About six-one, dark hair, gorgeous brown eyes. He and I are very close!"

"I see," Karl smiled as he quickly grasped what Wilhelm was implying. "Well, tell Captain Tannen that I will be forever grateful!"

"How grateful?" Wilhelm laughed sarcastically.

"Very," Karl replied solemnly. "But now I must be off to visit a sick friend."

"No, Karl!" Wilhelm shouted. "That was not part of the deal! He is still under guard and you are still being watched!"

"But surely…"

"No! Damn it, Karl! I'm serious! I was able to get him to a hospital, but if you try to see him now it will blow everything. I was able to make some real changes in that camp today, but I won't be able to go back in if you screw this up. They will take him back, Karl. Before he has had time to heal. And when he goes back, which he will, I have arranged for him to be the camp physician. That should keep him safe." Karl hung silently on the line. Wilhelm remained silent for a long time as well. Then eventually, he said softly, "Karl? Do you understand? You can't go to him."

"I understand," Karl whispered. "Thank you, Wilhelm. At least I know he is safe for now."

111

"And if you follow the plan, he will stay that way. I have to go now. I have a meeting in twenty minutes with Admiral Canaris. If I am late he'll have my head. Just follow the plan, Karl, and everything will be all right."

"I will, Wilhelm. Thank you again. Goodbye." *Yes, Wilhelm, I will follow the plan, but not yours. Klaus will never go back, not as long as I am alive.*

---

By June, 1934, Ernst Roehm and his S.A. Brownshirts had become more powerful than Hitler could remain comfortable with. They were constantly causing civil unrest, becoming drunk and disorderly and rioting when they didn't get what they wanted. Roehm had a reputation for being radical and Hitler knew that his troops were so numerous that they could threaten him if he lost their confidence, especially as he struggled to legitimize his position.

In addition, their undisciplined behavior was quite embarrassing to the Führer as he negotiated with Germany's top generals. Hitler had effectively taken over the civilian government, but had failed to enlist the cooperation of the military. Now that President Hindenburg was dead, the military was threatening to take control of the state. Hitler needed to find a way to validate his power and become the supreme commander of the German armed forces. For their loyalty, the army demanded the sacrifice of the S.A. and Goering and Himmler agreed. Together they drew up a long list of names for execution. Many of them were from the files of the *Institute for Sexual Science.*

On the night of June 29, 1934, the bloody purge began. Gestapo agents from Berlin to Munich crashed through the doors of many prominent S.A. leaders' homes and hotel rooms, slashing and shooting as they went. Edmund

Heines, the homosexual S.A. Obergruppenfuhrer of Silesia, was found in bed with his young lover. Both were beheaded where they lay. Karl Ernst, former bouncer of a gay bar and leader of the Berlin S.A., also lost his head that night. Other S.A. leaders, approximately a hundred and fifty of them, were rounded up and taken to the Cadet School at Lichterfelde. There they were lined up against the wall and shot to death by an S.S. firing squad.

The S.S. were Hitler's own personal security force. They assisted the Gestapo with the purge. By the time the bloody night was over four hundred men had been brutally murdered and the purge became known as "The Night of the Long Knives."

Ernst Roehm, Hitler's closest friend and supreme commander of the S.A. was found sleeping in his bed at the Hanslbauer Hotel, in Wiesseecafe. He was surrounded by his closest S.A. lieutenants when Himmler's men broke down the door. After the lieutenants had been taken out and shot, Hitler went into Roehm's room alone. The Führer gave him a stern dressing down and ordered him back to Munich, where he was held in Stadelheim prison. A few days later Hitler ordered that a pistol be left in Roehm's cell so he could commit suicide painlessly, but Roehm would have no part of it.

"If I am to be killed, let Adolf do it himself," Roehm hissed. Then two men entered his cell, drew their pistols and shot him several times in the chest.

Earlier, on that bloody night, Roehm had sent Heinrich out for beer. When he returned he saw the S.A. lieutenants being hauled out of the Hanslbauer Hotel. He started to run to them, but then he saw the Führer. Instantly, he froze. Seconds later, when the first lieutenant was shot through the head right in front of the Führer, Heinrich dove behind a tree. He watched silently as each one of the lieutenants fell. *My God! What is happening? Why is the Führer allowing this?*

113

Then he saw Hitler enter the hotel. Heinrich waited. A few minutes later he saw his master being drug out by several Gestapo agents. *Run!* Heinrich's mind screamed at him. *Run!* But he could not. He was frozen, watching Roehm being pushed into the back seat of a car. As it sped away, again Heinrich's mind yelled, *Run, you idiot, run!* Finally, when the car's taillights faded into the night, Heinrich's legs moved. He bolted into the woods as fast as he could, his mind reeling from what he had witnessed.

---

"What's happening, Doctor Schiller?" Anneliese shouted over the commotion in the emergency room.

"I'm not sure, Nurse," he shouted back as he directed ambulance drivers where to put the wounded men they were bringing in. "Someone said the Gestapo moved against the S.A. tonight and this is the result!"

"Do you need me to help?"

The doctor glanced over at Anneliese. Her purse was slung over her shoulder, and her coat draped over her arm. "How long have you been on duty?" he shouted over the noise of the screaming sirens and men.

"Since six this morning. I have already worked two shifts!" she yelled back.

"No, you go on home and get some rest. We'll call you if it gets any worse!"

Anneliese stood there for a moment staring at the confusion and the mess. The wounded were shouting, the sirens were blaring, and every doctor and nurse on duty was being paged over the hospital loud speaker.

*This is perfect*, she thought. *He may not be ready to travel, but we're never going to get another chance like this.* She ran back up stairs and down the hall to where the guard stood by Klaus' door. "Sergeant," she exclaimed, "several

114

S.A. troops have been wounded in some kind of fight with the Gestapo! Do you know anything about what's going on?"

The S.A. sergeant was surprised by Anneliese's abrupt announcement. "What do you mean, Nurse. What fight with the Gestapo?"

"That's just what I asked you, you dummkopf! They are bringing in your soldiers right now! Down in the emergency room!"

The S.A. sergeant immediately charged down the hall toward the stairs. When he disappeared down the stairwell, Anneliese slipped into Klaus's room and rushed to his bedside. "Doctor Gessler, wake up!" she whispered. "Wake up!"

"Uhhh…" Klaus moaned.

"Doctor Gessler, its Anneliese! I've come to see you several times over the last few days. Do you remember what I told you, Doctor Gessler?"

*Where am I?* Klaus struggled to come to consciousness through his fever. *Not Sachsenhausen.*

"Doctor Gessler, do you remember me? I'm Anneliese. Herr von Rauthenau asked me to look in on you!" she whispered. "We met at the White Rose Ladies St. Valentine's Day Drag Ball!"

*Roses. Sweet roses. Karl. Music. Dancing. Lovely visions.*

Anneliese shook him. "Doctor Gessler, you must wake up! This is important! You must listen to me."

"Who are you?" Klaus choked.

"Open your eyes, Dr. Gessler!" Anneliese insisted a little more sternly as she turned on the light. "I am Anneliese, a friend of Herr von Rauthenau's."

Klaus squinted, throwing his arm over his face. "Where am I?"

"You are in the hospital, Doctor Gessler! You are in Berlin, in the hospital. St. Augustine's."

115

Klaus was surprised. "How did I get here?"

"That doesn't matter right now. All that matters now is that you must get up, Doctor Gessler. This is our only chance."

"I can't," he whispered as he drifted back into unconsciousness.

Anneliese shook Klaus again. When he didn't respond she wrapped her arms around his shoulders and pulled him up to a sitting position. "Doctor Gessler, we don't have time for this. You must wake up right now!" She pulled his legs over the bed and grabbed the glass of water on Klaus' night stand. Pressing it to his lips, she commanded, "Drink, Doctor Gessler."

Klaus' eyes were still shut, but he sipped the water as it trickled down his chin. Then he began to stir. Opening his eyes just a little, he focused on Anneliese. "Am I dreaming?" he whispered.

"No, Doctor Gessler! This is quite real. I am taking you to Herr von Rauthenau, but you must help me! You must stand, and you must walk!" she commanded.

*Karl?* Klaus was still not sure if he was dreaming. "We are going to see Karl?"

"Yes, Doctor Gessler. We are going to see Karl. He is waiting for you, but you have got to help me. You have got to stand up. Can you do that?"

"I don't think so. Too weak."

"You must, Doctor Gessler, or they will take you back to the concentration camp!"

*Sachsenhausen!* The mere thought of it jolted Klaus to full consciousness. "Sachsenhausen!" he whispered.

"That's right, Doctor Gessler. You were in Sachsenhausen and if you don't move your ass right now, that's where you will be again! Now stand up!" Fear shot a surge of adrenaline though Klaus' body and he stood up immediately, but his legs were shaky at best. He grabbed for the night stand as Anneliese helped him put on a bath robe. Then she reached over and switched off the light. "I'm sorry I don't have any clothes for you, Doctor Gessler, but there wasn't time. We have to leave right now, before the guard gets back. Here, lean on me. I'll guide you."

Together they managed to shuffle through the door and down the hall, but just as they reached the elevator Anneliese heard the guard trudging up the stairs. "Shhhh, Doctor Gessler," she whispered. Then she pushed the elevator button fiercely. "Come on! Come on!" Suddenly, just as the guard reached the top of the stairs, the elevator doors opened and she pushed Klaus inside.

"Going home?" the guard asked Anneliese as she stood there, innocently holding the elevator door open.

"Yes," she sighed. "It's been a hell of a day. Did you find out what was going on down stairs."

"Yeah! Those guys aren't S.A., they're Gestapo. Seems our boys cleaned a few of their clocks," laughed the guard.

"Well, that's a relief. Everybody hates the Gestapo. Good night, then."

"Good night, Nurse," the guard winked. "See you tomorrow night?"

"I'll be here!"

Anneliese almost fainted as the elevator doors closed behind her. *My God, that was close. Now we just have to make it out the front door.* The elevator opened on the main floor and she poked her head out to see if the way was clear. Then Anneliese looked at Dr. Gessler. He was close to passing out. "Stay with me, Doctor," she said as she threw his arm over her shoulder. "Just a little farther. Now try to keep your head up and your eyes on the front door." Together they stepped out of the elevator and headed for the main lobby. "Just a few more steps," Anneliese whispered in his ear. "Just keep walking. You're doing fine."

Anneliese pushed the huge glass doors open just enough for them to squeeze through. Then she led Klaus to a bench on the sidewalk and hailed the cab that was parked down the street. When it pulled up she open the door and shoved Klaus in.

"What's with him?" the cabby asked.

"Drunk!" Anneliese grumbled as she crawled in behind Klaus. "Dead drunk! Papa is always drunk! Gets picked up by the police and they bring him here because they know I work here. He's such an embarrassment, but what can I do? He's my father."

"Let him sleep it off in the drunk tank?"

"Wish I could! Cafe Nolle, bitte."

Cafe Nolle was around the corner and down several blocks from Karl's mansion, but Anneliese didn't want to take the chance that the cabby might be questioned later. When he pulled up outside the cafe she paid him and told him to keep the change. "Come on, Papa, let's get you some coffee."

Klaus groaned and then pulled himself from the cab saying, "I'd rather have a beer!"

Anneliese was surprised that Klaus was conscious enough to play along, but the cabby laughed and said, "I'm with him! Good night, now. Take care."

"Good night," Anneliese grumbled, slamming the door. When the cab drove away she smiled and said, "Very good, Doctor Gessler. I'm glad you are so awake. We have a way to walk. Can you make it?"

"If it will keep me from returning to Sachsenhausen, I will force myself to walk to Munich," Klaus moaned.

"Just lean on me, Doctor Gessler. It's really not that far. I promise." But it was farther than Anneliese had promised. By the time they reached Karl's front door the sun was almost up. Quickly she rang the bell, and kept ringing it until Manfred finally opened the door.

"Who in God's name is..." he started to say. Then he recognized Anneliese, with Klaus collapsed in her arms.

118

"Quick! Get him inside before someone sees us," she commanded.

"Of course, Fraulein!" Manfred scooped Klaus up and carried him inside. Anneliese followed, quickly shutting the door behind them.

Just then Karl came stumbling down the staircase in his bath robe. "Who in the hell is calling at this hour!" he yelled. When Manfred turned, cradling Klaus in his arms, Karl stopped short. His mouth fell open as he realized what had happened. He ran to Klaus. Taking him in his own arms, Karl carried him into the study and held him in his lap. "Klaus," Karl whispered. "Klaus, open your eyes."

Klaus opened his eyes and smiled briefly. "Karl," he whispered. "Is that you?"

"Yes, my darling. It's me. Everything is all right now. You are going to be fine. You are safe. I will never let anything happen to you, ever again." Karl looked up at Anneliese and smiled through his tears. "Danke!"

---

In the fall of 1934 the Gestapo sent out a letter to every police station in Germany. The letter demanded that each police station compile a list of all the men they had ever arrested on homosexual charges, or whom they knew to be practicing homosexuals, regardless of whether or not they had ever been arrested. The letter further ordered that these lists be forwarded to the Gestapo headquarters in Berlin. The Berlin police department alone, sent in a list of more than thirty thousand. By the end of the year, after compiling these lists, the Gestapo arrested approximately seventy thousand men, effectively crushing the gay community in Germany.

# Chapter Nine

## Christmas in the Tyrol
## 1935

Since that bloody night in June Heinrich had tried contacting several leaders in the S.A., but to no avail. *Kill the root, and the vine dies*, he thought as he downed a beer at the Hofbrauhaus in Munich. *With the leadership gone the troops have scattered. A good move on the Führer's part.* It had been months since he'd seen anyone in a Brownshirt uniform. Himmler's S.S. had quickly replaced them as the dominant private military organization in Germany. *Their sleek black uniforms are quite handsome, and their numbers are growing.*

After he'd failed to reach anyone in the S.A. leadership, Heinrich remembered the files from Dr. Hirschfeld's office that he'd stashed away. Hermann Goering's file was at the top of the list. Goering had been privy to everything Roehm and Heinrich had ever done for the Führer; after all, Heinrich had used the tunnel that led from his home to the Reichstag, the night of the fire. When he explained to Goering that he was in possession of his file, Goering was more than willing to help him.

"The Führer holds no malice toward you, Heinrich. He knows how valuable you have been to our cause. Believe me, he still needs your services. I believe the Nazi party in Austria would benefit from your vast experience! I could write a letter of introduction for you. A man with your particular talents could go a long way in the party."

Heinrich knew exactly what talents Goering was referring to. Over the past four years he had been trained by the best. Espionage, arson, blackmail, surveillance, assassination, and crowd manipulation were his specialties.

If the Führer wanted to take Austria, Heinrich was just the man to go in and pave the way.

"Another beer, bitte!" Heinrich called. But the bartender was engrossed in a newspaper and hadn't heard him. "Max! Beer!"

"Oh! Sorry! Coming right up."

"What's so interesting?" Heinrich asked.

"Some new Department the Führer is appointing."

"Uh huh. And what's so interesting about another governmental department?"

"This one's about sex!" Max winked.

"Sex?"

"Yes, sex!"

"Let me see that rag!" Heinrich snatched the newspaper out from under Max's arm.

*"Oct 26, 1934, Department for the Prevention of Abortion and Homosexuality is set up in Gestapo Headquarters in Berlin."* Heinrich glanced up at Max and began to laugh. "Department for the Prevention of Abortion and Homosexuality? The Führer is going to regulate sex?"

"Ja, that seems to be the plan," Max grinned. "Just think, soon the Gestapo and S.S. will be crashing through bedroom doors all over the country!"

"Ja," Heinrich laughed bitterly. *You think it's a joke, huh Max? Laugh all you want, but that's exactly what they will do. I saw it with my own eyes. The Führer cleared out all the S.A. so the Army would support him. Powerful move. Good counter measure.* Heinrich tossed Max the newspaper and spun around on his bar stool. He hated the loss of Roehm, but appreciated the tactic Hitler used. *Hell, I would have done it myself had I been in his position.* Just then a familiar face came through the door. *Johan? I haven't seen him...since that night!* "Johan!" Heinrich shouted with a wave of his hand.

"Heinrich?" Johan squinted, "I thought you were…"

Heinrich jumped up and gave Johan a big bear hug. "I thought you were too."

The two of them ordered beers and moved to a table in the garden. "I thought they shot you that night!" Johan exclaimed as he glanced around to see if anyone had heard.

"No. Ernst sent me out for beer. By the time I got back everything was going crazy. How did you escape?"

"I dove out the window!" Johan roared. "Buck naked!" They had a good laugh at that thought and then their mood turned solemn. "I haven't seen anyone since that night."

"I've seen a few of the guys, mostly the lower ranking ones. But everybody's pretty much keeping a low profile. Especially the ones like us. Have you heard the news about the new department against homosexuality?"

"Ja, I guess we got a little too flamboyant for the Führer's taste."

"Too powerful is more like it!" Heinrich grunted.

"So, what are you doing now?"

"I'm heading for Austria. In fact, my train leaves in an hour."

"Austria? What for? Because of the new department against homosexuality?"

Heinrich grinned. "Ja."

Johan nodded his head with understanding. "The pickings are getting pretty slim here. I haven't seen any of the regular boys around. When was the last time you got laid?"

Heinrich laughed. "Last night, in the park!"

Johan looked surprised. "You're taking an awful risk, Heinrich. If they catch you, you'll end up in a concentration camp, or worse!"

"What could be worse than that?

"You could be dead!" Johan whispered sternly.

Heinrich laughed out load. "They wouldn't dare shoot me. I've done great things for the Führer. Things you can't even imagine!"

"Did Roehm know about them?"

Heinrich didn't respond. *Yes, my master knew. But now it is time for the slave to become the master. I will not make his mistakes. He became part of the structure. Let himself become too entangled in the politics. He became too visible. I will not!*

"There are Nazis in Austria, you know," Johan grunted. "Hell, we could start over. With our experience, we could become party leaders there! We could be important again."

Heinrich grunted. "I have no interest in leadership, Johan. I lead no one but myself."

"Vienna is a nice city though, or so I've heard. And, the men!" he laughed.

"Ja, the men!" Heinrich smiled.

---

It had been almost a year since Anneliese helped Klaus escape from the hospital. The road to recovery had been long and hard. Klaus' fever had raged uncontrollable for a week after his escape. The secret room behind one of the bookcases in Karl's study became his sanctuary every time the Gestapo came searching for him. The room was just big enough for a cot, a table, and a chair, which Karl sat in hour after hour, sponging Klaus' burning forehead. Each night Anneliese had come to check on them. She usually brought medicine that she managed to steal from the hospital, and gave it to Karl to administer during the day.

Naturally Karl's home was the first place the Gestapo headed for when Klaus' escape was reported. Thankfully, Klaus had slept quietly through each search. They came at odd hours. Sometimes in the midmorning and sometimes late at night. Each time they came Karl politely followed them through the mansion as they peeked in closets, looked under beds, and searched the attic and basement. Finally, after a month and a half they gave up entirely. The secret room had saved Klaus' life.

When his fever finally broke it took Klaus months to regain his strength. His body had been completely decimated by the Typhus, loss of weight, dysentery, and the beatings and rapes. In the concentration camps homosexual prisoners were considered free game for sexual exploitation by the guards and tougher prisoners. Over the months, Karl tended Klaus as if he were a fragile baby bird. He sat with him each day, spooning only a few drops of soup into his mouth at a time. The only time he took a break was when Katrine or Manfred insisted he rest. Katrine was also very good with Klaus. She fed him and sponged him while Karl slept.

After a few weeks Klaus was finally able to take some solid food. Slowly, he began growing a stronger. When the Gestapo searches eventually ended, Klaus was ready to test his legs. At first he could only stand with Karl and Katrine's help, but as time went by he was able to take a few steps on his own. First to the end of his cot and back. Then finally, on Christmas day, 1934, Klaus made it all the way into the study. Manfred had a beautiful dinner of spatzle soup, roasted lamb, asparagus vinaigrette, and plum dumplings waiting for him.

Now after almost a year, Klaus was going stir crazy from hiding in the mansion. "I haven't seen the sun in a year, Karl. Look at me, my skin has the pallor of death. If I don't get out soon I shall go absolutely mad."

Karl sat reading the May, 1935, edition of *Das Schwarze Korp*, the S.S. newspaper. "Uh huh," he replied without really listening. "Have you read this?" he asked casually.

"What?" Klaus groaned.

"The new edition of the S.S. newspaper."

"No! I have read everything in this library, but I refuse to read that rag!" Klaus snapped.

"You should, you know."

"Why?"

"Because it might encourage you to forget about going outside."

"Humph! Have the Nazis banned people from walking in the sunshine these days?"

"No. They're just calling for the death penalty for homosexuals, that's all."

Klaus hung his head. Karl knew the year of torture in Sachsenhausen, and then the year of recovery was weighing heavy on Klaus' spirit. Now that his body was strong and free, seclusion had almost become unbearable.

Karl put the newspaper down and went to sit by him on the couch. "I have an idea," he said. "It's something I've been thinking about for a while now. And as much as I would hate it, I think it's what is best for you. Why don't we move you to Vienna? You could stay with Leeza. She has a beautiful apartment not far from the Musikverein. You would be free to walk in the sunshine. You could go out whenever you wanted. You could even start practicing medicine again. What do you think of that?"

Klaus leaned his head on Karl's shoulder and sighed, "Don't pay any attention to me. I'm just feeling sorry for myself. I could never move back to Vienna. Not without you."

"Why not? Of course you could. Vienna is really not that far away. I could come and visit once a month, and..."

"No, Karl! I will not leave you!" Karl didn't say anything. He just let Klaus have some time to think about the idea. Finally, Klaus said, "And besides, I don't have the proper papers to cross the border. In all practicality I'm a man without an identity."

Karl stood up and walked over to his desk. Pulling open a drawer, he said "No, you're not. You're Doctor Klaus Streicher, an Austrian citizen." Then he tossed Klaus an envelope from the drawer.

Shocked, Klaus glanced at the envelope and then back to Karl. "What's this?"

"Your new identity papers."

Klaus opened the envelope and pulled out a worn looking passport and visa. Inside the passport he was shocked to see his own photograph, along with the stamps of several different countries. The visa stated that a Doctor Klaus Streicher had been allowed to work in Berlin for the past three years. "Where did you get this?" Klaus whispered in amazement.

"It doesn't matter. The only thing that matters is that the visa will run out by the end of the year. By then you must return to Austria."

Klaus looked down at the visa to verify the date. Then he looked up at Karl standing over him. With grief in his voice he whispered, "I can't leave you, Karl. I just can't."

Karl pulled him up from the couch. Taking Klaus' face in his hands, he kissed him passionately, but gently. Then he led Klaus up to the bedroom. After they had made love, Karl held Klaus and whispered in his ear. "You don't have to go right away. But by the end of the year you must be in Austria. You have your whole life ahead of you, Klaus. You can't spend it locked up here, waiting for Hitler to do what ever he's going to do. I love you too much for that."

---

The clatter of musicians tuning their instruments back stage could be heard by the audience at the Musikverein as they took their seats in the concert hall. From his seat in the balcony, Heinrich watched as the well to do of Austrian society fussed with their satins and furs. *This is a summer concert for Christ's sake! What in the hell are they all wearing their furs for? Fucking Jews, always have to show*

*off how rich they all are. The Führer will take care of them
when he gets here, that's for sure.*

Suddenly the house lights dimmed and rose again, and
then went out completely. Moments later the musicians
began quietly taking their places on stage. Heinrich
watched enthusiastically. He had never been one for
attending the symphony, but when the leader of the Nazi
party in Vienna had given him the concert tickets as a show
of gratitude for all the hard work he had done over the past
couple of months, Heinrich appreciated the gesture and
decided it was time he began elevating his level of
sophistication.

He watched intently as the concert master came out,
bowed to the audience, and then tapped his baton on one of
the violinist's music stand as he passed her. She smiled in
return. It seemed as if she wanted to laugh at him. That
smile caught Heinrich's attention *I know her from
somewhere. But, where?*

The audience applauded wildly as Julius took center
stage. The normal conductor had taken ill and Julius was
asked to stand in for the evening. This was an unexpected
treat for the usual Musikverein crowd. It was rare that they
got to hear Julius' particular influence. His direction was
sure to bring a new flare and style to the evening's
performance. The Austrians loved their music. After all,
Mozart had been Austrian. Most of all they loved hearing
new and fresh nuances in the classical pieces. This was
exactly what Julius intended to give them tonight.

As Leeza sat waiting for the cue to begin, she smiled as
she remembered how Julius had conducted his practice
session that morning.

"Now, Leeza darling, in the third movement…Here,
listen!" Julius flipped his Stradivarius up to his chin and
played a few fast and furious notes. "See? I want you to
play it just like that."

"Jules, dear, don't you think your head is getting just a little big?" Leeza quipped. "It's just one concert, you know."

"Oh, shut up! You're just as bored with the piece as I am! I'm just the one to inject a little life into the program. What could be wrong with that?"

"Nothing! All I am saying is that you think you're the only one with talent around here! I could just as easily conduct the concert myself."

"So, that's it! You're jealous," Julius exclaimed. "Green is not your color, Leeza. You don't wear it well, darling. Now, be a good girl and tune up that little fiddle of yours. And don't forget to make the changes on your sheet music!"

Leeza rolled her eyes at Julius. *Why do I love him so much? He's such a pompous ass sometimes.* Then she giggled as she watched him making his rounds to instruct the other musicians how to alter their sheet music. *He just can't help himself. He's like a kid in a candy shop, with an incredible sweet tooth. It's a good thing he's as talented as he thinks or they'd be ready to kill him right about now.*

When the music began Heinrich continued to stare at Leeza, trying to figure out where he knew her from. *Berlin? Must be. Maybe Munich.* But he just couldn't place her until he glanced at the evening's program. *"Second Violinist - Leeza von Rauthenau." So, this is where you play, Fraulein von Rauthenau. I've seen your picture in the bars in Berlin. But alas, there are no more bars in Berlin. No more gay bars in all of Germany, now that the Reichstag has changed the language of Paragraph 175 to include any touching between men. Did you know that, Fraulein? Men like your Uncle will either come to Austria, as I have, or they will be in a concentration camp, like the good Doctor Gessler. I look forward to meeting your uncle, Fraulein. I understand he's an incredibly willful man.*

128

After the May edition of *Das Schwarze Korp* came out, calling for the death penalty for all homosexuals, the Reichstag failed to meet the S.S. demands. However, in June, 1935, the Reichstag was pressured enough to consent to changing and clarifying the language of the Paragraph 175. The change stated that any touching, anything more than a hand shake, could be considered a homosexual act and was therefore illegal. The changes in the law sent shock waves throughout the gay community in Germany, and many began making plans to leave the country.

By September, 1935, when the Nuremberg laws were passed, Leeza begged her Uncle to move to Vienna. "Has the world has gone mad, Uncle Karl?" Leeza asked during her weekly telephone call home. "First Klaus is imprisoned for no reason. Then they say that Julius can no longer travel with the orchestra when it tours in Germany because he is a Jew! Next the damn *Department for the Prevention of Abortion and Homosexuality* is set up, and then the S.S. demands the death penalty for all homosexuals. Now the language of Paragraph 175 is changed, and the Nuremberg laws dictate who you can marry. Thank God none of us are Jewish! You and Klaus and Mama simply must come to Vienna at once! I couldn't bare it if something happened to any of you. And with everything that's going on, it surely will!"

"Leeza," Karl sighed. "I can't leave the factory. Hundreds of people depend on Rauthenau Steel for their survival. And besides, Hitler needs me too much. He won't do anything to jeopardize his precious rearmament program."

"Well, what about Klaus? Surely he needs to get out of that house."

"Yes, he does. But he won't leave. That's why I have arranged a holiday for us. Your mother and Klaus and I are going to the Tyrol for Christmas. I was hoping you would join us."

"Oh, Uncle Karl, that sounds wonderful! But is Klaus ready for a holiday in the Alps. Is he strong enough to ski?"

"I doubt it! But then you never know. He may just surprise us. Anyway, that's not why I'm taking him there," Karl sighed. "Leeza, I need your help with something. You're right about Klaus needing to get out of the house. He needs to be in the sunshine again. He needs to be free to move about and to be among people. Your mother and I are simply not enough. If he's going to heal completely it will have to be in Austria. I was hoping I could send him home with you after Christmas. I was hoping you would watch over him until he can get on his feet?"

"Of course, Uncle Karl. Of course Klaus can stay with me. But what about you and Mama? Why don't you all come too?"

"Leeza, please! Don't make this any harder than it already is. I have to stay here, and you know why!"

"The damn U-boats!" Leeza realized.

Karl hung silently on the telephone for a long while. "Yes, the submarines. I can't let them use our steel to produce those death traps ever again. I saw too many good men die in those things, and I simply can't allow it to happen again. As long as I am in Germany, and remain at the head of the company, I can make sure that Rauthenau Steel never produces U-boats as we did during the Great War! I would rather see the factory destroyed than to see it produce those damned steel coffins again."

Leeza knew of her Uncle's pain. His own design had produced the very U-boats he had captained. And for all his genius on the production line, the U-boat submarines had been a disaster that had cost thousands of lives, both

130

German and Allied. His conscience would never allow him to forget that fact.

"What of Klaus? Does he know why you are choosing to stay?" Leeza asked.

"No! How can I tell a man who has dedicated his life to preserving life, that I have taken so many. Hell, he can't even comprehend that he isn't coming back with me after our holiday."

"What do you mean?"

"Every time I bring the subject up, he changes it, and says he won't leave me."

"So, he thinks this holiday in the Tyrol is just another holiday?" Leeza asked.

Karl thought about that for a moment and then replied, "No. I think deep down inside he knows, he just chooses to ignore it."

"What about Mama? Will she be coming to Vienna with us?"

"No. We have discussed it, and for the sake of appearances she is returning with me."

"I see."

"Leeza, I want you to know how grateful I am that you'll help Klaus. I don't think I could stand loosing him if I didn't know that you were with him."

"He'll be fine, Uncle. Don't you worry about a thing. I'll get a room ready for him, and I'll ask Julius to make sure the apartment is stocked with plenty of food for when we return."

"How is Julius?" Karl asked casually.

"He's fine. Self-centered as always, but I love him," Leeza laughed. "Now where are we staying in the Tyrol? I haven't skied in years."

"There's a chalet just above Innsbruck, in a little village called Jenbach. A fellow by the name of Hans Hagen owns it. Nice man. I met him on a business trip a couple of years ago. I remembered it just a few weeks ago, and called him. We all have reservations for Christmas."

"An old flame, perhaps?" Leeza giggled.

"No, nothing like that. He's straight. Just a nice man who makes no judgments about his guests, if you know what I mean."

"It sounds wonderful, Uncle. I'll meet you there!"

---

The train from Vienna chugged leisurely along the southern slope of the Alps, stopping occasionally in picturesque little villages with a resounding blast of its whistle. Mist swelled and swirled between the jagged peaks of the mountains, and seemed to roll down the slopes like giant snowballs into the valleys below. Leeza leaned back in her seat and watched the majestic mountains as they ran past her window, relaxing with the clickity-clack rhythm of the train. After a while the sun broke through the morning clouds and reflected brilliantly off the snow covered trees. They seemed to dance with life. Soft colors of pink and gold and blue twinkled on their snow covered branches like starlight, as the train rushed past. *Even nature celebrates Christmas*, Leeza thought. *How far away the Nazis, and their gloom, seem today.*

"Jenbach!" the conductor called. "Next stop, Jenbach!"

Leeza reach down to gathered the packages she brought from Vienna. *Let's see, here's Mama's gifts, and Uncle Karl's. Where's...?* "Ah, there you are. Klaus would feel left out if I lost you," Leeza whispered to herself as she reached for a small red box that had slid far behind her seat. *I hope he likes you. I know I do.*

Leeza smiled as she gave the little box a shake. Then she grabbed Julius' violin and frowned. *When will that man ever learn to manage his money?* Julius always hocked the

132

Stradivarius to Leeza whenever he needed a few extra schillings. She patted the violin affectionately. "One of these days I'm not going to sell you back to him," she whispered as she stroked the case with envy. "He doesn't deserve such a fine instrument as you!"

Soon the train blew its whistle and chugged to a stop. Leeza stacked the packages in her arms and headed for the door. Only a few passengers followed her. They too were juggling Christmas packages. *There are a lot of hard Berlin accents*, she thought. *Everyone wants out of Germany these days. Who can blame them?* When Leeza stepped into the crisp mountain air of Jenbach, she took a deep breath and smiled brilliantly as she watched the steam swirl out of her mouth.

"You must be Leeza von Rauthenau," she heard a man's voice say from behind her.

Leeza spun around a little too quickly and almost spilled her packages. "Yes! I am Leeza von Rauthenau," she replied as she clumsily juggled the packages back into place.

Hans Hagen had recognized Leeza from Karl's description. Karl had told Hans that Leeza was tall, had dark hair and blue eyes, and would almost certainly be carrying a violin case. "Allow me, Fraulein." Hans smiled as he took a few of the packages off the top of the stack, while Leeza struggled to keep them balanced. "I am Hans Hagen."

"Hello!" Leeza flashed another brilliant smile. "I must look like a bumbling idiot," she laughed.

"On the contrary, Fraulein, you are lovely! In fact, your uncle failed to tell me just how beautiful you are." *She's the spitting image of her mother.*

Leeza blushed and ran her free hand through her hair. "You are too kind, Herr Hagen. I must look a fright from traveling all morning."

"You look like an angel from heaven, Fraulein von Rauthenau. Now, if you will follow me, my sleigh is right over there," Hans pointed.

"What about my suitcases?" Leeza asked, almost forgetting them.

"It will take a few minutes for the porter to bring them from the baggage car. We can put your packages in the sleigh while we wait."

"That would be wonderful!" Leeza grinned, still feeling a little off balance. "How far is the chalet?"

"Not far. About three miles."

When the porter set Leeza's bags on the platform, Hans immediately picked them up and carried them to the sleigh. Once everything was loaded he climbed into the front seat and gave the reigns a little flick. The sleigh bells jingled as the little mare broke into a trot down the snowy path. She loved making the short run down to Jenbach, but the trip back up the hill was a different matter all together. When the sleigh was loaded with guests and their baggage, she always needed a little coaxing to make it home.

"Are you cold, Fraulein? I have a blanket!"

"No, Herr Hagen. I'm fine. The cool air is invigorating." Leeza took in a deep breath and giggled again as the steam escaped her mouth. "It is so beautiful!"

"Ja!" Hans agreed, but he wasn't thinking about the scenery. *She's beautiful! Almost as exquisite as her mother!*

"Have my mother and Uncle Karl, and Klaus arrived?"

"Ja, Fraulein. They arrived last night."

"I can't wait to see them."

"I know they are thinking the same thing."

Klaus was the first to hear the sleigh bells coming up the road. Moments later he had everyone out on the front porch waving. "Merry Christmas, Leeza!" he called.

"Merry Christmas!" Leeza waved, beaming from the sleigh ride. "Merry Christmas!"

Hugs and kisses went all around while Hans unloaded the sleigh and took Leeza's things up to her room. "Merry Christmas, Mama," Leeza whispered as she gave Katrine a big hug. "I have missed you so much."

"Merry Christmas, Leeza dear!" Katrine replied joyously. Then she cupped Leeza's face in her hands and said, "You look as beautiful as ever. A little thin, but still beautiful! I am so happy to see you!"

Then Leeza looked over at Karl. "Uncle!" Leeza grinned. "Merry Christmas!"

Karl opened his arms and pulled her in close. "Merry Christmas, Leeza," he whispered.

Next it was Klaus' turn. They stretched out their hands toward each other and held each other at a distance while they gave each other a good looking over. "Look at you, Klaus!" Leeza exclaimed. "You look so handsome, and..."

"Well?" Klaus asked.

"Yes! Well and healthy! And wonderful. Give me a hug!"

"Merry Christmas, Leeza," Klaus said as he wrapped his arms around her gently.

"Merry Christmas, Klaus," she whispered back. "I am so happy you are with us!"

The Hagen Chalet was almost as beautiful as the Alps. Inside, the open beam ceiling was high and magnificent. The old framing timbers were visible in the walls and the huge stone fireplace roared with a blazing fire. The giant windows gave stunning views of the ski slops, and the great room was filled with the warm aroma of spiced cider.

Over the next week the healing atmosphere of the Tyrol soothed away all the cares of the von Rauthenau family.

135

They laughed, they danced, they played music, and Klaus was even able to ski. On Christmas morning Leeza was as giddy as a little child. She gleamed as she passed out her gifts to Klaus, Karl, and her mother. Katrine was overjoyed with her matching cashmere hat, scarf, and gloves. Karl loved his new pipe and smoking jacket. And his new gold pocket watch brought tears to Klaus' eyes.

"I haven't had a watch since..." Klaus held the pocket watch up to the light. His eyes glistening as it spun on it's fob. "Since..." Everyone watched him and knew what he was thinking.

"Well!" Karl interjected as he felt a lump rise in his throat. "It's time for you to open a gift, little girl." Then he reach under the Christmas tree and pulled out a long slender box and tossed it to Leeza. "Here, open this one!"

Excitedly, Leeza tore off the red bow and ripped through the bright green wrapping paper. The box was from Lindheim's Music Shop in Salzburg. Leeza's eyes grew wide as she opened the lid. "Oh, Uncle Karl! It's gorgeous!" she exclaimed in amazement.

Karl felt the pure joy of her pleasure. "You seemed to like the one I got for Julius, so I thought..."

"Oh, Yes! But this one is...It's incredible, Uncle Karl!" Leeza cried as she pulled the new violin case from the box. "When did you...?"

"I special ordered it over a month ago. Lindheim got it just right, don't you think?"

"Oh, Yes! He is a master craftsman!"

Leeza ran her fingers over the thin gold inlay and small diamond that formed a white rose on the lid of the new case. Closing her eyes, she breathed in the aroma of the rich warm burgundy leather and smiled. "Never have I seen a more magnificent case! Thank you!" she sighed in ecstasy.

Then she clicked open the locks to see what color the velvet was. Never in her wildest dreams could she have imagined what lay inside. Instantly, her eyes grew wide, her mouth dropped open, and her breath caught in her throat. "An Amati!" she whispered in awe. "But where…?"

Karl grinned at Katrine, who was just as awestruck as Leeza was. "Lindheim called me the minute it came into his shop. He always manages to come up with the finest instruments in the world. I understand Amati is quite rare. Why don't you play something for us, Leeza."

Leeza, with her mouth still hanging open, glanced up at Karl and then back at the little Amati. She was obviously overwhelmed at the sight of it. She looked as if she were seeing a holy vision. As if she was afraid to touch such a sacred object, she ran her fingers over the plush red velvet next to the violin and blinked in amazement.

"Go ahead, Leeza," Karl softly whispered. "Take it out and play something for us."

Ever so carefully, Leeza lifted the little Amati from its case. She could hardly breath as she placed the rest under her chin and reached for the new bow. Closing her eyes she gently drew the bow over the strings. *My God! Listen to that tone. Such quality. So rich*! Tears began streaming down her face as she stood and began playing in earnest. The melody of *Jesu, Joy of Man's Desire*, suddenly filled the great room of the chalet. All the other guests stopped what they were doing to listen as Leeza made the little violin sing to life.

When she finished, and lifted the bow off the strings, everyone stared silently in amazement. Neither Karl nor Katrine had ever seen Leeza play with such passion. When she finally opened her eyes, Karl stood up slowly and began clapping his hands in astonishment. Slowly, all the other guests joined in the applause. Soon the room was roaring with cheers of delight. Hans burst in from the kitchen yelling "Bravo! Bravo," and Klaus wept from the sheer joy of the moment.

That Christmas healed them all. It had chased away all the demons that Karl, Klaus, Katrine, and Leeza had lived with for so long. The sunshine and skiing had returned Klaus' strength to him. Karl had forgotten all about submarines as he watched Klaus return to life. Katrine had been romanced by Hans and they had fallen in love. For Leeza, seeing her mother return to the living was the greatest gift she could have ever received. They reveled in the love and warmth of their family, as their holiday brought joy back into their lives and hope into their hearts. None of them would ever forget the magic of this wonderful Tyrolian Christmas.

# Chapter Ten

## The Games
## 1936

Sending Klaus back to Vienna with Leeza had been pure agony for Karl. The long, dark, lonely nights without him were unbearable, but worth the sacrifice, for Klaus was thriving in Vienna. Only weeks after his return he started a small medical practice above the Cafe Savoy, a bar frequented by the gay men of Vienna. Now, six months later the practice was flourishing and Klaus was on the platform of the train station saying goodbye to Leeza and Julius.

"Give Karl my love," Klaus said as he brushed the tears from his eyes. "Tell him how much I love him, and that I miss him."

"He knows," Leeza reassured Klaus with a hug, "but I will tell him anyway. I just wish you could come with us!"

"I do too, but we both know that just because Hitler has reopened the bars for the Olympic Games doesn't mean it's safe for me to return to Germany."

"I know," Leeza sighed. Then she smiled and patted his stomach. "Just make sure there's food in the apartment when I get home. Your appetite has picked up quite a bit in the last couple of months."

Klaus laughed and carried Leeza's bag to the porter. "See you when you get back! Give Karl my love!"

"I will," Leeza called over her shoulder as she followed the rest of the orchestra members onto the train. "Be well!"

In August of 1936, Germany hosted the Olympic Games in Berlin. This was Hitler's chance to show how superior his master Aryan race was when compared to the dark skinned athletes that the other countries sent to

139

compete. Hitler intended the outside world to see a unified German people in a clean, cheerful, prosperous Germany. The signs, *"Juden Verbotten"* were taken down from hotels, restaurants, bars, theaters, and all other public places. All persecution of Jews, Christians, Gypsies, and homosexuals was stopped while the foreigners were in town. Goering, Ribbentrop, and Goebbels all hosted lavish parties for foreign dignitaries and made sure there was a tremendous amount of extravagant public entertainment. They also ensured that the gay and lesbian bars were reopened for the homosexual tourists. Even the Vienna Symphony, along with it's Jewish members, had been asked to play in the closing ceremonies of the games.

"This is fabulous!" Julius exclaimed as he sipped his beer. "Berlin is alive again! Who would have thought they would reopen the Eldorado Klub!"

"Isn't it wonderful?" Leeza grinned. "This place is packed, just like old times!"

Karl looked around suspiciously. "I don't mean to burst your bubble, but do you see anyone you recognize? For that matter, did you notice the Gestapo agent stationed across the street. I'm sure he's taking down the names of anyone he recognizes."

Leeza frowned as she took a good look around the bar. She didn't see anyone she knew. Then she listened to the crowd as they chatted in one language or another. "They are all foreigners?"

Karl took as sip of his beer. "Yes."

"Well, things can't be that bad if the bars are open again! Maybe the Olympics will infuse an attitude in the Reich. Surely the games are bringing in a tremendous amount of money? Maybe that will take some of the pressure off."

"Maybe," Karl shrugged. "Now tell me all about Klaus! I want to know everything."

"He's doing do well, Uncle Karl. You should see his little office above Cafe Savoy! It's so cute. He has his desk and his examining table, and all the new equipment you had delivered to him. His appointment book is full almost every day."

"And is he…is he seeing…I mean, does he…?"

"He sees patients, Karl," Julius chimed in flippantly. "That's all. Only patients. The man is a saint. As celibate as the pope. He won't even go to the bar with us for a drink. Just pines away, all night long, for you!"

Karl smiled in relief. "I just want him to be happy that's all."

"He'll be happy when you come for a visit!" Leeza smiled. "He loves you and misses you terribly." Just then a beautiful blond woman caught her eye. *It's her!*

Leeza had thought of Amy many times since the St. Valentine's Day Drag Ball. Many nights she had fallen asleep remembering their one dance. She remembered the way their bodies had moved as one, and the way their eyes had caressed each other.

*She probably doesn't remember.* Leeza sighed with the thought. *How could she, she ran away so fast we never had the chance to introduced ourselves.* Leeza watched Amy strolled up to the bar and order a beer. "Excuse me, bitte. I'm going for another beer. Anyone want one while I'm up?"

"Yes," Julius started to say, but Leeza was gone before he could get the words out. "Well, isn't that just like a women. Tease you and leave you. Honestly!"

"That's okay," Karl chuckled, "I've been wanting to talk to you alone anyway. How's that new violin case been working out?"

"It works beautifully when I have the chance to use it!"

"I presume you have seen Leeza's?"

"Yes! It's gorgeous! Why doesn't mine have a little gold and diamond rose?" Julius pouted.

141

"Sorry, old man. I didn't think it was your style. You know, it's exactly like yours in every other way."

"Yes, I know. But, it took me a while to get her to let me look at it closely. She guards it with her life."

"Let's hope it will guard hers!"

Leeza walked over to the opposite end of the bar from where Amy was. "Beer, bitte," she said to the bartender. From where she stood, Leeza strained to overhear Amy's conversation.

"You boys enjoying the games?" she asked the men next to her.

"Yeah! We're havin' a great time! Too bad it'll all be over tomorrow," they replied.

*English! Their Americans*, Leeza thought.

"So what do you think of Hitler's Germany?"

*That's the strange accent! She's American too!*

"It's great. Everybody's friendly and the place is spic-n-span! Sure ain't like the newspaper reports," one of them answered.

"Yeah! The streets are clean and the country is beautiful, and everyone seems to be really happy," the other one said.

"Happy! Oh yes, they're happy all right. Everyone had better look happy or they'll find themselves in a concentration camp. Have you heard of the concentration camps, fellas? That's where Herr Hitler sends anyone who disagrees with him. You've read about the Nazi camps, haven't you?"

"Naw, we don't read too much."

"Too bad. You'd be reading my stuff."

*She's a journalist?* Leeza thought.

"It's a good thing you're Americans and not Germans. Otherwise you might be in one of those camps right now. Hitler hates gays, you know, just as much as he hates Jews. The only reason this bar is open tonight is because he wants to make sure he gets as much money from the tourists as he

142

can. That's why this bar is open tonight, fellas. Otherwise, we'd all be in Sachsenhausen or Dachau, or some other stinking, rotting place. And you should hear what they do to gay boys in those camps. Geez fellas, it makes my hair stand on end." Then Amy took a sip of her beer, nodded her head, and said, "Goodnight boys."

Leeza watched as the color drained from the men's faces and became even more intrigued by this beautiful woman. *She taught those men a lesson, but what does she know of concentration camps?* Leeza watched her cross the room. *She's American! Still, she sounds like she knows what Hitler is capable of. But how? Her job probably. God, she is beautiful.*

Leeza noticed that Karl and Julius were watching her watch Amy. She was blushing as she returned to the table."

"Where's mine?" Julius whined.

"Yours?" Leeza frowned.

"Yes, mine! You were so busy watching that pretty woman that you forgot my beer."

"What woman?" Leeza blushed.

"That woman over there!" Julius pointed. "Now give me the beer and you go over there and introduce yourself!"

"I couldn't," Leeza squealed.

"Oh yes you can! Now go!"

"Jules, I can't. She's...I...We..."

"Gorgeous! Yes, I know. I have eyes, Leeza. Now go over and introduce yourself."

Leeza squirmed in her chair uncomfortably and then looked at Karl for help. He just laughed and said, "Leave her alone, Julius. She's obviously not the whore you are!"

"Well! I never," Julius cried.

"Never? Oh, my boy, that's not what I've heard." Karl laughed and winked at Leeza. "It took her three days just to bring me up to date on your love life!"

Julius glared at Leeza. She burst out laughing. "I never...really...honestly!"

Everyone had a good laugh as they drank their beer, but it wasn't long before Julius proved Karl right. He had spotted a striking young man across the room. "Well, if you won't buy me a beer, Leeza darling, I'm sure he will! Don't wait up for me."

"Julius, don't be late for the closing ceremony tomorrow," Leeza shouted, but it was too late. He was off like a moth to the flame. "Whore is right!" she laughed. "That man just can't help himself!"

"He's young! He should enjoy life! And so should you. Go! Enjoy yourself. This old man is going home and going to bed. I'll see you in the morning. Good night," Karl said as he leaned over to kiss her on the forehead.

Leeza smiled up at him and said, "Good night, Uncle Karl. Sweet dreams."

But Leeza didn't stay long either. From across the room she watched the beautiful woman she had dreamed of. Amy was chatting with friends and drinking her beer. *Why can't I just walk up and introduce myself,* she wondered. *Why can't I just say "Hello, my name is Leeza, what's yours."* Feeling frustrated with herself, she left. *No use torturing myself with something I can't have. Besides, she's American. She'll probably be going home tomorrow like everyone else.*

---

The next morning the orchestra played beautifully, as always. The concert for the closing ceremony of the Olympic Games was a great success, and the orchestra members were exhausted. That night at the train station the weary musicians lounged about waiting for their various trains. Most were taking a brief holiday. Some were going to Paris, some to Rome, others to Venice and Zurich, but

Julius and Leeza, along with a few others, were returning home to recover from the games in their own beds.

Among the sleepy musician who were traveling back to Vienna were Thomas and Marcus, the trombone players from Bavaria. As identical twins, they were extraordinary in their own right. But what made them even more exceptional was their size. They were giants. The brothers were huge men from a timber working family. Leeza had always wondered how they ever managed to find their talent in the woods, but because they were so menacingly quiet off stage she never had the courage to ask.

Sitting beside Thomas and Marcus were Elsa and Herman. Everyone knew they were an item even though they tried to hide it. Elsa was a very talented flautist, and Herman was an adequate clarinet player. However, what he lacked in talent, he made up for in spirit. His humor had kept the orchestra going through many weary times. As the clown of the group, Herman felt it was his duty to pull practical jokes on everyone in the orchestra. His jokes had become legendary. One time he even put a frog in Clara's cymbal case, which caused her to faint when she opened it. No one thought she would be able to play that night. Clara was the shyest member of the orchestra. Every time she walked on stage Leeza was sure she was going to faint. Albert was another shy one. He played the cello and was a perfect match for Clara, or so Herman thought. He had certainly teased Albert enough about it. But Leeza agreed with Herman. One time she tried talking Albert into asking Clara out on a date, but everyone was betting that he was too shy to make the first move, and they were right.

Suddenly the stationmaster called out over the loud speaker, "Passengers traveling to Dresden, Prague, and Vienna may now board at track one."

Slowly but surely the orchestra members nudged one another and started gathering up their belongings. "I get the window seat," yawned Elsa.

"Why do you want the window seat?" Herman yawned back. "It's dark outside. You won't be able to see anything anyway."

"I want it because you always get it. Tonight I called it first."

"Well that's a fine bit of reasoning. Women!" Herman grumped as he kicked the bottom of Julius' foot to wake him.

"What! What is it?" Julius exclaimed as he tumbled from his perch atop Frank's big base drum case.

"The train is here. Time to wake up, maestro!"

Julius tugged on the shoulder of Leeza's blouse as she slept, curled up with her violin case under her chin. "Leeza," he whispered. "Leeza, it's time to go." When she failed to respond right away he brushed the hair back out of her face and said a little more sternly, "Leeza, darling, I can't carry all of your stuff, and you too! You are going to have to wake up and carry some of this stuff yourself."

"Jules, be a dear and put my bags on a freight cart," Leeza mumbled. "I'll crawl up on top and you can push us to a baggage car and pour us in."

Julius smiled warmly and whispered in her ear, "Don't tempt me, you know I'll do it!"

Leeza's eyes popped open and she immediately jumped up. "You would, wouldn't you?" Jules just nodded.

Once on board everyone slept peacefully all the way to the German border. It wasn't until the train lurched into the Dresden station that the trouble began. Disembarking passengers left as quietly as they could, but the boarding passengers included five rowdy Nazi militiamen, Brownshirt leftovers from the purge of 1934.

Since the end of the Great War the people had had to put up with paramilitary groups along the borders. These militia groups were formed by men who couldn't find a place for themselves in peacetime. They were constantly looking for someone to take out their aggressions on. They

146

had a reputation for being violent, ruthless, and undisciplined. So much so that even the regular army didn't want them. When the Nazi party was formed, the Brownshirts, or S.A. Sturmabteilung Storm Troops became the party's private army. However, since the purge most members just romed the country side looking for trouble. Civilians wanted nothing to do with them, and would go out of their way to avoid them whenever possible.

When the new passengers became aware that the Brownshirts intended to stay in their car, they moved to another. The Brownshirts were drunk, loud, and obnoxious, making their presence known to everyone around them except the exhausted orchestra members. They were used to noisy travelers and slept right through the stop in Dresden. After the train departed the station and the lights were dimmed, the five Storm Troopers began looking for something to help pass the hours to Prague. Their leader immediately took notice of Leeza, sleeping quietly next to Julius.

Without warning the big lug hoisted Julius up and threw him into the empty seat behind Leeza. "Hey!" Julius cried out, barely conscious. "What is the meaning of this?"

"The meaning of this," hissed the leader of the pack, "is that we like the pretty little Fraulein here and we don't require your presence." Then he hauled off and slugged Julius across the chin.

"I beg your pardon!" Leeza exclaimed, although she was only half conscious.

Before she could bring herself to full awareness the leader had thrust himself into the seat next to her and ripped open her blouse. "You don't have to beg, my pretty! I'll give it to you!" Leeza was completely surprised by the assault and slapped the man across the face. Instantly, his fist came crashing down on her eye.

Horrified at the speed with which things had gotten out of control, Julius scrambled to his feet in an attempt to defend Leeza. Suddenly he felt a crushing blow to the back of his head and fell to the floor in the center isle. Again, he tried to scrambled to his feet, but as he struggled to gain his footing the heel of one of the other Brownshirt's boots came crashing down on his hand, smashing it to pieces. He screamed out in pain just as the leader was penetrating Leeza. Her agonizing scream echoed Julius'.

Their screams aroused the other musicians. Angrily, they turned to see what all the commotion was about. When Thomas and Marcus, the huge pair of trombone players, realized what was happening they jumped up and headed for the back of the car. With one punch Thomas knocked out the first Brownshirt who came up the isle to stop them.

Marcus was right behind him, vaulting over two empty seats to tackle the two who were sadistically watching their leader as he forced himself into Leeza. With each thrust they shouted words of encouragement. When Marcus came crashing down on top of them, they never knew what hit them. He bashed their heads together and threw them into the empty seat behind Leeza. Then he reached over the seat and grabbed the collar of the filthy, grunting leader and hoisted him off of Leeza. Half a second later he found himself dangling from the ceiling, pinned by the huge hulk of a man, with his throbbing member still bulging out of his pants.

Thomas rushed past Marcus and the leader. The last drunken Brownshirt, who was too busy going through Julius' wallet to notice that he was the only one left standing, looked up just in time to see Thomas' fist come smashing into his face. As he fell, Thomas called to Marcus, "What do you want me to do with this trash?"

"Throw it out," Marcus barked.

Thomas pulled open the train door. Then he hoisted the Brownshirts, two at a time, and threw them from the train. By that time Marcus' right arm was getting tired of holding the rapist up to the ceiling so he switched hands and looked down at Leeza. Tears streamed from her swollen eyes as she tried to pull her blouse over her bare breasts while at the same time trying to conceal her battered pelvis.

"What about him?" Thomas called.

Marcus glared up into the eyes of the terrified Brownshirt. "That is up to Leeza," he spat. Then tenderly he looked down at Leeza and asked, "What do you want me to do with him? Shall we hold him for the police in Prague or throw him off the train?" Marcus turned his flaming eyes on the sniveling beast he held. "Or, perhaps you want me to kill him here and now?"

Leeza looked up at Marcus standing there, pinning the drunken, stinking, animal to the ceiling of the train car. She watched as he squirmed and choked, clinging desperately to Marcus' wrist for his very life. Then she let her eyes run up and down his disgusting body. Rage filled her soul. Her eyes locked on the still throbbing member that dangled in front of Marcus' chest. "I want those," she hissed. "I want those so he can never do this to anyone again."

Slowly, Marcus' scowl turned to an almost evil grin. "That can be arranged."

The Brownshirt tried to protest, kicking and writhing, as his fate became clear. Marcus closed his massive hand around the animal's throat, squeezing off his air supply while he reached into his pocket and pulled out his knife. He glanced at Thomas and motioned for his help. Thomas quickly grabbed the animal's balls, pulling them taunt. In one swift motion Marcus flipped open his knife and sliced them off. Pure shock register on the rapist's face before Marcus let him fall to the floor in a pool of his own blood. Thomas drug the writhing animal to the open door and threw him, screaming from the train.

The other musicians just stood by their seat. They were in complete shock. Marcus looked at them and shouted, "Well, what are you all waiting for!"

Immediately, they rushed to help their injured friends. Clara and Elsa wrapped their arms around Leeza and helped her to the rest room. She was bleeding horribly, so they washed her, and Elsa gave her a pad from her purse. Then they helped her changed her clothes.

Julius was still unconscious when Herman and Albert picked him up off the floor. They wrapped his bleeding hand with their handkerchiefs while Marcus and Thomas retrieved some dirty laundry from their suitcases. Quickly, everyone worked to wiped up the blood from the floor before the conductor made his way in to check their tickets.

Later, when the conductor finally did come around, no one in the car said a word to him about what had happened. When the train pulled into Prague, Marcus and Thomas, Clara and Elsa, and the rest of the musicians took up all the seats surrounding Leeza and Julius. Everyone kept watch over them to make sure no one bothered them, but Elsa and Clara were really worried and kept a closer watch. Julius slept fitfully so they covered him with a blanket, but Leeza was growing very pale. She was in and out of consciousness throughout the trip to Vienna. Each time she woke up she called for Dr. Gessler, and Elsa noticed that she was bleeding through the pad.

"Herman," she whispered, "when we get to the station call Doctor Gessler immediately. Tell him to meet us at his office."

After Klaus gave Leeza and Julius a brief examination he came out to tell the musicians what they needed to do. "Their injuries are more than I can deal with here. Julius will need surgery on his hand. I think Leeza might need surgery as well. She has lost a lot of blood. I'm sure she's been torn inside. She was a virgin, but there is so much blood I can't tell if that's all it is. I have given them both sedatives so they are asleep right now, but we need to get them to the hospital, immediately! Thomas, I need you to call for an ambulance?" Klaus pointed to the telephone.

"Of course, Herr Doctor!"

"Elsa and Clara, I need your help to get them dressed. They are both pretty well sedated. I don't think I can manage it on my own."

"Absolutely, Doctor Gessler," they answered. "Anything we can do to help."

"And, Herman, you know Herr von Rauthenau, Leeza's uncle, right?"

"Yes, Doctor, I know him." Herman squirmed, knowing what the doctor was asking him to do. "But shouldn't you be the one to call him?"

"Yes, under any other circumstances I would, but I will be in surgery and this can't wait. Here is his telephone number. I want you to tell him what has happened. You don't have to go into the details. Tell him that he and Leeza's mother should come right away. Tell him I said it is serious. Can you do that, Herman?"

"Yes, Doctor. I will take care of it," Herman answered.

A few minutes later, just as Clara and Elsa had finished dressing Leeza, they all heard the ambulance pull up with its siren blaring. Thomas and Marcus went into the examining room and picked up Leeza and Julius to carry them down the stairs. Klaus followed them out and said to the rest of the horrified musicians, "Go home, now. Get some rest. There is nothing more you can do for them tonight. If you want, you can come by the hospital tomorrow. I'll be there."

# Chapter Eleven

## The Night Train

With all of the tourist leaving Germany after the Olympic Games the train station was almost crowded beyond capacity. Karl hadn't anticipated the crowds, but was grateful for them. Their presence made it quite simple to loose the Gestapo agent that tailed him. He and Katrine simply pressed into the crowd and followed them onto the train.

When they arrived in Vienna, Leeza and Julius were out of surgery and doing well. After a few weeks of recovery at home they were ready to be cared for in the lap of luxury. Karlovy Vary, in Czechoslovakia, was Europe's most renowned spa town and just what the doctor ordered. Kings and queens had made the river valley famous as their own personal playground. Peter the Great, J.S. Bach, Casanova, and Karl Marx were all among Karlovy Vary's most distinguished visitors. Its twelve mineral springs, with their celebrated healing waters and the beautiful mountain scenery were just the thing to rejuvenate Leeza and Julius. After three weeks of soaking in the medicinal thermal pools and being waited on hand and foot, they were looking like themselves again.

"A girl could get used to this," Leeza laughed as she sipped Champagne by the pool.

"This place is not for just any girl," Karl protested. "I am quite sure that God himself created this place for a girl such as you, Leeza. Your beauty and grace are unsurpassed."

Leeza self-consciously touched her face. The bruises had faded by then, but she still felt their presence. "You must think me very vain, Uncle, if you feel the need to flatter me so."

"Not at all!"

"It's true, Leeza darling," Katrine said, trying to be encouraging. "You know your Uncle Karl doesn't flatter many women. If he says you are beautiful, it's because you are."

"Thank you," Leeza smiled. *They have to say that because they're my family.* "Come on Jules, let's take a walk by the river."

"But I have to pack."

"We're not leaving until morning, come on!" she commanded.

The full moon lit up the small waves in the river. They sparkled like watery stars. After a while of walking in comfortable silence Leeza asked, "Jules, how is your hand?"

"It's sore."

"Will you be able to play again?" she asked hesitantly.

"Oh, heavens yes! Just last night Karl sent the most handsome man to my room. We played all night."

Leeza slapped him on the shoulder and grinned. "No, you idiot!" Then she turned somber. "I meant, the violin?"

"Oh! The violin! Yes, of course. Only one bone was broken. It is healing nicely. Thank God it was my bow hand and not my left. A few more weeks and I shall be good as new."

Tears welled up in Leeza's eyes. "Thank God," she whispered. "I've been so afraid to ask. If you had not been able to play again because of me, I would never have forgiven myself."

Julius was astonished. "Is that what's been troubling you all these weeks? Oh God, Leeza, I've been so afraid that you blamed me for what happened. I'm so sorry I couldn't stop them."

153

"No, Julius! I would never blame you for what those pigs did! I thought you might blame me for the loss of your career!"

"How could you think such a thing?"

"Well, how could you think such a thing?"

Half laughing and half crying they collapsed into each other's arms, apologizing to one another for what had happened. Then Julius grabbed Leeza and raced with her back to the hotel. "I have something for you," he panted. "I wasn't sure if I should give it to you, but now I think it might be the right time." Together they ran back along the riverbank as the moon began setting behind the mountains.

Julius whisked Leeza up to his suite and closed the door firmly behind them. She watched as he rushed to his bureau and pulled open a drawer. Gently, he took something out that was wrapped in a man's handkerchief and tied with a lady's hair ribbon. Slowly he walked over to her and sat down beside her on the couch. Cautiously, he placed the package on the coffee table.

"What is it, Jules?" Leeza laughed. "A package of dynamite or something?" Julius' face grew more serious than she had ever seen it. She glanced from his face to the package, and then back again. "What is it?" she whispered.

"I don't know if you really want this or not. And I don't know if it's the time or not. But it is yours to do with as you please," Julius groaned.

Confused, and a little more than curious, Leeza picked up the package cautiously and felt it. It was obviously some kind of jar. She unwrapped it slowly and was surprised by its contents. "A jar of pickles?" she laughed.

"Not just a jar of pickles," Julius whispered as if he were afraid to tell her. Tenderly, he said, "I'm afraid you wouldn't want to eat these pickles. Look closer."

Leeza read the label. Not seeing anything special about it she turned the jar over to examine its contents. Confused, she stared at the pickles. Just when she was about to say "so what," one of the pickles caught her eye. It had an odd shape about it. Suddenly she realized what it was and erupted in laughter. "It's a pickled penis!" she roared.

Puzzled at first, and then relieved by her reaction, Julius began laughing with Leeza. "Yes! So it is! A pickled penis. With testicles," he added.

After a few minutes they were exhausted with laughter. "Where on earth did you get this?" Leeza gasped.

"While I was in the hospital Marcus and Thomas came to see me. They brought it. They were not sure you really wanted it. So they gave it to me."

Leeza's eyes grew wide as the color drained from her face. "You mean…You mean this is…But surely this can't be the…" Suddenly the image of that horrible night came flooding into her mind. Tears welled up in her eyes and spilled down her face. She began heaving huge sobs of pain out onto Julius' shoulder.

He just held her until she finally wept it all out. After a while he smiled and said, "You know Marcus and Thomas. They are so literal. It must be a Bavarian trait. Anyway, when you said you wanted it, they thought you meant it. So when the conductor came around Thomas ordered a jar of pickles from the dining car. It was the only thing he could think of at the time." Julius grinned as he wiped the tears from Leeza's face. "So there you have it. A pickled penis."

After crying so hard Leeza couldn't help but chuckle. Then after of few minutes of staring at the jar she picked it up in one hand and took Julius' hand in the other. She led him over to the balcony that overlooked the river. There, she leaned back and heaved the thing into the night. A second later they heard the splash.

Turning to her best friend in the whole world, Leeza said, "Can you play something sweet for me, Jules. Your music comforts me so."

Julius went inside smiling to himself. He knew in his heart that Leeza would heal, just as his hand would. A few seconds later he retrieved his Stradivarius from its case and began playing for the first time in over a month.

"It may not be smooth," he called to Leeza on the balcony. "But it will be sweet." The soft mellow tones filled the room and lofted out onto the balcony, healing both their wounds in the cool night air.

---

When the night train from Prague to Berlin pulled into the station in Dresden, there were no more Olympic Games tourists to distract the Gestapo. Only a week after the games were over the Gestapo returned to its practice of checking papers and harassing travelers. Now, over a month later, checks were mandatory. Suddenly there was a banging on Karl and Katrine's compartment door. "Papers!" shouted a gruff agent. "Papers!"

"Yes, yes! all right! Just a minute, bitte!" Karl yelled back as he pulled on his robe before opening the door.

"Papers," the Gestapo agent grumped.

Karl fumbled through his brief case for his and Katrine's passports with out switching on the lights. He handed them to the agent.

"Herr von Rauthenau?" the agent asked.

Karl yawned. "Yes, who else would be giving you my passport?"

The agent eyed Karl suspiciously. "Herr Karl von Rauthenau?"

"Yes, yes. I know the picture isn't very…"

"You will get dressed and come with me, Herr von Rauthenau," the agent barked.

"What? Why?" Karl questioned.

"My superiors have a few questions for you."

"What questions? What is the meaning of this? As you can plainly see my documents are in order!" Karl snapped.

"You did not receive permission to leave Germany, Herr von Rauthenau. And there is some question about large sums of money missing from your accounts in Germany. It is against the law to transfer funds out of the country. You know that, don't you? You will come with me now."

"I most certainly will not," Karl exclaimed. "If your superiors have any questions for me they can contact me in Berlin! Good night, Herr…"

"What is it Karl?" Katrine whispered hoarsely from the darkness behind him.

"Nothing, Katrine. Go back to sleep."

"Herr von Rauthenau, you will get dressed and come with me!" ordered the agent.

"Karl?" Katrine asked anxiously as she became more aware of the Gestapo agent standing in the doorway.

"Herr von Rauthenau, if you do not get dressed immediately, I will be forced to drag you from this train in your pajamas. Is that what you want?" the Gestapo agent asked sternly.

"All right," Karl hissed. "Just give me a few minutes."

"You have one minute."

Karl closed the door and switched on the lights to get dressed. Katrine got up and started to dress as well. "What are you doing?" he asked.

"I'm going with you, of course!"

"No, you're not. You're staying right here on this train. You are going home," Karl commanded.

"But…"

"Katrine, I'll just go and answer their questions. Everything will be all right. I'll be home tomorrow."

"But…"

"Katrine," Karl pleaded as he stood up to zip his pants. "I need you at home, where I know you'll be safe. Don't argue with me. I'm sure they just want to harass me, but I couldn't bear the thought of them harassing you too, not

157

after what happened to Leeza." Then tying his shoes he whispered, "Besides, I can take care of myself. I don't need you to come along." He leaned over and kissed her on the forehead, then opened the door to face the Gestapo agent. "I'm ready."

---

When three days had gone by without any word from Karl, Katrine was beside herself with worry. He had always been there to take care of everything, and now when he needed her to hold things together, she couldn't. She simply didn't know how.

"Manfred, we have to do something," she exclaimed nervously as she paced back and forth in front of Karl's desk. "We have to call someone or do something!"

"Yes, Frau von Rauthenau," Manfred answered calmly. And just as he was about to suggest that they call Gestapo headquarters there was a knock on the front door. A few moments later, he returned to announce that Herr Leber of the Gestapo was there to see Katrine.

"Good day, Frau von Rauthenau," the nasty little man grinned.

Katrine drew her handkerchief to her lips. With halting breath she replied, "Good day, Herr Leber. Have you brought news of my brother-in-law?"

"Yes, as a matter of fact I have. Frau von Rauthenau, your brother-in-law has been most uncooperative in providing us with the information we require, and I thought you might be able to help us in this matter."

"Is Karl all right?" Katrine quickly asked.

"Of course, Frau von Rauthenau. Of course!," agent Leber smiled. "Herr von Rauthenau is very important to the Führer. We would not let anything happen to him. It's just this business about your sudden trip to Austria, and then to

158

Czechoslovakia. Herr von Rauthenau didn't obtain permission to leave the country and the Führer was concerned about him. Perhaps you can tell us why you felt it necessary to leave so suddenly?"

Katrine shook all over. "My daughter...Leeza...she took ill very suddenly. Her doctor, in Vienna, called to tell us that she was having emergency surgery. That is why we left as quickly as we did. Her life was in danger, Herr Leber."

"And your trip to Czechoslovakia?"

"To Karlovy Vary? We took Leeza there to recover from her ordeal, that's all."

The Gestapo agent grinned. "Yes, Frau von Rauthenau, that is exactly what Herr von Rauthenau told us."

Waiving her hand in the air, Katrine said, "Well there you have it. There is nothing so mysterious about the matter. It was a family emergency, that's all. Now we are back and everything will be fine."

"Frau von Rauthenau, there is another matter," the agent said with a devilish grin. "The money?"

"Money?" Katrine shrugged. "I don't know what you are talking about, Herr Leber."

"Oh, come now, Frau von Rauthenau. Surely you know that Herr von Rauthenau's accounts are down a tremendous amount."

"I know of no such thing," Katrine innocently remarked. "I know Karl withdrew several thousand marks for our trip, but that couldn't have been enough to cause concern."

"We are not talking about several thousand marks, Frau von Rauthenau. We are talking about several million marks."

"I know nothing about millions, Herr Leber. Have you asked Karl?"

"Yes, we have, and he has told us nothing. He claims there has been a mistake."

Katrine breathed a sigh of relief. "Yes, I'm sure that's it. As soon as he comes home he'll be able to clear this all up for you, Herr Leber."

"I'm afraid, Frau von Rauthenau, that your brother-in-law will not be released until this matter has been cleared up."

"Well how do you expect to clear it up if you don't release him?" Katrine cried.

"Actually, there is a way. You can surrender Herr von Rauthenau's account books. We will have our accountants look them over to see if there has been a mistake. Only then we can release Herr von Rauthenau."

Katrine glanced toward the safe behind the painting that hung over the mantle in the study. She wasn't sure she should turn over Karl's books. Then she glanced at Manfred, who stood in the door way. He nodded. Biting her thumbnail, Katrine walked slowly over to the safe and turned out the combination. When the door clicked open she reached in a pulled out a black account books.

"Is this what you need, Herr Leber?" she asked hesitantly.

"Yes, Frau von Rauthenau. That is exactly what I need."

Katrine had expected that Karl would be home by the next morning, but when he did not showed up she went into hysterics. Manfred feared that she was near an emotional collapse and he knew it was time to call Leeza in Vienna.

"She needs you, Fraulein. With the Herr von Rauthenau away, she can't manage. I don't know what else to do for her."

"Did the agent say where they took Uncle Karl?" Leeza's asked calmly.

"No, Fraulein. He only said that Herr von Rauthenau would be held until the matter of the missing money could be cleared up."

"Very well, Manfred. I'll be on the next train out. Tell Mama not to worry. I'm coming home, and I'll take care of everything."

"Very good, Fraulein."

"Oh, and Manfred, I want you to pack some of Mama's things. I'm going to send her to the Herr Hagen's chalet, in the Tyrol. She doesn't need to be in Berlin right now, not at least until I can get this cleared up."

# Chapter Twelve

# The White Rose

"No one wants to read doom and gloom," Amy mumbled to herself as she scanned her article in the *New York Times* while she waited in the Munich train station for her connection to Salzburg. Her editor had cut her column in half, and warned her that she needed to do more human interest stuff. It seemed the folks back home were weary of all the talk about Hitler, and how bad things were in Germany. They were more interested in President Roosevelt, and how he was going to bring America out of the depression.

*Salzburg's just the place for human interest stuff. Maybe I'll discover the next virtuoso or great writer. Huh. That'll certainly take their minds off Germany. The world's going to hell in a hand basket and nobody gives a damn.*

The train from Salzburg was just pulling into the station in Munich when Amy slammed the paper down on the bench next to her. She watched as the passengers stumbled from the train, gathering children and luggage, and trying to get their bearings. *Everyone's always a little disoriented when they get off a train or a plane. I wonder if that's a human interest story.* Then her eye caught sight of a familiar face. *My God, it's her! Leeza von Rauthenau!* Amy's heart began to race as she watched Leeza from a distance. *She just came from Salzburg. Must be on her way to Berlin. Why didn't she take the train through Czechoslovakia? Who cares, you idiot! There she is, go after her!*

"Danke!" Leeza said as she tipped the porter and took her bags. "What platform will the train to Berlin leave from?"

162

"Track three, Fraulein. It leaves in fifteen minutes. You have plenty of time to make it," replied the porter.

Amy watched Leeza gather her bags and head for track three. *God she's beautiful.* Then she noticed that Leeza was looking around anxiously. *She seems nervous about something.* She got up and followed Leeza to track three. Leeza was dressed in a navy blue tailored skirt and jacket that accentuated her hour glass figure perfectly. The outfit accented her grace and elegance. Amy's insides churned with delight as she watched Leeza walk. *Her legs are gorgeous, lean and sensual. She could wrap those around me anytime.*

Leeza glanced around anxiously and then took a seat on a bench. She placed her luggage strategically on both sides of her so no one could sit next to her. Crossing her legs, she cradled her violin case on her lap.

*What are you doing, Trevor?* Amy thought to herself. *You are on your way to Salzburg and she's obviously going back to Berlin. And besides, you already blew it with her. You haven't got a snow ball's chance in hell.*

Just then the station master called out, "Passengers traveling to Berlin may now board at track three. All aboard!"

As Leeza rose and started gathering her things, three men dressed in trench coats stepped out of the shadows and approached her. They looked like the average Gestapo types that hung around Germany's train stations. Most people were use to their presence these days, and counted themselves lucky if they got away unmolested.

"Fraulein von Rauthenau," Amy heard the shortest one say. "I am Gestapo agent Reinberger. These are my associates, agents Gukelch and Beck. Where are you traveling today?"

Leeza's heart began pounding. "I am on my way to Berlin. But then I assume you know that."

"We thought that might be the case. However, we need you to open your bags, bitte."

"For what reason?" Leeza snapped.

"We are searching for…contraband," the little agent grinned.

Leeza became indignant. "I can assure you, Herr…"

"Reinberger."

"Herr Reinberger. I am not carrying any contraband. At least not today!"

Agent Reinberger smiled politely and then he pointed to her bags. The other agents grabbed them and started rummaging through them. The tall one pulled out one of Leeza's fine silk bras and twirled it around his finger. The other one came across a garter belt and whistled as he smiled up at her. Leeza hugged her violin case to her breast and began to shake.

Amy was still watching Leeza as the Gestapo agents toyed with her and pawed through her things. She could see that Leeza was visibly shaken by the Gestapo agents' games. Immediately, she pulled out her press pass and note book, and walked right up to them and asked, "Are lady's undergarments now considered contraband in the Third Reich?"

The little Gestapo agent was surprised by her abrupt and direct question. "Who are you?"

"Amy Trevor. International News Service. So, how long has lingerie been illegal in Germany? I'm sure my American readers will be interested to know."

"This is none of your concern, Fraulein Trevor. Move along," the little Gestapo ordered.

"Oh, but it is my concern," Amy eyed the agent harshly. "If underwear is illegal in Germany, then my readers in America need to know. It's my job to tell them."

Herr Reinberger was obviously frustrated at being observed by an American newspaper reporter. "Underwear is not illegal in Germany, Fraulein Trevor!" he snapped.

164

"Oh, I see. So it's just that the Führer's police like to play with lady's lingerie. Is that it?" Amy grinned.

"Fraulein Trevor, this is not your concern. My men and I are…"

"Harassing one of Germany's finest violinists," she interrupted. "If that can happen to one of Germany's best, then it can most certainly happen to American tourists. I shall have to report this in my column. Now, how do you spell your name, Herr Reinberger? Is that with a 'U' or an 'E'?"

The little agent huffed and marched off in frustration, with his men trotting along after him. Amy chuckled. Then she looked at Leeza, who had been holding her breath the whole time. She was pale. Amy could she her shaking. "It's okay, Fraulein von Rauthenau. They're gone now." Amy had no way of knowing the state of terror Leeza was in. Leeza just stared at her empty bags and her things scattered all over the floor.

"Hey, let me help you with this," Amy chirped as she bent down and started folding Leeza's clothes and placing them in her suitcase. "Those Gestapo guys are creeps, but they're not that hard to manipulate, especially if you're with the press." Leeza just stared at the floor, unmoved. Amy nervously kept rattling on as she packed Leeza's luggage. "The Führer wants to make a good impression on America, so most of the time the Gestapo steers clear of us reporters." She glanced up at Leeza. Leeza still didn't move. "Most of the time I can bully my way around them. They're so afraid they'll get their name in the paper." As she closed the lids of the suitcases and stood up, Amy smiled brightly. "I just ask them how they spell their names and that usually sends them packin'."

Leeza shook her head as if trying to wake from a deep sleep. Then she noticed that her bags were all packed and sitting on the bench. *How did…*Leeza turned to Amy, focusing on her for the first time. Instantly, she recognized

165

her. Her eyes filled with tears. "Thank you," she whispered in English.

"You're welcome," Amy smiled. "I didn't know you spoke English." *She looks like a deer caught in the headlights.*

"A little," Leeza answered in a halting voice. Just then the station master gave the last call for the train to Berlin. "I have to go!" Leeza pick up her bags and rushed off without saying another word.

"Well, thank you very much for saving my ass," Amy snapped to herself. "How wonderful you were to be so kind. If you're ever in Berlin, look me up!"

Irritated, Amy watched Leeza scurry onto the train. Then she felt a sudden urge to follow her. *She might need help again. I should go with her, just in case.*

Amy was remembering the St. Valentine's Day Ball, and how she had run away from Leeza. *She didn't even remember you, Trevor. Or maybe she remembers how you treated her the last time she met you. She doesn't want anything to do with you. Let her go, you fool!* Then Amy remembered the soft silk bra she had folded and put into the suitcase. *Would that I were it,* she thought as she made a dash for the moving train.

Amy reached Leeza's car just in time to see her disappear into compartment 3E. Just then she spotted the conductor making his rounds to check tickets. "Excuse me, bitte," she panted as if she were out of breath. "I was late for the train and didn't have a chance to buy my ticket."

"This is not a problem, Fraulein. I can sell you a ticket," he smiled.

"Danke," Amy panted some more. Then she smiled and said, "My sister is in compartment 3E. I don't suppose you would have a seat available in her compartment?"

"But of course, Fraulein. Your sister is the only one in that compartment."

"Danke, danke very much, Herr Conductor," Amy grinned.

When she opened the door to the compartment Leeza didn't look away from the window. She just sat there staring at the sun as it sank low in the sky. "Beautiful sunset," Amy remarked. Leeza hadn't heard the door open and jumped with fright. "I'm sorry," Amy said sympathetically. "I didn't mean to startle you, Fraulein von Rauthenau."

Leeza was relieved to see that it was Amy and not the Gestapo. She took a deep breath and smiled nervously. "That's quite all right, Fraulein...?"

"Trevor. Amy Trevor."

"Fraulein Trevor."

"You can call me Amy, if you like."

*Amy. A lovely name.* Leeza smiled and nodded slightly. "Amy."

"The Gestapo shook you up quite a bit back there, Fraulein von Rauthenau."

"Leeza. Yes, the Gestapo have a way of..." She breathed a hesitant laugh.

*Somethin's goin' on here,* Amy thought. *I can smell it.* "Have you been harassed by them before?"

"Not me," Leeza shook her head. "My uncle. They..." her voice cracked and tears began to run down her face.

Amy wanted to rush to her side, to hold her and let her cry her eyes out on her shoulder, but she held back. "He's had some trouble? Is that why they were harassing you, because of your uncle?"

Leeza was surprised by Amy's direct questions. "Yes, something like that."

*Be cool, Trevor. Don't get too personal. Not until she let's you know it's okay.* "I see."

Slowly, as the rhythm of the train soothed away Leeza's tension, she began to open up a little. "The Gestapo took him. That's why I'm on my way to Berlin." Amy pulled a

167

clean handkerchief from her duffel bag and handed it to Leeza. "Danke," she whispered as their eyes met and their hands touched, sending a shiver up both of their spines. Leeza broke down and began to cry again.

Amy scooted over in the seat next to Leeza and pulled her close. Leeza allowed herself to be drawn in and sobbed even harder when Amy cooed, "It's okay. It's okay. Let it all out." *The uncle must be in some serious trouble.* "I know some people in Berlin. They might be able to help." Amy put as much sympathy in her voice as she could muster.

Leeza sniffed and pulled away. "Thank you,...Amy. But you have been too kind already. First you helped me get away from the Gestapo, and now I have cried all over you. Look at the mess I've made of your shirt." Leeza rubbed the handkerchief on Amy's shoulder.

Amy felt a rush of warmth serge through body when Leeza touched her. "Well," she said softly, "I figure I owe you." Leeza looked confused. "For that night at the ball."

Leeza pulled away and blushed. "Oh that. Well..."

"I wanted to apologize for that," Amy quickly said. "I don't know what came over me. I just..."

"I understand, Fraulein Amy. One never knows what will happen when one asks a stranger to dance. You just...I mean...We...Maybe I wasn't..." Leeza blushed with frustration.

"You were wonderful!" Amy exclaimed. "It was me. I was the one who blew it! And it's just Amy."

"Well Amy, all is forgotten," Leeza sniffed. "Don't worry about what happened three years ago, not when things are so..."

*She does remember! But obviously she thinks it was her fault. What an idiot I was.* Then Amy decided to come clean. "Leeza, about that night...I just wanted you to know that I haven't forgotten it. I think about it all the time. I...I think about you all the time," she whispered.

Leeza was surprised by this stranger. "But you don' t even know me."

*What are you doing, Trevor? Are you out of your mind?* "I just wanted to tell you how sorry I was. I didn't mean to disappear like that. It's just that I hadn't...I mean...it had been a long time since I..." Amy's voice trailed off as the sun disappeared over the horizon and darkness filled the sky.

Neither she nor Leeza moved to switch on the light. *What can I say to get her back in my arms,* Amy wondered. But she couldn't think of anything. Eventually she heard Leeza's breath slow to a rhythmic pace. *She's asleep. That's good. She probably needs it. I wonder if Elizabeth can help her?* Finally Amy drifted off to sleep next to Leeza.

When the train pulled into the Berlin station Amy rubbed her eyes and sat up stretching. Suddenly she remembered that Leeza was right next to her and reached out to wake her, but she was already gone. "Where did she go?" Amy groaned as she grabbed her duffel bag and stumbled from the train.

---

It didn't take long for the Gestapo to pay a visit to Leeza once she arrived in Berlin. "We trust you have recovered from your recent illness, Fraulein von Rauthenau," Herr Leber remarked. But before she could answer he continued, "Now, about this matter of your uncle's accounts."

"I really don't know anything about my uncle's business," Leeza answered flatly. "As you probably know already, I live in Vienna most of the year. I am with the orchestra there. I can't tell you anything about Uncle Karl's accounts or about how he manages his money."

"Awe, but it is not just his money, Fraulein. It is yours as well. Are you not the heir of Wolfgang von Rauthenau?"

"Yes, I am."

"Well then, you see what I mean. Much of your money has disappeared under Herr von Rauthenau's management. You should be just as concerned as we are."

"I trust my uncle completely. He has always taken very good care of the estate," Leeza insisted.

"Be that as it may, Fraulein, we need to make sure that the money is returned to Germany. Do you know where your uncle has put it?"

"No."

"Then we have a problem," the agent grinned.

"My mother tells me you have examined Uncle Karl's account books?"

"Yes, we have."

"Well, what did you find?"

"Nothing out of the ordinary."

"If your accountants can't find anything wrong, then what makes you think I can tell you anything?"

"Surely you don't think that we believe you don't know anything about your own money, Fraulein von Rauthenau?"

"I don't," Leeza groaned. "I told you that already. Uncle Karl manages everything for me. If I could just see him I'm sure we could work this out."

"That is quite impossible. Herr von Rauthenau is being held in…in protective custody."

"Protective custody? Who are you protecting him from?" Leeza hissed.

"From himself, Fraulein," grinned the Gestapo agent. "Now, to another matter. Production at Rauthenau Steel has steadily decreased over the last month."

"I'm sure that's because Uncle Karl was with me during my…illness. Once he's back at the factory things will improve."

170

"That's just it, Fraulein, he won't be going back to the factory until we can clear up this matter about the missing money. We think someone from the family should stand in for him until he is released."

Leeza was shocked. "What are you saying Herr Leber? That I should run the factory in my uncle's place?"

"That is exactly what we are saying, Fraulein von Rauthenau."

"But that is absurd! I don't know anything about the family business. I am a musician, Herr Leber, not a business woman."

"You will eventually have to learn, Fraulein. Your uncle will not live forever!"

Leeza looked into his eyes and knew immediately what the weasely little Gestapo agent was implying. Taking a deep breath, she said flatly, "So, am I to understand that if I take over at the factory, Uncle Karl will live a longer life?"

"All I am saying is that a man of his age should know that he can depend on his family."

"I see. And if the factory should produce enough to replace the missing funds from my uncle's accounts, then he would be free to resume his leadership of Rauthenau Steel?"

"I think we understand one another very well, Fraulein. You have a sharp mind. You learn quickly." With that understanding, Agent Leber stood up. "Well, I must be going. So much to do these days. Good day, Fraulein von Rauthenau. I'll be seeing you soon."

"Uh, Herr Leber. Bitte, a moment more of your time. I'm thinking I need to know that my uncle is well before I can start to work. You know how worry can distract one from their business."

"I think that can be arranged, Fraulein." Then Herr Leber tipped his hat and strolled out of the study.

Moments later Manfred came in. "Are you all right, Fraulein Leeza?"

Leeza paced back and forth in front of Karl's desk. "Yes, Manfred. Is Mama ready to leave for the train station?"

"Yes, Fraulein."

"Good. I want you to go with her to Herr Hagen's chalet, Manfred. It's up to you to stay with her and take care of her."

"Of course, Fraulein. But who will take care of you?"

Leeza smiled tenderly at Manfred. "I'm not as fragile as Mama is. I'm use to being on my own, remember?"

Manfred smiled. "The little girl has grown up. Your uncle would be proud of you, Fraulein Leeza."

---

The next morning Leeza received a note from Karl. Herr Leber made sure she read it before she left for Rauthenau Steel.

*Dearest Leeza,*

*I'm so very sorry you have to be involved in this mess. Know that I am well, and miss you. Herr Weisman and Hanna will give you all the help you need. Should you have an hour of need, remember how your little violin case soothes your worries. Julius knows.*

*All my love,*
*Uncle Karl.*

Leeza hadn't been to the factory in years. She wondered how in the world she would ever manage to increase production enough to replace the millions the Gestapo said was missing. Shortly after she arrived she asked Hanna, Karl's secretary, to gather all the employees together in the break room.

172

"Most of you don't know me." Leeza tried to look strong and confident. Inside she trembled. "But you all know my Uncle Karl. You know what a good man he is."

"Herr Karl is the salt of the earth," called Albert Weisman from the back of the room. Everyone nodded their heads in agreement.

"Well, the Gestapo doesn't seem to agree with you. They have accused him of embezzling from the company!" Leeza let her voice sound indignant.

"Herr Karl would never do that," Hanna shouted, "unless he was trying to keep the money out of the Gestapo's coffers!"

"Ja!" everyone shouted. "Herr Karl is a good man, a decent man. He has always been good to everyone who works here. He would never intentionally hurt the company!"

"Then we are in agreement," Leeza said calmly. "However, the Gestapo is holding him until we can replace the money that is missing." A hush fell over the workers. Leeza looked around at each face. "They will hold Karl until we have replaced what is missing without touching our current income. This means that we are going to have to produce like we have never produced before." Leeza paused to watch their reaction, but there was none. *What are they thinking?* "You know that I don't know anything about the steel business. However, the Gestapo has ordered me to fill my uncle's shoes." Again she paused for their reaction, and again the workers were stone faced. "We all know this is impossible." Leeza grinned, and the workers erupted in laughter.

"Don't worry, Fraulein Leeza!" Albert called out. "We will teach you everything you need to know! Right Fellows?"

"Ja!" they shouted. "Ja! We'll teach you, Fraulein. Soon you'll know how to stoke the furnaces and mix in the coke!"

"And I'll teach you everything you need to know about the business end of the operation," Hanna called out with a smile.

Relieved, Leeza nodded. "Danke. Danke for me, and for Uncle Karl."

"Don't you worry about a thing, Fraulein Leeza. We'll work day and night until we have raised the money for Herr Karl. We'll bring him home in no time! You'll see!" shouted the workers.

———————

By the end of the year Leeza had, in fact, learned to stoke the furnaces and mix in the coke. She had also learned what a valuable friend Hanna was. Every morning Hanna brought the books into Karl's office so she could show Leeza the previous day's production increases and where they stood on raising the money needed to free Karl.

"We need to increase production by fifteen percent if we are ever going to see the extra income," Hanna barked.

"How much has it increased to date?" Leeza asked hesitantly.

"Since you took over two months ago, we have realized a three percent increase." Hanna tried to answer enthusiastically. "That's very good."

"My God, at that rate it'll be a year before we raise the funds. Some Christmas this is going to be," Leeza sighed. She was exhausted from the long hours she was putting in loading rail cars. "I was really hoping we could bring Uncle Karl home for the holiday."

"Go home," Hanna urged. "You are dead on your feet."

"No, Hanna. I can't. If the men are putting in such long hours, how can I not? I've got to get back out there and help them load those rail cars. If they don't go out this morning we'll loose another day's revenue."

174

Hanna grabbed Leeza by her grubby coveralls. "I won't let you go out there today. Even Albert is worried about you. You have been at this factory everyday for two months. You can't keep pushing yourself this hard. Karl wouldn't want that!"

"Hanna, I can't just go home! I have to…"

"No you don't!" Hanna snapped. "I won't let you! Besides, it will all be here tomorrow."

Leeza was too tired to argue with her any more. "Maybe you are right," she sighed. "I'll go, but I'll be back here bright and early in the morning."

After she changed out of her coveralls, Leeza decided to take a stroll down the Kunfurstendamn. All of the old bars were boarded up with signs over the windows that said "CLOSED." *Just like the rest of Germany. Closed for the duration.* Eventually she strolled down Unter den Linden and past the Adlon Hotel.

From her window on the fourth floor, Amy sat watching the traffic as it crawled up the street. Suddenly her heart skipped a beat. *Leeza!* She grabbed her coat and ran out the door. Not wanting to wait for the slowest elevator in Berlin, she flew down the four flights of stairs and crashed through the front doors of the Adlon. Quickly looking right and then left, she scanned the sidewalk for Leeza, but she wasn't there. *Where did she go?* Then she bolted around the corner to see if Leeza might have gone that way, but she didn't see her anywhere. *Tough luck, Trevor,* Amy sighed to herself. *It's just not in the cards.*

Amy hung her head and walked slowly back to the bar in the Adlon. *The only thing that's gonna keep you warm is a bottle of bourbon.* Suddenly her heart skipped a beat again as her eyes fell on Leeza's profile. She was sitting at the bar. Amy just stood there frozen, staring at her soft pale skin.

"Hey, Amy!" the bartender called. "Ya want the usual?" Leeza glanced over and saw her standing there.

*Shit!* Amy thought. *Not the approach I was hoping for.* "Naw, John. Just a beer," she called as she strolled casually up to the bar.

"Hello," Leeza said in English. Then she flashed Amy a brilliant smile.

*This is encouraging*, Amy thought. "Hi! Long time no see!"

Leeza frowned. "Long time no see? What does this mean, bitte? My English is not very good."

"Oh! Sorry!" Amy stammered. "It means, 'it has been a long time since I have seen you.' Long time no see. Get it?"

"Yes, I understand now. Danke"

"Sure," Amy grinned. "How have you been?"

"I have been fine. I am very tired," Leeza ran her hand through her hair, "but I am fine."

Amy was mesmerized by the graceful way Leeza's hair fell over her shoulders. "What...uh, what has you so tired?" *What a dumb question, you idiot!*

"I have been working long hours."

"But I thought you were a musician in Vienna?"

"Yes, I am." Leeza gave her a sideways glance. "But recently I have taken over my uncle's job in our steel factory."

Amy sipped her beer. *Way to go, Trevor. You sounded like you didn't appreciate the fact that musicians worked for a living.* "I see." Then she really saw. Glancing down at Leeza's hands, Amy noticed how rough and red they were. *Geesh. What the hell is she doing working in a steel plant?* "How's your uncle?"

Leeza took a sip of her beer and hung her head. "He is not well, Fraulein Amy."

"Just Amy. Did he get things worked out with the..." *There you go again! Don't talk about the tough stuff. Keep it light!*

176

Leeza glanced around the room. "No. He didn't. He never came home." Then she hung her head again.

"Listen, I have a friend. I started to tell you about her that night on the train. Anyway, she works at the..." Amy stopped suddenly and took a look around the bar. "You wanna grab a table?" she asked as she pointed to one in the back.

Leeza looked grateful. "Yes. Danke."

When they had huddled close together in the back, Amy continued whispering. "I have this friend. She works at Gestapo headquarters." Leeza's eyes flew open in fright. "No! Wait! It's not what you think. She's a secretary there, but she's one of us. She's a friend of mine. You know, an informant. She hates the Nazis as much as I do, so she leaks me information when she can. Maybe she can tell us something about your uncle."

Leeza was visibly frightened. "No. They would find out! It isn't safe."

"Sure it is!" Amy smiled. "She gets off work in a couple of hours. We could arrange to meet her at Pauli's Dance Palace. I'm sure she'll help if she can."

"You don't understand, Fraulein Amy. The Gestapo is blackmailing me. They will keep my uncle alive as long as I work at the factory and increase its production."

"Just Amy. Where are they holding him?"

"I don't know," Leeza cried. Then tears began spilling down her face.

Amy took Leeza's hands in hers. Tenderly, she brushed the hair back from her eyes and lifted her chin. "Leeza, let me help you. I'm sure we can find out where they're holding him. Elizabeth will help if we ask her. I know she will."

Leeza smiled weakly and nodded.

Later that evening they found Elizabeth at Pauli's Dance Palace. Lesbians had been meeting secretly in the

177

back room of Pauli's ever since Hitler closed all the gay bars in town.

"We just knock like this." Amy rapped her knuckles on the back door twice, then paused and rapped three more times. "Pauli likes the extra money we bring in."

The door opened and the sound of soft music spilled into the alley. Once inside Leeza was amazed by the number of women crammed into the little room. *There must be a hundred of them.*

Amy smiled when she saw the expression on Leeza's face. "Who says Hitler got rid of all the dykes?"

Leeza glanced around the smoke filled room and smiled. There were women everywhere, many of whom she knew. "There's Helene Stocker from the White Rose Ladies Society," she whispered in Amy's ear.

Amy felt a warm sensation rush through her body as Leeza's breath brushed her ear. *Okay Trevor, keep your mind on business.* Trying to ignore the sensation, Amy frowned. "Hitler outlawed the White Rose Ladies Society a few years back, or hadn't you heard? Now it's strictly back rooms and dark corners for us."

# Chapter Thirteen

# Conflicting Messages
# 1937

"If I were the King of England, I can tell you I wouldn't let no dame pull me off my throne," Jim Newman grumped as Amy packed her bags to leave for France. "Edward's a fuckin' idiot!"

Marshall Turner laughed. "Spoken like a true romantic!"

Amy smiled. "What's the matter, Jim, don't like spring weddings?"

Jim took another swig from his bottle of bourbon and grinned at Amy. "Let's just say, I'm glad I'm not the one who got this assignment. I hate human interest stuff. That's the only thing women reporters are good for. Weddings, funerals, all the social crap!"

"It's more than social, ol' man," Marshall Turner chimed in. "Edward's abdication has serious ramifications for my country. It has meant the political death of Winston Churchill, and he's the only man in the country who's had the good sense to keep his eye on Hitler."

"Ya see!" Jim yelled, "that's what I'm talking about. Churchill and the King were buddies, right? So Churchill supports the King and this Simpson broad, right? Well look what it got him. The House of Commons wants to string him up and the *Arms and the Covenant*, England's rearmament program, is out the window. They were the only organization that showed any backbone when Hitler marched into the Rhineland last year. Now because Edward falls in love with a divorcee, no one gives a shit what Hitler's doing. He's probably laughing his ass off right now."

"Yes, I confess, many of my countrymen are pacifists," Marshall sighed.

"They're not the only ones," Amy said as she closed up her duffel bag. "Most Americans don't want anything to do with the outside world either. And I'll tell you what, this isolationist position is gonna come back and bite everybody in the ass." Then she glanced at Jim. "But I really don't think the King's love affair has much to do with any of this."

Jim rolled his eyes and lit a cigarette. "Just like a dame. The world is going to hell and she thinks a little love can change everything."

"Ya never know, Newman," Amy replied as she threw her bag over her shoulder and headed for the door. "Ya just never know. Lock up when you leave, and if you order room service put it on your own tab this time."

"Yeah, yeah!" Jim waved, taking another slug of bourbon.

Amy hated that she had to go just when she had the chance to get to know Leeza. *Geesh. Between her working fourteen hours a day at the steel plant, and me being sent away on assignment every other week, and with her being so worried all the time, when are we ever gonna be able to get together? I hope Elizabeth comes up with some news about her uncle soon. I don't know how much longer Leeza can keep up this pace.*

It had been several months since Leeza and Amy talked to Elizabeth that night in the back of Pauli's Dance Palace. Elizabeth had told them to be patient, that it might take some time for her to find out where Karl was being held. After all, she just couldn't walk up to the chief and ask about him. She had to be careful not to jeopardize her position at Gestapo headquarters. Patience and timing were everything. Eventually, Karl's name would come across her desk and when it did, Elizabeth would have all the information Leeza needed.

Leeza stumbled into her office and collapsed in the chair behind her desk. She had been helping load rail cars since five o'clock in the morning, and by ten o'clock her head was pounding and her feet were sore. Moments later Hanna appeared in the doorway with a cigarette dangling from the corner of her mouth, and the account books in her hands.

"Not this morning, Hanna," Leeza sighed. "I have a splitting headache." She leaned back in her chair and put her feet up on the desk.

Hanna looked intense. "You'll want to see this, Leeza."

"I'm not sure I can even focus on the numbers today. I'm just too tired." Leeza closed her eyes and folded her arms over her chest, hoping Hanna would leave her alone long enough to grab a few minutes rest.

Hanna took the cigarette out of her mouth and flicked the ashes on the floor. Then she dumped the books on the desk next to Leeza's feet. "Well, these should put a spring back in your step."

Leeza's eyes popped open. "What do you mean?"

"We're close," Hanna grinned.

"How close?"

"Real close."

"How close is real close?"

"Take a look for yourself!" Hanna grumped. Leeza swung her legs off the desk and opened the general ledger. "That one's not important. Take a look at the accounts receivable."

Leeza quickly rummaged through the books. "Which one is that?"

Hanna reached for the red one and opened it to the last page. "There, you see! Once the invoice is paid from this

181

mornings shipment, we'll only have another two hundred thousand to go!"

Leeza's eyes sparkled in amazement. "That close?" she whispered.

"That close," Hanna smiled. "Shouldn't take much more than two weeks to cap it off."

"Do we have that many orders to fill in the next two weeks?"

"Honey, as fast as Hitler is laying track and building up the army, we'll have enough orders to last for the next fifty years!"

"Thank God!" Leeza exclaimed as tears of joy and exhaustion filled her eyes. "Just two weeks and Uncle Karl will be a free! How can I ever thank the crew. They have worked so hard, and they never even complained once."

Hanna hated it when Leeza cried. She was a crusty old dyke who had buried her own emotions long ago. She did not quite know what to do when Leeza got emotional. "Awe, don't worry about them, kid. They're a tough bunch. Hard as nails. Just give 'em a nice beer party when Karl gets home. That'll make 'em happy." Hanna was relieved when the telephone rang and ran off to answer it. Leeza just sat back and smiled through her tears.

"Leeza!" Hanna called from the front office. "It's for you. You know someone named Elizabeth?"

Leeza sat bolt upright. "Yes!" she cried. "I'll take it." Her hand shook as she picked up the receiver. "Hello! This is Leeza."

Elizabeth spoke in a whisper. "Are you free for lunch?"
"Yes. You've got news?"
"Yes."
"Where shall we meet?"
"Eddi's Cafe?"
"I'll be there! What time?"
"Noon."

182

"Is he…?" Leeza started to ask, but Elizabeth quickly interrupted.

"I'll see you there. Good bye."

As she hung up the telephone Leeza ran her fingers through her hair. *Greasy! Yuck!* Then she looked down at her coveralls. *No wonder. Look at me, I'm a mess.* She glanced up at the clock on the wall. *Great! I've got just enough time to go home and get cleaned up.* "Hanna!" she shouted. "I've got to go somewhere! I'll be back this afternoon."

"Fine with me," Hanna yelled back. "Take all the time you need."

*I swear, sometime I feel like I'm the one who's working for her*, Leeza thought as she tore off her coveralls and ran out the side door.

Eddi's Cafe was pretty busy around the noon hour. People were buzzing in and out, taking any open table they could find or picking up lunch orders to go. Leeza was lucky to get a table near the front window so she could watch for Elizabeth. A few minutes later she saw her coming up the sidewalk. Leeza waved. Elizabeth nodded slightly. When she came in, she headed for the only open table in the back. Leeza followed.

"Can't be too careful. Who knows who's watching," Elizabeth said as Leeza took a seat across from her.

Leeza looked around anxiously. "I'm not used to all the cloak and dagger stuff," she whispered.

Elizabeth handed Leeza a menu. "You should be by now. You know they're watching every move you make." Leeza nervously looked over her shoulder again. "Don't worry," Elizabeth winked. "Even Gestapo agents take a lunch break. Your guy is down the block and across the street. Right about now he's stuffing his face with a bratwurst. What are you going to have?"

183

Leeza glanced down at the menu in front of her and then up to Elizabeth. "I'm too excited to eat. What news have you brought?"

"Leeza, you really need to eat something. You're looking very pale these days."

Just then the waitress came over to take their orders. "I'll have the special." Elizabeth said. "And coffee."

The waitress looked at Leeza, who was staring blindly at the menu, but could not think of anything except what Elizabeth had to say. "I'll have the same," she finally said so the waitress would go away. When she did, Leeza gasped, "Tell me before I go crazy!" Elizabeth frowned. She really didn't want to give Leeza this news. "What is it?" Leeza cried. "He's not dead?"

"No!" Elizabeth exclaimed. "No, he's not dead. He is alive."

"Then what is it? Where is he?"

"Leeza, this is not good news," Elizabeth sighed. "He's in Dachau."

Leeza slowly leaned back in her seat. As the reality hit her she closed her eyes. *All of the months of waiting! What did you expect, that they were holding him at a health resort?* Tears slipped through her closed eyelids.

"I'm sorry," Elizabeth whispered. Then she reached out to hold Leeza hand. "But the good news is that he's alive. You should be grateful for that."

Leeza nodded her head, unable to speak because of the lump in her throat. She took a handkerchief out of her purse and wiped her nose. Finally, she took in a deep breath and said, "Thank you for your help, Elizabeth. Yes, at least I know he's alive. And for that I am eternally grateful." Then she managed to work up a smile. "We are quite close to raising his ransom money. It won't be much longer if he can just hold on."

"He has held on this long, there's no reason to expect that he can't make it a little while longer." Elizabeth was

184

trying to be as sympathetic as she could. "I wish there was something more I could do."

Leeza smiled through her grief. "You've done everything you can, Elizabeth. The rest is up to me." She tucked away her handkerchief just as the waitress brought their order of sausage with sweet-hot mustard.

---

Admiral Canaris had Wilhelm's best interests in mind when he called him into his office. "You received a call from Fraulein Leeza von Rauthenau today?"

"Yes, Sir. I did." Wilhelm answered smartly.

"And how is the Fraulein?"

"She is concerned about her uncle," Wilhelm replied coldly.

"And you agreed to help her, Captain Schroeder?"

"I most certainly did not, Admiral."

"Why not?" Canaris barked. "You helped the uncle's lover!"

Wilhelm felt the sweat bead up on his forehead. "I don't know what you mean, Admiral."

"Did you think I wouldn't be notified that one of my officers made a refit inspection at Sachsenhausen?"

*Admiral Canaris is obviously testing me.* Wilhelm tried to look as confused as possible. "Sachsenhausen?"

"Don't play dumb with me, Wilhelm!" Canaris snapped. "The camp commander described you perfectly. It was very foolish of you! But at least you didn't use your own name. I was able to deny that a Captain Tannen worked in my office."

"Admiral!" Wilhelm exclaimed vehemently, "I never..."

Admiral Canaris lifted his hand to cut Wilhelm off before he could say any more. Then he ran is hand over his silver hair and sighed. "Karl von Rauthenau was a friend of mine too, Wilhelm. I was his commanding officer long before I was yours. But you should have saved your efforts for him, and not his..." Canaris' voice trailed off.

"My conscience..."

"Your conscience, yes. Well, there's a matter we should have all thought about back in 1933. Now it's too late." Canaris eyed Wilhelm carefully to gauge his reaction. Wilhelm just held his stare. "What do you think about that?"

"Every man must follow his conscience, Admiral."

"And if his conscience should oppose the law?"

"The laws change every day."

Canaris' face was intense. "But what of truth?"

"Truth. Lies. I don't know anymore. When a man like Karl von Rauthenau is thrown into a place like Dachau, what difference does the truth make? He was a loyal son of Germany."

Admiral Canaris stood up and pulled his shoulders back. He towered over Wilhelm. "Many loyal sons of Germany have learned to lie, Wilhelm. Have you?"

Wilhelm stared into the Admiral's eyes. *He's testing me. Testing my loyalty.* "What must I do to prove myself?"

"Tell the Fraulein that her uncle is dead."

Wilhelm began to shake inside. "Is it true?" he whispered.

"Truth is a relative thing, Wilhelm." Canaris paused for a moment. "Sometimes a lie is more real than the truth."

Wilhelm's heart sank.

"After you have spoken with Fraulein von Rauthenau, you will report to our Embassy in Paris."

"You are transferring me to Paris? Why?" Wilhelm questioned.

"Men who have not learned to lie well don't need to be in Berlin. It is for your own sake that I'm transferring you.

One day, Wilhelm, I may call upon you to follow your conscience, but not today."

As Wilhelm boarded the plane for Paris that night, he never felt more broken hearted or alone in his life. It had almost killed him to tell Leeza that Karl had died in Dachau. She went into a rage such as he had never seen before. He remembered her fury as she pounded his chest with her fists and screamed how much she hated him. "You murdered him, Wilhelm! You, and your Nazi assassins. You murdered the man you loved! And I will hate your forever for it."

Wilhelm had tried to calm her. "Leeza," he had whispered as he wrapped his arms around her to control her. "Leeza."

"Let go of me!" she had screamed. "Get out! Get out of my home! I never want to see you again! Get out! I hate you!"

He had no choice but to leave. His presence only upset her further. Walking out, he knew indeed, that she would never forgive him. He knew that he would never be able to regain her love or receive her forgiveness. *Lies are sometimes more real than the truth, but both can devastate*, Wilhelm thought as he buckled himself into the airplane seat.

---

Darkness fell over the von Rauthenau mansion as Leeza sat alone, curled up on the couch in Karl's study staring at the walls, and longing for sleep. But sleep wouldn't come. She could still smell Karl's pipe tobacco on the afghan she clutched to her breast. The months of worry and laboring in the factory had taken their toll. Leeza was physically and emotionally exhausted. The bitter joy of learning that Karl was alive in Dachau was suddenly and unexpectedly crushed by the news that he had died that very day. *How can it be? We were so close!* Leeza groaned from the very depths of her soul, but she couldn't cry another tear. She felt cold and empty inside. *I have nothing left to give, Uncle Karl. You should have come to Austria when I begged you to. Now it's too late.* Eventually Leeza fell asleep there on the couch. She simply didn't have the energy to continue thinking about what had happened or about what to do next.

When she opened her eyes the next morning another wave of grief washed over her, but this time Leeza let the grief turn to anger. *Those Nazi bastards! Those blood sucking Nazi bastards. I'll show them that they can't...*Then her thought halted. *Can't what, Leeza? Just what do you think you can do to them? Nothing! That's what!*

Leeza thought about the workers at the factory. *Hanna, Albert, how am I going to tell you? You've worked so hard. And for what? For what?* Leeza stormed through the house getting ready for work. Angrily, she splashed water on her face to wash the sleep from her eyes and ripped a comb through her hair. *They worked so hard and never took a Deutsche Mark's worth of overtime money. God, we were so close to raising the money.*

Then an idea struck her. *The Führer is never going to see one precious Deutsche Mark of that money. After all, they earned it.* "Fuck Hitler and his whole fucking government." Leeza yelled. Then she smiled a bitter, angry smile as she slammed the door on her way out.

When she got to the office she slammed that door too. "Hanna! I want to see you in my office, now!"

Hanna appeared in the doorway and said, "Yeah, what about?"

"How long will it take you to cut a check for every worker in the factory?" Leeza barked.

Hanna was dumbfounded. "What in the hell are you talking about, it's not pay day?"

Leeza threw her hands in the air and shouted bitingly, "It is today!"

Hanna could see that Leeza was very upset about something. "What's going on, kid?" The gentleness in Hanna's voice took Leeza by surprise. It froze her where she stood. She looked up at Hanna's warm gray eyes and the sight of them melted her rage instantly. Her bottom lip began to quiver, but she couldn't bring herself to say the words. Hanna knew by the look on her face. "He's dead, isn't he?"

Leeza just stood there shaking. Tears streamed down her cheeks as she nodded her head. "Yes," she finally whispered. Hanna walked slowly over to Leeza with her arms stretched out. Leeza collapsed against Hanna's full, round breasts and began sobbing.

"There, there," Hanna sighed. "It's all right." But only a second later she was sobbing too. Together, they stood there weeping in each others arms.

Finally, when they both had cried themselves out, Leeza sniffed and rubbed her eyes. "I want the workers to have the money. I'll be damned if I'll give it to Hitler for murdering Uncle Karl."

Hanna sniffed and rubbed the tears off her face. "I know how you feel, honey. But you can't do that."

Leeza pulled back indignantly. "You just watch me!"

"No," Hanna sighed. "Do you want to sign their death warrants?"

Leeza was stunned. "What do you mean?"

"Honey, I know how much you want to avenge Karl's death, but this is not the way. The Gestapo will be in here in two seconds flat if that money disappears again. You just can't do this, Leeza. There are better ways of getting even."

"Like how?" Leeza shouted.

189

"Think about it! Besides the money, what else are we giving the Führer?"

Leeza paused and thought about it for a moment. Then the lights came on in her eyes. "Steel?"

"Steel!" Hanna grinned. "Let's get Albert in here."

After giving Albert the time to adjust to Karl's death, Hanna and Leeza told him what was on their mind. "What happens if the coke isn't mixed in with the iron just right? Or what happens if the heat in the furnace isn't right?"

"Oh! That is not good, Fraulein," Albert exclaimed. "Too much coke and the steel doesn't harden right. It becomes brittle. Too little and it doesn't harden enough. And if the temperature in the furnace is not right, there remains too many impurities in the finished product! It would break very quickly."

Hanna winked at Leeza. "So if there are impurities in the steel of say, a tank?"

"This is not good. The tracks would fall apart a couple of miles down the road!"

"Perfect," Leeza grinned. "Just what the doctor ordered."

"I don't understand, Fraulein Leeza," Albert rubbed his balding head.

Hanna groaned. "It's kind of like baking a cake, Albert. You put in too much flour and the cake turns out like a brick. Too little and it turns out like soup." Albert still didn't understand. "It's like this, Albert, we want to bake a cake for the Führer and we don't want him to enjoy it! Got it?"

The quizzical look on Albert's face disappeared slowly as he realized what they were up to. "Ja," he smiled. "I think you Frauleins want Albert to bake a steel cake for the Führer. One that goes flat, ja?" Albert squashed his hands together and laughed.

"Ja! Now you understand," Leeza giggled. "I want the ships to rust, the tanks to run off their tracks, and the machine guns to explode. You understand?"

Albert laughed again, "I understand, Fraulein Leeza. Albert can make this happen."

"Thank you, Albert. You are a good friend."

The smile on Albert's face faded. "Karl was my friend. I know he would do this himself if he were here. He once told me he would rather blow up the factory than allow Hitler to take it. Well, I'd better get out there and make those changes." But before he got to the door he turned around. "Fraulein Leeza, may I speak with you a few more minutes?"

"Of course, Albert!" Leeza exclaimed.

Hanna got up. "I have to get back to work."

Leeza nodded as Albert sat down. "What's on your mind?"

Albert looked pained. He hesitated. Then he said, "Your uncle, Herr Karl, he once told me that I should ask him if I needed help with anything." He waited for Leeza's response.

"Albert, anything you need, just ask! You were not only my uncle's friend, you are mine as well."

Albert smiled shyly. "I have four grandchildren, Fraulein Leeza. Did you know that?" Leeza nodded. "Well, Herr Karl once asked me if I had made arrangements to leave the country. At the time I didn't think that it would be necessary, but now I..."

"Where do you want to send them?" Leeza smiled gently.

"I have a sister in America. I think maybe it would be best if they were to stay with her for a while. But I have not been able to obtain visas for them. America has closed its doors to Jews."

"Say no more Albert. Give me a few days and I'll see what I can come up with."

"Thank you, Fraulein Leeza," Albert smiled gratefully. When he left the office, Leeza leaned back in her chair and thought about what to do with Albert's grandchildren. That night she arranged to meet Anneliese and Margo at Pauli's Dance Palace.

Coming in through the ally entrance wasn't a good idea anymore. With the Gestapo watching her, Leeza decided it would be better to go in through the front door and slowly make her way to the back room. She stopped at the bar and ordered a beer. No one followed her in so she moved to the back of the bar and gave the designated knock. She was admitted quickly. Anneliese and Margo were already there. They were devastated by the news of Karl's death, and agreed to find a way to help Albert's grandchildren.

"I can get them Austrian passports, but that won't get them to America," Margo said.

Leeza was excited at the idea. "At least that would get them out of the country!"

"Yes, but who's going to stay with them until they can get visas?" Anneliese asked.

"My mother and Hans!" Leeza exclaimed. "They can stay at the chalet."

Anneliese sighed, "I hate to be the one to throw cold water on the plan, but who's going to take them across the border? You can't."

Margo looked around the back room. "Hey, anyone got a kindercare permit?"

"I do!" a young blond woman shouted.

---

A week later, Albert's four grandchildren were running and tumbling in a grassy meadow in the Tyrol. Leeza had given the blond woman a letter for Katrine. It explained who the children were, how they had gotten there, and what

192

needed to be done for them. The letter also told Katrine about Karl's death.

> *Mama, I know how much you loved Karl, but you must not loose heart. Uncle Karl would want you to be strong and help these children. He would have done this himself had he been able to. Do this in remembrance of him.*
>
> > *Love always,*
> > *Leeza*

Tears ran down Katrine's face as she and Hans watched Albert's grandchildren playing in the meadow. Hans put his arm around her as she wiped the tears from her face. She smiled sadly. "They are beautiful children."

"Ja," Hans agreed.

"Is this all right with you, Hans?" she asked hesitantly.

Hans smiled brilliantly. "Ja, of course. Children are a blessing no matter where they come from. I enjoy having them around!"

Now Katrine's only fear was for Leeza. *What has that girl gotten herself into? I wish she would leave Germany. She should have come with the children.*

# Chapter Fourteen

# Hanukkah Lights

Albert's head snapped back as the little Gestapo agent hit him in the face. "What are you doing here, Jew?"

"I am working, Sir," Albert replied, rubbing his chin.

"Jews are not allowed to work here anymore!" The little agent slugged Albert in the stomach, and he folded up like a rag doll. The other workers in the furnace room watched in horror as the two other Gestapo agents grabbed Albert by the arms and pulled him back up. "Jews are not allowed to work anywhere anymore!" The little agent punched Albert in the face again. This time blood spurted from his nose.

The other agents laughed. "The Führer has forbidden it!" They continued what the little agent had started. Soon Albert was on the floor gasping for breath as they kicked him in the ribs. "Jews cannot earn wages from Aryans!" they yelled.

One of the men working the furnace ducked out unnoticed and ran to Leeza's office. Moments later she came tearing into the furnace room screaming, "Stop it! Stop it right now! What in God's name are you doing to him? Stop it!"

Herr Leber motioned for his men to stop.

Leeza ran to Albert and knelt down beside him. Cradling him in her lap, she glared up at the grinning agents. "Animals!" she spat. "Why would you do this to him? He has done nothing wrong!"

"He is a Jew, Fraulein von Rauthenau! That is what is wrong here!"

Leeza was enraged. Her face turned several shades of red. She wanted to jump up and beat the little man

194

senseless. Breathing hard, she hissed, "He may be a Jew, but he is also my foreman!"

"Jews are not allowed to work for Aryan employers, or give orders to Aryan workers! Didn't you know that, Fraulein von Rauthenau?"

Leeza wiped the blood from Albert's nose with her sleeve, but it wouldn't stop gushing. "I don't keep up with politics, Herr Leber!"

"This is not politics, Fraulein! It is the law. The Führer's law!" barked the little Gestapo agent.

"This man has worked at Rauthenau Steel for as long as I can remember. He has never failed in his duties to this company, or to Germany!"

"Germany does not need Jews!" Agent Leber snapped. Then he looked at his men and yelled, "Take him away!"

"Wait!" Leeza screamed. Gently she laid Albert's head on the floor and stood up in the little agents face. Standing nose to nose with him, she stared him in the eye. "You can't take him." Her lips pursed. Her jaw was tight. "I need him!"

"He can be replaced!" the little agent barked.

Leeza glared at him. "No he can't! There is not a man alive who knows this factory like he does! If the Führer wants his steel, then I need Albert!"

"Are you saying that production will fall without this Jewish pig?"

"Yes!" Leeza spit.

The little agent removed his glasses and cleaned off the spray. Then replacing them on his pinched little face, he grunted, "Hurmph."

Leeza saw her only chance and she took it. "You know very well that production has increased by thirty-five percent over the last year. This is due strictly to Albert's ingenuity. If you take him, I can assure you that production will fall fifty percent the day he leaves, and I won't be able to stop it from falling even lower. I am not an expert, Herr Leber! He is!"

The little agent stepped back away from Leeza. He looked around the furnace room slowly. The workers were all staring at him and nodding their heads. "Very well, Fraulein. You may have your Jew," he sighed. "But production will increase by another fifteen percent, or he will be removed from his position! Do I make myself clear?"

"That is impossible," Leeza snapped. "We are already thirty-five percent over the normal production."

"Then you will raise it to a full fifty percent," Agent Leber barked.

"That's blackmail!" Leeza yelled.

The little agent just grinned. Then he snapped his fingers at the other two agents. They all did an about face and marched out of the furnace room.

Leeza watched them leave the factory and then called for some of the men to help Albert. "Take him into my office," she directed. "Lay him on the couch."

After Leeza and Hanna washed Albert's bloody face and wrapped his broken ribs, they let him sleep the rest of the day on the couch in her office. Quietly, they went into the other room to talk. "I don't know how we're ever going to boost production another fifteen percent," Hanna grumped.

Leeza groaned. "I don't know how either, but we had better think of something because now Albert's life depends on it."

"We'll need more workers, that's for sure."

Leeza sat on the floor and laid her head against her knees. "How many do you think we'll need?"

"At least twenty, maybe more."

Leeza nodded her head. "I'll see what I can do."

"There's another matter I've been wanting to talk to you about."

"What is it, Hanna," Leeza sighed.

"I've been thinking about ordering some new equipment."

"New equipment?"

"Uh huh."

"Why do we need new equipment?"

"We don't."

Leeza looked confused. "Hanna, what are you talking about?"

"Money," Hanna grinned. Now Leeza was more confused than ever, but was too tired to figure it out. "I've been thinking about what to do with all the extra money. Equipment is always a good investment. It looks good on the books."

"I don't give a damn how the books look anymore," Leeza moaned.

"Let me spell it out for you, kid. The Swiss make fine conveyor systems. Half the conveyors in this factory came from Switzerland. I just happen to know someone in the business. I can transfer funds to him and he can put them in a Swiss bank account for you. That way we can shelter at least some of your cash. I'm sure he would do it for us."

Leeza still looked confused. "But what about the equipment?"

"Well, as I see it, the Nazis can't complain about us buying new equipment. My friend can charge us double for everything he ships to us, and the rest can go safely into a Swiss account. All we have to do is make sure the invoices and the transfers match up."

"I like it!" Leeza grinned. "How long will it take you to set it up?"

"I'd have to make a trip to Switzerland. But that shouldn't be a problem. Hell, they just ordered us to increase production. That's a good excuse to buy new equipment." Hanna winked.

"Do it!"

Paris was beautiful, but being assigned to the city of love when one didn't have a lover was like drowning in a sea of longing. Amy had strolled up and down the Champs-Elysees for months watching lovers holding hands, and whimsically gazing into jewelry store windows dreaming of the wedding rings they would some day wear. Then they would kiss, there on the sidewalk, and giggle as if they hadn't a care in the world. Invariably, the man would wrap his arm around his beautiful young lover, and together they would stroll on to the next store window. Amy would always think of Leeza as she watched the lovers of Paris. *Some day I'll wrap my arm around her and she'll lay her head on my shoulder, just like that couple. Some day, she'll gaze into my eyes the way that woman looks into his, and I'll tell her how much I love her.*

Amy was thrilled when her editor finally reassigned her to Berlin. With the arrival of the new British Ambassador to Berlin came her chance to write real news stories again. It was also her chance to see Leeza. *I'll be there just in time for Christmas. Christmas! Oh hell, I need a gift. What should I get?* Amy looked at her watch. *I have time for one last stroll down the Champs-Elysees.* Amy gazed in store window after store window looking for just the right gift. *A box of Chocolates? Naw, doesn't say what I want it to say.* Moving on she saw a nice necklace in a jewelry store window. *It's lovely, but it's not right either.* The next store was a lingerie shop. Amy remembered holding Leeza's silk bra at the train station in Munich. *I know she likes nice lingerie.* She stood in front of the window gazing up at a black silk negligee. *That would look great on her!*

Amy smiled as she let her imagination play out the scene. Leeza came to her in the still of the night. She stood gracefully, silhouetted in front of a roaring fire. Amy slowly walked over to her. They gazed into each others eyes for a few longing moments and then Amy gently brushed the thin strap off Leeza's elegant shoulder. The negligee fell, revealing only the top of Leeza's smooth breast. Amy caressed Leeza's thin shoulder and moved to kiss her tenderly at the base of her neck. Amy's body flushed with warmth as her passion began to rise.

Suddenly, Amy shook her head to bring herself out of the day dream. *Pull yourself together, Trevor. You haven't even had a first date with her yet!* Then she looked back up to the negligee. *Nope, too presumptuous.* She moved on to the next store, and the next, and the next. Then she came to another jewelry store. There is the window was a beautiful little blue star sapphire ring. *And you thought the negligee was too presumptuous!* But still, she couldn't take her eyes off the ring. *Some day...She might.* Amy let her impulse override her logic. She went straight in and asked to see the ring in the window. When the clerk brought it to the counter Amy held it up to the light. The star sparkled like crystal, and the blue reminded Amy of Leeza's eyes.

"I'll take it," she declared.

"You have made a fine choice, Madame!" the clerk smiled.

---

Love was the last thing on Leeza's mind when Amy called to ask if they could meet before she attended the reception at the British Embassy. Helping Albert's grandchildren escape from Germany had given Leeza a new energy. Finding ways to thwart the Nazis was all she could talk about when they finally met in the Adlon Hotel bar.

"Leeza, your getting in too deep!" Amy cried. "You have to get out of Germany before you get caught."

"I can't," Leeza remarked casually. "Too many people are counting on me. I can't just leave Germany."

"You don't get it, do you?" Amy yelled. "Churchill is out of favor in England, France won't move until England does, and America's isolationist. Who else does that leave to stop Hitler? Mussolini? I don't think so! Hell, Hitler provided him with arms and men in Spain. They're bosom buddies now."

"None of that matters."

"Why?" Amy groaned. "Your uncle is dead. There's no reason for you to stay any longer."

Leeza looked crushed. "Yes, my uncle is dead." Tears welled up in her eyes. "But there are a million other reasons to stay!" *She doesn't understand.*

Amy took Leeza's hand. She pulled it away. "I'm sorry. I didn't mean to sound callous about your uncle. I know he was a good man. And I know how much you loved him. But he would tell you the same thing I'm telling you. Get out! Get out while you still can!"

Leeza just looked blank.

*She doesn't understand*, Amy thought. "Look, I have to go to that reception, but can we meet later?" Amy fingered the ring in her cloak pocket.

"I don't think so," Leeza sighed. "You go on to your reception. I have a long day ahead of me tomorrow. By the way, you look wonderful."

"Yeah, right," Amy grunted as she got up and stormed out of the Adlon. Feeling hurt and rejected, she fingered the ring in her pocket again. *Stupid idiot. What did you think, she was just going to wait for you? You've been gone for over six months. She's probably fallen in love with someone else by now! I hope they have plenty of booze at this damn reception.*

The reception for the new British Ambassador to Germany, Nevile Henderson, was a formal affair. Amy was dressed in the same evening gown she had worn to the last St. Valentine's Day Drag Ball. She thought of that night, and how they had danced so perfectly together. *I hate dresses. At least on me! And I hate dancing.* "Just because you danced with her doesn't mean she's yours, Trevor," Amy mumbled to herself as she crossed the street.

The Embassy was just across the street from the Adlon Hotel, and every reporter in Germany was there. Outside sat Hermann Goering's limousine that he had stolen from some Jewish industrialist. A swastika flag flapped from its antenna. Inside the Embassy was typically British. King George's picture replaced his brother's, and he didn't look too happy about being king.

Amy scanned the room hoping to get a look at the new ambassador. The pop of flash bulbs drew her attention to the top of the stair case. Nevile Henderson was a tall, stoop shouldered, pale man who looked as if a stiff wind could blow him over. Goering stood by his side all puffed up in his military uniform bedecked with ribbon and medals. He was even wearing rouge on his cheeks. *What a picture! A skeleton and a peacock!* Amy thought. *I can't believe that's who England sent to deal with Hitler.* Henderson and Goering descended the staircase together, shoulder to shoulder, laughing and smiling for the cameras.

Amy took a glass of Champagne from one of the mingling waiters and listened as Goering blew smoke up Henderson's ass. "We consider England one of our greatest allies, Ambassador. After all, we are all Aryan brothers."

Henderson smiled and raised his glass. "To Field Marshal Hermann Goering, whom England considers a valuable friend!"

Amy didn't drink the toast. Her stomach was churning. She noticed Marshall Turner standing in the corner and made her way over to him. "Hi, Marshall."

Marshall Turner just scowled at the scene before him. "He's a bloody little weasel, that Henderson is!"

"Shhh! Somebody will hear you," Amy whispered with a grin.

"I don't give a bloody damn," Marshall snapped. "What was Whitehall thinking when they assigned this...this...this imbecile to negotiate with Hitler?"

"Obviously they didn't want to send anyone too threatening!" Amy giggled.

Marshall threw Amy a sideways glance. Then he caught himself before he burst out laughing. "The ol' chap probably has to brace himself before he passes wind."

That did it. Amy pictured the skeleton farting and blowing himself off the crapper. She couldn't contain herself. She burst out laughing for all she was worth. Luckily, Henderson had just said something mildly amusing and the crowd started laughing out of courtesy. "Come on Marshall, let's hit the buffet before we get ourselves thrown out of here."

"Good idea, Miss Trevor," Marshall chuckled. "Lead the way."

Standing in the buffet line, Amy leaned over and whispered to Marshall. "What else can you do? You just have to laugh at the absurdity of the situation. Instead of sending a lion to deal with the Nazis, England sends a mouse?"

"Did you see the way he was staring at Goering's medals?"

Amy chucked. "Goering sure had him mesmerized."

"He's a fool!"

"Yeah, but he's not threatening. Just the kind of guy Hitler likes to squash."

"Well if this is England's appeasement plan, it's a damn good one," Marshall replied as he angrily speared a piece of roast beef.

Just then Henderson and Goering passed the buffet table. "I'm not an anti-Semite, Herr Goering. I just don't like Jews, that's all. And Herr Hitler's policy on homosexuality is perfectly acceptable to me. I despise faggots, myself."

Amy's blood began to boil. Her face turned red and her hands began to shake. "Easy there, Miss Trevor," Marshall warned. "You can't do much with a butter knife."

Amy looked up at Marshall defiantly. "Hold this!" she said as she shoved her plate into his chest. "Excuse me, Ambassador! Amy Trevor. International News Service." Marshall rolled his eyes.

Ambassador Henderson turned to acknowledge Amy. "Miss Trevor," he smiling as he offered his hand.

Amy declined the gesture. "Ambassador, are you aware of the harsh treatment that hundreds of thousands of Jews are receiving in the Nazi concentration camp?" Henderson was aghast. "And are you aware, Sir, that their property is being confiscated. Their fortunes now finance much of Hitler's ability to wage war?"

"Uh...uh," was all Henderson could get out before Amy laid into him again.

"And, Sir, are you aware that thousands of homosexuals are being raped daily by the heroes of Herr Hitler's master race? And furthermore, are you aware, Sir, that many of Germany's leading citizens, men such as Karl von Rauthenau, one of Germany's foremost industrialists, has been murdered in Dachau Concentration Camp because he would not finance Hitler's fraudulent political campaign?"

Nevile Henderson was beside himself with frustration. "I know no such thing, young lady!"

Goering stepped in to cut Amy off before she could attack the Ambassador again. "Fraulein, you are obviously mistaken. Jews are leaving Germany of their own free will. Those who are in work camps are there because they are indigent and can't provide for themselves. The German government is providing them with work in the camps. It's the only way we can afford to feed them. And as for Herr von Rauthenau, he was arrested on charges of embezzlement. He stole a significant amount of money from his own workers."

"That's bullshit," Amy howled.

But before she could start in again, Marshall stepped up from behind and cupped his hand over her mouth. "You must forgive the young lady, Ambassador, Herr Goering. She has obviously had to much to drink. I shall escort her to her hotel. It is just across the way. If you'll pardon us?" Marshall nodded his head.

"Of course!" Ambassador Henderson gasped. "Of course!"

Marshall spun Amy around and said, "Let's go, my dear, you look pale."

On their way out Amy huffed and sputtered and cussed at Marshall. "Why the hell did you do that? I was just about to nail that son of a bitch!"

"Do you still want to work in Germany?" Marshall grinned. "Goering could have your visa revoked just like that!" He snapped his fingers.

Amy halted in her tracks. "Okay, okay" she spat as she jerked her arm away from Marshall. "I'll be good. But I don't want to leave yet. I'm gonna get drunk tonight one way or another. And it might as well be on free booze!"

Marshall smiled. "Very well. But you promise you'll behave yourself?"

"I'll be a perfect angel."

"Hey, Trevor!" Jim Newman called out from behind them. "Way to hit, slugger!"

"I'm not in the mood, Newman!"

"What do ya mean, not in the mood? It looked like you were gonna tear that poor little toad apart! What's the matter? Didn't like his remark about faggots?

"Fuck you!" Amy cursed.

"Hey, any time, any where. All ya have to do is ask!" Jim laughed.

"God, you're such an ass, Newman."

"Better to be an ass than take it in the ass, I always say."

Amy rolled her eyes. Despite everything she really did like Jim Newman. But she couldn't figure out why. *Maybe because he keeps me on my toes.* "You just can't help yourself, can you Jim? It drives you crazy that you can't get me into bed."

"Some day, Trevor, you'll beg me," Jim grinned.

"When hell freezes over! Come on Marshall, let's find a drink."

Later that evening Amy and Marshall saw the Austrian Ambassador stumble into the lobby. They followed him. He was as white as a ghost and he was clutching his chest. "Ambassador?" Marshall rushed over. "Are you all right, Sir?"

The Austrian Ambassador looked up into Marshall's eyes. "Nevile Henderson just told Hermann Goering that Germany could have Austria," he gasped. "That it makes no difference to England! How can England turn it's back on us like that?"

Marshall was just as surprised by the announcement as the Austrian Ambassador was. "I don't believe it, Sir! I can assure you the majority in England will oppose Hitler should he move against your country!"

The Austrian just shook his head and stumbled for the door. Amy looked at Marshall and shrugged her shoulders. "You should have let me have him for dinner."

Marshall was just as pale as the Austrian. "How can they do this?" he stammered.

"The same way they let Hitler waltz into the Rhineland with his army. Come on ol' man, I can't stomach any more of this masquerade. Let's get out of here!"

"I'm with you," Marshall groaned. The shock was still evident on his face. "I need a real drink."

"The bar is just across the street. I could use a bourbon myself."

---

Vienna was beautiful at Christmas time. All of the shops around St. Stephan's square had special decorations in their windows, which caused children and adults alike to stop and watch as miniature trains ran around their tracks under Christmas trees. Carved angels and crèches were on display as well. Garland and wreaths were strung up between street lamps, and during the day the smell of gingerbread from all the bakeries filled the air.

Snow was falling as Heinrich stood in the shadows watching the boys coming out of the bar. Vienna was not nearly as open as Berlin had been, but there were enough bars and cafes to satisfy most needs. Soon, he spotted who he was looking for. The couple stumbled out of the bar laughing. Heinrich reached into his pocket and fingered the cold steel of his blade. *I could kill you now, but Berlin doesn't have enough evidence.*

"You naughty boy," the younger one giggled.

The older one threw his arm around his companion's shoulder. "I can be more naughty than that!" he laughed.

Heinrich was growing impatient waiting on Berlin. *Look at you. A distinguished Aryan man running around with your little Jewish faggot. How I would love to slit your throat tonight. How can you defile yourself with that pig? And how can you be such a traitor to your own people?* Again Heinrich fingered the knife in his pocket. *I bet you*

206

*let that Jew fuck you in the ass.* Heinrich let his imagination run wild, and decided to ignore his orders. He started to step out of the shadow when his foot crunched the ice under the new snow. He glance quickly down at his foot and then back to his prey. The older one stopped and cocked his head to listen.

"What is it, Dieter?" the younger one asked.

Heinrich froze. The older man put his finger to his lips. He stared into the shadows, listening again. When he didn't hear anything, he said, "Nothing. I thought I heard something, but it was nothing. Probably snow falling off the roof. Come on, let's go." They wandered off down the street laughing and playing grab ass with each other. Neither of them noticed that a small package had fallen out of the younger man's pocket.

Dieter von Kleist was from one of Austria's minor noble houses. He was a relatively unimportant politician who worked in the diplomatic corps. In the scheme of things he was easily expendable. High enough to be useful, but not important enough to impair the government's function should he suddenly die. He was just the sort of man Berlin was looking for.

Heinrich saw the small package fall. When the couple was far enough down the street he crept out and picked it up. Ripping it open, he found several passports inside. There were no pictures inside the covers, but they had several stamps. Heinrich glanced down the street. He could still hear the couple laughing. *Lucky for you. If Berlin had this right now, you would both have died here tonight. I wouldn't have let a little ice stop me. Your red blood would have looked beautiful in the white snow. Perfect Christmas colors.*

---

On top of the huge, cold stone walls of Dachau Concentration Camp stood the menacing barbed wire and guard towers. Each tower had a machine-gun mounted inside, with a flood light that constantly illuminated the stark white walls of the barracks, giving the exhausted prisoner no darkness to sleep in. Karl rushed to the window when he heard the guards shouting and the dogs barking. From the end of the barracks he could see the frail man as he walked intently toward the forbidden zone, blinking up into the floodlights that now illuminated his black and white stripped uniform. The forbidden zone was a ten foot area marked off by a low wire around the inside perimeter of the wall. A number of signs warned that anyone who crossed the wire would be shot immediately. The skeleton of a man paused in front of Karl's window. He smiled up into the lights. He didn't seem to hear the guards shouting, "Halt!"

Karl placed his palm against the window and called to the man, urging him to stop. The man looked over at Karl and smiled warmly. Karl noticed his pink triangle. Then the man turned toward the forbidden zone and Karl saw the blood stains on the seat of the man's pants. Instantly he knew what had happened. The camp guards and some of the prisoners targeted the men with the pink triangles for rape. Karl had heard the horror stories that circulated through the camp. Some of the pink triangles had been raped to death. Other were used as sport. Sadistic guards sometimes used broom handles and other object to penetrate their victims in order to see who could scream the loudest. Karl had thought himself fortunate when he heard these rumors. He wore the red triangle of a political prisoner.

The whole incident took only a few seconds. The man with the pink triangle walked peacefully to the wire. The guards shouted, "Halt," a final time. The man looked over his shoulder at Karl. For a moment their eyes locked. "Remember me," the man with the pink triangle shouted. Then he stepped over the wire. Instantly, the machine-guns started to rattle and the man jerked in an odd little dance until he collapsed to the ground. Tears streamed down Karl's face as he pressed his hands to the glass. "I will remember," he sobbed.

The Rabbi who stood beside Karl at the window put his arm around him. "Come, Karl. It's time to light the candles," he said quietly.

Karl let the Rabbi lead him. They sat down next to several other men who huddled around nine little make shift candles. Actually they were hollowed out turnips that one of the men had smuggled out of the camp kitchen. It had taken days to acquire all nine. Another of the men smuggled in an oil rag from the work shop, and they had torn it into nine pieces. The hardest thing to acquire for the ceremony was the match. One of the guards had dropped it from the tower when he was trying to light his cigarette. It had laid in the forbidden zone for two days before anyone had a chance to retrieve it. Luckily it had not snowed before another prisoner decided to commit suicide by crossing the wire. Karl volunteered to pick up the corpse and carry it to the crematorium the next morning. When he knelt down he was able to reach the match without being noticed by the guards.

"We only have this one chance," the Rabbi whispered. "Everyone, huddle in close and hold your breath." The Rabbi struck the match. It sputtered to life. One of the men next to Karl held up a piece of the oily rag. It lit.

He handed it to the rabbi who lit the rest of the candles. As the Rabbi lit the candles, he sang quietly in Hebrew. "Baruch ata adoni elohainu melech ha-olam. Blessed art Thou, Lord our God, King of the universe who has sanctified us with His commandments and commanded us to kindle the Hanukah lights. Blessed art Thou, Lord our God, King of the universe who has performed miracles for our forefathers in those day, and at this time."

209

Karl prayed, *God, we could use a miracle here in Dachau!*

# Chapter Fifteen

## Lesbian Law
## 1938

The stack of paper on Elizabeth Kroll's desk was rather high this morning. Each day she came to work at the Gestapo Headquarters in Berlin hoping to see her in-basket empty, but usually it was overflowing with memos to be filed or forwarded to field offices, or routed through the interoffice mail. This morning was no exception. *My God, will it never end? You'd think that it being the first of the year and all, these guys would still be on holiday. What else can they possibly have to say to one another? It must make them feel damned important to write all these directives and bulletins. Geesh.*

Elizabeth was a pretty girl with auburn hair and hazel eyes. She was tall and slim, with very shapely legs, and the way she filled out her sweaters had caught Himmler's eye. His secretarial pool was filled with young women who projected just the right image of beauty that represented the health and vitality of the nation that Himmler wanted to see each day.

The state employment agency had sent Elizabeth to work for the Gestapo when it was first created. She had started in the mail room, and was promoted to file clerk the day Himmler saw her. Elizabeth hated the job. She hated the way the agents ogled her, and the way Himmler eyed her. She hated the very nature of what the Gestapo was. It went against everything she believed in, but when the Reich told her where to work, that's where she worked. She didn't have a choice in the matter. When people asked, Elizabeth often lied about where she worked. She was uncomfortable with the fear that crept into people's eyes

211

when she said the word "Gestapo." Most people didn't make the distinction between being a secretary and being an agent. When the subject came up she just said she worked for one of the other state agencies.

*So, what's up this morning,* Elizabeth wondered as she took a sip from her coffee cup and started sorting through the stack of paperwork on her desk. *One for the Munich office - three for Agent Leber - one for the Hamburg office - one to be typed up and forwarded to all field offices - wait a minute - hello - what's this?* Elizabeth's jaw dropped open as she began to read the bulletin marked # 49, BAKNSD 17/12. It was issued by the Intelligence Service of the Race Policy Bureau.

*Sufficient material is now available about the scale and spread of homosexuality to be able also to combat female homosexuality (lesbianism). We urgently require information about observations made by our colleagues themselves, or reports given to our colleagues from elsewhere. For this purpose, addresses of individuals known as lesbians should be provided wherever possible. The reports should be forwarded to: Rassenpolitisches Amt - Feichsleitung - Rechtsselle Berlin W8, Wilhemstr, 63.*

Elizabeth couldn't believe her eyes. For the first time lesbians were being targeted for arrest. *My God, we've got to do something. This is insane.* Elizabeth folded the bulletin and slipped it under the blotter on her desk. She nervously sipped her coffee and looked around to see if anyone had seen her do it. Then she continued sorting through the paperwork while she thought about what to do with the bulletin. She remembered what had happened to the gay men in Germany and dreaded the thought of it happening to the women. *If I don't forward the bulletin they will most certainly be able to trace it back to me. If I send the bulletin, thousands of women are going to be picked up. Damn! What can I do?* As the morning wore on Elizabeth became more and more agitated. Beads of sweat budded on her forehead. Her stomach churned and she felt like throwing up. She took a deep breath and put her head down on her desk for a moment.

"Are you all right?" asked the woman who sat at the desk across from Elizabeth's. The woman noticed that Elizabeth was pale and looked as if she were going to pass out.

Elizabeth smiled nervously. "I don't feel well, Gerta. I think I'm going to be sick. Excuse me." Elizabeth ran for the restroom.

When she came back Gerta smiled gently and said, "You should go home if you're sick. You can't work like this."

"But I have to file these memos," Elizabeth groaned.

"They will be there tomorrow, and the next day. You know the paperwork around here never ends. You shouldn't kill yourself trying to get it all done. Go home!"

"Maybe you're right, Gerta, but I think I'm going to be sick again."

Gerta grinned suspiciously. "Maybe you're not sick?"

Elizabeth knit her brow quizzically. "What do you mean?"

"Maybe it's morning sickness. Maybe you're pregnant!"

Elizabeth frowned. *Fat chance*! Then she made another run for the restroom. This time when she came back she gathered up her things to leave. Gerta's telephone rang and Elizabeth took the opportunity to slip the bulletin into her handbag. When Gerta hung up the phone, Elizabeth groaned, "I'm going home, but I'm sure this will pass by tomorrow."

Gerta smiled, "We'll see!"

Elizabeth took a few deep breaths when she got outside. That seemed to clear her head. Then she took off for Eddi's Cafe. Elizabeth and Eddi had been seeing each other for a little over a year. They met when Elizabeth moved into the apartment across the hall, in Eddi's building. Eddi was in her mid forties, with dishwater blond hair and brown eyes. She was the maternal type and loved owning her own cafe. She often joked about feeding half the lesbians in Berlin.

Eddi saw Elizabeth come through the door and knew right away that something was terribly wrong. Elizabeth never took time off from work. "What's wrong?" she called out.

"I'm not feeling well," Elizabeth sighed as she took a stool at the counter. She quickly glanced around the room. Luckily it was midmorning and the cafe was empty. "I have something I think you should see." When Eddi brought her a cup of coffee, Elizabeth handed her the bulletin. "Take a look at this." As Eddi read her face grew pale. "We'd better call Helene right away."

Helene shuddered at the news Eddi told her over the telephone. "Damn it! This is not the way I planned to bring in the New Year! My God, do we have to fight this battle again?" she asked with an angry tone of voice. Eddi gave her a few minutes to calm down. "All right, I'll call around and see who I can get a hold of. You do the same. Have everyone meet at Pauli's tonight around eight o'clock." Eddi agreed.

That night several dozen women crammed into the dark and smoky back room at Pauli's Dance Palace. Anneliese, Margo, Amy, and Leeza sat together around a table near the back door. Everyone listen intently as Helene read the bulletin. When she finished the room erupted into a clatter

of angry voices. Fists pounded the tables, beer sloshed out
of mugs, and cigarettes were ground into ashtrays that were
overflowing. Many women jumped to their feet in rage.
"She can't forward that memo!" they yelled. Other's yelled
back, "What choice does she have?" "There's always a
choice!" angry voices answered back.

Helene pounded her empty beer mug on the table.
"Order! Order!" she called. The room grew quiet after a
few seconds. "The question," Helene said, "is not whether
Elizabeth should forward the bulletin. She must forward it.
Her safety requires it. She has no other real choice. The
question before us is what are we going to do about it?"

Most of the women were really angry and ready to take
action. "We should riot!" one of them shouted. "We
should demonstrate peacefully," someone called back. "I'm
leaving the country," another one called out.

"What do you think, Lotte?" Helene asked calmly.

Lotte's face was stern. "I think we should hold a
demonstration. We have to protest this action. There has
never been a law in Germany pertaining to lesbians, and we
can't let them issue one now."

"I agree," Helene sighed. "We fought this issue before,
and we won. There's no reason to believe that a
demonstration would not be effective now."

"What about Leeza," Amy shouted from the back of the
room. Everyone turned to stare. "She can't take part in a
demonstration. The Gestapo would pick her up in a
heartbeat!"

Leeza turned bright red with anger. *How dare she
presume to speak for me!* But before she could speak on her
own behalf, Lotte called back.

"Of course she can't participate in the demonstration!
No one should demonstrate if they are already being
watched or if they are Jewish." That seemed to settle
everyone down. "I think only German women without any
kind of record should be the one's to demonstrate."

Leeza was fuming by this time. She raised her hand and shot a threatening glance at Amy. "I want to…"

"Lotte is right," Helene interjected. "We're not asking anyone to risk their lives here. If you don't feel good about the action, don't do it." Helene looked directly at Leeza and shook her head. "You shouldn't do it!" The rest of the evening was spent debating strategy and planning the protest demonstration. They decided to give Elizabeth plenty of time to forward the bulletin to the field offices of the Gestapo, and that the demonstration should take place the following week at Brandenburg Gate.

Throughout the meeting, Leeza sat with her arms folded across her chest. Sensing that she was upset about something, Amy leaned over and said, "Is there something wrong?"

Leeza flashed her an angry glare. "How dare you speak for me," she exclaimed as she jumped out of her chair. "What gives you the right to dictate what I can and can't do?" Leeza was furious at being cut out of the demonstration. "I already have the Gestapo telling me how much steel I have to produce, and who can work for me and who can't, and whom I can be seen with and whom I can't! I don't need anyone else watching over my shoulder!" she snapped.

Amy was cool under Leeza's angry gaze. "That's exactly what I said. They are watching you too close! You think you could get away with marching in this demonstration?"

Leeza stared hard into Amy's eyes. "That should have been my decision to make. Not yours!" Then she spun on her heels and left.

Amy looked over at Margo and shrugged her shoulders. "What's up with her?"

Margo shrugged her shoulders. "She's under a lot of pressure. She just needs a little breathing room. That's all." Margo knew right away by the look in Amy's eye that she

216

was in love with Leeza.  She had the same protective look for Anneliese.

---

It was extremely cold the morning the women gathered at the Brandenburg Gate with their signs of protests.  No one could see the great bronze horses shrouded in snow drifts high atop the gate.  Snow flurries whipped around the marchers in little swirls of white mist as they began their hike toward the Reichstag.  Word had spread through the lesbian community like wildfire, and thousands of women showed up to support the demonstration.  They lined the opposite side of the street and cheered as the march began.  Their collective breath raised tumultuous swirls of fog above their heads, giving them the appearance of a great smoke breathing dragon.

Helene Stocker, Lotte Hahm, Hilde Wolfe, Isa Vermehren, Liebe Posen, Margarete Rosenburg, and Maximiliane Ackers led at least one hundred women up and down the sidewalk leading from Brandenburg to the Reichstag.  They waved their signs and shouted chants of protest against the new persecution of lesbians.  Amy stood on the opposite side of the street in the crowd of supporters.  She was taking notes for an article she knew would never be published.

Not long after the marchers made their first pass by the Reichstag, Amy noticed Elizabeth in the crowd.  From her vantage point she could tell that she wasn't watching the demonstrators.  Amy followed Elizabeth's gaze to a little man in a trench coat.  Elizabeth was frowning.  *Gestapo, I'll bet!*  When she looked back, Elizabeth was gone.  Amy began looking over the crowd herself.  *One - two - three - four - five of them.  Shit.  They're taking notes.  At least Leeza's not here.*

Amy pulled out her press pass and hung it around her neck. She worked her way through the crowd saying, "Excuse me, bitte. Excuse please. Excuse me. So sorry. Pardon me." Eventually she made her way to the curb and dashed across the street. The crowd cheered and another layer of fog rose above their heads. They must have thought that Amy was running over to join the demonstrators because several women followed her. Moments later the ranks of the marchers were bolstered by another one hundred women or so.

Amy caught up with Helene and pulled her off to the side. She cupped her hand around her mouth and whispered loudly in Helene's ear. "I counted five Gestapo agents in the crowd. They're taking notes."

Helene frowned as she scanned the crowd across the street. Defiantly she shouted, "They can go straight to hell! What are they going to do, arrest us right here on the street?"

"They might," Amy called over the noise of the chants. "Elizabeth has already left."

"That's good! We can't afford to loose the information she brings us!"

"Yeah, and these women can't afford to loose your leadership either. You and the others should get out of here."

"We can't leave!" Helene shouted. "If we do, how can we expect anyone else to stay?"

The marchers continued on, chanting and waving their signs. Suddenly a truck filled with troops roared up to the Reichstag. Amy saw them pile out of the back of the truck. "I don't think you have a choice now!" She pointed toward the truck. "I think we all had better get out of here right now. Run!" she shouted over the chants of the women. "Run!"

When the women who were marching realized that Amy was issuing a command, they looked around to where she was pointing and saw the troops marching up the street behind them. Immediately they started screaming for their friends and lovers to run. Most bolted across the street and disappeared into the crowd without looking back. Seconds latter, the crowd itself was scattering in every conceivable direction and the troops were confused on just who they were supposed to arrest.

Amy giggled to herself as she watched them scrambling about looking for the dykes they had seen marching. One of them grabbed someone from behind. When he spun the person around, he was stunned to see that he had grabbed a man instead of a woman. She couldn't hear what the trooper was saying, but Amy was sure he was cussing a blue streak. It seemed that most of the women had just vanished into thin air. Amy counted only three women being hauled back to the truck, but she didn't know who they were. She quickly wrote down their appearance so she could describe them to Helene later.

---

The next morning Elizabeth went to work as if nothing had happened. She sat at her desk sipping coffee and sorting through the stack of paperwork from her in-box. "Gerta, I have to take these down to the mail room. I'll be right back."

"Take your time," Gerta waved without looking up from her own stack of paperwork.

Elizabeth was just coming out of the mail room when she saw Helene being dragged out of an interrogation room down the hall. She froze in her tracks. Helene had been beaten black and blue, and could barely walk. Two agents had to drag her limp body up the hall. They were heading for the back door, near where Elizabeth was standing.

As they came closer, Elizabeth began to panic. She didn't know what to do. A second later Helene looked up and saw her standing there. Their eyes met, and in those few seconds Helene told Elizabeth everything that had happened. The Gestapo had burst through her door sometime during the night and arrested her and Lotte. Helene's nightgown was spattered with blood, obviously from her broken nose. They had brutally interrogated her for several hours, but she had told them nothing. She hadn't revealed the names of any other protesters.

Elizabeth started to reach out and touch Helene as she passed, but Helene defiantly shook her head, indicating that Elizabeth should not acknowledge she knew her.

"Move along, Fraulein," one of the agents said, "Do not waste your compassion on one such as this. She is not worthy to be in your fine feminine presence. She's a lesbian. She defiles German womanhood."

Elizabeth was frightened by how bad Helene looked. "Where are you taking her?" she whispered almost hysterically.

The other agent called over his shoulder, "Ravensbruck! She deserves no less!"

Tears welled up in Elizabeth's eyes as she watched them haul Helene out through the back door and shove her into a waiting truck. *Ravensbruck!* Elizabeth's mind screamed. *Not Ravensbruck!* Ravensbruck Concentration Camp was a camp for woman in Northeastern Germany. Elizabeth had heard the horror stories about how the women were treated there, and feared for Helene's life. But there was nothing she could do. Her hands were tied. Grief and guilt set in immediately. *If I had just kept quiet about the bulletin maybe none of this would have happened.*

---

Over the next few weeks Elizabeth learned that nothing she could have done would have made any difference. She had read dozens of reports from all over Germany. Helene and Lotte, and the rest of the old White Rose leadership were not the only one's who'd been taken to Ravensbruck. Women were being arrested right and left, and the camp was filling up quickly.

"Two school teachers in Munich were arrested," Elizabeth told the group gathered at Pauli's. "One of them, Johanna, I think her name was, she was the headmistress of a school. She was denounced for having lesbian tendencies."

"And just what the hell are lesbian tendencies?" Margo growled.

Everyone laughed nervously, but they knew exactly what lesbian tendencies meant. Anyone with short hair or who wore pants was considered to have lesbian tendencies.

"They also said the one teacher approached several other teachers in 'that way.'"

Margo slammed her beer on the table. "Tendencies, 'that way,' is that what they're being charged with?"

"No," Elizabeth answered. "They are charging them both with violating Paragraph 176!"

"What the hell is Paragraph 176?"

Elizabeth explained. "Paragraph 176 is the section of the German legal code that deals with having sexual relationships with dependent minors. Because the children were in her care at the school, and therefore dependent on her, they are charging her with violating that statute. They are also charging the other teacher with the same thing."

"That's bull shit!" Margo barked.

"My God, what next?" Anneliese sighed.

"They also made raids at the *Reich Labor Service for Young Women* and the *Bund Deutscher Madle*. Five women were arrested at the *Reich,* and four at the *Bund*," Elizabeth told them.

221

"I don't think I can take hearing any more," Leeza moaned.

Vera Lackmann, the lyricist, was one of the few leaders in the White Rose Ladies Society to escape arrest. She sympathized with Leeza. "I'm getting out!" she announced. "I know they took down my name at the demonstration because when I came home the next day my door had been kicked in. I don't have a choice anymore. I've got to leave. I can't expect my friends to hide me forever. I've got to get out, and soon."

"I'm thinking of leaving too," Dr. Charlotte Wolff responded. "I'm getting a lot of pressure to work in one of the Lebensborn houses and I just can't bring myself to do that."

"What's a Lebensborn house?" Eddi asked.

"It's Hitler's selective breeding program. He's trying to create the master Aryan race. He gets tall, blond, blue eyed young girls to basically serve as prostitutes to tall, blond, blue eyed men. When the girls produce a child that meets the master race's criteria, she gets a large bonus. It's disgusting. Most of the time the girls don't even get to raise their babies. They are shipped off to other childless homes and the girls get pregnant again."

"What happens if the baby isn't blond and blue eyed?" Eddi asked.

"They are sent to orphanages," Charlotte answered bitterly. Then she sighed. "My daughter is studying in England. I think I'm going to go stay with her for a while. Maybe I can get a visa to practice there. I don't know. All I really know is that I can't stay here much longer. If I do, they'll force me to go to work in the Lebensborn project."

"Well," Elizabeth lamented, "we had all better think about doing something pretty soon. There's a rumor going through the office that Himmler's going to lay down a dress and appearance code for women. Pretty soon they'll be telling us how to dress and what kind of make-up and jewelry to wear, and how long our hair should be."

"Fuck Himmler," Margo yelled as she slammed her beer on the table again.

"Ja," the rest of the women shouted back.

"No thanks!" Anneliese grinned. Everyone roared with laughter. When they finally quieted down, Anneliese spoke in a serious tone of voice. "Listen, we really need to get organized if we are going to protect ourselves."

"But what can we do without Helene and Lotte, and the rest?" Elizabeth asked.

Eddi gave that some thought. "Do you think you can get a list of the women who are being watched?"

"Yes, I think so," Elizabeth answered hesitantly.

"Good! If we could get them new papers they might have a chance of getting out of the country, or a least moving to another town and starting over."

Margo spoke up. "I could probably get a few of the girls new passports if they wanted to go to Austria."

"I could give them new jobs at the factory," Leeza exclaimed. "It's hard work, but it's good money, and we need all the workers we can get right now. I don't think the Gestapo would look for them there. They're too busy watching me."

Margo chuckled. "We can send all the butches to you, Leeza. I know a lot of women who could pass!"

The room exploded with laughter again. "That's not a bad idea!" Eddi shouted. "Does anyone work at the Reich Labor Office?"

"My girlfriend does," shouted a woman from the back of the room.

"Would she be willing to falsify a few papers?" Margo asked.

"I think she would do it! I'll ask her when I get home tonight."

"Great," Eddi replied. "Looks like we might have a real resistance group forming here. What does everyone else do?"

Everyone began shouting out their occupations and their connections. There were two more nurses besides Anneliese, several factory workers, one mechanic, one teacher, three store clerks, four who worked in government offices, one who worked in a print shop, and three who were unemployed.

Eddi was writing down the occupations and names as they were called out. "This is a good start. But I think everyone should have a chance to think about this very carefully. Why don't we meet at my cafe on Thursday night. I'll buy dinner. Anyone who really wants to do this, meet there at nine o'clock. I'll close down early so we'll have the place to ourselves."

Margo stood up and raised her beer. "To the White Rose underground."

A hush fell over the back room at Pauli's. Then everyone lifted their beers and shouted, "To the White Rose!"

Eddi raised her stein next. "Here's to defying the lesbian law!"

Leeza quickly stood up and raised her beer. "Here's to creating our own law!"

Everyone cheered, "To the law of the lesbians!"

---

The next Thursday night, at the first official meeting of the White Rose underground, eleven women showed up at Eddi's cafe, including the woman who worked at the Reich Labor Office. Her girlfriend introduced her to the group. "For those of you who don't know, this is Heidi, and I am

224

Luise. I work at the post office, and you know where Heidi works."

"This is a good idea," Eddi smiled as she passed around the coffee pot. "Most of us know each other, but for the sake those who are new to the group we should all introduce ourselves."

Leeza went first. "I am Leeza and I work at Rauthenau Steel." Then Anneliese, Margo, and Elizabeth introduced themselves. Next came Elli, who worked in a weapons factory, Gertrude who worked in a department store, and Olga who worked at one of the train stations selling tickets. The last woman to introduce herself was Claire, who worked as a cabaret singer. During dinner, everyone chatted about their jobs and old lovers and how long they'd been out, and how they had come out. It seemed everyone had a different story to tell, but somehow they were all the same.

After dinner Eddi pretty much led the meeting. "I think we should keep our membership to the twelve of us gathered here tonight. We can always ask friends for help when the need arises, but we do need to think of security."

"Absolutely!" Elizabeth agreed. "It will be very important for all of us to know each other, but for no one else to know all of us."

Olga spoke up just then. "I had an uncle who was in the resistance during the Great War. He always said that it was important to have his own contacts, and that his group never met together all at once. He always said that it was better to pass information rather than meet in a group. It was just too dangerous otherwise."

"That's a good idea," Eddi replied. "We can use the cafe as a message center."

"So, does this mean you'll hold this?" Margo asked as she tossed a brand new passport out onto the table.

Everyone stared at it in amazement. Eddi just smiled. "You work fast." She reached for the passport and opened it. "No picture, no name, but its got all the official stamps. Very good."

"We need a photographer who won't ask any questions," Anneliese mused.

"And someone with access to a typewriter. We'll need to be able to fill in new names and addresses without being seen," Eddi added.

"I think I can handle that," Leeza replied. "I'll have Hanna, my secretary, do it. But I don't know any photographers."

"I have a camera," Gertrude grinned sheepishly, "but I don't have a dark room. I don't think we can have the pictures developed at the photo shop."

Claire's eyes sparked. "We have a dark room in the back of the cabaret. The owner makes money by taking photographs of customers enjoying the show, and sells them back to the customer at a healthy profit. It's good publicity, and it makes him money. We could develop the film there."

Eddi grinned. "Well, it sounds like we're in business. Margo, you can bring the passports by here when you stop in for lunch. I can hand them off to Leeza to be typed. Gertrude can take the pictures and develop them at the cabaret. Claire, you'll have to stand watch for her."

"No problem!" Claire exclaimed. "The dark room is right by my dressing room."

"Fine. After Claire and Gertrude develop the pictures they can bring them back here, and I can affix the photographs to the passports in the kitchen. Now what about new work papers and identification cards?"

"I have been giving that some thought," Heidi answered. "Whenever a worker dies, my office is notified. I am the one who records that the person is no longer working. I make arrangements for that person's pension to be transferred to their spouse. If there is no living spouse, I terminate their account. If we used the names of people who have died and who have no living spouse, we could simply give the name to a person who needs a new identity. We could also use the same process for the passports. I could bring you a stack of identity cards. All you would have to do is type in a new name and address, and affix a new picture. Then give me the new addresses and I will create a file for them. That's basically what happens when people change jobs or move to new addresses. Only in this case we'll be using the names of dead people."

"Brilliant!" Eddi exclaimed. "We're lucky to have you working with us, Heidi."

"Thank you," Heidi replied with a sigh. "Helene was a good friend of mine. Anything I can do to help, I'll do it. I know she'd want me to."

"But how do we know who needs the new papers?" asked Anneliese.

Elizabeth grinned. "I've got a partial list right here." She reached into her pocket and pulled out a crumpled sheet of paper. "These are the names of women here in Berlin who are being watched. It's a relatively short list right now. After all, Helene and the rest are already gone." Then she frowned. "But Leeza, I'm sorry to say you are at the top of the list. Of course you know that already. And you're not being watched because you are a lesbian. It's because of your uncle and the factory."

"I know," Leeza frowned.

"That's why I think you should have this first passport!"

"I agree," Eddi replied.

"You do?" Leeza frowned again.

"Yes," Eddi smiled. "We are grateful that you are willing to help, Leeza. But you should have an Austrian passport just in case."

"And you should also have a train ticket on hand," Olga smiled gently. "I'll get you one."

Leeza was overwhelmed by the generosity of the women she sat with. *They are incredible. They think of my safety before their own.* "Thank you," she replied humbly.

Then Eddi looked at Luise. "If I gave you this list, could you mail a note to these women and explain that they are being watched?"

Luise nodded her head. "But what should I tell them to do?"

"Tell them that if they want new identity papers or if they want to leave the country they should come here for lunch. If they want new papers, tell them to carry one white rose. If they want an Austrian passport, they should carry two white roses. Then I'll set them up at the back table and they'll have to wait for Gertrude to take their picture. I'll tell them to come back in a few days and order the 'special of the day to go.' I'll put their new papers inside the bag along with a train ticket if they're leaving the country. Olga, I'll need you to bring me several tickets to Salzburg or Vienna. Can you do that?"

"Sure thing, Eddi, but I'm gonna need some money to pay for all the tickets."

"Don't worry about that," Leeza spoke up. "I'll supply what you need. Let's meet here, at the café, for lunch tomorrow."

"I'll be here," Olga replied.

"There's just one other thing," Leeza chirped. "If anyone needs a job, tell them to bring their work permit and a white rose to the factory. Tell them they can either speak to me or Hanna, or Albert."

"Thank you, Leeza," Eddi smiled. "Well, I think that about does it for tonight, unless anyone else has any questions."

Anneliese and Elli piped up. "We don't have anything to do," they complained.

Eddi rubbed her head. "I can't think of anything right now, but I'm sure we'll find something for you to do along the way. Don't worry about it right now. I think we should take things slowly. Let's see how it goes." Everyone agreed.

The next morning Leeza met with Albert and Hanna. "Should anyone come in looking for a job, and they have a white rose, I want you to put them to work right away."

"You got it, boss," Albert saluted.

"Sure thing, Leeza. No problem. But what's with the white rose bit?" Hanna asked.

Leeza smiled. "It's just a little sign that tells us that person needs our help. That's all."

# Chapter Sixteen

## Rose Petals

Everyone at the Austrian Embassy in Berlin was tense these days. Margo had heard the reports from Vienna and shuddered to think what the Nazis were doing to her beloved homeland. Every day there were reports of explosions rocking the mountain lands surrounding Vienna. Everyone was getting very nervous. The Embassy was on a high state of alert. Margo glanced around the lobby of the Embassy to see if anyone was watching. As she slipped two new Austrian passports into her vest pocket, she thought, *What good will these do if Hitler consumes little Austria? We'll be sending our refugees right into the lion's den.*

---

Heidi was a little nervous as she jotted down the names of the three people who had been reported dead this morning. Quickly she pulled the three files to see if they had living spouses. Two did not. *Hilde Franc and Joseph Gaus. Fine names. I just hope someone can pass as a Joseph.* Heidi giggled to herself. Replacing the files in the cabinet, she tried to imagine what a female Joseph Gaus might look like. Then she took a small stack of new identity cards out of her desk drawer and typed in the names. *I'll give these blank ones to Eddi just in case an emergency comes up.*

---

Eddi looked up from pouring a cup of coffee and was surprised by the young dyke standing in front of her with a white rose. "Uh...would you like to take the table in the back?" she stammered, pointing to the corner table near the kitchen door. *I didn't think they would come so soon.*

"Ja." answered the young dyke without moving.

Eddi smiled. She could see the girl was nervous. "I've been expecting you," she whispered, hoping her comment would soothe the girl's fears. "I see you have brought me one white rose."

The young dyke shifted her feet apprehensively, as if she might bolt. "Ja." She thrust the rose into Eddi's hand.

"Danke," Eddi smiled. "Would you like some coffee or maybe some breakfast. You might have to wait a while for our friend to come."

"Ja."

---

Around lunch time Gerta came by the cafe with her camera. She glanced to the back table by the kitchen door and saw a pretty young woman waiting there. Then she glanced over to Eddi who was taking an order at a table by the windows. Gerta smiled and Eddi nodded her head to the back table.

Gerta plunked herself down at the table as if she knew the young woman. "Hello! It's good to see you! Sorry I'm late," she smiled. "My boss is a tyrant! Honestly, he is!" Gerta had done this enough times by now to know that if she sat down talking, it usually comforted the person waiting for her. This time it was an extremely feminine girl with long dark hair, polished nails, and gold earrings. "Have you washed up yet? I just can't relax and enjoy my lunch if I haven't washed my hands."

The young woman looked confused, but when Gerta nodded toward the restroom door, she took the hint. "Uh...no, not yet."

"Well, lets do it, shall we?"

Gerta led the way. Once they were inside she checked the stalls to see if anyone was using the facilities. "Good, we're alone!" she breathed a sigh of relief. Then she slid the trash can in front of the bathroom door and walked over to the last stall. She pulled open the stall door which Eddi had covered to look like the screen that passport photos were taken against.

"Stand over here while I take your picture," Gerta instructed. The flash bulb popped and she said, "Great! Now lets go have some lunch."

———————

Claire lit up a cigarette in the hallway outside her dressing room at the cabaret. She kept an eye on the door of the dark room. Gerta was inside developing her latest passport photos. Suddenly the manager of the Cabaret came down the hall. He was headed straight for the dark room.

"What's going on, Frederic?" Claire asked coyly.

"I was just going to develop the pictures of the show I took last night."

"Now?"

"Ja, now. Anything wrong with that?"

Claire took a drag off her cigarette and quickly tried to think of some excuse to keep Frederic from going into the dark room. She seductively blew the smoke in his face. Then she leaned up against the wall and pushed her shoulders back. She pulled the tie of her dressing gown and it slipped open just enough to reveal the top of her round breasts. Claire nodded toward her dressing room. "Would you like to come in for a drink?" Frederic grinned.

232

Hanna lit a cigarette and carefully rolled the new passport into her typewriter. Cautiously she aligned the page and began typing. *M -a-r-g-a-r-e-t-t-e—R-a-d-u-s-c-h. That's a good solid German name*, she thought as she pulled the passport out of the typewriter. *You shouldn't have any trouble, Margarette Radusch. This baby should slide you right through the inspection station at the Austrian border.* Hanna smiled to herself and took a drag of the cigarette that dangled from the corner of her mouth. *Now for Walter Gruhn. Hum. I wonder what the new Walter Gruhn will look like?*

In between delivering meals to tables and giving orders to her cook, Eddi cut photos and brushed rubber cement onto their backs. She carefully placed them on the inside covers of the new passports, and on the faces of the new identification cards. Then she wiped them down with a clean towel. Today Eddi smiled. *Four more, ready for Margo to stamp.* So far, that had been the only hitch in their plan. They had forgotten that all passports needed to have the Austrian seal stamped over half the picture. Each new passport had to go back to the Embassy for their seal of approval.

Eddi glanced up from the passports. Through the kitchen window that opened up into the dining room she saw a man with a neatly trimmed beard taking a seat at the counter. He was carrying a white rose. She tucked the passports into her apron and went out to take his order.

"I'll have the special of the day, to go." he said in an oddly feminine voice.

Eddi grinned. "Good choice."

She went into the kitchen and wrapped up four stuffed cabbage rolls and placed them in a paper sack. Then she opened the knife drawer and lifted out the tray. Under the tray were several passports and identification cards. Eddi glanced through the window again and back down into the drawer. *Beard. Beard. Where's the beard. Ah, here you are.* She looked at the name on the card. *Gustav Held. Now, lets find your new work permit.* When she matched the name on the identification card with the name on the work permit, she pushed them both into the bottom of the bag.

"Here's your order, Herr Held. I hear you are looking for work?" The man at the counter just nodded. Eddi leaned in closer and whispered. "If you take that rose to Rauthenau Steel I'm sure they'll have a job for you." The man tipped his hat and smiled.

---

At the train station, Olga was busily discussing the schedules with a gentleman who had stepped up to her window. "If you hurry, mein Herr, you can make the Paris train. It's just about to leave. However, it will take you a few minutes to get through document inspection. If you miss this train, there will be another one at nine o'clock this evening." The man hurried away grumbling about having to have his bags searched every time he made business trip to Paris. Olga shrugged as she watched him walk away. Then her eye fell on a familiar face. She knew the woman who was stepping up to have her bags inspected by the Gestapo.

"Where are you traveling, Fraulein?" the agent asked.

"To Munich, and then onto Salzburg," the woman answered.

"Papers, bitte. Would you hand your bags to the officer there," he pointed to the man who sat next to him at the inspection table. The woman lifted her suitcase onto the table and then handed her passport to the Gestapo agent. He looked at it curiously. "This is an Austrian passport, but your accent is Berliner."

Olga held her breath.

"Yes," the woman replied. "I have been in Berlin since I was a child. My father is an engineer for a manufacturing company here. Now I have gotten word that my grandmother is very ill, in Salzburg. My father wants me to go and attend to her."

The Gestapo agent looked her up one side and down the other. Then he looked at the officer who searched her bags. "Nothing," he shrugged.

"Very well, Fraulein, you may pass."

Olga breathed a sigh of relief. "Goodbye, Edith," she whispered. "Have a safe journey."

---

Leeza introduced Albert to a young man who had come to the factory with a white rose. "Albert, this is Herr Rudolf Hilgard. Herr Hilgard, this is Albert. Albert is the foreman here at Rauthenau Steel."

Rudolf stuck out his hand, offering it to Albert. "I'm please to make your acquaintance."

Albert grinned as he shook Rudolf's hand. He hadn't quite gotten used to hearing the higher pitch in the voices of the men who were coming to work at the factory lately. "So, Rudolf, you ever worked in a steel factory before?"

"No," Rudolf grumped, trying to lower his voice.

"That's not a problem, Herr Hilgard," Leeza grinned, knowing what Albert was thinking. "Albert will show you just what to do. Right Albert?"

"Oh, Ja!" Albert laughed as he threw his arm around Rudolf's shoulders and walked him back to the loading docks. "I train all of Fraulein Leeza's friends."

---

*This is lovely stationary*, Luise thought as she folded the last of this week's letters. *The soft white rose is just perfect.* Then she licked the stamps and stuck them to all the envelopes. There was no return address. Luise caressed them lovingly. *I just hope you reach them in time, my little messengers.*

The next morning Luise slipped her little messengers past the Gestapo inspector who glanced over every piece of mail that came through the post office. She waited for him to make his morning trip to the men's room, where she knew he would sit for at least fifteen minutes. Luise quickly sorted through the addresses on her messages and hid each of them in the bottom of their appropriate mail bag. By the time the Gestapo inspector returned Luise had time to stack up his desk with the outgoing parcels, which she knew he would quickly glance over and toss into the bags. Most mornings he was anxious to get to his coffee and pastry.

Luise grinned as she stamped the envelope a lady had just handed her. She quickly handed it back to the inspector. "I don't need to see that one," he mumbled, his mouth full of pastry. "Just put it in the bag."

"Danke, Herr Inspector. How's your breakfast."

"Very good," he said as he stuffed his mouth again.

Luise just smiled. *What a pig!*

236

Elli watched the forty-five caliber pistols roll down the conveyor belt. Her job was to force a cleaning rod through the barrel one last time and then pack it neatly into the wooden crate for shipping. Every day the weapon changed. One day it was pistols, the next it was rifles. Once a week it was machine guns. With the way the army was growing she was sure she'd have a job for long time. Within a few weeks she was able to smuggle out a few of the pistols. *I wish I could think of a way to get a few of the rifles out. They might come in handy one day. But my lunch box just isn't big enough,* Elli grinned to herself.

Marta winced as Anneliese cleaned the cut above her eye. "How did this happen, Marta?" Anneliese whispered so the other nurses wouldn't hear them.

"Anneliese, we were just walking down the street. We were not holding hands or anything. We were on our way to get something to eat when they came out of the shadows. How is Anna?" Marta cried.

"She is unconscious," Anneliese whispered softly.

"What's going to happen to her?"

"I don't know. The doctor is examining her right now. I'm sure she has a concussion."

"Oh God, I have to get her out of here!" Marta brushed Anneliese's hand away.

"She can't be moved right now, Marta! She needs her rest!" Anneliese raised a bandage to Marta forehead.

Marta grabbed her hand and pleaded. "Anneliese, you don't understand. Anna is Jewish! They'll take her away!"

"Shhhh," Anneliese whispered. "Don't worry Marta, everything will be all right. Herr Doctor does not turn in Jews when they come to this emergency room. As soon as she can be moved, we'll get you both out of the country."

"How can you do that?"

"I have a way. Don't worry. Until then, we'll put you in a room together up on the third floor. Now let me bandage your forehead."

---

Elizabeth scanned each document carefully as it came across her desk. She was always on the lookout for the names of lesbians that were being investigated. However, this morning she was shocked to see so many on one page. She held a transport order in her hands. Twenty-eight women were being transferred to Ravensbruck. All of the names listed were deemed anti-social, a code word for lesbian, and therefore were assigned to wear the black triangle.

*Oh my God, I know some of these women. Joanna, Lilly, Grettle, Hedwig. You've all been arrested? This can't be. We can't let this happen. I've got to talk to Eddi!*

At lunch time Elizabeth raced over to Eddi's cafe. Eddi was just handing a lady one of her special orders to go. Eddi glanced up and saw the look on Elizabeth's face. She knew right away that something was very wrong.

"Come into the kitchen." Eddi sat Elizabeth down at a work table in the back and ladled her a bowl of soup. "Here, eat this. You look terrible." Then she sliced open a roll and spread butter on it. "Eat this too!"

Elizabeth pushed the bowl of soup away. "Eddi, you have to listen to me," she gasped.

Eddi pushed the bowl of soup back to her. "Whatever it is, it can wait until you have had some lunch."

238

"Eddi, you don't understand. Look at this." Elizabeth unfolded the transport order and held it up for Eddi to read.

Eddi wiped her hands on her apron and took the document. "Transport number 3147. Destination, Ravensbruck. All black triangle prisoners. See following names." Eddi let her eyes drift down the list of names. She recognized a few of them as well. "Oh God, they've got Joanna and Gretchen!"

"And Lilly and Grettle!" Elizabeth exclaimed. "Here we are saving all these strangers and we can't even save our friends."

"We've got to do something about this!" Eddi glanced back down at the transport order. "When are they scheduled to leave?"

Elizabeth grabbed the document. "In three days. They'll be transported at night."

"How?" Eddi asked.

"Probably by truck to the freight yard, and then by train."

"We've got to get to them before they make it to the train yard!"

"How?"

Eddi walked over to the flour barrel and reached way down into the bottom. A second later she pulled up some kind of package.

Elizabeth looked confused. "What is it?"

"Open it."

Elizabeth didn't like the look on Eddi's face. "What is it?"

"Just open it."

Elizabeth untied the string that held the brown wrapping paper. Inside was a cigar box. "What's in it, Eddi?"

"Open it!"

"I'm not sure I want too," Elizabeth groaned.

"Go ahead!"

Elizabeth opened the box. Inside lay a forty-five caliber pistol. "Oh shit," she whispered.

Eddi put her hands on her hips and smiled. "We are going to take out that transport truck before it gets to the freight yard."

"With one pistol!" Elizabeth cried.

"No. With five, and a little ingenuity," Eddi said defiantly.

Elizabeth glanced back to the pistol in the cigar box, and then squinted up at Eddi. "Five?"

Eddi walked over and tapped the rice barrel, then the bean barrel, then the sugar barrel, and finally the lard barrel. "Get the picture?"

"Oh Eddi," Elizabeth grinned. "Elli?"

Eddi just nodded her head. "Now eat your soup before it gets cold. I've got some calls to make."

---

Amy was sick every time she thought about how things had gone with Leeza. *Maybe it's better that I'm being transferred to Vienna. There's so much happening there that it's bound to take my mind off of her. Damn I wish she'd go with me. But she'll never leave that fuckin' factory, or Karl's memory.* Amy crammed everything she owned into her duffel bag and cussed some more. "You just had to go and open your damn mouth, didn't you Trevor! And look what it got you. A big fat zero. This dame ain't worth it. She'll never leave. She's too stubborn."

Every time Amy had seen Leeza at Pauli's or one of the other underground clubs, she had tried to talk her into leaving Germany, but each time Leeza had grown more distant than before.

"The women in Vienna are gorgeous, you know. I'm sure one of them will appreciate me," she yelled at the ring

240

on her night stand. Then she walked over and picked it up. Slowly, she sat down on the bed and stared into the star sapphire. Then she heaved a huge sigh. "Oh what are you talking about, Trevor? Fraulein Leeza von Rauthenau has stolen your heart and there's not a damn thing you can do about it. And she's entirely worth it. You just have to use a softer approach next time."

---

Albert knocked on Leeza's office door. It was open. She looked up and saw him standing in the doorway with his hat in his hand.

"Come in, Albert." she waved.

"Fraulein Leeza, may I talk to you in private?"

"Of course. Close the door if you like."

Albert closed the door and sat down on the couch. "Fraulein Leeza. I...Well, I..." He was obviously nervous about something.

Leeza leaned forward and looked him straight in the eye. "What is it Albert?" *He's having a hard time. The last time he wanted to talk privately it was about his grandchildren.* Then Leeza realized what Albert wanted. "Are there more children?"

"Ja," Albert nodded his head. "I see these...our new employees coming in with brand new work permits and identification cards. I..."

"Albert," Leeza smiled warmly, "how many are there?"

Tears welled up in his eyes. "More than you can imagine, Fraulein Leeza. More than you can imagine."

"Tell me," she whispered.

For the next hour Albert told Leeza how the Jewish community in Berlin had managed to hide so many of its own. "We hide them in the woods, in cellars, in abandoned buildings. But it is so cold, and they get so little food.

Many of the children will die if they can't get better shelter."

"What about their parents? Where are they?"

"In the camps, or dead. Some are in hiding also."

Leeza poured Albert a glass of schnapps. "Albert, why didn't you come to me sooner? I want you to bring as many as you can here, to the factory. Put the adults in overalls and put them to work. Have my friends build some bunks down in the furnace room. The little ones can stay down there where it's warm. I'll have a friend of mine deliver bread and soup every day. Then we'll work on getting them safely out of the country. But that's going to take some time."

"Danke, Fraulein Leeza." Albert cried. "Danke. I don't know what to say. You are so generous."

Leeza went over and sat beside Albert on the couch. She put her are around his shoulders tear filled her eyes. "Albert, the only thing that counts in this world," she whispered, "is what we have done for each other. You helped my friends when they needed it. Now it's time I helped yours. Don't worry about a thing," she sniffed.

# Chapter Seventeen

# The Austrian Connection

Mist rose up in swirls from the Danube Canal shrouding the bridge in an eerie fog. Night was falling quickly. Bernhard ran toward St. Stephan's Cathedral, his feet kicking at the mist which parted before him. He was late. *I hope the old man waits. Damn, I shouldn't have had that last beer.* Bernhard ran until he was out of breath. He slowed to a brisk walk, clutching the little package in his pocket. In the distance he heard the bells of St. Stephan's. The six o'clock mass was begining. *Surely he'll wait a few minutes more.* Then he broke into a run again.

Outside St. Stephan's, Heinrich crushed out a cigarette on the sidewalk across the square. He watched as Bernhard raced around the corner and headed for the massive doors of the cathedral. Bernhard stopped before entering and quickly removed the Nazi party pin from his collar.

*He's not there, traitor! You'll have to make your delivery to me.* Heinrich grinned as he lit another cigarette and waited for Bernhard to come out again.

As Bernhard enter the cathedral he dipped his finger into the holy water fount and crossed himself. He was out of breath from running and tried to quiet his gasping heaves before he made his way up the north aisle to the spiral staircase of the side pulpit.

There he knelt and crossed himself before he took a seat in the pew. His heart was racing. Again he clutched at the little package in his pocket and glanced at the carvings of Saints Gregory, Jerome, and Ambrose on the pulpit. They seemed to be staring at him with pity. Bernhard shuddered.

His eyes drifted down to the carving of the man in the window at the base of the pulpit. The master carver had left his own self-portrait there in the stone. The man in the window seemed to be saying, "God sees what you do, Bernhard." *I'm not doing anything wrong*, Bernhard's mind screamed at the man in the window. He looked around nervously. *Where is the old man? I'm not that late!*

Bernhard had joined the underground Nazi movement in Vienna the year before. He was a minor clerk at the passport office who didn't make very much money, and had believed the Nazi promise of prosperity. He was not the only one. Many young men had believed them. Now Bernhard was having second thoughts. When he was approached about selling a few passports, the hole in the bottom of his shoe convinced him that he could not wait for the Nazis to come to power. Nervously, he looked down at his new shinny shoes. *What difference does it make to the party if a few Jews get Austrian passports? I get a new pair of shoes, and possibly a coat.* Glancing at his watch and then around the cathedral, his heart began to race again. *The old man has already left. Damn! Now, what do I do with these?* He fingered the bundle of passports in his pocket. *I'll just have to come back tomorrow. The old man will come again, I'm sure. I just hope he has the money.* Bernhard decided to leave, remembering that he still had enough money for another beer.

Heinrich followed Bernhard at a discreet distance until they got to the bridge over the Danube Canal. Then he quickened his pace.

Bernhard heard the footsteps coming up from behind him and glanced over his shoulders. He couldn't see anyone in the darkness, but the footsteps were getting closer. He quickened his pace also. Suddenly the footsteps sounded like they were running. They were very close now. A moment later he felt a strong grip on his shoulder that spun him around.

"Heinrich!" Bernhard cried. "Oh, thank God it's you!"

"Hello, Bernhard," Heinrich hissed. "Going somewhere?"

"Uh, yes," Bernhard wheezed. He had always been secretly afraid of Heinrich. "To the beer hall."

"Where are you coming from? I see you don't have your party pin on." Heinrich was toying with Bernhard.

He glanced down at his collar. "I was just at St. Stephan's for mass. I didn't think…"

"I didn't know you were a religious man." Heinrich teased playfully.

Bernhard blushed a little and shrugged his shoulders. "Well, I'm not really. I just…"

"Perhaps you were meeting someone?" Heinrich stared hard at him.

"No! I…"

Heinrich grinned. "Herr Dieter von Kleist, perhaps?"

Bernhard's eyes grew wide and his hands began to tremble. *He knows.*

"Yes, Bernhard. We know all about your little arrangement with Dieter von Kleist." Then suddenly Heinrich backhanded Bernhard and blood flew from his mouth. "Imagine our surprise when we traced him to you! One of our own, selling passports to Jews! Traitor!" Heinrich backhanded him again.

"Herr von Kleist is not a Jew!" Bernhard gasped as blood filled his mouth. "He is an Austrian official."

"Who has a Jewish boyfriend!" Heinrich yelled. Then he calmed himself and grinned. "However, Dieter von Kleist is no more. And soon his Jewish boyfriend will take the blame for his murder. He will be joining him in hell shortly. Just as soon as I hunt down his connection." Then Heinrich smirked. "Give me the passports, Bernhard."

"I don't know what you mean, Heinrich!" Bernhard exclaimed. "Honestly, I…"

In the flash of an eye, Heinrich pulled out his blade and sliced Bernhard's throat. Quickly, he pushed Bernhard's head and shoulders over the bridge railing and reached into his pocket to retrieve the little package. Then he shoved Bernhard's body over the railing and listened for the splash in the darkness.

---

Amy missed her gang of reporters back in Berlin, but the way things were going in Vienna she figured it wouldn't be long before Jim Newman and Marshall Turner, and the rest of the guys would join her. It seemed every eye was on Austria, especially after Dieter von Kleist's body had been discovered in his apartment early that morning. The teletype at the International News Service office was abuzz with the stories reporting that von Kleist had been found tied up, execution style, with his throat cut. The police weren't saying if they had any suspects in the murder, but the Nazis were screaming that the murder of a government official was a Jewish plot to take over the country.

Tired and hungry, Amy headed back to her hotel. The string quartet in the dining room of the Sacher Hotel played softly as Amy entered. The maitre d' squared his shoulders and clicked his heels. "Is the Fraulein dining alone this evening?"

"Yes," she nodded.

The maitre d' clucked his tongue. "Unfortunate."

Amy frowned. The snow was piling up outside and the cold damp night only added misery to her solitude. She knew that it was considered almost a sin in Austria to eat alone. "Yes, unfortunate."

The maitre d' gave Amy a slight bow and escorted her to a table against the side wall. Above the table hung a portrait of Emperor Franz Joseph in his military uniform. *Too bad you're not in charge anymore,* Amy thought as the maitre d' pulled out her chair. *Maybe you'd tell Hitler to*

246

*take a flyin'...* The maitre d' snapped open the linen napkin and laid it in Amy's lap as she sat down.

"Tonight, our special is roasted veal in red wine sauce with asparagus. It's lovely."

The maitre d' was quite proper and polite, but still Amy felt uncomfortable with his pity. *I know, I know. What's a nice girl like me doing dining alone.* "Yes, danke. The veal sounds good. I'll have that." Then she smiled, trying to seem perfectly at ease with dining alone. "The orchestra plays beautifully."

"You like the music, Fraulein?"

"Yes. The music in Vienna is wonderful."

The maitre d' smiled. "I'm sure the concierge will have tickets to the symphony, if the Fraulein wishes to attend this evening."

Amy thought of Leeza. She had never seen her play, except at the St. Valentine's Day Ball. "Will he have tickets to the Musikverein?"

"Of course, Fraulein!"

"Danke. I'll stop by and see him after diner."

"No need, Fraulein. I will arrange for your ticket." The maitre d' smiled brightly Amy grinned. "Danke."

"It is my pleasure, Fraulein."

---

The idea of seeing where Leeza used to perform thrilled Amy. Somehow just the thought of seeing her orchestra play made her feel closer to Leeza. The doorman at the Sacher hailed a cab for her while she waited under the awning. The ride to the Musikverein wasn't long, although the cab moved slowly in the snow. Amy's ticket was for the tenth row, second seat. A man was already sitting in the aisle seat when she arrived. Obviously he was alone. Amy frowned, wondering if the maitre d' had set her up.

"Pardon me, bitte," she smiled. "I believe I am sitting next to you." The gentleman stood up and allowed Amy to pass. "Danke."

The musicians could be heard tuning up back stage as the audience filled the concert hall. Handsome gentlemen in black ties and shiny black shoes escorted beautiful ladies in flowing evening gowns and furs to their seats. Amy felt completely out of place. Most of her gang entertained themselves in beer halls and bars. Americans loved to listen to the tunes of Duke Ellington and Glen Miller. She hadn't been to the symphony in years. Not since college. *College. Now that seems like a long time ago. Kerry and I went to the symphony with her parents. That was the night they told her they had arranged for her to marry Michael Dumont. God, we fought about that. Damn, I hope this is a better night than that was.* Amy glanced down at her program. Unconsciously she was looking for Leeza's name. It wasn't there. Then she looked up to the empty stage and sighed. "If only you were really here," Amy said to herself.

"Pardon me, Fraulein?" The gentleman next to her asked, thinking she had spoken to him.

Amy blushed. "Oh, excuse me. I was just thinking out loud. I have a friend who used to play with the orchestra. Now she's in Berlin."

"I too have a friend who used to perform with this orchestra. She is also in Berlin," the man smiled.

*Oh sure you do, fella.* "Hum, imagine that. What a coincidence."

The man looked longingly at the empty stage. "Her name is Leeza von Rauthenau."

Amy's heart skipped a beat. "Leeza! You know Leeza? She was the friend I was talking about."

"Yes," the man smiled. "I know Leeza. I am her...uh uncle."

Amy frowned. "But her uncle is..."

"I am Leeza's...Uh...I am Captain Wilhelm Schroeder."

"Oh, Karl's old..." Amy blushed, thinking she had just put her foot in her mouth.

Wilhelm frowned. "Yes. Karl's old lover."

"I'm so sorry, Captain Schroeder. I mean about Karl." *Way to go, Trevor. Why don't you just dig a hole and jump in?*

"I am too, Fraulein..."

"Amy Trevor." *Change the subject, Trevor.*

"Have you seen Leeza lately, Fraulein Trevor?"

"I saw her last week," Amy grinned.

"And she is well?"

"Yes. She works long hours so she is very tired, but she is healthy and is doing quite well at the steel factory from what I understand."

"Then you are not close to her?" Wilhelm frowned.

Amy blushed. "I...She...We..." Amy stuttered.

"Ah, so that's how it is between you!" Wilhelm smiled. "I was hoping she would take a lover. Especially after everything that has happened. I hope the child does not remain a virgin forever."

*Virgin! You mean to tell me she's a virgin?* Amy was really blushing now. "No! Herr Schroeder, that's not how it is between us. I mean, yes I would love to, but she..."

Wilhelm grinned. "Chased you away, did she?"

Amy reluctantly nodded her head. "Something like that."

"She's a wonderful girl, Fraulein Trevor. You should try again. Don't let her scare you off."

"Got any more great advice?" Amy groaned.

"As a matter of fact I do," Wilhelm winked.

"Well let's hear it. I'm willing to try anything."

Wilhelm leaned back in his seat and sighed out loud. "Leeza is a passionate girl. Woman, really. I still think of her as a little girl most of the time." Wilhelm chuckled.

249

"Obviously you haven't seen her lately!" Amy flashed Wilhelm a wry grin.

"No, I suppose I haven't. But I do know how stubborn she can be. When she was a little girl and her music teachers suggested she study here in Vienna or Salzburg, and Karl said that she was too young to be alone in Austria. She was so stubborn that she just set her mind on Vienna and wouldn't eat for three days. Finally, Karl had to soothe her another way before she would consent to eat again." Wilhelm laughed at the memory.

"What did he do?" Amy asked. She was more than a little curious.

"He had to handle her very gingerly. He went up to her room and begged her to stay. He cried and said how much he would miss her. That she was the sunshine of his days and the starlight of his nights. He told her that he didn't think he could live without her, at least until she was eighteen, and that if she wouldn't eat, he wasn't going to eat either."

Amy laughed, imagining the scene. "And she bought that?"

"Oh yes," Wilhelm chuckled. "Telling her no, straight out, only makes her more determined to do whatever it is that you don't want her to do. Karl knew he had to focus her attention on him. He had to make her think it was her own idea to eat again."

Amy thought about how she had nearly ordered Leeza not to participate in the demonstration, and how she had driven Leeza farther away by insisting that she leave Germany. "So, you're saying that if I want her to do something, I have to make her think she's doing it for me?"

"Sometimes, yes. Especially when it's something she won't do for herself."

"Boy, does that sound familiar!" Amy sighed.

Just then the house lights dimmed, indicating that the concert was about to begin. The audience quieted down and the musicians paraded onto the stage. Wilhelm leaned close to Amy's ear and whispered. "If you want to know how to win her heart, Fraulein Trevor, you should talk to him." Wilhelm pointed to Julius. "He probably knows Leeza better than anyone in the world. He's her best friend."

"Danke, Captain Schroeder. I'll do that," Amy winked, "right after the concert."

---

It was bitter cold the night the women were led from their prison cells to the truck waiting at the gate. The freezing steel of their handcuffs burned the tender skin around their wrists. They shuffled along, one after the other, to the shouts of the guards who demanded they moved faster. Their bruised and battered bodies were weary from their long interrogation sessions. Many had to carry their cell mates because they simply couldn't walk on their own. Some of the women led other women by the hand because their eyes were swollen shut.

Lesbians were the lowest form of life to the Nazis. The way they saw it, these women simply chose not to sleep with men in order to defy German ideology. To the Nazis there was no higher honor for a woman than to be a wife and mother. When these women chose to reject men, they were choosing to thumb their noses at proper German womanhood. The Nazi mind could not conceive of the fact that a woman could naturally be attracted to another woman. Women who chose to reject men were simply being rebellious, and the Nazis prided themselves on their ability to break rebellious people.

"Ravensbruck will teach you to behave like proper women!" one of the guards shouted as the women stumbled to the truck.

"I could teach them!" laughed another guard.

"Ja, I thought you already had!" laughed the first one.

"Hum, let me see." The second guard looked up and down the line of women. Then he pointed to one of them. "I don't think I had a chance to teach her!" All the guards roared with laughter. The women just kept their eyes down and shuffled along without looking up at the laughing guards.

"Hurry up you bitches. It's freezing out here!" yelled the driver of the truck. "Schnell, schnell!" Then he glanced over at the guards who were still snickering. "Which one of you is riding in the back?"

The first guard jerked his thumb at the second one and yelled, "He is!"

The second one grinned. "It will be my pleasure!"

---

Anneliese stood outside the prison in the woods. She had seen the women struggling to climb into the back of the truck. When she heard the roar of the big diesel motor start up and saw the gate being to open, she quickly ran out and pointed her flash light down the road. She blinked it on and off once, indicating that there was only one truck. She waited until she saw the taillights of Leeza's Mercedes take off down the road before she ran back into the woods. Then she waited for the truck to pass before she got on Margo's motorcycle and pressed on the starter. Anneliese tailed the truck, but didn't turn on the headlights.

Up the road, Margo and Elli had picked out the spot where they planned to ambush the truck. They had thought of an all out attack, something like shooting out the tires as the truck went by. But Anneliese and Leeza weren't to happy with that idea. Claire suggested that the old fashioned way might work best, and it was certainly less dangerous.

"What's the old fashioned way," Margo barked.

Claire batted her eyes. "Why sex of course!"

So that was their plan. About halfway between the prison and the freight yard, just before the edge of the woods, Claire parked her car on the road. She lifted the hood when Leeza's Mercedes came by flashing its lights.

Leeza turned right on the next dirt road that led into the woods. It was about one hundred yards up and thick with trees. Leeza parked her car in line with the others. She and Eddi, Luise, Heidi, Gertrud, and Olga all ran back to the tree line beside Claire's car, and waited. Claire had worn a low cut sweater and very tight skirt for the occasion. And sure enough, when she stepped into the headlights of the oncoming truck and smiled brightly, it stopped.

The driver stuck his head out of the window and shouted, "What is wrong, Fraulein?"

Claire batted her big blue eyes and smiled. "I don't know. It just stopped."

When the guard in the back of the truck heard Claire's voice, he lifted the tarp to take a look. By this time Anneliese was coming up on the truck and saw that the plan was working, at least this far. She turned off the key and coasted to a stop before anyone could hear the motorcycle.

The guard shouted, "I'll take a look at it for her," as he jumped out of the back of the truck with his machine-gun.

The driver saw the guard in his side mirror and yelled, "No, I'll look at it for her!" The two of them argued all the way over to the front of Claire's car. Claire just grinned at Margo and Elli who were peeping out of the trunk.

"What seems to be the trouble, Fraulein?" asked the guard as he stuck his head under the hood.

Claire leaned over the fender and shoved her breasts near his face. In the most seductive voice she could manage without laughing, she sighed, "Why, I don't know. It just went clunk, clunk. And then it seemed to choke. Then it just stopped."

The driver watched the expression on the guard's face. Then he slapped him on the shoulder and said, "Move over." Squeezing in between Claire's breasts and the guard, the said, "You don't know anything about engines!"

When both the driver and the guard had their faces under the hood, Margo and Elli slipped out of the trunk. Quickly and quietly, they snuck around and slammed the hood down on Nazi's heads. Both were out like lights. Cheers rose up from the woods, and the hiding women ran out to the road.

Anneliese ran to the back of the truck and called to the women inside. "Everything is all right," she cried as she threw open the tarp. "Hurry, we have come to get you out of here. We are friends. Hurry, come with us."

A moment later Leeza, Elizabeth, Eddi, Heidi, Luise, and Gertrude were helping Anneliese with the women. Many of them were hysterical, not understanding what was happening. The rescuers were horrified to see how battered the women were.

"Shhh. Shhh," Anneliese tried to calm them. "Everything is all right now. We're friends. We're here to help you."

"Lilly. Joanna. Hedwig. Grettle. It's Elizabeth. Elizabeth Kroll. You remember me. Eddi is here too. You must trust us. Hurry! We have to get you out of here."

Eddi peeked around the side of the truck. "Margo, we need the keys. They're handcuffed!"

Margo rolled the driver over and started rummaging through his pockets for the keys. Leeza ran up to see what was taking so long. "I don't know," Margo barked. "He doesn't have any keys."

Leeza looked at Elli. "What about him?"

Elli tucked her pistol in the back of her pants and rolled the guard over. Then she knelt down and reached into his coat pocket. "Here they are," she smiled. But just then the guard grabbed her by the throat with one hand and reached

254

for his machine-gun with the other. Elli dropped the keys as she grabbed at the hand around her throat. Margo threw herself on the machine-gun and wrestled it away from the guard. Suddenly everyone heard a loud BANG!

Instantly, the hand around Elli's throat loosened and fell to the ground. She gasped for breath as she scrambled to back away from the dead guard. Then Elli and Margo glanced at each other in confusion. Neither of them had shot the guard.

Leeza whispered hoarsely, "Give me the keys."

Margo and Elli looked up at Leeza. She stood there frozen. The pistol barrel was still smoking in her hand. "Leeza," Margo whispered.

"Elli, give Eddi the keys," Leeza commanded.

Elli looked around for the keys. They were laying in a pool of blood by the guard's head. She picked them up and ran them back to Eddi.

"What happened up there?" Eddi whispered frantically.

"Leeza just saved my life," Elli gasped, still trying to catch her breath.

Eddi stared at her in amazement. *Leeza? Leeza shot one of them?* Then she shook her head and focused on the keys. "We've got to hurry. Someone could come along any minute. As I unlock them, you all start taking them through the woods to the cars. Put the seriously injured ones in Claire's car."

"What about the truck and the guards?" Anneliese asked.

"Don't worry about that. Margo and I will take care of them," Elli answered.

"Anneliese, make sure you ride back with Claire!" Eddi directed. "Those women will need your care first!"

"Right," Anneliese responded. "But what about Leeza? I'm sure she's in no shape to drive. She's never killed anyone before tonight."

"I'll ride back with her. Don't worry!" Eddi answered compassionately. "Now get moving. We'll all meet up at the factory later."

Once the women were in the cars, Elli and Margo cleaned up the scene. They threw the bodies in the back of the truck. "You'd better ride back here and keep an eye on the driver," Margo grumped. Then she fired up the truck and drove it off down one of the side roads, deep in the woods. When she finally pulled off, she pitched the keys as far as she could throw them.

Elli kicked the driver's boot and whispered, "What do we do about this guy? He got a real good look at Claire."

Margo reached in the back of her pants and pulled out her forty-five. "Did you see what these animals did to those women?" Then she fired. "Come on. Lets get back to my bike."

---

Amy had been up all night thinking about what Wilhelm and Julius had told her about Leeza. *I've got to see her again. I'll take it easy this time. I won't even bring up leaving the country. I'll just invite her out to dinner, and we can talk about anything she wants to talk about.*

That was the thought that had run through Amy's mind as she boarded the morning flight for Berlin. *I'll just go to Rauthenau Steel and sweetly ask her to dinner.* But that had been at six o'clock this morning. Now it was eleven-thirty and she was standing in Leeza's office facing her. "I uh...I uh..." *God, she's so beautiful. Even in coveralls.* Amy smiled and shrugged her shoulders shyly.

For the first time, Leeza saw something in Amy that she didn't know existed. *She looks like a little girl. Cute and shy.* Then she remembered how gentle Amy had been at the ball. Leeza just stood there staring at her, dressed in khaki tan pants and blue blouse. *She looks very modern. Typically American.* Unexpectedly, the image of her questioning the Gestapo agent about lingerie laws in Germany filled her mind and she smiled. *She was wonderful. Brave. Strong.* Then she flashed back to their dance. *She was so gentle. Her skin was so soft in my hand. And her smell. So sweet and warm.* Then she remembered how demanding and overbearing Amy had been about leaving Germany. *Still, she was only trying to protect me.* Leeza smiled warmly.

Amy took Leeza's smile as a sign of encouragement. "I'm being transferred to Austria. Actually, I've already moved to Vienna. But I just wanted to tell you that I was sorry for being so domineering. I was hoping we could have dinner so I could apologize properly."

"You live in Vienna now?"

"Yes. Well I don't actually live there. I'm staying at the Sacher Hotel."

"I know the Sacher very well. I used to go there for coffee. They make the most wonderful Viennese Coffee."

"Yes," Amy smiled, "I've had it."

"So, when are you returning to Austria?" Leeza toyed with an idea in the back of her mind.

Amy shrugged her shoulders. "I guess that depends on if you'll have dinner with me."

"Do you mean you came all the way to Berlin just to have dinner with me."

"I took the morning flight." *Does that mean you'll have dinner with me? Slow down, Trevor. Remember, nice and slow.*

Leeza smiled brightly. "Yes. We can have dinner together. Right now as a matter of fact. If that's all right with you?"

Amy was surprised, but pleased. "Uh…Absolutely! Where would you like to go?"

"How about the furnace room?"

257

Amy's scrunched her eyebrows together. "I've never heard of it."

Leeza strolled over and put her arm through Amy's. "It's not far. And the food's not bad."

Amy's heart beat faster when Leeza touched her. "Sure!"

A few minutes later they were down in the furnace room facing fourteen Jewish children. There were also nine injured lesbian women laying unconscious in the bunks. Eddi was happily serving soup and bread from behind a table in the corner.

Amy looked around in amazement. "Who are they?" she whispered.

"They are the million little reasons I must stay in Germany," Leeza smiled.

"What have you gotten yourself into, Leeza?" Amy asked softly.

"I do what I can to help, but they need more." Leeza squeezed Amy's arm and looked into her eyes. "They need your help too."

Amy's first reaction was to tense up. Leeza felt it and pulled away. *Take it easy, Trevor. Don't go blowin' up or anything.* Amy followed Leeza over to the soup line.

"We'll take two bowls, Eddi. And some bread, bitte."

Eddi handed the bowls to Leeza. "I'll bring the bread over in a minute. You go on and sit down."

Leeza led Amy over to a small table. As they sat down she said, "They are Jewish children. And the women over there, they are lesbians the Gestapo nearly killed. We helped them escape last night."

Amy nearly bit her tongue off trying to keep from yelling about what a dangerous thing that was to do. "And you need my help, how?"

"We need someone who can move about freely enough to take them across the border to Austria." Leeza smiled warmly and touched Amy's hand. "I was hoping you would do this for me."

Amy sipped her soup. *Is she nuts? How the hell am I supposed to get fourteen Jewish kids across the border?*

"We have secured new Austrian passports for all of them."

*Yeah, but fourteen!* Amy sipped her soup again.

"Of course you couldn't take them all at once. It will require several trips. But we will pay for all of your expenses."

*Now I know she's nuts. Even if I could get them across, what would I do with them when we got there? Take it easy, Trevor. Just keep sippin' your soup.*

"I have made arrangement for them to stay with my mother in the Tyrol."

*Just how am I supposed to handle screaming babies and toddlers? Sip the soup.*

"We have sleeping medication for the small ones. So they won't be a problem for you."

*What, is she reading my mind? Soup. Keep sippin' the soup!*

"This would mean so much to them."

*Yeah, but what about to you?*

"You would be saving their lives."

Amy shrugged her shoulders and smiled humbly. "That's me, the life saving news reporter."

"So you'll do it?" Leeza touched Amy's hand.

*No, Trevor.* "Yeah, sure. I'll do it." *You idiot. What did ya go and say that for? She's only touching you because you have an American passport! You idiot, she's using you!*

Leeza leaned over and took Amy's face in her hands. Then she kissed her gently on the lips. "Thank you," she whispered in her ear. "This means the world to me."

Amy grinned. *Well, maybe it's a little more than my passport.*

# Chapter Eighteen

## Swiss Account

The next morning Amy found herself carrying a kindercare permit and boarding the early flight to Vienna with five Jewish children. In her arms she rocked a tiny baby girl. "Shhh, shhh. Stay asleep, little one. Aunt Amy needs you to sleep quietly all the way home."

Getting through the inspection at the airport had been easier than Amy had anticipated. When the Gestapo agent looked at the children's Austrian passports and then at her American passport, the only thing he asked was where the parents were.

"Their father is here on business," Amy replied. "After a few days, the children grew restless and so their mother asked me to take them home."

"And you are their…"

"Nanny!" Amy quickly answered. She put the baby up on her shoulder and pulled out her kindercare permit. "I am their nanny." The Gestapo agent eyed her suspiciously, but finally waved her through. "Come along children," she smiled, "we're going home now. Hans, take Mary's hand. Fritz, take Gretchen's hand. Everyone stay together now."

Thankfully the boys were old enough to help their little sisters onto the plane, because Amy had her hands full trying to manage the baby and their little bags. *It's a good thing these kids don't have much to bring along.* Actually, only two of the children were related. One of the boys was the brother of the baby.

Once they were all buckled into their seats Amy gave the little girls a teaspoon each of cough medicine. Soon they were fast asleep. The boys just sat quietly, looking out the windows in fascination as the plane soared over the

260

mountains. Amy held the baby gently in her arms, stroking her little head and cooing softly. She smiled to herself as she watched the baby sleep. *What a beautiful little girl you are. How proud your parents must be.*

Suddenly, tears filled her eyes. The baby's parents were almost certainly dead. Their names had appeared on the weekly deportation list, and everyone knew what that meant. The baby's mother had taken her children to a church the night before she and her husband had boarded the train for a concentration camp. She left them with the priest, begging him to help them escape. Luckily, the priest was working with the Jewish underground. He wanted her to go with the children, but she knew that if she didn't show up to the deportation center the next morning, the S.S. would turn their neighborhood upside down looking for them. There were too many others in hiding to risk it. The parents sacrificed themselves to save not only their own children, but the lives of countless other children as well.

"Hush little baby, don't you cry," Amy sang, but her voice cracked and the boys looked at her sadly. *Their young eyes have seen too much. Dear God, help me watch over them.* She smiled at the boys warmly and said, "We're going to a very beautiful place. You'll love Herr Hagen's chalet. Aunt Leeza tells me its the most wonderful place on earth." The boys didn't smile. Their hearts were too heavy. Amy knew they missed their parents, and she could not think of any words that would comfort them.

Things had happened so fast that no preparations had been made for when Amy and the children landed in Vienna. Leeza's only thought had been to get the children out as fast as they could. Now it was up to Amy to get the children to Jenbach and deliver them to Frau von Rauthenau. The airport was packed with impatient travelers and the medication was starting to wear off. The little girls started crying and Amy didn't quite know what to do at that point. If she medicated them again they would not be able to walk, and she certainly couldn't carry all three of the little girls to the train station by herself. Desperately, she tried to comfort the girls, but they just cried louder.

"May I be of some assistance, Fraulein?" Amy heard a familiar man's voice behind her. She looked around and saw Julius standing there grinning.

"Herr Barkowski!"

"I didn't know you had children," Julius laughed.

The little girls cried louder. "Shhh, shhh. There, there." Amy desperately tried to calm them, but they were so frightened they couldn't stop. Amy looked up at Julius, her eyes were pleading. "Obviously, they are not my children. Our mutual friend has asked me to look after them."

Julius looked hard at Amy. "Our mutual friend?"

Amy nodded her head ominously.

"Leeza?" he whispered.

Amy nodded again. "I have to get them to Jenbach. To Leeza's mother. It's just north of Innsbruck. But as you can see, I'm having a little problem."

"I was just on my way to Zurich," Julius rubbed his chin. "But I suppose I could take the train with you."

Amy stood up and shoved the baby into Julius' arms. "You got yourself a deal!" Then she knelt down and pulled the girls close to her. "Come on, little ones. Let's have some medicine. That will make you feel better."

Julius looked like a fish out of water holding the sleeping baby girl. He held her out stiffly, as if she was going to bite him. His violin case dangled from his finger tip. "I don't know how to do this," he whispered gruffly. "I just meant that I could walk with the boys while you managed the girls."

"Sorry, pal. I need a little more help than that. Just hold her like you would your violin. Gently, and close." Amy pushed Julius' arms into his chest. "There, just like that." He still looked extremely uncomfortable.

262

"She doesn't feel like a violin!" Julius said with an exasperated tone in his voice.

Amy grinned. "Too bad!" Then she turned to the children and picked up the girls. "Hans, Fritz, can you get the bags?" The boys nodded. "Well then, we're off to the train station."

———————

From the shadows Heinrich watched as Julius spoke with the woman. He took a long drag off his cigarette and blew smoke rings into the air. *Who is the Fraulein, Herr Barkowski? Your contact, perhaps? I'll have to keep an eye on her.*

———————

Julius purchased a whole compartment for Amy and the children. As soon as the door was closed behind them, Amy took out the little medicine bottle and gave each of the children a teaspoon full. Now they slept quietly as the train chugged through the foothills on its way to Salzburg and then up through the Alps.

Finally, Julius was able to ask the questions he had been waiting to ask. "What in God's name is Leeza doing?" he barked.

Amy barked right back. "You know her better than I do. You tell me!"

"I thought you were going back to win her heart, darling, not sneak children across the border for her!"

"She never gave me the chance," Amy hissed. "As soon as I got there she took me down to the furnace room."

"The furnace room?"

"Yeah, she has turned it into a regular dormitory."

263

"What do you mean?"

"I mean, she is hiding Jews down there."

"Oh my God!" Julius growled. "With the Gestapo watching her every move?"

"I know, but you know how she is," Amy grinned. After Julius thought about it for a moment he burst of laughing. "What's so funny?" she asked.

Julius rubbed his chin and sighed. "It's not funny, darling, it's brilliant!"

"What do you mean?"

"Well, think about it. The Gestapo think they are watching her so closely that she'd never try anything like this. They would never imagine she could sneak Jews in right under their noses. It's perfect. The factory is the last place they'd think of searching for Jews. How many is she hiding?"

Amy looked at the children. "These are only five of fourteen, plus some of their parents and the lesbians the White Rose broke out of prison."

"The White Rose Ladies Society? I thought they were outlawed years ago?"

"They were, but when Himmler issued the new law against lesbianism, the old leaders of the White Rose protested. Most of them were arrested. They're in Ravensbruck now. Anyway, after that happened, Leeza and some of her friends revived the White Rose Ladies Society and turned it into the White Rose resistance. I don't know all of the details, but somehow they are able to get Austrian passports and new German identification cards with work permits."

Julius laughed again. "So, how does she get the Jews in and out?"

"In the coal cars."

Julius looked puzzled. "Coal cars?"

"Yeah, the train delivers coal to the factory every day. Apparently Albert has quite an underground going himself.

Some of his associates put the Jews in the coal cars after they are loaded and tagged for Rauthenau Steel. When the coal cars pull up, Albert's dykes help them out and lead them down to the furnace room."

"Wait a minute. Albert's dykes?"

"Yup. Ever since Himmler's lesbian law came out earlier this month, Leeza has had dykes working at the factory."

"How did this happen?" Julius asked.

"It's a long story, so I'll give you the short version. The White Rose is hiding more than Jews. They hide homosexuals as well. Both men and women. The women who don't want to leave the country, and who can pass as men, well, Leeza gives them jobs at the factory." Amy laughed. "You should see them, Julius. You would never know they were women! Some even have beards and mustaches. Albert trains them and they work really hard for him and Leeza."

Julius shook his head in amazement. "Who would have thought our darling Leeza could ever be a resistance leader. She has always been so..."

Amy leaned forward. "Tell me."

Julius thought for a moment. "I don't know. She is so lovely."

"You can say that again," Amy chirped.

Julius grinned. Then his face became puzzled. "She's beautiful, charming, talented. And she's not shy when it comes to performing, but when it comes to..." Julius couldn't think of what he wanted to say.

"Relationships?" Amy offered.

"Relationships yes, but it's more than that. Somehow, I think she believes that her music is all she has to give. In the other areas of her life, she lacks confidence in herself. She seems almost sad. Perhaps it was loosing her father at such a young age. Maybe that has caused her to be afraid to love. But that's not it either. I know she loves deeply. Her love for Karl is overwhelming. And I know she loves me. Maybe it's the fact that she has never been loved in a romantic way. Everyone loves her music, but they never approach her romantically. Maybe it's a matter of trust. I know she dreams of being loved."

"I love her, Julius." Amy's voice trembled "I don't know how or why, but I do."

"Then you must tell her, darling!" Julius beamed.

"How can I? Right now all she wants from me is my American passport!" Amy groaned.

"That is not true!" Julius barked. "If I know Leeza, and I do, she would never have asked for your help if she didn't know she could trust you."

Amy looked up at Julius hopefully. "She kissed me yesterday after I told her I would take the children. It was just once, but she did kiss me."

"There, you see," Julius sighed. "I think with Leeza it's a matter of trust. The more she trusts you, the more she will let herself love you."

Amy's eyes filled with tears. "But the only way I can earn her trust is to keep bringing the children across the border. If I keep doing that, she'll stay in Germany and keep risking her life."

Julius leaned forward. "So, you're like everyone else. You love her music and not who she really is."

"What do you mean?"

"Leeza is a loving woman. She is so much more than just her music. She is complicated. Is it the music or the woman you love?"

Amy smiled and brushed away her tears. "I have only heard her play once, at the Valentine's Day Ball."

"That was nothing!" Julius grinned. "A few little ditties."

"Then it must be the women I love," Amy sniffed.

Julius leaned forward and took Amy's hands. "And it is the woman who is driven to do what she is doing. You have fallen in love with her compassion and her courage, and all the other qualities she carries in her soul. Don't try and stop her. Just help her, and love her for what she is doing.

"And what if I loose her?"

"Darling, you can't change her mind about this, so I suggest you ask yourself if you are willing to love her even though there are risks."

Amy leaned back in her seat and stared out the window. Images of Leeza filled her mind. Leeza in a tuxedo at the ball. Leeza in her navy blue tailored skirt and jacket at the Munich train station. Leeza in a sweater and slacks at Pauli's. Leeza in coveralls at the factory. Leeza in the black negligee. *God, there are so many facets to this woman. How can I refuse to love her? There is no way I could.* Amy leaned her head against the window and fell asleep thinking about what a rare kind of woman Leeza really was.

Late that evening the train screeched to a halt in Jenbach station. Julius helped Amy and the children off the train and into a cab, bidding them farewell. "I would love to go with you, but I have a business meeting in Zurich. I'm afraid I am already late. Give Frau von Rauthenau my love. And when you see Leeza again, give her a hug for me. I know how much she misses me."

"I will," Amy called as she waved goodbye. "And thank you!" Julius waved as the cab pulled away. Then he got back on the train. *You are a good woman, Amy Trevor. And you are good for Leeza, I think.*

———————

Needless to say Hans Hagen and Katrine were very surprised by Amy's arrival. Especially with five Jewish children in tow. They had faithfully taken care of Albert's grandchildren until they had flown off to be with their family in America. Since then the chalet had felt quite empty, even when it had been overflowing with visitors. Katrine and Hans had thoroughly enjoyed having children of their own, even if it was only for a short time. Katrine had been reborn at the chalet. She and Hans were planning to marry as soon as Leeza could come for the wedding.

Once the children had eaten and were tucked into big fluffy feather beds, Amy explained as much as she could to Katrine and Hans. "She has many more children," Amy told them. "Most of them don't have parents any more. So, we'll need to find homes for them."

Hans ran his fingers through his beard. "I know a Jewish doctor in Innsbruck. I will go see him tomorrow. I'm sure he'll be able to make the arrangements we need. Until then, you must bring all the children here. We have plenty of room and plenty of food."

"And plenty of love," Katrine beamed. "We loved having Albert's grandchildren here. I almost didn't want to let them go to America."

"When will you be going back to Germany, Fraulein Amy?" Hans asked.

"In the morning," Amy yawned. "Excuse me."

"You must get some rest before you leave," Katrine patted Amy's hand.

Amy smiled. *Leeza looks just like her. Same long dark hair. Same sparkling blue eyes. Same shapely figure and fine features. Just a little older, that's all.* "Danke, Frau von Rauthenau."

"You must call me Katrine," she smiled.

"All right, Katrine. Danke. I could use a good night's rest. Your daughter kept me up most of last night."

"How is Leeza, really?" Katrine asked sadly.

Amy could see the concern in her eyes. "She is tired from working such long hours in the factory, Katrine. But honestly, Leeza is beautiful and healthy, and seems to be very happy helping these children. She has a lot of courage. More than anyone I know."

Perhaps it was the tone in Amy's voice when she spoke Leeza's name, or maybe it was just a mother's intuition. "Do you love my daughter, Fraulein Amy?"

Amy was completely surprised by the question. She didn't know what to say. "I...Well. I..."

"It's all right if you do," Katrine smiled. "I like you very much, Amy." Katrine took her hand again.

*I had no idea she knew Leeza was...*Amy squeezed Katrine's hand. "Yes I do, Frau von Rauthenau." Then she blushed. "But it remains to be seen if she loves me."

"How could she not love you, Amy. Just look at your beautiful blond hair and your pretty green eyes. Look Hans! Look how her eyes shine."

"Ja, they are beautiful, Fraulein. And the love makes them sparkle." Hans grinned.

---

The next morning Julius stepped off the train with only his violin case. His suit was wrinkled from sleeping on the train, and his face was stubbled with a morning beard. Needless to say, he hadn't packed for an overnight trip. He glanced at his watch. *Good, Herr Meyer should be arriving at the bank just about now.*

Out on Bahnhofstrass Julius caught the tram south to Burkliplatz, on the edge of Zurichsee. The people on the tram were well dressed and seemed to enjoy the ride through the old section of Zurich. The city beautifully contrasted the old with the new. Downtown, the side roads were old cobblestone streets lined with timber framed houses that ran right into the more modern thoroughfare of Bahnhofstrass. There, new department stores, coffeehouses, and banks lined the boulevard. Yet the new blended with the old perfectly. The street was dotted with large planters and huge towering trees which gave the shopping and banking district a feeling of age and continuity.

Zurich was the international banking capital of the world. Anyone could walk into any bank with a suitcase full of cash and anonymously open an account. No one asked any questions, especially after the Nazis came to power. American businessmen, Nazi party leaders, German industrialists, Jewish refugees, it didn't matter. The Swiss were neutral when it came to international politics and anyone with money was grateful to have a safe place to stash their cash. The Swiss certainly didn't mind the sudden increase in business since 1933. A crisp breeze blew in off the lake and fishing boats dotted the horizon. Julius pulled his overcoat closed around his neck and headed across the street to Zurich National Bank.

"Good morning, Herr Meyer," Julius called as he entered the safe-deposit office.

Herr Meyer looked up at Julius' stubbled face. "You didn't pack a razor in your violin case I see."

Julius rubbed the whiskers on his chin and smiled. "My trip took an unexpected detour I'm afraid. Is anyone in the vault?"

"No," Herr Meyer answered. "You can have it all to yourself."

"Danke," Julius grinned.

Herr Meyer took the master keys out of his vest pocket and slipped the proper one into the lock on box 214. After he turned it, he pulled the key out and bowed to Julius with a click of his heels. Then he left him alone in the vault room.

Julius placed his violin case on the table and opened it. He removed his box key and slid it into the second lock. *You would be proud of Leeza, Karl. She is following in your footsteps.*

270

# Chapter Nineteen

# The Englishman

Amy was exhausted by the time she delivered the next five children to Katrine and Hans in Jenbach. They had taken the train all the way this time, through Munich. Amy wasn't sure she could talk her way past the Gestapo agent at the airport so soon after her first trip with five children. He would surely have remembered her. At least on this trip the children were all big enough to carry themselves and their little bags.

"Will you be bringing the last four tomorrow?" Hans asked as he poured Amy a cup of coffee the next morning.

"No. I've got to get back to Vienna and check in at the International News Service office. I'm sure they're going crazy wondering where I am. But I should be back two days after that. I'll send you a wire when I leave Berlin."

Katrine smiled warmly. "Hans spoke with Doctor Feldman in Innsbruck yesterday."

"Ja! He is willing to help. He has connections through a Zionist organization he belongs to. They will help the children immigrate to Palestine. I don't know the details, but the children will be able to stay together. They will be living on something called a 'kibbutz.' I don't know what that is, but he said it will be good for them."

Amy grinned. "A kibbutz is a farm. A cooperative farm. Several families live and work together to increase their security and their chances for successful production. But what about their immigration papers? I thought the British Mandate government was slowing down immigration these days?"

271

"I don't know," Hans shrugged. "Doctor Feldman didn't seem to think it would be a problem. But if it turns out that it is, the children can always stay here with us."

Amy's thoughts turned to the British Mandate in Palestine. *I know that Palestine has filled it's immigration quota every year since Hitler came to power. How in the hell are they going to get these kids into the country. And if they do manage to get them in, what about the Arabs? Things aren't very cozy over there either.* Amy decided she wouldn't mention the Palestinian situation to Hans and Katrine. *They have enough to worry about.*

"Doctor Feldman asked about the children's parents," Katrine commented. "Will they be coming after the children?"

"I don't know," Amy answered. "I don't know how many are still alive. I know some of them are, but Leeza hasn't said if she will be sending them the same way as the children. I'm not sure they have thought that far ahead. Right now, everyone seems to be concentrating on getting the children out."

"And what about Leeza. When will she be coming?" Katrine asked hesitantly.

Amy frowned. "I don't know about that either. I've asked her to leave, but she refuses. As long as she can help I don't think she'll leave."

"This is a good thing she is doing." Hans smiled and wrapped his arm around Katrine's shoulder. "Not only is she as lovely as her mother, she is also very courageous."

"Yes, but her hands were not made to work in a factory. They were made to play the violin," Katrine lamented. "She has such talent. When was the last time she played?"

Amy hung her head. "I don't know, Katrine. I'm not sure she's even had time to think about it."

"She should make the time," Katrine moaned. "Her music brings her such joy. It will help her through the days ahead."

272

Amy smiled softly. "I'll remind her."

Katrine took Amy's hand and gazed into her eyes. "Please tell her that...tell her how very proud of her I am. And how much I love her."

"I will," Amy whispered. "But I'm sure she knows."

"I don't know," Katrine replied. Then she hung her head. "I was not a very good mother to Leeza. I was too lost in my own pain to be there for her. Now..."

"Now, you are there for her. And that's all that matters. You are helping her more than you can imagine," Amy replied. "But I will give her your message anyway. Now I have to get going. There's no rest for the weary."

---

The teletype machines in the INS office were clattering away as Amy entered the building. *Ah, home sweet home*, she thought. *The wheels are grinding, the typewriters are clanking, and the place smells like an ashtray. Nothing ever changes.* Amy felt like she had been away for years.

"There you are!" yelled Jim Newman. "Where the hell have you been, Trevor?"

"I had some things I had to take care of. What's it to you?" Amy grumped, surprised to see Jim Newman.

"Nothin'," Jim shrugged. "Just wondered if you were gonna take this assignment or not." He waved a telegram in her face.

"What's New York want now, a piece on the Winter Music Festival?" Amy scowled. "More human interest stuff?" She was tired and the last thing she wanted was to fight with Jim, or any of the other reporters who had come from Berlin.

"No, it's not human interest stuff," Jim grinned. "But, if you don't want it, I'll take it."

273

Amy eyed him suspiciously and then snatched the telegram from his hand. "Give me that!"

"Take it easy there, Trevor. There's no need to get all bent out of shape about it. I was just offerin' to help ya out on this one."

Amy glared at Jim and then read the telegram. Her eyes grew wide.

"What do ya think of that, Trevor?" Jim teased. "Straight from the old bulldog himself."

"Churchill? Winston Churchill wants to see me?" Amy whistled long and low. "I wonder what's up?"

"I don't know, but whatever it is, I'd be packin' my bags if I were you." There was obvious envy in Jim's voice.

"But why me?" Amy asked herself.

Jim grinned. "Not that it's gonna do him any good with you, Trevor, but he does like the ladies."

Amy scowled. *That's not what I've heard.*

"Maybe he thinks that talkin' to a female reporter would be less noticed than if he was talkin' to a man. You'd be keeping up his reputation as a lady killer."

"Well, whatever he wants, I'm damn well gonna find out," Amy grinned. "If anybody needs me I'll be in London."

In all the excitement about Churchill's telegram Amy had forgotten her promise to Leeza. She was suppose to return to Berlin and take the last four children back to Jenbach. *Okay, just pack up a few things and stop by Berlin on the way to London. Leeza will understand. I'll take the rest of the kids as soon as I get back.*

"London!" Leeza cried. "You can't go to London now! What about the children? They need to get out of Germany now, not next week!"

*Okay, so she doesn't understand*, Amy thought as she watched Leeza pace around the furnace room. "It's my job," she sighed. "I have to go. I can't just tell them what I'm doing here, ya know. Not if you want to keep a lid on this thing." Leeza kept pacing. Amy was frustrated.

"Would you be willing to take the children with you to London?" Albert asked.

Leeza glanced up at Albert and then over to Amy. "Yes, then you could fly straight into Zurich from London, and from there take the train to Jenbach!"

"Now wait a minute!" Amy cried. "I just can't take four kids to Churchill's home in the country and say 'Oh, by the way, I'm illegally transporting Jewish children out of Germany!' He would never be willing to talk to me in front of the children."

"You wouldn't have to take the children with you, Fraulein Amy," Albert remarked. "I know a rabbi in London. I'm sure he would be willing to take the children."

"And what if he's not?"

"They are better off with you in London than they are here with us in Berlin!" Leeza shouted. "But, if it is to much to ask..." Leeza felt bad for trying to manipulate Amy, but she had no choice.

Amy followed Leeza's gaze over to the anxious children. She smiled at them. "So, have any of you ever been to London?"

———————

London was cold and gray, and miserable in January. Umbrellas dripped over the shoulders of people running here and there doing their afternoon shopping. Amy and the children had no umbrellas. By the time they found the synagogue in north London, they were soaked to the bone. Rabbi Moshe had been more than obliging when Amy explained that it was Albert who had sent the children to him. They were old friends it seemed, and he quickly agreed to help.

Amy bid the rabbi and the children farewell and proceeded on to Chartwell, the country estate of Winston Churchill. Since his downfall, Churchill had spent most of his exile tending his garden and supporting himself by writing political commentary. His position on India, Russia, and British rearmament had cost him his seat in parliament. Not to mention that his support for King Edward's relationship with Mrs. Simpson had driven the final political nail in his coffin. Now no one in England wanted to listen to his doomsday cries about Hitler. England had had enough of war, and was holding staunchly to a policy of appeasement.

The butler escorted Amy into Churchill's library. "Miss Amy Trevor to see you, Sir."

Churchill didn't turn around, but continued stoking the roaring fire in the fireplace. Amy stood nervously in the doorway. She could see the billows of cigar smoke rise above the old bulldog's head. He was dressed in a smoking jacket and khaki trousers. "Good day, Miss Trevor," he growled. "I expected to see you two days ago."

Amy stuffed her hands in her pockets and shuffled her feet. "I'm sorry, Mr. Churchill. I didn't receive your telegram until yesterday. I came as fast as I could."

Finally he turned to look at her. "I hear you are in Austria now. Vienna, is it?"

"Yes, Sir."

Churchill eyed Amy. "And how do you like Austria, Miss Trevor?"

"It is very nice," she replied.

Churchill smiled a bitter smile. "Herr Hitler thinks it's nice as well. What do you say to that, Miss Trevor?"

Amy flashed Churchill a wry grin. "The better question is, what do you think of that, Sir?"

Churchill walked away from the huge fireplace and waved his hand toward a comfortable looking wing-back chair. "Have a seat, won't you."

"Thank you," Amy smiled.

"Would you care for some tea, Miss Trevor?"

"Yes, thanks."

"Hobson, we'll have tea now," the old bulldog growled. Then he stared at Amy. He seemed to be scrutinizing her. "You have been writing about flowers and romance, Miss Trevor. Did your editor assign you those stories, or is that what you prefer to write about?"

Amy flushed with embarrassment. "I prefer to write the truth, Mr. Churchill. However, most Americans, like the British, don't want to hear the truth. My editor assigned the stories."

"I thought as much," Churchill growled. "No one cared when Hitler rearmed Germany, and no one cared when he marched into the Rhineland. I can almost guarantee that no one will care if he annexes Austria either. Anything to avoid a war."

A chill ran down Amy's spine. She thought about Julius, and about the Jewish children in Jenbach, and about Austria's gay and Jewish communities.

"Anthony Eden, our foreign minister, is the only one left in His Majesty's government who has any backbone."

"But according to the Rome Protocols," Amy argued, "Italy is committed to Austrian independence. It has vowed to defend Austria, along with France and Britain."

"The Prime Minister," Churchill looked disgusted, "Mr. Neville Chamberlain courts both fascist dictators. Did you know that, Miss Trevor?" Churchill didn't wait for Amy to respond. "Last year he invited the Italian Ambassador,

Count Grandi, to Ten Downing Street, while Nevile Henderson went to Hermann Goering's hunting lodge for the weekend. Yes, Miss Trevor, Chamberlain, and the rest of Whitehall seem hell bent on befriending Mussolini and Hitler while the rest of us can only sit on our hands and watch."

Amy was almost afraid to ask, but she had to. "What about the Rome Protocols?"

"You are, of course, aware of what happened in Spain?" Amy nodded her head. "Obviously Mussolini is in bed with Hitler."

"What about Britain and France?"

"There are those in parliament who feel that Austria is a small sacrifice to make for the cause of peace," Churchill growled. "Many in France feel the same way."

"Then Austria is already lost." Amy whispered.

"It is only a matter of time." Churchill leaned forward in his chair and stared hard at Amy. "When Mr. Henderson was in Herr Goering's lodge he saw a map of Europe. There was no border line between Austria and Germany. Hitler has been planning to annex Austria for a very long time now."

"Is there no hope at all?" Amy groaned.

"We can only hope that Anthony Eden can make his case in parliament. As the foreign minister, his opinion still counts for something. But there are many who oppose him. He and Chamberlain hate each other. Unfortunately, the Prime Minister's opinion carries more weight than Anthony's does. Needless to say Anthony was not invited to Ten Downing Street with the Italian Ambassador. While Chamberlain was making nice with Count Grandi, Anthony was demanding that the piracy in the Mediterranean be stopped immediately. The Italians and the Germans hate Anthony Eden because he has the courage to face them down. This whole business could be stopped at the German border if Anthony were the prime minister. But

Chamberlain has promised peace. My only question is, what will that peace cost? Peace without freedom is worthless, and that's just what Mr. Chamberlain will give us." Churchill puffed on his cigar impatiently. Billows of smoke rose above his head. "The little corporal thumbs his nose at us, and all Chamberlain is willing to do is smile."

Amy was furiously taking notes. "So, you think England should rearm?"

"Absolutely. Along with France and America!" Churchill slammed his fist down on the arm of his chair. "There are those who say Germany is already too strong to defeat. I say that if we don't rearm now, we probably won't have the chance to do it later. By then, we might all be speaking German."

"Lindbergh would like that," Amy whispered under her breath.

"Yes, your Colonel Charles Lindbergh is singing the praises of the German Luftwaffe these days. I read that he and Joseph Kennedy, your American Ambassador to Britain, think that appeasement is the only policy. That the German Luftwaffe is the best air force in the world. Kennedy said, 'No one can beat them.' Well obviously Mr. Kennedy does not remember what His Majesty's Royal Air Corps did to the Germans in the last great war."

Amy was embarrassed and sorry she ever brought up Lindbergh's name. She didn't want to get into the fact that Charles Lindbergh, America's hero, was totally anti-Semitic and probably hated homosexuals as well. *Should I ask him about his opinion on that subject? Naw, it's irrelevant. It would never make it to print.* "Do you think America should get involved in this conflict, Mr. Churchill?"

"I think Hitler's propaganda is working perfectly in America, Miss Trevor. He used the Olympic Games and Colonel Lindbergh's tour to keep America quiet and passive. Have you not read *Mein Kampf*?"

Amy shook her head. "Afraid not. Couldn't bring myself to do it."

Churchill trained his steely eyes on Amy and growled. "You should, Miss Trevor. That is, if you want to understand how Hitler's mind works. It is wise to know your enemy and the only way you can do that is to read what he has written. Let me quote for you. *'The skillful and unremitting use of propaganda can persuade people to believe that Heaven is Hell...For the masses of people, in the primitive simplicity of its heart, more readily falls victim to a big lie than to a small one...'* You see, Miss Trevor, how Hitler used the Olympic Games and Colonel Lindbergh's tour to seduce the world into believing he has peaceful intentions?"

"Has the Prime Minister read *Mein Kampf*?"

"Humph," Churchill grunted. "Anthony suggested he read it and Chamberlain told him to go home and have a lie down."

Amy leaned back in her chair and watched Churchill chew on the stub of his cigar. "Mr. Churchill, why did you ask to see me?"

"Because you needed to know about the map. Someone needs to report it, and frankly, I don't think anyone in Britain is reading these days."

"No, Sir. That's not what I meant," Amy grinned. "Why did you ask to see me and not one of the male reporters."

Churchill coughed on his cigar smoke. "Hmm hmm, well yes, I see your point." Then he took another long drag off the cigar and blew the smoke out slowly, giving himself time to consider his answer. "As you may have heard, Mrs. Trevor. I have somewhat of a reputation with the ladies. Let me assure you that reputation is unwarranted. However, when one is in political exile it is frowned upon if he speaks out against the present Prime Minister. You can't quote me on anything I've said here today. But, I do want you to report what I have told you." Churchill puffed on his cigar and coughed again. "Do you understand what I am trying to say, Miss Trevor?"

Amy shot him a wry grin. "Yes, Mr. Churchill, I think I do. Just in case someone should see us talking, you hoped they would think that we were having an affair. A male reporter wouldn't be able to give you that cover. Is that about it?"

Churchill cleared his throat. "Yes, quite. I'm sorry to use you this way, Miss Trevor, but one can't be too careful these days."

Amy smiled. "Of course. I just wanted to make sure I had my facts straight. It has nothing to do with the fact that I'm a good reporter."

Churchill didn't look embarrassed at all by Amy's obvious slam. "Indeed it does, Miss Trevor. There are a number of female reporters I could have called upon. However, I chose you because you are one of the few who can truly write."

"Yes I can!"

Just then the butler brought in their tea and poured two cups. When he left the room, Amy cleared her throat. "Mr. Churchill, would you mind if I ask you a question, off the record of course?"

Churchill sipped his tea. "You may ask me anything you like, Miss Trevor. My life is an open book."

Amy grinned sheepishly. "You are, of course, aware of Hitler's policy about Jews, but are you aware of his policy on homosexuality?"

"Yes, I know his policy. It disgusts me. Hatred for its own sake is a dangerous thing. Jews, homosexuals, it does not matter. Hatred is like a plague, no one is quite sure where it comes from. Nevertheless it consumes everything in it's path. My fear is that Herr Hitler's irrational hatred is spreading, and not only in his own country."

281

Amy shot Churchill another wry grin. "If you will allow me another question of a more personal nature?"

Churchill nodded his head. "Of course."

"I have heard rumors that in your youth, you...uh, you had several affairs with other young men. Are the rumors true?"

"Not true," Churchill shook his head. Then he grinned. "But I once went to bed with a man to see what it was like. He was a musician by the name of Ivor Novello."

"And what was it like?"

"Musical," Churchill smiled.

---

It was only at this morning's rehearsal that the new concertmaster announced the change in the evening's performance. Chancellor Schuschnigg's secretary had called at the last minute to request a special performance of Respigi's *Pini di Roma*. Julius was happy to oblige. Some Italian dignitary was visiting and the Chancellor wanted to honor him with an Italian score. A concert in Vienna was a mainstay in Austrian diplomacy. While dignitaries were taken on hunting trips in Germany, Schuschnigg hoped to soothe the savage beast with music.

"It could be Count Grandi," Clara giggled.

"It might even be Mussolini, himself," Elsa smiled. "Imagine, playing for him."

"Calm yourself, ladies," Julius exclaimed, with a stomp of his foot. Then he started marching around back stage in an imitation of Mussolini's high stepping soldiers. "I'm sure Mussolini is goose-stepping his troops out of Spain right now. It's probably just the king."

"The king!" Elsa and Clara squealed. "The king! We'll just die if it's the king."

"Now girls, you mustn't die before you tune up. Come on, schnell, schnell," Julius clapped his hands. "We can't keep His Majesty waiting," he quipped.

Clara and Elsa giggled as they ran off to fetch their instruments. Julius' grin faded to a frowned as he watched them scurry away. *So, has the Italian come with good news or bad? Will he say to Chancellor Schuschnigg, "Thank you for the lovely concert, but Italy is going to feed little Austria to Germany, like a mouse to a python," or will he tell Schuschnigg that Italy will stand with Austria? That Italy will honor its agreement to defend Austrian independence.*

Klaus tucked his program into his tuxedo pocket as the house lights dimmed off and on. He had purchased two season tickets at the Musikverein the moment his practice had provided the funds. Tonight, Karl's seat still remained empty. Even though Leeza said that Karl had died in Dachau, Klaus still hoped for a miracle. *One day soon, my love, Leeza will return to the stage, and we will be here to greet her. And she will play for you, Karl. Just for you. She will play her Amati, and it will sound just as sweet as it did on that Christmas morning, there in the Alps. Do you remember, my darling? Can you still hear the music as I do? Remember the music, Karl. Wherever you are tonight, I pray you can still hear the music.*

Moments later the musicians walked out. The audience applauded gleefully as Julius took center stage. The old concertmaster had taken a new position in New York and Julius was asked to take his place. *Look at him, Karl. So dignified and formal. You would be so proud of him. He is really taking this job seriously. If the audience only knew the real Julius.* Klaus chuckled to himself.

Julius bowed to the audience and lifted his Stradivarius to his chin. When he drew back on his bow a clear resounding note filled the auditorium, and the other musicians found their pitch. The concert was off to a great success.

Then suddenly a man in the balcony sprang to his feet and shouted out, "We don't want a Jew on the stage! Get out! Get out! Heil Hitler! Heil to the Third Reich! Austrians are Germans!"

The music stopped abruptly. The audience, along with most of the orchestra members, stared up into the balcony, straining to see who had dared to interrupt the music. Several people in the balcony yelled, "Sit down and shut up!"

Then the man pulled out a revolver and shouted, "Austria is part of the Reich!" He aimed at the stage and the shot rang out. Julius heard the bullet whistle past his ear and hit the floor behind him.

Music stands and instruments went toppling onto the stage as the musicians dove for cover. Women in the audience screamed as they threw their furs over their heads and crouched down in their seats. Several men clambered toward the man in the balcony, but he was able to fire several more rounds before they could wrestled him to the floor. Security guards ran up the stairs toward the balcony, and their chief yelled, "Everyone stay down!"

A woman who was sitting in the front of the auditorium screamed, "Help! Oh my God, someone call a doctor. Help!"

Klaus immediately looked up to the front of the auditorium. Then he glanced toward the balcony. The security guards were just handcuffing the maniac shooter. He sprang from his crouching position and scurried to the woman screaming for help. Her husband was laying in the aisle holding his shoulder. "I am a doctor," Klaus smiled. "Everything is going to be all right. Where were you hit?"

284

The man groaned. "In my arm."

"Help me get him up," Klaus instructed the man's wife. "We need to get his jacket off so I can see the wound."

The man was obviously in pain, but he refused to cry out. "It's just a flesh wound, I'm sure," he grumbled as Klaus gently removed his jacket and tore away the sleeve of his shirt. "I was hit worse during the war, Herr Doctor. I'm sure this is nothing."

"You are probably right, my good man. But as long as I'm here I might as well take a look at it, just to be sure," Klaus winked.

As the security guards started dragging the would-be assassin from the balcony, he screamed out again. "Austrians are Germans! We are of the same blood! How can you allow a Jew to entertain you like that? Listen to the Führer. Cleanse Austria of the Jews. Death to the Jews. Life to Aryans! Death to Jews! Life to Aryans!"

As Klaus wrapped the man's bleeding arm with his torn sleeve, the man shouted up toward the balcony, "I'm an Aryan, you idiot!" Then he looked at Klaus. "Sheesh! Some master race, huh. Hitler's little Nazis can't even tell an Aryan from a stinking Jew."

Klaus frowned. *He's more concerned about being mistaken for a Jew than he is about being shot!* "I don't think he was aiming for you, mein Herr," Klaus tried to smile. "I think Herr Barkowski was his target."

"Well, that explains it!" the man spat. "He's the Jew!"

Klaus synched down the bandage real tight over the man's wound. He winced in pain. "It's a flesh wound, just as you said. You should go to the hospital for stitches, but you will be fine. Let's just hope your doctor isn't Jewish. Some madman might shoot him before he has the chance to stitch you up." Then Klaus slapped the man on the shoulder, and he cried out in pain. "Oh! Sorry old man. I hope that didn't hurt," he grinned.

From the back row of the balcony Heinrich grinned. Johan had done and said just what Heinrich had told him to. *Now we'll see if this makes our Jewish faggot nervous enough to make a mistake. Almost being shot should make him run straight to his friends. He'll lead me right to their nest.*

# Chapter Twenty

## Prayer At Notre Dame

*Paris will always be Paris, at least to the Parisians,* Wilhelm thought as he strolled the Champs Elysees in his double-breasted blue suit. The cafes and sidewalks were teaming with people sipping strong cups of coffee and gazing into store windows. *Look at them. Are they even aware of the outsiders among them? Do they even suspect what their apathy means?* Wilhelm walked with his eyes wide open. He was aware of the refugees among the Parisians. Mostly Jews. Others were political dissidents, criminals, gypsies, gays, and anyone else not fitting the perfect Aryan model of the Reich. The political attitude in the city was "live and let live," but Wilhelm preferred to wear his civilian clothes when he was off duty, and walking around Paris. His German military uniform brought him cold looks and slow service. He enjoyed the freedom he felt when blending in with the crowds. He knew Paris was filled with Gestapo agents, each tailing their own particular mark. He had seen many of their files. And yes, he was quite sure that he too was being watched. But none of that mattered now.

The beauty of Paris did not blind Wilhelm to the agony he saw around him. The glamour of the Champs Elysees did not erase the frightened faces of the refugees. The shadow of the Eiffel Tower did not mask the look of terror in their eyes. The banks of the Seine did not nourish their tortured, half starved bodies. He saw them all. Their tattered rags. Their scuffed suitcases. Their ghostly eyes and blank stares. He was remembering the horrors he had seen in Sachsenhausen. *Wake up Parisians!* he screamed in his head. Then his thoughts turned to Karl. *This is not what*

*I wanted. It's not what Hitler promised. That kind of misery will not restore Germany. You were right all along, Karl. I was such a fool. Pride comes with the freedom to live as we choose, not through degradation and suffering.*

Admiral Canaris had banished Wilhelm to Paris to save his life. He also probably hoped that the distance would give Wilhelm the perspective he needed to clear his thoughts and determine what his motivations really were. The transfer had done just that. Now Wilhelm was able to see the big picture. He understood that Hitler was a madman who was going to destroy Germany in the end. But what could he do about it? It all seemed so far away now that he was in Paris.

Wilhelm stopped in a cafe and ordered a cup of strong black coffee. He watched two young men at the table next to him. Only his eyes would have noticed that the two were lovers. By their accents he could tell that they were German. Berliners probably. But the waiters of the Parisian cafes had stopped asking people where they were from, desperately trying to avoid any discussion of what was happening in Germany. They knew the masses of people flooding into the city were refugees, but took them all in stride as they clung to the illusion of Paris. "Paris will always be Paris," they often remarked to each other.

As Wilhelm watched the two young men he thought of Karl. *We should have come here, you and I. We could have been happy in Paris. Why didn't we come, Karl?* Then he thought about Klaus Gessler and remembered how he found him in Sachsenhausen. Wilhelm's heart ached with longing for Karl. *How could I have saved him and not you, my dear sweet love? How could I have let them take you without so much as a word in your defense? My God, what have I done?*

Wilhelm's haunting grief began to set in. Now that he could see clearly what Karl had tried to tell him, it was too late. Wilhelm sipped his coffee and watched the young lovers. *Enjoy your freedom. Paris is the city of love. Don't forget that. And don't let anyone ever steal that freedom from you. Fight for it! Hold on to it! No matter what the cost! Where I come from the state owns a man's heart. Don't let that happen here.*

Wilhelm looked at his watch and finished the last of his coffee. Leaving the cafe he headed for the subway, clutching the letter in his pocket. His meeting with Ernst von Rath was in a half hour and he didn't want to be late. Ernst von Rath was the third secretary in the German Embassy in Paris. Because of his position he was privy to almost every communiqué that came into Paris. He had given Wilhelm a copy of a letter issued by Nazi Party Headquarters in Berlin. The communiqué gave orders that terrorist actions in Vienna were to be increased by the local Nazis there.

Wilhelm got off the subway at the Hotel de Ville and walked across the beautiful bridge spanning the Seine River. Notre Dame towered on the island in the middle of the river. Its huge towers and flying buttresses were the most prominent feature on the skyline. Wilhelm entered through the huge central arch. Inside the brilliant stained glass rose windows flooded the interior with a rainbow of colors. Rays of sunlight, filtered through hues of red, blue, green, gold, and purple cast streams of flowing color over the faces of the saints and the virgin mother, and finally onto the floor.

Wilhelm crossed himself and walked to the altar where the Virgin Mary held the crucified Christ in her arms. He knelt beside Ernst von Rath and stared up into the eyes of Mary. *I weep for Karl as you weep for him*, Wilhelm thought.

Ernst crossed himself and looked up at the cross looming behind Mary and the crucified Christ. "Admiral Canaris sends word from Berlin," he whispered.

"The Admiral?" Wilhelm whispered back.

289

"Yes. He wants to know if you have learned how to lie yet?"

Suddenly the conversation from over a year ago crashed into Wilhelm's mind. With perfect clarity he recalled every word that had passed between them.

"*Every man must follow his conscious, Admiral.*"

"*And if his conscience should oppose the law?*" the Admiral had asked.

"*The laws change every day.*" Wilhelm had replied.

"*But what of truth?*"

"*Truth. Lies. I don't know anymore. When a man like Karl von Rauthenau is thrown into a place like Dachau, what difference does the truth make? He was a loyal son of Germany.*"

"*Many loyal sons of German have learned to lie, Wilhelm. Have you?*"

"*What must I do to prove myself?*"

"*Tell the Fraulein that her uncle is dead.*"

Wilhelm had asked the Admiral if Karl was really dead and he had responded, "*Sometimes a lie is more real than the truth.*" For Karl's sake, Wilhelm hoped that the lie had become the truth. Life inside a concentration camp was like a living death with no peace. The Admiral had transferred Wilhelm to Paris saying, "*Men who have not learned to lie well don't need to be in Berlin. It is for your own sake that I'm transferring you.*" Wilhelm remembered the ominous words that came next. "*One day I may call upon you to follow your conscience, but not today.*"

"Every day I put on my uniform, I lie. You can tell the Admiral that I have learned to lie very well," Wilhelm whispered.

"If this is the case, then he has told me to instruct you to follow your conscience."

*My conscience.* "It is time for every man to follow his conscience," Wilhelm replied, staring at the Christ as if he were praying.

290

"And you are ready to do that, Wilhelm?" von Rath asked.

Wilhelm's heart raced. His year in exile had prepared him for this day. "The madman must be stopped."

Ernst von Rath smiled hesitantly. "It would seem you are not alone in that thought. Von Fritsch, Blomburg, and the other generals are in agreement. They are ready to move against the Führer and arrest him."

*So, the High Command is finally going to put a stop to Hitler!* Wilhelm wanted to shout for joy. *Karl, if you are still alive, hang on. This insanity will soon be over!*

"They are making plans for his trial as we speak," von Rath whispered.

"What must I do?"

"The generals won't move to arrest the Führer until they know that England and France will stand with them."

"But how are they going to know what the generals are planning?"

"Admiral Canaris wants you to go to Cannes."

"Why Cannes?"

"Because the British Foreign Minister, Anthony Eden, is in Cannes on holiday. Winston Churchill will be joining him there in a few days."

"The Admiral wants me to inform them of the plan?"

"Exactly," von Rath whispered hoarsely.

Wilhelm quickly played the scenario out in his mind. "They will want proof!"

"And they shall have it!"

"How?"

"The S.S. has sent a communiqué to Vienna, to the Nazis in Austria."

"What does it say?" Wilhelm asked impatiently.

"Hitler and Himmler have come up with a plan that they hope will move the Anschluss forward. They are planning to assassinate their own man, Ambassador von Papen."

"But he is a German, and a Nazi! Why would they do that?"

"No one in the party particularly likes von Papen. The S.S. hate him."

"I still don't understand. What will assassinating von Papen prove?"

"They have chosen a Jew to do it," von Rath whispered.

Suddenly everything made sense. If a Jew killed a German Ambassador in Austria, Hitler could justify going in and taking control. He could claim that Germans were not safe in Austria and that they need the protection of the Reich. "My God! When is this going to happen?"

Beads of sweat rose on von Rath's forehead. "Soon!"

"Then I'll leave right away."

"You must go to Cannes, and you must tell Anthony Eden about this plot." Von Rath crossed himself and reached into his breast pocket while doing so. He laid a note on the altar rail. "This is the secret address of the Nazi headquarters in Vienna. Give it to Eden. Tell him about the communiqué. Tell him to go to Vienna, to warn the Austrians." For the first time Ernst von Rath took his eyes away from the cross and looked at Wilhelm. "Wilhelm, you must make them understand! Everything depends on England and France! They must be willing to make a stand. If they won't back the generals, then the generals won't risk themselves in an arrest attempt at this time!"

"I will make them understand, Ernst! I promise," Wilhelm smiled.

Von Rath smiled back, "God go with you." Then he crossed himself again and said, "Wait here for five minutes. We can't afford to be seen leaving together."

Wilhelm nodded and then looked back up at Mary as he slid the note along the rail. He listened as Ernst's footsteps echoed through the cathedral and finally faded as he walked out into the cold sunlight of Paris. "God, please make them understand," he prayed.

292

A few days with Winston Churchill and Anthony Eden in Cannes was just what the doctor ordered for Amy's travel weary aches and pains. After all, she hadn't had a real vacation in years. How could her editor in New York begrudge her a few days in the sun and surf of the French Riviera, especially after she had filed the map story? After enjoying a shrimp cocktail at a seaside cafe, she was ready to return to the hotel for an afternoon nap. When the elevator doors opened on her floor, to her surprise, there stood Captain Wilhelm Schroeder. He was just as surprised to see her there.

"Captain Schroeder! How wonderful to see you again," Amy beamed as she stepped off the elevator.

Wilhelm glanced down the hallway to where Churchill and Eden were standing in their doorway watching him leave. He pulled his shoulders back and replied, "Excuse me, Fraulein, you must have mistaken me for someone else!" Then he stepped into the elevator just as the doors were closing.

Amy stood there in shock, her mouth open and shopping bags dangling at the end of her arms. She glanced at Churchill and then back at the elevator. "Wasn't that Captain Schro...?"

"Why don't you come in, Miss Trevor," Churchill interrupted. "We have some things to discuss."

Amy was confused. She knew the man was Captain Wilhelm Schroeder, but why had he pretended not to know her? She headed for the open door of Anthony Eden's suite, but kept glancing back toward the elevator.

"Here, let me help you with your bags." Churchill took a couple of Amy's shopping bags and closed the door behind her.

293

"Would you care for something to drink, Miss Trevor?" Anthony Eden asked.

Amy's mouth was still hanging open. She glanced at the door and then over at Churchill. "Wasn't that man, who got on the elevator, Captain Wilhelm Schroeder?"

Eden smiled and said, "Scotch?"

Amy frowned. "No, bourbon please. Was he here to see you?" Eden poured the bourbon and took it over to Amy. "What was he doing here?"

Eden walked away without answering. "Winston, drink?"

"Yes, please," Churchill growled.

"Okay, you guys, what's going on?" Amy squirmed. "I know that was Captain Wilhelm Schroeder. I met him in Vienna less than a month ago. We attended a concert together. He is a good friend of my...of a friend of mine. Now I want to know what's going on. What was he doing here? And why did he pretend he didn't know me?"

Eden looked at Churchill and grinned. "She's your contact, old man!"

Churchill took his drink from Eden and lit a cigar. Then he took a seat next to Amy on the couch. "Yes, that was Captain Wilhelm Schroeder," he sighed. "But you were not supposed to see him. And you must not tell anyone that you did. Do you understand, Miss Trevor?"

"Yes, but why?"

"Because he is working on our side, and we can't afford to..."

"Wilhelm's a spy!" Amy shrieked.

Churchill looked at Eden. Eden looked at Churchill. Both shrugged their shoulders and then Eden took the lead. "Miss Trevor, I assure you it's not as mysterious as you might think. Captain Schroeder was simply delivering a message to me. That's all."

294

Churchill jumped in. "However, should anyone become aware that Captain Schroeder delivered the message, his life would be in jeopardy."

Amy took a slug of her bourbon. "Come on fellas. You were the one's who invited me to this party, remember?" Then she leaned forward and asked with a gleam in her eye, "What did the message say? Where did it come from? Who sent it?"

Churchill frowned. "Miss Trevor, I assure you we will..."

"Hey, I'm a reporter. You can't expect me not to ask!" Amy grinned.

Anthony Eden smiled. "Yes, we are quite aware of the fact that you are a reporter, Miss Trevor. However, why don't you give us a few days to follow up on the information Captain Schroeder gave us and then we'll..."

"So! It was information and not just a message!" Amy exclaimed.

Churchill and Eden were growing frustrated. The more they said, the more Amy picked up on. "Let's just say, we have to make a trip to Austria," Eden interjected. "I believe you are heading that way yourself?"

Amy smiled. "So you guys promise I'll get the scoop when the time comes?"

"Agreed," Churchill said with relief. "We'll leave in the morning."

---

That evening Churchill and Eden escorted Amy to the hotel's casino. They were having a marvelous time at the roulette table when Amy spotted Wilhelm watching her from across the room. When their eyes met Wilhelm nodded toward the door. Amy stretched and yawned.

Smiling at Churchill and Eden, she gathered up her chips and said, "Thank you gentlemen for a lovely evening, but you will have to excuse me. It's getting late and I'm very tired. It's been a long day. I think I'll go up to my room and get some sleep. It's going to be another long day tomorrow."

Eden stood. "Good night, Miss Trevor."

Churchill smiled. "Sleep well, my dear."

Amy glanced to where Wilhelm had been standing. He was gone. "Now where the hell did he go," she muttered under her breath.

In the lobby she looked around and saw Wilhelm heading for the main exit. She followed him. He waited for her around the corner. "Shall we go for a walk," he said as he stepped out of the shadows.

"Damn it, Wilhelm! You scared me to death," she gasped.

Together they walked arm in arm to the beach. There, with the waves crashing on the sand, Wilhelm was sure that no one could overhear them. If anyone was watching, they would simply look like lovers taking a moonlight stroll.

"What are you doing here?" he asked sharply.

"What are you doing here?" she fired back.

"That does not concern you!"

"The hell it doesn't!"

"What are you doing with Churchill?" Wilhelm glared.

"I'm a reporter! It's what I do. He's a British dignitary. I'm interested in what he has to say."

"You can't report that you saw me here!" Wilhelm barked.

"I know that! I'm not an idiot!" Amy snapped back.

From a distance they looked as if they were having a lovers spat. At least that's what anyone would have seen, were they watching. They both stood there in the sand and glared at each other. Finally, Amy began to laugh. She put

296

her arm through Wilhelm's and led him down the beach. If anyone was looking, the lovers had obviously made up.

"So, you are a spy?" Amy asked coyly.

Wilhelm laughed. "Is that what Churchill told you?"

"No. He wouldn't tell me anything."

"And I'm sure you pressured him to tell you, didn't you?"

"Of course. After the way you pretended not to know me, I had to ask a lot of questions," Amy grinned. "But they wouldn't tell me anything. Just that I would get the scoop when, and if, the information panned out. So are you going to tell me what the information was, or do I have to drag it out of you?" Amy tickled Wilhelm's sides and he roared with laughter. Someone watching would have thought they were going to fall down in the sand and make love there on the spot.

When she finally stopped tickling him, Wilhelm sighed. "I can't tell you, Fraulein Amy. As much as I would like to, I can't. There are too many lives at stake, and I don't want yours to become one of them. I have too much blood on my hands already."

"What do you mean?"

Wilhelm gazed off over the ocean. "Karl," he whispered.

"Was there anything you could have done?"

Wilhelm leaned down and picked up a stone. He tossed it out over the waves. "It all happened so fast. I wanted to help him, but Admiral Canaris transferred me to Paris. If I had gone back to Germany to help him escape, the Gestapo would have put me in Dachau with Karl, and what good would that have done?"

"Wait a minute," Amy hissed. She eyed Wilhelm suspiciously. "Karl was still alive after you got transferred to Paris? Leeza told me that you were the one that told her Karl was dead." Wilhelm hung his head. Amy took a step back as the realization came to her. "He's alive?"

297

Wilhelm's head jerked up as if she had slapped him in the face. "No!" he cried. "No. I'm sure by now he has…"

"Has what, Wilhelm?" Amy snapped. "You're sure he's dead by now?" Wilhelm began to shake with his own guilt. His tears did little to soften Amy's judgment.

"You don't understand," he whispered in agony.

"You damned right I don't understand. Leeza told me you were in love with him. And you just let him die in Dachau? How could you? Explain it to me!" she demanded.

Wilhelm fell to his knees and wept bitter tears of apology. "I'm so sorry! My God, if I could undo what I have done, I would. But I can't. Karl is dead, and I can't change it! I will have to live with the guilt for the rest of my life!"

Amy wanted to scream at him, to condemn him to hell. *How could he have betrayed Leeza like that. She needed his help and he just walked away from her.*

"In the beginning, I truly believed that Karl would be ransomed. I thought Hitler just wanted to teach him a lesson. I never thought it would go as far as it did. When they ordered me to tell Leeza her uncle was dead, I realized that they were not going to ransom him. That was the same day Admiral Canaris transferred me to Paris. I knew it was too late to help Karl. They were seeing to that. So I agreed to tell Leeza that Karl was dead. I thought it was the merciful thing to do. I didn't want her to live with the agony of knowing where he was. I knew it was too late for me to help Karl, but if Leeza believed he was dead already, at least she could grieve and then get on with her life. I only did what I thought was best for her!"

Amy slowly began to absorb what Wilhelm was telling her. His thoughts weren't on saving his own skin. They were on saving Leeza the agony of not knowing. Wilhelm had been right. Leeza had grieved and then gotten on with her life, such as it was. Now it was Wilhelm who lived with the pain of knowing.

Calmly and compassionately, Amy asked, "Do you know for sure if Karl is alive or dead?"

Wilhelm shook his head. "No. If I put in a request for information on him, the Gestapo would know instantly and my position would be jeopardized."

"Jeopardized!" Amy exploded again. "Jeopardized. Leeza's uncle could be rotting away in Dachau and you are worried about your position!"

"You don't understand!" Wilhelm shouted. "There is more at stake here than you realize!"

The image of Wilhelm stepping quickly onto the elevator without acknowledging her ran through Amy's mind. *What does he mean, "There's more at stake?"* Amy looked him hard in the eyes.

"You must think me a coward, Fraulein Amy," Wilhelm sniffed. "But I assure you I am not. I would give my life gladly if I thought Karl were still alive and it would do any good. But I can't risk an inquiry. Especially now. It has been two years since Karl was taken. Most don't last six months in the concentration camps. Believe me, Fraulein Amy, if Karl knew what I was doing in Cannes, he wouldn't want me to risk everything for him. I am doing exactly what he would want."

"And what is that?" Amy barked.

"I can't tell you!"

"Yes, you can. I am not asking as a reporter. I'm asking as someone who loves Leeza. I'm asking for her. She hates you, you know. She hates you for not helping Karl. Maybe if she understood the reasons you are doing what you are doing, she might be able to forgive you."

Suddenly the weight of the guilt bent Wilhelm's knees to the sand. Tears welled up in his eyes again. *Leeza!* his mind screamed. *I love you so much. You are like a daughter to me.* Then Wilhelm's mind flashed to an image

299

of a gun barrel being placed against his head. He saw his body fall on the bloody pavement. *I may never get the chance to tell her again. If things go wrong...This may be my only chance. If I don't tell now, she may never know what I tried to do today. I don't want to die without her forgiveness!*

Then Wilhelm stared up at Amy. "If I tell you, you must give me your word that you will tell Leeza, and only Leeza. And you must wait until after what is going to happen, happens."

Amy knelt in the sand in front of Wilhelm. She saw the agony he was going through. "I promise."

"Thousands of lives may depend on your promise, Fraulein. Leeza's included."

# Chapter Twenty-One

## Forgotten Date

As much as Amy wanted to head straight back to Berlin, she couldn't. She had given her word that she would wait for Wilhelm's hand to be played out. By the time she arrived in Vienna, Julius was already on stage at the Musikverein. She wanted to talk to him, to warn him that actions against the Jews were being stepped up in Austria, and that he should leave the country. But that would have to wait until after the evening's concert. She decided to check in at the INS office.

"Hey, Trevor!" shouted Jim as Amy walked in the office. "Nice piece about Goering's hunting lodge and the map. Too bad you couldn't quote Churchill as the source."

Amy smiled and waved. *Why's he being so nice?* "Thanks!"

"So how was the old bulldog?" Jim asked.

"Charming!"

"Charming?" Jim's face scrunched up. "Huh! Who would have thought he was charming?" Amy just grinned. "So what'd he tell ya?"

"You obviously read the article. He told me about the map," Amy chirped.

Jim grinned and lit up a cigarette. He blew smoke in her face. "Yeah, but he must have had more to say. You've been gone for almost a week."

Amy just smiled. "So, what's been going on around here since I've been gone?"

Marshall Turner stepped up. "Things are really quite tense in Vienna, Miss Trevor. Did you hear about the shooting at the Musikverein?"

Amy's jaw dropped open. "What happened? Was anyone hurt?"

"It was a bloody mess," Marshall answered. "Some Nazi chap started screaming about the Jews in Austria and then he just blasted away! A man in the audience was wounded slightly."

"What about the musicians?" Amy gasped.

"Naw," Jim interjected. "They're all fine. The Nazi couldn't shoot straight."

"Thank God! Did they get the guy?"

"Yeah, they hauled him off to jail." Amy quickly shoved her bags under a desk in the corner and made a beeline for the door. "Where ya goin' now, Trevor?" Jim called out.

"To the Musikverein!"

"You're too late, that's old news!" Jim shouted over the teletype.

Amy stopped dead in her tracks. She spun around. *This could be it!* "What do you mean?"

"We just received word," Marshall jumped in, "that two German generals have been relieved of command!"

Amy's heart sank. "Who? Which ones?"

"Blomburg and von Fritsch. They were from the old Prussian Army," Marshall frowned.

"Why were they relieved?"

Jim laughed. "Seems old Blomburg married a prostitute after the death of his first wife, and it turns out that von Fritsch is a faggot!"

"A what?" Amy exclaimed.

"You know, Trevor. A homosexual. Seems they found out he's been being blackmailed for years. It makes sense. He's been a bachelor all his life."

"So have you, ol' chap!" Marshall laughed.

Jim scowled at him. "That don't mean nothin'." He turned to look at the teletype.

302

Amy's mind was racing a mile a minute. *Blomburg and von Fritsch! Oh God no! Those were the generals Wilhelm said were going to arrest Hitler! Without them the plan is down the tubes.* "When did this happen?"

Marshall answered, "Today, I'm afraid."

Just then they all heard sirens screaming down the street and everyone grabbed their pens and note pads and ran for the door. The reporters followed the police cars to a run down building on Taborstrass, across the river. By the time they got there the police were already hauling out most of the leaders of the underground Nazi party. Boxes of files were also being carried out, and the news reporters were furiously taking notes as their photographers were snapping pictures. The next morning Chancellor Schuschnigg held a press conference in the Chancellery building. Amy gathered with the other reporters to hear what the police had found the night before.

"Last evening, police officers, acting on a reliable tip, raided a warehouse on Taborstrass. There they found the headquarters of the underground Nazi party in Austria and arrested its leaders. These men are suspected of carrying out the recent bombings around our fair city. Also, the police uncovered a plot to assassinate Ambassador von Papen, of the German Embassy. Investigators are still sorting through the evidence gathered in last night's raid, and all suspects are being held without bond."

The Chancellor turned and left the conference room without answering any of the reporters as they shouted out question. Amy didn't bother. She headed straight for the Musikverein after the press conference. *I've got to talk to Julius. He has to leave Vienna. With von Fritsch and Blomburg out of the picture, no one can arrest Hitler now. But at least they stopped the assassination. That might buy us some time.*

Amy knew the Musikverein's front doors would be locked at this time of day so she headed down the alley to the stage door. She knocked and the stage manager opened it.

"I would like to speak with Julius Barkowski, bitte."

"He is practicing right now, Fraulein. You'll have to call another time." The stage manager was used to young women wanting to see Julius. It was his job to make sure that they didn't get in. He started to close the door.

"Bitte, Sir!" Amy called as she stuck her food in the door. "It is a matter of the utmost urgency. I must speak with Herr Barkowski right away!" The stage manager looked weary. "Bitte, it's a matter of life and death."

Something in her voice must have convinced him and he opened the door wider. Amy stepped inside. "You will wait here. I'll tell Herr Barkowski you are here. Your name, bitte?"

"Amy Trevor."

The stage manager turned on his heels and marched off down a hall. A few minutes later he returned and said, "Herr Barkowski will see you in practice room six. It's straight down that hall, to the right."

"Danke," Amy smiled. Moments later she entered the little practice room where Julius was just putting the Stradivarius back in its case.

He smiled and threw open his arms. "Ah, Fraulein Amy. So good it is to see you! Are we still playing the part of the nanny?" he said with a wink.

Amy smiled hesitantly. "For now, my charges are all tucked safely away. But that's not why I've come to see you!"

"No doubt you have heard about my brush with death," he grinned. "But as you can see, I am quite well. There's no need for you to worry."

"Oh yes there is!" Amy gasped.

"No there isn't. Look, I am fine." Julius spun around laughing.

Amy wasn't laughing. "Stop it! I need you to listen to me!"

Julius frowned in surprise. When he took the time to look at the expression on her face he could clearly see that she was terribly worried about something. "Leeza? Has something happened to Leeza?"

"No! Leeza is fine! As far as I know. But you won't be if you don't get out of here!"

Julius had a puzzled look on his face. "Why? Is the Musikverein going to blow up or something?"

"No. It's because you are a Jew. The Nazis are coming!"

Julius put his hands on his hips. "Nazis, Smatzis. This is Austria, my dear. Nazis are not welcome here, or haven't you heard?"

"I have heard a lot more than you have. I can assure you of that! Hitler is planning on taking over Austria, so the generals were going to arrest him, but he relieved them of command and now they can't arrest him, and the police raided the Nazi headquarters last night and they stopped the assassination plot. But you've still got to get out of Austria!"

Amy was rambling so fast that Julius couldn't make sense out of anything she was saying. "Darling, have a seat and slow down. I don't understand." Amy took a seat at the table in the little practice room. "There, that's better. Now what's this all about? What raid? What assassination plot?"

Amy took a minute to catch her breath and collect her thoughts. It took her a while to explain everything that had happened over the last few days, but Julius finally understood the chain of events and why she was so upset.

"I'm heading back to Berlin tonight. I've got to tell Leeza what's been going on. Perhaps I can convince her to

305

leave Germany now. Maybe she would be willing to go to
Paris or Prague."

"If she goes anywhere, she'll come here, to Vienna,"
Julius grinned.

Amy threw her hands in the air. "Haven't you been
listening to a thing I've been telling you?"

"Yes, Darling. I heard every word. And now I'm
telling you. Austria is perfectly safe. Schuschnigg will
never surrender Vienna. Don't worry your pretty head
about me, I'm fine. Vienna is my home. I simply can't
leave and return to Poland. I'm not a star there!"

Amy stood up in a huff. "Well if you stay here you
won't be a star much longer! You'll be dead!" Then she
spun on her heels and stormed out of the practice room.

Julius tapped his violin case. "There are a million other
reasons I must stay, Fraulein Amy. A million."

---

Before she caught the afternoon flight to Berlin, Amy
had called Leeza to ask her to meet her at the Adlon Hotel
for dinner. Leeza had agreed. During the flight Amy
considered how much she should tell her. *I'll tell her that I
met Wilhelm in Cannes and why we were both there. But I
don't think I should tell her about Karl. After all, he
probably is dead by now, and there's no use putting her
through all that again. Especially when no one knows for
sure. But then what if he is alive?* After giving it further
thought, she decide to stick with her original idea. *Even if
he's alive, there's nothing she can do to get him out.*

---

Leeza sat in her office beaming. The thought of having
dinner alone with Amy excited her. *What should I wear? I*

306

*want to look just right. Not too assuming, and yet not too unreachable. Hum, maybe my blue skirt and jacket. No, too business like. Perhaps the blue skirt with my cable-knit sweater. No, too school girl.* Leeza ran her fingers though her hair. *Greasy! What time is it? Three o'clock. Just enough time to go home and bathe. Perhaps a blouse with the skirt!*

Leeza took a long hot bath when she got home. She washed her thick dark hair with lavender scented soap. *So sweet and warm. I hope she likes lavender. Of course she likes lavender. Who doesn't?*

After she bathed, Leeza brushed out her hair until it was dry. Tonight she would let it hang loose about her shoulders rather than tying it back as she normally did. Then she spritzed her shoulders with perfume and smiled. *A touch of lipstick and that should do it. Now, what to wear?* She pulled the tailored blue skirt out of the closet and laid it across the bed. Then she looked intently at the blouses that hung in the closet. *Red? No, too provocative. Cream? Yes, perhaps the cream blouse.* She took it out and laid it next to the blue skirt. *Yes, that's just right. Now, what about...? Lets see. Cream silk bra, or perhaps a teddy.* Leeza looked down at her bare breasts. *Teddy, I think. Cream slip. Silk stockings, and of course, the pearls. They are so elegant.* She held them to her neck and looked in the mirror. *Too virginal. No pearls.*

Leeza took her time dressings, letting her imagination take her into a night of long awaited passion and romance. She dreamt that each item she was putting on, Amy would later remove very slowly. Then the phone rang. It startled her out of her fantasy. *Maybe her plane was early!* Leeza's heart skipped a beat with anticipation.

"Hello," she said as she picked up the receiver, fully expecting to hear Amy's voice.

"Leeza!" The voice on the other end of the line sounded panicked.

"Yes, this is Leeza."

"Leeza, it's Anneliese!"

"Anneliese, what's wrong?" Leeza could tell that she was crying.

"It's Margo! She was attacked! They've beat her!"

Leeza sank to the bed. "Where are you?"

Anneliese was near hysterics. "We're at the hospital! Leeza, it's bad. Her arm is broken and she has a concussion. I need you."

"I'll be right there," Leeza cried. "Just hang on!"

Leeza grabbed her overcoat and ran out the door, completely forgetting her date with Amy.

---

By the time Leeza got to the hospital Margo had been taken upstairs to a private room. Anneliese sat by her bedside and stroked her hand as she slept. Leeza crept into the darkened room quietly and stood behind Anneliese. She reached out and stroked Anneliese's hair. Then she whispered, "How is she doing?"

Anneliese looked up with tears in her eyes. "She has not regained consciousness yet." Anneliese let her head fall back against Leeza's stomach. "We won't know anything until she does."

Leeza continued stroking her hair and softly asked, "How did this happen?" Anneliese stood up and motioned toward the door. Stepping out into the brightly lit corridor, Leeza immediately saw the bruises on Anneliese's face. "Oh Anneliese!" she cried as she reached out to touch her face.

Anneliese collapsed into Leeza's arms and sobbed. "We were just walking in the Kunfurstendamn, reminiscing about the old days when things were so different. We were just walking and talking when these men, boys really, started following us. They were Hitler youth, from the university probably. They started harassing us, and then…" Anneliese couldn't go on.

Leeza just held her and let her cry. Suddenly, flashes of Leeza's own rape came crashing into her mind. She could see the Nazi bastard all over her, hitting and hurting. She pulled Anneliese even closer. "They didn't…"

"No," Anneliese whispered. "But I'm sure that's what they were after. It was me they wanted initially, but Margo fought them off. Then when they realized she was a woman, they really went berserk. One of them knocked me down and before I knew it they were all on top of her. They punched her to the ground and then they started kicking her. When I started screaming they finally ran away. Ever since the General von Fritsch incident yesterday, the Nazis have been ranting and raving about homosexuals again. There were three beatings in the Kunfurstendamn last night. I should have known better than to go walking there. This is all my fault."

Leeza gently pulled Anneliese's face back and looked down into her eyes. She was remembering the night she had shot the Nazi guard. The night the White Rose had rescued the black triangled women. "No it's not. This is not your fault. You did not cause this to happen. It was the Nazis. This is their fault, all of it!" Then she pulled Anneliese's face back to her shoulder and they cried together. "I'm so sorry, Anneliese. I'm so, so sorry this happened," she whispered.

Anneliese finally sniffed and pulled herself together. "We should probably go back in now. I don't want Margo to wake up in a strange place alone."

Leeza nodded and dabbed her handkerchief to her eyes. "Yes. She shouldn't be alone." Together they walked back into Margo's room and sat by her bedside. Occasionally, Anneliese would stand and lean over Margo and whisper to her. "Margo, it's time to wake up. Open your eyes sleepy head." Eventually, around eleven o'clock, Margo finally opened her eyes and looked at Anneliese in confusion. "Where am I?" she whispered hoarsely.

Anneliese lifted Margo's head and placed a glass of water to her lips. Margo sipped the water and immediately fell back to sleep. Leeza looked at Anneliese. She was smiling. "Is this a good thing?"

"Yes," Anneliese whispered as tears ran down her face. "The fact that she came to consciousness at all means that she's not in a coma. But the fact that she was conscious enough to know that she wasn't in her own bed, well it means her mind is working. That's a really good sign. The pain is what drove her back to sleep. When she wakes up next time she will be more aware. And she will probably have one hell of a head ache," Anneliese smiled.

"And that's good?" Leeza questioned.

Anneliese nodded her head as she wiped the tears from her face. "It's better than feeling nothing at all," she whispered.

Leeza nodded in understanding. "Then she is going to be all right?"

"Yes, I think so. I have seen a lot of beatings lately. Those who wake up early after their attacks usually make a full recovery." Anneliese pushed the hair back out of her face and winced.

"Hey," Leeza whispered urgingly, "You need to get some rest. Have you had those bruises looked at?"

Anneliese nodded and yawned. "They're superficial."

Leeza came around the bed and held Anneliese by the shoulders. "Not to me, they're not. Look at you, you're exhausted. You need to get some sleep."

Anneliese shook her head. "I'm all right. I'll just get a blanket at the nurses station and curl up in this chair. But you should go. I know you have to be at the factory early in the morning. You need your rest." For the first time Anneliese noticed what Leeza was wearing and how she

310

looked. She knit her eyebrows. "Why are you so dressed up?"

Leeza looked down at her skirt and blouse. "Oh my God," she cried. "I forgot about Amy. Oh Anneliese, I have to go. I had a date with Amy at the Adlon Hotel for dinner. That was four hours ago. Damn it! I was so worried about Margo that I forgot to leave Amy a message. I'm sorry I have to leave you like this, but..."

"Go," Anneliese smiled as she push Leeza out the door. "We'll be just fine. Don't worry, go!"

Leeza smiled and hugged Anneliese. "I'll be back as soon as I can. But I've got to go and apologize in person."

Anneliese scolded Leeza teasingly. "You've got better things to do tonight than sit around a hospital. I have seen the way you look when you talk about her. Go on! Go to her for heaven's sake."

"Am I that obvious?" Leeza grinned.

"Yes! Everyone knows that you're in love with the American, now go! We're going to be just fine without you. Hurry up!"

Leeza hesitated one last time. "Are you sure?"

Anneliese pointed her finger down the hall toward the elevator. "Go!"

Leeza turned and started running down the corridor. She called over her shoulder, "She's probably gone to bed already."

Anneliese laughed and ran after her. When they reached the elevator Anneliese giggled and hugged Leeza. "When she gets a look at you, believe me, she'll invite you to bed with her."

Leeza blushed as the elevator doors opened. "Oh Anneliese, it's too soon for that!"

"It's never too soon," Anneliese grinned. Then she shoved Leeza through the doors. "Have a good time!"

Amy sat at the bar in the Adlon Hotel nursing her beer. She glanced at her watch. *Ten-thirty. Face it, Trevor, she's obviously not coming. No one could be this late. The least she could have done was call and make up some excuse.* Amy chugged the rest of her beer. *What a fool I was. All she wanted was an American passport, and you knew it. Trevor, you idiot, you should have listened to your gut and not your heart.*

"You want another one?" the bartender asked.

"Yeah, Mike, but this time I'll have a bourbon. Straight up."

Mike set her shot on the bar and she toyed with it, swirling the glass round and round. *You knew it would happen this way. Why in the hell didn't you listen?* Suddenly the bile of her anger rose up in her throat and she swallowed it down with the bourbon. *What the hell are you waiting for, Trevor. Get out of here and never look back. The only reason she kissed you was so you'd take the children. She's probably with that Eddi woman right now.* The more Amy thought about it the madder she got. *Just pack your bags and hit the road. She doesn't want you. She never did. You're the idiot for not listening to your gut in the first place.*

"Hey, Mike!"

"Yeah, Amy. Ya need another?"

"No! When does the last train for Munich leave?"

Mike shrugged his shoulders. "I don't know. Maybe midnight."

Amy slammed a hundred Deutsche Marks on the bar. "This should cover my tab, Mike. Keep the change!"

"You can catch me next time, Amy," Mike smiled.

"There isn't going to be a next time, Mike. I'm out of here! See ya stateside."

Mike took the bill and waved. "Good Luck."

Leeza screeched to a halt in front of the Adlon Hotel lobby. The doorman opened the heavy glass door for her when he saw her running toward him. "Danke," she called as she ran past him to the dining room. Her heart sank when she saw that it was closed. Anxiously she looked toward the bar. From the dining room she could see Mike, the bartender, standing behind the bar and knew that at least it was still open. Anxiously, she scanned the empty tables, and her heart sank.

"Can I help you, Fraulein?" Mike asked.

"No, danke," Leeza groaned. "I was supposed to meet a friend here tonight, but I am very late."

"You talkin' about Amy?" Mike asked casually.

Leeza's heart leapt in her chest. "Yes. Amy Trevor, the journalist!"

"Yeah, she was here. But she left about an hour ago."

"Do you know what room she is staying in, bitte?"

"Sure. She was stayin' in room 311, her usual."

"Danke," Leeza exclaimed as she ran for the stairs.

"I don't think she's there!" Mike called after her, but it was to late. Leeza hadn't heard him in her excitement.

Halfway up the first flight of stairs Leeza reached down and slipped off her heels. Then she bolted up the stairs even faster. By the time she hit the third floor and ran down to room 311 she was out of breath, but still excited. She knocked on the door and anxiously waited for Amy to open it. She knocked again. Still Amy didn't answer. Then Leeza stepped back and looked closer at the number on the door. *"She's in room 311, her usual." That's what the bartender had said. "Room 311."* Leeza knocked again. *She's either not here or she's not answering the door.* Leeza decided to check with the desk clerk.

313

"I'm sorry, Fraulein," he said. "Miss Trevor checked out almost an hour ago."

"Checked out!" Leeza exclaimed. "Why would she check out at this time of night?"

The desk clerk shrugged his shoulders. "She did not say, Fraulein."

Leeza hung her head. Her heart sank into her stomach. "I see. Did she leave a forwarding address?"

"No, Fraulein, I'm afraid she didn't," the desk clerk sighed.

"Danke," Leeza whispered sadly as she turned to leave.

Suddenly, she heard the bartender call to her. "Fraulein! Fraulein! You didn't hear me when I called to you. Amy left. She's on her way to Munich, I think."

"Munich?"

"Yeah! She asked me about the midnight train to Munich. I don't know why, but she seemed like she was in a big hurry. Said she wasn't coming back. Paid off her bar tab and everything."

Tears welled up in Leeza's eyes. "Danke."

Mike glanced at his watch. "I got a quarter to twelve. If ya hurry, ya might still be able to catch her at the station!"

Leeza glanced at her watch and then made a dash for the door. "Danke," she called over her shoulder. "You have been most helpful."

Leeza skidded the Mercedes to a stop at the passenger loading dock in front of the train station. Slamming the door, she called to a porter. "The midnight train to Munich, bitte, what platform?"

The porter looked bewildered. "Platform three, Fraulein, but it is just about to leave."

"Danke," Leeza called as she raced past him.

Once inside, she ran toward the doors leading to the train platforms. She hadn't thought about getting through the inspection station. She didn't even have her passport with her. "Halt," the big hulk behind the desk shouted.

314

"I'm just trying to see a friend before she leaves, mein Herr. I'm not boarding a train!" she quickly tried to explain.

"I'm afraid I can't let you through, Fraulein, until I have seen your papers," barked the Gestapo agent.

Frustrated, Leeza anxiously looked through the huge glass doors. She could see the Munich train just beginning to pull out. It's whistle blew as a billowing puff of smoke rose from its stack. *I'm too late*, she thought. *Even if I could get through the Gestapo, I'd never make it onto the train.* "Never mind, Agent…"

"Colburg."

"Agent Colburg," Leeza sighed, wanting to cry. "I have missed my friend. She is gone."

# Chapter Twenty-Two

## False Accusation

It had been two weeks since Dieter von Kleist's body had been found tied, with his throat cut. The police investigators were no closer to solving the case than they were the morning the body was found. Heinrich watched as the detectives entered von Kleist's apartment to search it again. They were obviously frustrated by the clues he had left, and couldn't figure out how the pieces of the puzzle fit together.

Heinrich overheard the chief inspector talking to another investigator as they entered the building. "If we could find the matching cufflink," he said, "we would find the murderer. I have no doubt about that."

"What about the silk scarf?" the other investigator asked. "I know I have seen one like it somewhere, but I just can't remember where."

Heinrich crushed out his cigarette with the toe of his boot. He, himself, had narrowly escaped the raid at the Nazi Party headquarters and was frustrated at how slow things were moving. Most of his associates were in jail, pending the outcome of their trials. Heinrich felt responsible for getting them out quickly. *I suppose I am going to have to lead these fools where I want them to go*, he thought.

That afternoon he grinned as he sealed the two large envelopes and dropped them in the post box on the corner. One was addressed to police headquarters and the other was addressed to the local newspaper. *These should lead them right to him.*

The knock on Julius' door came early in the morning. He had barely gone to bed when the police inspectors arrived, insisting on searching his apartment. "What is this about?" Julius yawned as he tied his bath robe.

"You are the man in this photograph?" the chief inspector asked as he held up Julius' promotional photograph for the orchestra.

Julius rubbed the sleep from his eyes and looked at the photo. "Yes, obviously it is me. There are hundreds of these up all around the city. What about it?"

"Can you produce the scarf you are wearing in the photograph?" the other investigator asked.

"Yes," Julius yawned. "Do you gentlemen mind if I make some tea?"

"Go right ahead."

Julius walked into the kitchen and filled the kettle with water. The chief investigator watched as he lit the stove. "Would you gentlemen care for a cup?"

"Danke," the chief replied. "Now about this scarf, may we see it, bitte?"

Julius walked into the bedroom and rummaged through his closet. The inspectors followed him. "Is this what you are looking for?" Julius yawned as he pulled the scarf from its hanger.

The inspectors looked at each other in surprise. "This is the scarf in the photograph?"

"Yes, or maybe this one," Julius pulled another from the closet. "Or maybe this one, or this one, or this one. It's hard to say which one exactly it is. They are all the same. The Musikverein supplies them to all the members of the orchestra." Julius rubbed his head and yawned again as the tea kettle started to whistle. "Excuse me, bitte. I'll make our tea." Julius trudged to the kitchen and pulled three cups and saucers from the cupboard. "Now gentlemen, are you going to tell me what this is all about? Is there something I should be concerned over?" He handed the inspectors their tea and motioned for them to take a seat at the kitchen table.

The chief stirred his tea and eyed Julius suspiciously. "Did you know Dieter von Kleist, Herr Barkowski?"

Julius hung his head and sighed. "Yes. I knew Dieter. Terrible thing, his death. What a nightmare. Who could have done such a thing?"

"That's what we are trying to determine, Herr Barkowski. Do you see the cufflinks in the photograph?" the inspector said as he slid the picture across the table.

"Yes," Julius frowned, finally realizing that he was under suspicion for Dieter's murder.

"May we see them, bitte?" The inspector smiled warmly.

"Why?"

"Because we found one at the murder scene that looks just like those, Herr Barkowski. We also found a scarf that looks just like that one. Only ours had blood on it."

"I can assure you, gentlemen, I did not murder Dieter von Kleist, if that's what you are implying!" Julius snapped.

"May we see your cufflinks, Herr Barkowski?"

Julius sipped his tea calmly. "Are you aware that every man in the orchestra owns a pair of those cufflinks? Like the scarves, the Musikverein gives them to the musicians."

"No, Herr Barkowski, we were not aware of that fact. Now, may we please see your cufflinks?"

Julius smiled and walked to the bedroom. When he returned, he carried a small box and casually handed it to the chief inspector. He opened it and frowned. "I see there are two here."

Julius sat down. "As I told you, gentlemen, I did not kill Dieter von Kleist." He took a sip of his tea.

"We have just one more question, Herr Barkowski," the inspector grinned.

Julius shrugged his shoulders. "I have nothing to hide. Ask your question."

318

"What was the nature of your relationship with Herr von Kleist?"

Julius leaned back, crossed his legs, and stared at the inspector. "We were friends."

"We were told that you were quite close."

Julius nodded his head. "We were friends."

"What kind of friends?" the inspector asked with a wry grin.

"What are you implying, Inspector?" Julius asked calmly.

"We were told that you often visited Cafe Savoy together, and that you usually left together."

Julius cleared his throat and took a sip of tea. "That is true."

The inspector sat back and grinned. "So you and Herr von Kleist were lovers?"

Julius smiled. "We were friends."

"I asked if you were lovers. The Cafe Savoy is a known homosexual establishment."

"Have you been to the Cafe Savoy, Inspector?"

"No I have not!" the inspector barked, growing impatient with his game of cat and mouse.

"Then how do you know it is a homosexual establishment?" Julius shrugged.

"I have been to the Cafe Savoy, Herr Barkowski," the other investigator answered. "That is how we learned that you were seen leaving with Herr von Kleist on the night he was murdered."

"Gentlemen," Julius sighed. "I am very tired. You know that I work at night, and that I must get my rest. I did not kill Dieter von Kleist. Yes, we frequented the Cafe Savoy together, and yes we often left together. However, on some occasions we each left with different friends. On other occasions we left together in a group of friends. On a few occasions I left alone. I can only say that Dieter was my friend, and I miss him. I am saddened by his death, and

319

I hope very much that you catch his killer. But as you can see, I have both of my cufflinks, and obviously I have many scarves. Now, if there is nothing further, you must excuse me. I have to get some sleep before tonight's concert. We will be performing Mozart if you care to attend."

The investigators knew they didn't have enough evidence to hold Julius for the murder, but they said, "You will stay in Vienna, bitte, in case we should have any further questions for you, Herr Barkowski."

Julius yawned again. "Of course, of course. I perform every night at the Musikverein. Where else would I go?"

"Good day to you, then." Both inspectors tipped their hats and left.

Julius stood behind the door, listening to their footsteps as they echoed down the stairwell. Then he ran to the window and watched as they got in their car and drove away. Running into the bedroom, he pulled open his top dresser drawer. There in the corner were three little boxes like the one he had shown the police. Hesitantly, he opened the first one. There were two cufflinks inside. Slowly, he opened the next box. It also had two. Then he opened the last box. It contained only one. Julius sank to the floor. *Someone is trying to frame me for Dieter's murder.*

That morning Julius' orchestra photograph was on the front page of the Vienna newspaper. The headline read: *"Musikverein's Jewish Concertmaster Questioned In Murder Case!"*

---

The evening's performance had not gone well for the orchestra. Obviously the audience had read the morning headline and believed the innuendo. Even though the musicians had played their hearts out in support of Julius, and he had performed his solo superbly, the audience had

320

responded with only meager applause. This evening there was no standing ovation, no cheers, and no feeling of satisfaction for the musicians.

Immediately after the concert, Julius apologized to the orchestra back stage. "I can assure you that this is a false accusation. However, Vienna has evidently judged me guilty of this crime before all the facts are in. Nevertheless I have an obligation to you, my friends, and fellow musicians, to step down from the leadership of the orchestra until this sordid affair is resolved." Julius stood tall, pulled his shoulders back and clicked his heels together. "I profoundly apologize to you for this unfortunate incident." Then he gave his respected colleagues a slight bow and turned to leave the building. Thomas, Marcus, Clara, Herman, Elsa, and Albert looked at each other with concern. They knew Julius had nothing to do with the murder of Dieter von Kleist, but they could not do anything to prove his innocence. Sadly, they had to accept Vienna's judgment for now, but personally they were all outraged that one of their own had been the target of such a vicious accusation.

Julius stuffed his hands in his pockets and hung his head as he walked out of the Musikverein. Walking through the back alleys of Vienna he felt angry and hurt, frustrated and vengeful, and didn't want to see anyone he knew. *Who is framing me for this murder?* he wondered. *As soon as the police figure out that the Musikverein gave us several pairs of cufflinks, just like the silk scarves, they'll be back. Of course it's all circumstantial evidence, but still.* Suddenly Julius noticed the sound of footsteps coming up behind him. *Run!* his mind screamed. But it was too late. The last thing he felt was the searing pain of a knife in his lower back.

Heinrich wasn't satisfied with a relatively easy kill. He wanted to inflict much more pain on Julius. "I've been watching you, Jew!" he hissed. He was angry about the raid on his headquarters and wanted Julius to pay the price. He let his steel toed boot crash into Julius' ribs, and heard the muffled crack. The sound of breaking ribs only fueled his rage. "I have waited a long time for this, Jew! Don't you die on me before we have had our fun!"

Then Heinrich kicked Julius in the head. Blood oozed through his hair. "I saw you with your lover, von Kleist." Another kick to the head. "I was the one who retrieved the little package of passports you lost." Another blow to the ribs. "I enjoyed my time with von Kleist!" Heinrich brought his boot crashing down on Julius' hand. It shattered. "I fucked him good before I sliced his throat!" Julius' mouth filled with blood as another kick broke his jaw. "Oh, you are no fun, Jew. You died too quickly." Heinrich fingered the ring in his pocket and grinned. "When the police find Herr von Kleist's ring in your pocket, they will have their final piece of evidence. Too bad you won't live long enough to be tried." Heinrich bent down and placed von Kleist's ring in Julius' pocket. "Still, the Führer will be able to use your miserable case as evidence. He will be pleased that he doesn't have to wait for a trial."

---

The telephone on Leeza's night stand rang, pulling her from a sad dream about Amy. She fumbled for the lamp switch and picked up her clock. *Three o'clock! Who is calling at three o'clock in the morning?* Suddenly her mind was clear and alert. *Margo! It's Anneliese! Something is wrong with Margo!*

She quickly picked up the receiver. "Anneliese?"

Leeza could hear raspy breathing on the other end. "Leeza," the voice moaned.

"Who is this?" she asked in confusion.

"Julius," the voice whispered.

"Julius?"

"Leeza," Julius wheezed and then coughed.

Leeza heard him cry out after the cough. "Julius!" she shouted. "Julius, my God, what is wrong?" He didn't answer right away. Leeza could hear the rasp in his breath. "Julius!" she cried again.

"Leeza," he finally moaned. "Listen...to...me! Not much time. You have to listen...The Stradivarius...practice room six...Karl's documents...in the case...two clicks upward."

Leeza was listening intently, but his voice began to drift. "Julius!" she screamed. "Where are you?" She listened carefully for a response.

Finally it came. "Basement...Hotel Zohrer..." Then the line went dead.

Leeza looked at the receiver and then clicked the carriage a few times. "Hello? Julius? Hello!" she cried. But is was no use. He wasn't there. *My God, I have to do something.* Leeza sprang from her bed and threw on her robe. She began pacing back and forth beside the bed. *The Gestapo will never let me leave the country. How can I get to him?* Her mind raced. *Klaus! Yes, Klaus.* Leeza dove for the telephone. She clicked the receiver carriage again. "Operator, yes! I want to place a long distance call to Vienna, to Doctor Klaus Gessler. Yes I have the number."

Leeza waited while the call was put through. Finally the telephone rang at the other end. It rang several times before Klaus picked up. "Hello," he mumbled.

"Klaus, it's Leeza!" she exclaimed. "I'm calling about Julius. He needs your help." Leeza quickly explain about Julius' call and what he had said. "I don't know what's happened, but he sounds like he's dying. Please go to him, Klaus. I think he's in real trouble."

"Of course, Leeza. I'll go right away."

Klaus crept through the seedier part of Vienna, a section he was unfamiliar with. *The Zohrer Hotel, it's got to be around here somewhere.* Klaus kept walking and searching the names on the buildings. *There, on the corner! Zohrer Hotel.* He quickly ducked into the alley behind the hotel. *Let's see. The basement entrance should be around here somewhere.*

It was very dark in the alley so Klaus took his steps carefully, running his hand along the back wall. *There! A doorway.* He lit a match. Suddenly the doorway to the basement illuminated for an instant before the match blew out. Carefully, he made his way down the steps and opened the door. Stepping inside, he locked the door behind him. *Julius, this had better not be a practical joke. I could be arrested for this.* Klaus reached into his pocket for another match. The moment it flared Klaus saw Julius laying on the floor by the laundry desk. He had obviously made his call to Leeza from that desk.

Klaus ran to him and rolled him over. "My God, Julius! What happened?" he whispered. "Can you hear me? It's Klaus!" Julius moaned but did not come to consciousness. The match began to burn Klaus' fingers. He struck another and quickly examined Julius. He moaned again. "Julius, it's Klaus. I'm here! I'll get you to the hospital!"

Julius didn't know if he was dreaming or if he was conscious, but he gurgled, "No hospital."

"Julius, you'll die if I don't get you to the hospital!"

"No!" he rasped. Through his coughs, Julius managed to communicate what would happen if Klaus took him to the hospital.

"I understand! But we can't stay here. I'll take you to my place. After lighting several matches, Klaus called for a taxi to pick them up in front of the hotel. Then he took several clean towels from the maid's cart and tried to clean Julius up as much as possible. He stuffed one in Julius' pants to stop the bleeding from the knife wound in his back. Then he picked Julius up and carried him through the alley and around to the front of the building. When the taxi pulled up, Klaus dumped him in the back seat and joined the driver in the front.

The cab driver looked over the back seat at Julius and said, "What happened to him?"

"Jealous husband," Klaus mumbled. "Now drive!"

"Where to, mein Herr?"

Klaus thought better of the idea of taking Julius to his apartment. *I won't have the equipment I need. I need to get him to the office.* "Linke Wienzeile 42, and hurry, bitte."

---

During the long hours before sun up Klaus did as much as he could for Julius in his little clinic above Cafe Savoy. He stitched up the knife wound in Julius' back and prayed it hadn't pierced the kidney. Then he wrapped Julius' ribs tightly and hoped that none had punctured his lungs. Next he proceeded to shave Julius' scalp and stitch up the laceration above his temple. Then there was the matter of setting his jaw. Several of Julius' side teeth were broken, so Klaus removed them before he set the jaw and wired it shut.

"What do I do about his hand?" Klaus mumbled to himself. "It needs surgery again, but I can't operate on him here. And besides, the anesthetic could kill him. I'll just have to do the best I can without opening him up." Klaus began manipulating the small bones of Julius' right hand.

When the sun finally rose around seven-thirty Klaus had bandaged Julius' hand and washed the remaining blood from his face and body. Then he carried him into his private office and laid him on the couch, covering him with several blankets. The telephone rang. *It's probably Leeza.*

325

"Hello," Klaus sighed as he placed the receiver to his ear.

"Klaus?"

"Yes."

"It's Leeza. Did you find Julius?" she asked anxiously.

"Yes."

"Is he all right?"

"No, Leeza. I'm afraid he's in pretty bad shape."

"But he's going to be all right, isn't he?"

Klaus hesitated. "Leeza...I don't know. He has a knife wound in his back. His hand is broken again. He jaw is broken, along with several of his ribs. The bones are the least of my worry. He wouldn't let me take him to a hospital so I brought him here to the clinic. But I don't know if the knife wound hit his kidney, or if the ribs have punctured his lungs. The way he sounds, I'm sure that one of them did."

"Why wouldn't he let you take him to the hospital?" Leeza cried.

Again, Klaus hesitated on how much he should tell her. "Leeza, much has happened in the past couple of week. Have you read any of the news from Vienna?"

"No. Why? What has happened?"

"Two weeks ago, Herr Dieter von Kleist was murdered. This morning's paper reported that the police have questioned Julius about the murder. Apparently his is a suspect."

"That is insane!" Leeza barked. "Julius wouldn't hurt a fly. It's preposterous."

"All the same, I can understand why he didn't want to go to the hospital. Apparently this attack on his life proves that he is not safe. The city is pretty upset right now."

"But he's going to be all right with you, isn't he Klaus?"

"I don't know, Leeza. I'm doing everything I can. We'll just have to wait and see. I am monitoring his temperature and his breathing. I can't give him anything for the pain until he wakes up, or it might kill him." Klaus waited for Leeza to respond. She didn't. He heard her crying in the background.

When she finally spoke, she asked. "Did he say any more about Uncle Karl?"

"No. He was unconscious most of the time. What about Karl? I don't understand."

"I don't know," Leeza cried. "I could barely understand him when he called. Something about his violin, and practice room six, and about Uncle Karl's documents."

"What's practice room six?" Klaus asked.

"It's in the Musikverein. Julius practically owns practice room six. They're sound proof rooms backstage where the musicians practice. I think he was trying to tell me that his violin was in practice room six. He said something about Uncle Karl's documents, and then he talked about the case. And there was something else, but I don't remember."

"Hum, it doesn't make any sense," Klaus whispered.

"I know. Julius never goes anywhere without the Stradivarius. He wouldn't just leave it in the practice room. It's too valuable."

"Well, he didn't have it with him when I found him."

"None of this makes any sense," Leeza cried in frustration. "If I could only be there! If I could talk to him."

"I'm afraid he won't be talking for a while. I had to wire his jaw closed. But tell me again what he said about Karl."

Leeza sighed. "I don't know. Just something about Karl's documents."

"What documents could he be referring to?"

"I don't know. I can't imagine."

Klaus ran his hand over his head. "Well, I don't have any idea either. I guess we'll just have to wait and see when he wakes up."

"He'll be sick if he's lost the Stradivarius," Leeza groaned.

"He'll be lucky if he doesn't loose his life," Klaus replied flatly.

"Call me when he regains consciousness?"

"Of course. You know I will."

"Danke, Klaus. For everything"

---

Amy paced back and forth with yesterday's paper. *What evidence do they have? Where is he? The police are fools if they think Julius Barkowski killed von Kleist. He's too...too...Well he just couldn't do it, that's all.*

Amy had been at the concert the evening before. As soon as she saw the morning paper she tried to call Julius but he wasn't home. She had gone to look for him at the Musikverein, but he wasn't there either. Finally, she decided to purchase a ticket to the concert. The box office said there were plenty of tickets available. He had played brilliantly, but the audience hadn't responded to him. Amy could tell that most believed the accusations in the paper and were telling Julius so by their sparse applause. She saw the pained look in his eyes as he took his final bow. She had felt sorry for him and wanted to let him know that she didn't believe the news report. But he had disappeared before she could get to him.

*Leeza might know where he would go. I should call her.* "What, are you nuts, Trevor?" Amy said to herself. *But you're a reporter. This is news. It's your job to follow up on every lead you can.* "Yeah, but she isn't going to tell you anything. She made her point perfectly clear a few nights ago." *This isn't personal. It has nothing to do with your relationship.* "What relationship. We haven't got a relationship!" *She kissed you, didn't she?* "She just wanted the use of an American passport, that's all." *But the passport doesn't have anything to do with Julius. She loves him. They're practically siblings.* "They are best friends." *Then she should know what's going on with him, and that he's disappeared.* "Okay, I'll call."

A few minutes later Amy heard Leeza's voice on the other end of the line. "Hello."

*God, her voice is beautiful.* "Hello. Leeza?"

"Yes."

"This is…"

"Amy!" Leeza cried. "Thank God you called! Are you in Vienna?"

"Yes," Amy answered matter-of-factly, trying not to sound thrilled at hearing her gentle voice. "I was calling to talk to you about Julius."

"Julius?"

"Yes. I was wondering if you had heard the news about him?"

Leeza could tell by her voice that Amy was trying to be very business like. *You had better make this good, Leeza.* "Amy, I'm so glad you called. Yes, I know about Julius, but first I want to apologize for the other night."

Amy cut Leeza off before she could give her excuse. "That's okay, I had to leave anyway. Lots of news to report, ya know. Now, about Julius."

"Amy," Leeza whispered. "I'm so sorry. It was Margo. I got a call at the last minute, while I was getting dressed for our date. She was attacked in the Kunfurstendamn. Anneliese called from the hospital. I ran out without thinking. I went to the Adlon later, but you had already left. The bartender told me you were taking the midnight train to Munich, so I drove to the station hoping to catch you, but

329

the Gestapo wouldn't let me through to the platform. I watched your train pull out. I'm so sorry."

Amy's heart sank. "You were getting dressed for our date?"

"Yes," she whispered.

Amy cleared her throat. "Gee, you didn't have to get all dressed up just to have dinner with me."

"I wanted to."

*You idiot! You should have listened to your heart and not your head!* Amy cleared her throat again. "I, uh...I...We'll have to plan it again."

"I would like that very much."

"Yeah, me too. Hum, hum. How is Margo?"

"She is doing much better. Anneliese says she'll be able to go home in a day or two."

"That's great."

"Yes."

There was an awkward silence on the line. "Ah, anyway. The reason I called was to ask you if you might know where I could find Julius?"

"Julius? Have you seen him?" Leeza asked coyly.

"I saw him last night at the Musikverein. Listen, Leeza, have you read any news about Julius?"

*She knows something.* "Yes. I read the ridiculous accusations in the Vienna paper."

"Good, at least I don't have to give you that piece of bad news. But no one has seen him since last night. I was wondering if you knew where he hangs out?"

Leeza hesitated. "Amy, I need you to do something for me."

*Oh great. Here we go again.* "What is it?" she asked calmly.

"I know where Julius is, but I need you to go the Musikverein first."

"Why?"

330

"I need you to get into practice room six, alone. Julius might have left his violin there. I need you to pick it up if it is there, and take it to Doctor Klaus Gessler's office, above the Cafe Savoy."

"Why would he leave his fiddle in a practice room?"

"Amy," Leeza sighed.

*God I love it when she says my name.*

"Julius was attacked last night."

"What?"

"He is with Doctor Klaus Gessler, above Cafe Savoy." Leeza's voice cracked. "Klaus isn't sure Julius is going to live."

Amy heard Leeza break down and cry. "God I wish I were there with you. I'll get on the next plane."

"No!" Leeza exclaimed. "I need you to go to the Musikverein for me. See if his violin is there. Please!"

"Okay," Amy tried to calm her. "I'll go, but I don't understand. His violin should be safe at the Musikverein, shouldn't it?"

Leeza got a grip on herself. She sniffed. "Julius called me last night. I could barely understand what he was saying. I think he was near death," her voice broke. Amy waited while she took a minute and pulled herself together. "Julius said something about Uncle Karl's documents. I don't know what he was talking about, but he was insistent about his violin being at the Musikverein."

"Can you tell me exactly what he said?" Amy asked gently.

Leeza sniffed. "He said something like, 'Stradivarius - practice room six - Karl's documents - in the case."

"Is that all he said?"

"Yes," Leeza sighed and sniffed again. "There was something else. I can't remember. Something about two clicks. I don't know what that could mean."

"If he thought he was dying, it's probably something he thinks is pretty important," Amy answered.

331

"Yes, that's what I thought also. But I have been up all night thinking about it and I just don't understand. I know the Stradivarius is important to him." Leeza laughed a sad little laugh. "He once joked about leaving it to me in his will."

"That might be what he was talking about. Maybe his will is in the violin case," Amy suggested. "Maybe he thought he was going to die and wanted you to know where his will was."

"I don't think so," Leeza's voice broke again. "Why would he have mentioned my uncle?"

Amy ran her fingers through her hair as she paced beside her bed. "I don't know. It doesn't make any sense. I'll tell you what. I'll go over to the Musikverein tonight. I'll sneak back to the practice room and check it out. If the violin is there, I'll get it."

Leeza cried even harder. "Thank you, Amy. I will never be able to repay you."

Amy bounced her toe against the night stand. "Ah, don't worry about it. It's nothing. I'll take the violin to Doctor Gessler and then I'll come see you. How about that?"

Leeza stopped crying. "I'll be waiting for you. Come to my house."

"You got a deal!"

332

# Chapter Twenty-Three

## The Stradivarius Secret

The concert was underway by the time Amy took her seat in the Musikverein auditorium. The orchestra was well into Mozart's *Eine kleine Nachtmusik Allegro*. The lively and sweet melody filled the auditorium with resounding emotion. Tonight they played for Julius alone. They had canceled the previously scheduled performance of Bach's *Brandenburg Concertos* as a sign of protest to German aggression, and refused to play any German compositions until the Nazis in Austria were tried and convicted, and Hitler stopped threatening the Anschluss.

After all, Vienna was Mozart's city. He was completely Austrian. It was in Vienna that he had his greatest success and appreciation. Even though Mozart had begun his career in Salzburg, he felt constrained by his employer, the archbishop. He was invited to freelance in Vienna, where he gave piano lessons to the children of the nobility and wrote some of his greatest works. Most Viennese felt about Hitler the way Mozart felt about the archbishop.

By canceling their performance of Bach, the orchestra members were reminding Vienna that Austria would always be Austria, and not Germany, as Hitler wished it was. The audience was overwhelmed with the performance. The musicians played as they had never played before. The music was passionate, stirring, and filled with emotion as the orchestra synchronously moved from one piece to another without missing a note.

Amy sat in awe, watching the bows of the violinists and cellists dash back and forth over the strings of the instruments. She imagined Leeza sitting in the first violinists chair. *This is her home. This is where she should*

333

*be. She must be so very talented to have played with this orchestra. God I would give anything to hear her play tonight. I would give anything if she were here instead of in Berlin.*

Amy looked down at the program. The orchestra had just begun the tenth piece, *Violin Concerto, K 216: Allegro.* It was the next to the last piece to be performed. She decided it was time to make her move. The concert would end with *Serenade, K375: Menuetto.* By that time she hoped be waiting at the backstage door in the alley.

Amy heard the thunderous applause from the audience as the orchestra finished the last number. It seemed to go on forever. *Standing ovation,* she thought as she shivered in the shadow of the building. Finally, musicians started filtering out through the back door and Amy slipped in. Remembering the way to practice room six, she slid down the hall unnoticed by the remaining musicians who were standing around backstage congratulating themselves. She had her press pass handy just in case someone stopped her. But no one did.

Practice room six was pretty bare. Just a table, two chairs and a music stand. Amy looked under the table and chairs. No violin. She looked around the room slowly, not wanting to miss anything. Still no violin. Her heart sank. *What now? Should I ask someone if they picked it up for Julius?*

Frustrated, and just about to leave, she noticed a small pile of dust on the floor. *Huh, where did that come from? The rest of the room is spotless.* She glanced around again to see if she could find the source of the dust. Directly above it there was a ventilation duct. Amy looked down at the pile of dust on the floor and then back up the wall to the grate covering the duct. *You don't suppose he...* She quickly slid a chair next to the wall and climbed up. Pulling the grate away from the wall, a similar pile of dust fell on top of the one already on the floor. Amy stood on her tip-toes and peered in. There in the darkness she saw the violin case. She slid it out and replaced the grate. Then she climbed down and laid the case on the table.

Nervously, she open the lid. A white silk scarf covered the violin and she pulled it away, revealing the Stradivarius. *It's beautiful*, she thought. *Such a delicate thing. Rich, luxurious luster.* She gently picked up the instrument and peered into the case. *Nothing.* Then she opened the little box in the neck of the case. *Just resin.* In the lid were two bows. *There's nothing here except the violin. No documents. No will. Nothing.* She slid her fingers over the velvet interior. She didn't feel anything under the lining. *Nothing at all.*

Feeling like she had been led on a wild goose chase, Amy replaced the Stradivarius in its case and closed the lid. *Now what?* "Just take it and get the hell out of here, that's what!" she whispered to herself, forgetting she was in a soundproof room. She cracked the door and looked out. No one was in the hall. She tucked the Stradivarius under her coat and slithered down the hall, toward the stage door. A few of the musicians were still standing around talking about the evening's concert. Staying in the shadows along the wall, she slipped by them and out the into the cold night air.

---

"Doctor Gessler!" Amy had knocked on the clinic door several times, but Klaus didn't answer. *He's afraid.* She banged on the door again. "Doctor Gessler, it's Amy Trevor. I'm a friend of Leeza's. She asked me to bring you something!" Still there was no answer. Amy knocked again. "Doctor Gessler, I have the Stradivarius! Please, let me in."

A second later the clinic door cracked open and Klaus peeked out. Amy smiled. She raised Julius' violin case so Klaus could see it. "I spoke with Leeza this afternoon. She told me where to find it, and that I should bring it here to you."

"What was your name again, Fraulein?" Klaus asked hesitantly.

"Amy. Amy Trevor!"

"And you are Leeza's friend?"

"Yes," Amy smiled.

"And where did you get the violin?"

"At the Musikverein."

"Where in the Musi…"

"Practice room six," Amy insisted. "Bitte, please let me in. It's freezing out here."

Klaus opened the door cautiously and took a look around. Satisfied that no one was watching, he opened it wider and let Amy in.

"Danke," she smiled.

Klaus eyed her suspiciously. "Where was Leeza when you spoke with her?"

"She was in Berlin," Amy replied as she took off her overcoat. "I called her from my hotel. The Sacher Hotel. You can call her to verify it if you like."

"You are not German or Austrian?"

"No. I'm just plain ol' American," Amy smiled, trying to relieve Klaus of his suspicion. "I'm a newspaper reporter. You know, a journalist. I was assigned to Germany, but I was transferred to Vienna a couple of weeks ago."

"And how do you know Leeza?" Klaus was still not satisfied.

"I asked her to dance at the St. Valentine's Day Drag Ball, geesh, almost five years ago now."

Klaus frowned. "She has never mentioned you before."

Amy blushed. "Well, I'm only now getting to know her. We've kinda taken different paths over the last few years, but that seems to be changing. How is Julius?"

"Tell me more about Leeza, bitte. If you can," Klaus asked suspiciously.

Amy raised her eyebrows. "Well, lets see. Um...She has gorgeous dark hair that falls to about here." Amy pointed to her mid-back. "She has luscious blue eyes that shine like sapphires. She plays the violin, but I confess I haven't heard her play much. She's almost as tall as I am. About five-six. She's stubborn! Boy, is she stubborn," Amy grinned. "And..." Amy knew she was giving a pretty general description, "and she's a...vir...virtuous person."

Klaus began to smile. "That's just as I would have described her."

Amy smiled, too. "So, how's Julius?"

Klaus frowned again. "Not good. He hasn't regained consciousness. But at least he's still breathing." He glanced down at the violin case. "I see you retrieved the Stradivarius?"

"Yeah, it was in practice room six, just where Leeza told me it would be. He hid it in the ventilation duct. I almost missed it."

"Have you looked inside?"

Amy scrunched up her face. "Yes."

"And?"

She looked Klaus straight in the eye and shrugged her shoulders. "Nothing."

Klaus looked confused. "Nothing?"

"I was disappointed too," Amy sighed. "Leeza told me there were documents inside. Something to do with her uncle."

Klaus took a deep breath. "Yes, she told me the same thing. Are you sure there's nothing inside?"

"Look for yourself."

Klaus picked up the case and laid it on the table. He went through the same process Amy had. "I can't believe there's nothing here. Julius believed he was dying. He thought he was using his last breath to tell Leeza about the case. There's got to be something we're missing."

"I don't know," Amy shrugged. "As you can see, there's nothing there. Just the Stradivarius. I know Leeza's going to be disappointed when I tell her tomorrow."

"You going to Berlin?"

"Yes. She's pretty upset about Julius. I don't think she should be alone. Are you sure he hasn't said anything else?"

"No. He's been unconscious the whole time."

"Can I see him?"

"Yes, you can see him. But you will not recognize him."

"Is it that bad?"

"Yes. It is bad. He is lucky he has lived this long."

Klaus led Amy to his private office. There on the couch lay Julius. Amy could hardly believe her eyes. Julius' face was swollen to the size of a basketball, and his eyes, nose, and mouth were all black and blue. His noble features were indistinguishable. His right hand, also bandaged and swollen, lay across his stomach. Amy gasped. She hadn't imagined he could look so bad. *Is this the same man who just a few days ago held a baby in that hand?*

She slowly walked over to Julius and knelt on the floor beside him. A tuft of dark hair stuck out from underneath his bandaged forehead. She gently brushed it away from his face. Then she whispered, "Julius. Julius, it's Amy. I brought your violin. Leeza told me where to find it. Julius. Leeza sends her love."

Julius' breathing changed. Amy could see his eyes begin to move underneath their swollen lids. "Julius," she whispered again. Then she glanced back at Klaus. "Doctor Gessler, look." Klaus bolted to Amy's side. "Julius," she

338

whispered, almost singing. "Wake up." Julius' eyes fluttered.

Klaus said, "Excuse me, Fraulein Amy." She moved back and Klaus placed his stethoscope to Julius' chest. He listened carefully. Julius' right lung was making a rasping sound. Klaus frowned. "Julius. Julius can you hear me?" Julius' eyes fluttered open slightly. "Julius, it's Klaus Gessler. You are safe. We are in my office above the Cafe Savoy. You are safe. Don't worry."

Julius blinked his eyes uncomprehendingly. Then he tried to say something.

"Don't try to talk, Julius. Your jaw was broken. I had to wire it shut."

Julius blinked again but didn't move. He moaned.

"Do you understand what I just told you? If you do, blink your eyes."

Julius closed his eyes.

Klaus looked at Amy. "He responded to you. Maybe you can try to explain."

Amy nodded and knelt down. "Julius," she whispered. "I want you to open your eyes." Julius' eyes fluttered again and then opened. "I want you to listen carefully." Amy paused to give him time to adjust to the light. Julius moved his eyes and looked directly at her. She smiled warmly. "You are in Doctor Gessler's office. If you understand me, I want you to blink your eyes once for yes and twice for no. Is your name Julius?"

Julius blinked once. Amy smiled brightly and glanced at Klaus.

He smiled and said, "Test that."

Amy looked back at Julius. "Is your name Harry?"

Julius blinked twice.

She smiled and said, "Good, you do understand. You are safe. You are here in Doctor Gessler's office. He's going to explain what is going on, okay?"

Julius blinked once.

339

Klaus knelt down so Julius could see him. "Julius, I don't want you to try and talk or move your mouth. Your jaw was broken. I had to wire it shut. Do you understand?"

Julius blinked once.

"You also have a nasty knife wound in your lower back. Do you feel any pain there?"

Julius tried to shake his head, but the pain stopped him.

"Use your eyes, Julius," Klaus instructed. "Do you feel any pain in your lower back?"

Julius blinked twice.

"Are you sure?" Julius blinked once and then twice. Klaus looked up at Amy. "What does that mean?"

She smiled, "Yes and no, Doctor. I think he's trying to say that yes, he feels the pain, but it's not bad."

They both looked down at Julius. He blinked once.

"Oh! Yes, I see. That's very good. If there is not a tremendous amount of pain, that means it is just a flesh wound. The knife did not puncture your kidney. Now, you have several broken ribs. I want you to take a deep breath while I listen to your lungs with my stethoscope. Do you understand?"

Julius blinked once.

"Here we go then. Take as deep of a breath as you can."

Julius moaned as his chest began to rise.

"Stop," Klaus directed. Tears spilled out of Julius' swollen eyes. "I know that hurt, but the good news is that your left lung is clear." Klaus smiled tenderly. "The bad news is that we have to check your right lung. I need you to take another deep breath while I listen to it."

Julius blinked twice.

"I'm sorry, Julius, but you must. I have to know if the rib punctured your lung or not."

Julius blinked twice again. Klaus looked up at Amy and shrugged.

340

She knelt down and began talking to Julius. "I talked to Leeza this afternoon. She was the one who told Doctor Gessler how to find you. You know she is beside herself with worry. She would want you to do this."

Julius closed his eyes for a moment and then blinked once.

Klaus put the stethoscope to the right side of Julius' chest. "Take a deep breath now." Tears rolled out of his eyes as his chest rose again. He moaned. "Stop," Klaus said. Julius closed his eyes and more tears squeezed out. "I could hear fluid," Klaus whispered, "but I don't think the lung is punctured. It's probably very bruised."

Julius rolled his eyes.

"No, no!" Klaus cried. "That's a very good thing. If your lung was punctured, I'd have to operate. As it is, the fluid should dissipate on its own."

Amy smiled and gently stroked Julius' forehead. "Leeza is going to be very happy when I tell her the good news."

Julius' eyes darted back and forth.

"What is it?" Amy whispered.

Julius squinted his eyes in frustration. Then his eyes flew open and he began trying to hum Mozart.

Amy recognized it. It was a piece she had heard at the concert. "*Nachmusik*," she cried. Then she looked puzzled. "I don't understand."

Julius raised his bow hand and started to make like he was playing the violin and felt the pain in his hand. He stared at the bandage and knit his eyebrows together.

Amy took the bandaged hand in hers and whispered, "It is broken too."

Julius heard Klaus say, "But I have set it. Don't worry. It will heal."

Julius' eyebrows relaxed. Then he slowly raised his hand again and pretended to play.

341

"Oh!" Amy cried. "I see. Yes, I brought your Stradivarius. Leeza told me where it was. I brought it."

Julius blinked once.

"You want to see it?"

Julius blinked again.

Amy ran into the reception room to retrieve the violin. When she returned she held it out for him to see. "Here it is, safe and sound."

With his good hand, Julius motioned for her to bring it to him. Amy laid it gently on his stomach. With his good hand he fumbled with the lock but he couldn't manage it. He closed his eyes in frustration.

Amy asked softly, "Do you want me to open it, Julius?"

Julius blinked once.

Amy pushed down on the locks and the case opened. She lifted the lid and raised the Stradivarius out. "See! It's safe. No harm," she smiled.

Julius blinked twice. Amy looked confused. Julius blinked twice again.

"What do you mean? See! It's fine." She held the Stradivarius closer so he could see it clearly.

Julius reached up and took the violin from Amy's hand and then laid it on the back of the couch. Struggling not to move too much, he closed the lid of the case and flipped the locks down. Then he motioned with two fingers. He pointed them at his own eyes, indicating that he wanted Amy to watch closely. He felt for the locks again, and turned their casings counter clockwise. Then he motioned for her to put her finger on the second lock. Carefully, he pushed upward, twice, on his lock. Nothing happened. He motioned for Amy to do the same as he repeated the movement. When she did, the top of the case seemed to lift ever so slightly. Amy was astonished. Julius lifted the lid and there, in a false top, were several passports and a file of documents.

Amy smiled wryly at Julius. "You sly devil."

342

Julius' eyes smiled back and then he passed out.

"Julius!" she cried.

Klaus stepped up to her and put his hand on her shoulder. "It's all right, Fraulein Amy. I'm surprised he stayed awake as long as he did. It took every ounce of strength he had to show us this."

They both stared down into the false top of the violin case in awe. "My God, would you look at all this!" Amy exclaimed.

"Yes," Klaus whispered. "It seems our friend here is some kind of smuggler."

Amy shook her head. "Jewish underground is more like it." She reached for one of the passports and opened it. "Polish." She took out another one. "Austrian."

Klaus opened one. "It's French," he whispered in awe.

They took the violin case into the outer office and examined all the passports. There were American, Czech, Polish, Italian, Swiss, French, English, and Austrian. They were all blank, just waiting for new names and photographs to be filled in. There were thirty-five in all. In the bottom of the false lid was a small velvet bag. Klaus opened it and spilled it's contents onto the table. Several rubies, diamonds, and emeralds, along with some gold coins and several thousand in bills of Austrian and German currency spilled out. Amy and Klaus were speechless. Then their eyes fell on the file that Klaus had set aside.

"Do you want to open it, or should I?" Amy asked. They both feared what the file might contain.

Klaus hung his head and sighed. "No. I will look at it." Slowly he slid the file toward him and turned the cover. Inside he saw a photograph of Karl von Rauthenau. Tears instantly filled his eyes. "It's Karl's Gestapo file."

Amy was hesitant to ask. "What does it say?"

Klaus picked up the photo and turned away from the file. He couldn't bare to read what information the file might contain. If Karl was really dead the file would

343

contain that final determination, and if he was alive, it meant that he had lived too long in hell.

"You can read it," Klaus whispered. "I can't bear to know the truth." Amy quickly picked up the file and read Karl's Gestapo biography.

*Name:*        *Karl von Rauthenau*
*Prisoner number:*    *7761*
*Charge:*       *Political Dissident*
*DOB:*        *9 October, 1881*
*Occupation:*     *Steel Industrialist*
*Sentence:*      *Dachau Concentration Camp*
*Length of Sentence:*   *Unspecified*
*Date of Incarceration:*  *30 October, 1936*
*Date of Release:*
*Date of Death:*

Amy read through the brief description of Karl's supposed crimes and the surveillance notes taken by the Gestapo. Captain Wilhelm Schroeder's name was mentioned, as was Doctor Klaus Gessler's. The bio also gave the amount of money that was missing from Karl's accounts. The Gestapo suspected that he had a Swiss bank account, but they were unable to locate the account number. Karl had denied he had a Swiss account, and refused to answer most other questions during the Gestapo's interrogation.

Amy closed the file. She looked at Klaus and smiled sadly. "There is no date of release or death," she whispered softly.

Klaus heaved a sob and then covered his face with his hands. Eventually, he raised his head and looked at Amy. "I am truly grateful he is alive, but I know what he is living with. The agony he must be going through."

Amy got up and knelt in front of Klaus. She took his hands in hers and brushed the tears from his face. "As long as he is alive, there is hope," she whispered. "Dr. Gessler, we have to keep on hoping."

Klaus fell on Amy's shoulder and began sobbing again. "We have to get him out of there," he moaned. "It's been over a year. He can't last much longer. You have no idea what it's like."

"Come on," Amy whispered as she pulled Klaus out of his chair. "You need to rest. I'll bet you haven't slept since you rescued Julius." Klaus didn't respond. He just followed Amy blindly. She led him into his office and made up a bed on the floor next to the couch. As she covered Klaus with a blanket she smiled. "I'll watch over both of you tonight."

Amy sat at Klaus' desk and switched off the lamp. There in the darkness she listened to the two men breathing. Klaus had fallen asleep clinging to Karl's picture. Julius slept clinging to his life. Both were in more pain than she could imagine.

Through the long dark hours, Amy wondered what she should tell Leeza. She had seen the agony that knowing the truth had brought to Klaus. *How can I put her through that?* Then she thought about Wilhelm. *Now I'm standing in his shoes. Do I lie to her, or do I tell her the truth?* Amy ran her fingers through her hair in frustration. *If I tell her, she'll probably go off half cocked and try to rescue him too. And if I don't tell her, and she finds out later, she'll never trust me again. Damn it! What should I do?*

Amy's thought turned to Julius. *I wonder who his contacts were. One of them must have been Dieter von Kleist. But there had to be several more. Hell, he has passports from half a dozen countries, including the U.S. Shit, if he could only tell me. He must have an elaborate network.*

Suddenly, Amy realized that she had first hand knowledge of not one, but four underground organizations. *Wilhelm's. Julius'. Leeza and the White Rose. And then there's her foreman, Albert. He seems to have a pretty good underground stream going. Too bad they can't all work together, but it would probably get too complicated.* Then her thoughts returned to the dilemma of how much to tell Leeza. *No matter what the cost, I can't loose her trust now. I have to tell her the truth. The truth about Karl. The truth about Wilhelm. And the truth about how I feel.*

# Chapter Twenty-Four

# The Judenplatz

Eddi set a tray of meats and cheeses out on a table in the diner. The women of the White Rose were coming for breakfast. The time for expansion had come. After Margo was attacked in the Kunfurstendamn their vulnerability had become apparent. Up to that point their success had been phenomenal, but now it was obvious that more needed to be done. And if they were to loose one member of their team their whole operation might fall apart.

Elizabeth passed a basket of rolls around. "I don't think we can afford to wait. Things are getting worse every day. I saw a communiqué from Hamburg yesterday. One hundred and thirty-seven women have been denounced by their employers, neighbors, and relatives. Another one from Frankfurt listed ninety-four women, and Munich sent in a list of eighty-nine. If we had organizations in those cities we might have been able to prevent so many from being charged and sent to Ravensbrueck."

"Yes, but if we reveal ourselves too much we could find ourselves there!" Heide cried.

Elli stuffed slices of cheese and ham into her roll. "I don't know about all of you, but I think we should organize more cells of the White Rose. If we don't do something we'll never get our country back. I think it's time to do more, not less."

"What more can we do, Elli?" Anneliese asked.

Elli chewed her mouthful of sandwich and washed it down with some coffee. "I don't know. I just think we need to be doing more. Did you see that anti-Soviet exhibit the Nazis put up? Someone needs to burn that thing to the ground!" The women chuckled nervously as they sipped their coffee. "All I know is that getting people out of the country is not enough. What happens after they're all gone? Hitler will still be in control. The S.S. and Gestapo will still be here, and we'll be screwed. We aren't doing anything to really fight them."

Leeza grinned. "Oh we're doing a little more than you know."

Everyone looked at Leeza with questioning expressions. She just kept grinning. "Herr Hitler is in for a big surprise when his tanks start rolling and the tracks fall off five miles down the road."

"Leeza!" Anneliese exclaimed in amazement. "What are you doing?"

She laughed. "Oh, it's a little thing really. Let's just say that Rauthenau Steel isn't producing the finest quality of steel in Germany these days."

"You see, that's what I am talking about," Elli slammed her fist on the table. "Now that's fine work, Leeza. But imagine what we could do if we had people in all the factories. We could stop the rearmament."

Now the women grew quiet. The realization of how much they could really do began to set in. "When my uncle was in the resistance during the Great War," Olga smiled hesitantly, "they were able to pass on information to the allies."

"How did they do that?" Eddi asked.

"Through women," Olga answered. "Sometimes women were able to get information from their dates."

"Dates?" Margo hissed.

"I see where you're going with this, Olga," Claire grinned. "Pillow talk!"

"Exactly," Olga nodded.

"Ick!" Elizabeth shuddered.

"Well, I'm not sleeping with a man, and that's final," Margo barked.

"Me neither," Elli frowned. "Never have, and never will."

"Of course not," Claire insisted with a wry grin. "It takes a certain kind of woman to do that job!" Everyone broke out in laughter. "I'm sorry, Elli, but you and Margo are too, well um, too butch to handle it."

"Damn straight!" Margo grumped. "That's a femme job if there ever was one."

"Hey," Olga interjected, "I wasn't suggesting that we do it, I'm just saying that if we could make the right contacts we might be able to get some valuable information to England or France. You know, plans, that sort of thing!"

The women laughed uncomfortably. The thought of sleeping with Gestapo agents or S.S. officers turned their stomachs.

"Several of my customers at the department store are S.S. officers," Gertrud said thoughtfully. "They come in to have their uniforms altered, and to buy presents for their girlfriends and wives. I know a couple of them by name. They're always trying to get me to go out with them. I could try to get information through them. They're always friendly with me."

"I'll bet!" Elli grumped. "You have blond hair and blue eyes. Just the type of woman every S.S. officer is suppose to marry."

Gertrude frowned. "Well, I wasn't talking about marrying them!"

"Bitte, everyone," Eddi's voice rose, "let's just settle down for a minute. I think we're getting ahead of ourselves here. We haven't even decided to expand what we're doing, let alone sleep with S.S. men." Eddi gave everyone a moment to drink their coffee and eat their breakfast before she suggested putting the idea of expansion to a vote. "You all know what's at stake here. We've been very lucky so far, but this is a risky thing we're doing. I wouldn't blame anyone if they wanted out, or if they didn't want to take it

349

any farther. So, with that said, let's vote. How many think we should stop?" No one raised their hands. "How many think we should keep things the way they are?"

Hesitantly, Heide and Luise raised their hands. Then Heide said, "But, if everyone else wants to expand, I'll go along with it."

"Me too," Luise sighed.

Eddi nodded. "All those for expansion?" Everyone raised their hands. "Well then, it's agreed. Now how do we do it?"

"I have a friend in Munich," Anneliese said, raising her hand. "An ex-girlfriend really. She's a nurse too. I could contact her. She's bound to know other women in Munich." Margo frowned. She obviously wasn't thrilled with the idea of Anneliese talking to an old lover.

"I know a couple of women in Hamburg," Olga said.

Luise raised her hand. "I know someone in Trier. She works in the post office there."

"I'm dating a girl at the university," Elli grinned.

Pretty soon everyone started calling out people they knew in other towns and Eddi stood up. "All right. Let's all contact our friends, but let's be very cautious. I don't think that we should use the post. After all, Luise won't be there to watch over our little messengers. I suggest that we visit them personally, over the next couple of weeks. I also suggest that we don't reveal the names of anyone in our group until they have formed their own groups. Just tell them what we've been doing, but don't give our names. Let's just take it nice and slow."

"I agree," Heide exclaimed. "Just because you know someone doesn't mean they are willing to risk their lives."

"I have tomorrow off," Anneliese chirped. "I could take the morning train down to Munich and see my friend."

"I'll go with you," Margo groaned.

350

Anneliese grinned a patted Margo's hand. "What's the matter? Are you afraid for my safety or are you jealous that I'm going to see an old girlfriend?"

Margo grumped, but didn't answer.

"It's always better to travel with someone," Leeza said hesitantly, remembering her own experience. "And while you're there, I know someone you should look up. Her name is Hanna Jaeger. I heard she is teaching music at the university in Munich. Tell her I sent you."

"An old lover?" Margo grinned.

"No, just an old friend."

"Speaking of lovers," Anneliese giggled, "when is your American coming back?"

Leeza blushed. "Today."

———

Heinrich had rounded up the Nazis that had escaped the raid on their headquarters, and led them into the Judenplatz of Vienna. This was an old familiar pattern he had used many times, in many cities. Up Seitzergass they slithered with their cans of paint and clubs. The medieval street was narrow and their footsteps echoed through the alley-ways toward the Jewish square. The first rays of dawn cast long shadows across the square. This was the same square that had seen so much bloodshed in 1421, when the people of Vienna had massacred over two hundred Jews in the Judenplatz, burning them at the stake. In the ancient synagogue, rabbis had cut their own throats rather than allowing themselves to be taken alive. *Fear caused that massacre and fear will cause this one,* Heinrich thought. *Too bad we can't arrange another bout of the black plague to blame on the Jews.*

As Heinrich and his men stepped into the square, he shouted "Woe to the Jews of Vienna! Murderers and race defilers all." With that shout, Heinrich's men set out smashing in windows and scrawling huge red swastikas on the white facades of the buildings. One of them ran around the square painting a giant red line across every building, creating what looked like a huge ring of blood. Heinrich's heart began to race. "Death to the Jews," he cried.

As in Berlin, and a dozen other cities, he grabbed the first Jew he could and pounded him to the ground. Another went flying through a shop window. Soon the Judenplatz was erupting in blood and red paint. Jewish bodies lay under the slogans, *"Jew get out! Death to the Jews! Christ Killers! Race Defilers will be castrated!"* The Jews of Vienna could never have imagined the blood bath that would be unleashed on them that day, and Heinrich was just getting started. "When one of you murders one of us," he screamed, "we will kill a thousand of you in return!"

"Revenge!" screamed Heinrich's men. "Revenge for Dieter von Kleist!"

---

Amy had barely gotten out of Vienna when the Judenplatz riot broke out. Had she stayed just a few minutes longer she would have heard the Vienna police sirens wailing toward the little square in the Jewish district. If she had known, she would have been compelled to investigate the disturbance that was now being reported by Vienna radio stations. Instead, she held Julius' violin on her lap and dreamt of Leeza as she soared high above the rolling hills of Czechoslovakia, on her way to Berlin.

*Oh Leeza, what should I tell you?* Amy tapped the little violin case. *What should I show you? What will you do if you think Karl is alive?* Amy spent the entire flight debating with herself again, just as she had the night before. *You know what she's gonna do, Trevor. If you show her the*

352

*file, she'll head straight for Dachau. If you don't show it to
her, and she finds out from Klaus later, well, you're dead.*

The flight picked up a tail wind and landed in Berlin
sooner than expected. Amy took a cab straight to the von
Rauthenau mansion and knocked on the door. "Nice place,"
she mumbled nervously to herself while she waited for
someone to answer. A few moments later Leeza opened the
door. They just stood there staring at one another. Leeza
was wearing the same tailored blue skirt and cream silk
blouse she had planned to wear the night of their date.

"Hi," Amy breathed.

"Hello," Leeza smiled invitingly. A few more seconds
went by. *She is incredibly beautiful,* Leeza thought. *The
same flowing blond hair, those same flashing green eyes.
God I would love to run my fingers through that hair. To
touch...*

"May I come in?" Amy asked softly.

"Oh! Yes, of course," Leeza blushed, tearing herself
from her daydream. "Come in. I'm so sorry." Once inside,
Amy set her duffel bag by the front door and handed the
violin case to Leeza. "You found it!" she cried in
amazement.

Amy smiled. "It was at the Musikverein just like Julius
said it would be."

"How is he?" Leeza asked anxiously.

"He's in pretty bad shape."

Leeza hung her head and looked at the Stradivarius.
Then slowly she looked back to Amy. "Thank you for
bringing it."

Amy stepped forward and lifted Leeza's chin with one
hand. "You are very welcome."

Leeza's heart skipped a beat at Amy's touch. "Forgive
me," she sputtered shyly. "Won't you please take off your
coat and come in and sit down. I made some tea."

"That would be great."

353

Leeza escorted Amy into the study. She scanned the ceiling high bookcases in awe while Leeza poured the tea. "Do you take sugar?"

"Yes. Please," she answered as she ran her index finger over the spines of several classics. "Your library is quite impressive."

"It's not mine," Leeza sighed. "My father and uncle were the book enthusiasts in the family. My passion has always been music."

"Have you had a chance to play?" Amy asked, turning from the bookcases to look at her.

Her expression was sad. "I have not picked up my violin since I returned to Berlin. I find no joy in it any more," Leeza replied as she handed Amy her tea.

"Julius wouldn't want that," Amy whispered softly. "And neither would your mother. She asked me to remind you of the joy your music brings you." Leeza just hung her head. Again, Amy lifted her chin. "Would you play something for me?"

Leeza blushed. "It's been so long since I have played, I'm not sure I would…"

"It will be fine," Amy sighed.

Leeza set her tea cup on the desk and picked up Julius' violin. Tears filled her eyes. "Will he live?"

Amy cleared her throat, but she didn't say anything.

Leeza brought her eyes up to meet Amy's. She could see that the news she brought was not good. "What does Klaus say?" Now it was Amy's turn to avoid eye contact. "Please tell me," Leeza whispered anxiously.

Amy took a sip of her tea. "He doesn't know."

"But you saw Julius?"

"Yes. His jaw was broken. Klaus wired it shut so communicating was kind of difficult." Amy explained about how she and Julius communicated. "At first Klaus was worried about the knife wound. Then it was his lungs."

"Klaus told me his hand was broken?"

354

"Yes. He set it without surgery. He's not sure how it's going to affect…"

Leeza burst out crying. "He'll play again. He has to!"

Amy set her tea cup down and took Leeza in her arms. Gently, she rocked her from side to side and then led her over to the couch. Leeza continued crying out all of her fears and frustrations on Amy's shoulder as they sat down together. *Just let her cry it all out, Trevor. Then you've got to tell her about the file. She'll never trust you again if you don't.*

Leeza's heart was breaking wide open in front of Amy. The news that Julius might not live opened the flood gates of her pent-up emotions. From Klaus' arrest and sentence to Sachsenhausen to the loss of several of her friends in the bar raids, and on to her own rape and Karl's arrest, the images that now flooded her mind were more than she could bare alone.

Slowly at first, Leeza began unconsciously pouring out her nightmares between sobs. For what seemed like hours Leeza clung to Amy as if she were a life line. While Leeza laid her head in Amy's lap, Amy stroked her hair and listened compassionately. When she told her about the rape, Amy tensed. In that instant she wanted to kill someone with her bare hands. But Leeza was on to her next horror. The night Karl was arrested. *Tell her now, Trevor, while she's willing to let you to hold her. Maybe you can help her through this.* But Leeza had moved on to the night the women of the White Rose ambushed the prisoner transport.

"I reached in the back of my pants and pulled out the pistol. I just pointed it at him and pulled the trigger. It was so easy," she whispered. "So easy. I just pulled the trigger and shot a man dead. I didn't know I had that much hate in me. But when I saw what they had done to those women, I began reliving my own experience and I was filled with rage. I just stood there and shot him. I didn't feel anything for him. I was so cold inside." Leeza's voice trembled.

Amy could feel her body shudder, as if she was reliving it all over again. Desperately, she tried to think of something to say, but she knew nothing she could say would ease Leeza's pain, so she said nothing. She simply held her, there on her lap, stroking her hair.

When Leeza had talked herself out, Amy took a deep breath. "Leeza," she whispered, not wanting to spoil the tenderness they were sharing, "there's something else I have to tell you."

Leeza brushed the tears from her eyes and sniffed. "What is it?"

She looked up into Amy's eyes with such warmth and appreciation that Amy could barely get the words out. "It's about your uncle. Karl."

Leeza sat up as if bracing herself for another blow. "Was something in the case?" she hesitantly.

"Yes," Amy whispered softly as she reached out and brushed the hair from Leeza's face. "Karl's Gestapo file is in the violin case."

Leeza glanced at the Stradivarius. "His Gestapo file? But how?"

"I don't know. There are some other things in the case as well as the file."

"Show me," Leeza whispered nervously.

Amy got up from the couch and fetched the violin case. Setting it on the coffee table in front of them, she said, "The case has a false top. Normally you open the case like this." Amy pushed both thumbs down on the little locks. They popped open. She lifted the lid to reveal the white scarf covering the Stradivarius. Then she closed it. "To open the secret compartment you go like this." She spun the lock casings counter clockwise and pressed her thumbs upward twice. The false top popped up ever so slightly. She lifted the lid again and this time the passports slid out.

356

Leeza gasped in amazement. "Where in the world did Julius get all of these?"

"I don't know for sure, but Klaus and I figure that he's been working with the Jewish underground in Vienna. There are blank passports from just about every country in Europe. Even a couple from the United States."

"Julius!" Leeza whispered in awe.

"This little bags has all kinds of jewels in it, as well as a fist full of cash. I think he's been buying passports in every country the orchestra visits. But I'll be damned if I know how he got the American ones."

Then Leeza's eyes fell on the file stuck in the lid of the violin case. She looked at Amy as if to ask if it was Karl's. Amy nodded her head. "What does it say?"

"I think you should read it for yourself," Amy whispered gently.

Leeza's hand shook as she reached for the file. Amy didn't say any more as Leeza began to read. She read each page slowly, afraid she might miss something that would give her some important little bit of information. Amy stood up and paced back and forth, sipping her cold tea as Leeza poured over the file without saying a word. Eventually tears began running down her face as she closed the cover.

Looking up at Amy, she bit her lip. "He's alive?"

Amy sat down and took Leeza's hands in hers. "We don't know," she said nervously. "Klaus and I simply don't know. Julius passed out before we had a chance to ask him where he got the file. I don't think he could have told us even if he was awake."

"I see," Leeza sniffed.

"We don't know how long he has had the file, or where he got it from. For all we know it could be a forgery." Amy was doing her best to keep Leeza calm. "Until Julius is out of the woods, he won't be able to tell us anything. I know this file seems to offer hope, but..."

"But you don't want me to do something crazy until I find out. Is that it?" Leeza sighed.

Amy wanted nothing more than to take Leeza in her arms and kiss away all of the pain. She wanted desperately to tell her that Karl was alive and that together they'd find a way to bring him home safely, but she couldn't. She knew Leeza needed to come to that conclusion on her own. *Don't blow it now, Trevor.* "I'll do anything you want me to," Amy whispered. "Anything."

Leeza was exhausted from crying. She fell back in Amy's arms. "Just hold me for a while."

Amy reached out and pulled Leeza close. Gently, she laid her down in her lap and pulled the afghan off the back of the couch. Spreading it over her, she whispered, "Just rest now. Just rest. I'll stay right here." Leeza began to cry again, but sleep overtook her quickly.

Amy sat mesmerized, watching Leeza's breasts rise and fall with each low, sleep-filled breath. She felt desire rise within her. *How I would love to carry you up the stairs to your bedroom and make love to you, tenderly and passionately. You deserve to be loved with a gentle touch. Oh God, how could they have raped such a beautiful woman? Couldn't they see the tenderness in her eyes, in her soul?* Amy gently stroked Leeza's hair down to her shoulder. Then she laid her hand on Leeza's chest, at the base of her throat. *Why did her first time have to be with one of those animals? God, why did it have to be so brutal?*

---

Klaus headed for the Judenplatz as soon as he heard the news reports on the radio. He had several friends there and wanted to help them if they were hurt. He quickly gave Julius a shot to keep him asleep. Grabbing his medical bag, he ran for the trolley. When it stopped at St. Stephan's

358

square, Klaus jumped off and ran up the sidewalk, north, to the Jewish district. By then the police had barricaded off the streets and were in the process of arresting several of the Nazi they had trapped in the square.

Klaus couldn't believe the destruction he saw from behind the police barricade. *My God, how could they do this here, in Vienna?* He quickly flagged down a policeman and held up his medical bag. "I'm a doctor!" he shouted over the din of the crowd. "I've come to help!" The policeman waved him through the barricade and he ran up one of the side streets toward his friend's flat. *I hope to God that Moshe and Isaac had the good sense to stay inside!*

Suddenly a huge hand reached out and grabbed Klaus as he ran past a dark alley. "Doctor Gessler!" Heinrich hissed. "Imagine my surprise at finding you here."

Klaus never knew what hit him. All of a sudden he found himself laying on the ground staring up into a face he had never seen before. "Do I know you?" he panted.

"No, Doctor Gessler. But I know you!" Heinrich grinned an evil smile. "The last time I saw you, you were on your way to Sachsenhausen, I believe. How did you come to be here in Vienna? I thought you would be dead by now!"

Klaus was shocked that this stranger knew everything about him. "How do you know who I am?"

Heinrich laughed. "I was the one who sent you to Sachsenhausen, Herr Doctor. I was the one who bashed in your skull, there at the Institute." Klaus panicked and scrambled to get up. "I can see now that I should have finished you that day!" Heinrich kicked Klaus in the stomach and then hoisted him off the ground. "But maybe we can have some fun before I finish my work." Grabbing Klaus by his belt and by the hair on the back of his head, Heinrich spun him around and rammed his face into the brick wall. Then dragging him farther down the alley and

359

around behind the apartment building, he tossed Klaus over to a trash can.

Klaus was regaining consciousness when he realized his pants were down around his ankles. He struggled against Heinrich's hold, but Heinrich just laughed, grabbing his head and smashed it into the lid of the trash can. Then he unzipped his pants and pulled out his huge throbbing member. "Oh, you deserved this, Doctor Gessler. I'm glad you woke up for it."

Klaus screamed as Heinrich thrust his himself inside and began pumping, banging his head against the trash can lid with each stroke. Klaus moaned when Heinrich punched him in the ribs to silence him. "Take it like a man, Doctor Gessler. Keep your mouth shut or you will die with me inside of you!"

Klaus was on the verge of passing out when Heinrich heard footsteps running up behind him. It was the Vienna police. They shouted at Heinrich to freeze. He did, inside Klaus. Klaus moaned again.

"Step away from him," one of the policemen shouted.

Heinrich stepped back, pulling himself out of Klaus.

"Put your hands in the air!" another policeman yelled.

Heinrich looked over his shoulder and grinned. "Do you mind if I zip up first?"

"Do it!" the policeman said in disgust.

Heinrich shoved his dick back in his pants and turned around slowly. He smiled at the policemen. "I was just teaching this Jewish faggot a lesson, boys. Nothing to be alarmed about."

"Turn around and get on your knees," the policeman barked. Heinrich complied with a grin. "Now, put your hands behind your back!" One policeman handcuffed Heinrich while the other held a pistol to his head. "I should blow your brains out right here," the policeman with the pistol spat. Then he hauled Heinrich out of the alley.

360

Klaus moaned as the remaining policeman helped him stand. Pulling up his pants, she said "Danke," in a whisper of embarrassment.

"You are the doctor, yes?"

"Yes," Klaus groaned.

"Well, doctor. I think we had better get you to the hospital."

"No. Just get me a cab."

# Chapter Twenty-Five

## Goodwill Party

The endless digging and building never seemed to stop. In 1933, when Dachau opened, it was supposed to hold five thousand prisoners. By 1937, that number had doubled and there was simply no more room. The camp commandant ordered the prisoners to triple the size of Dachau. Eventually two hundred and six thousand prisoners were to be registered there. The order was unbelievable to Karl as he continued digging the foundation for a new barrack. His hands were blistered and bleeding as he hoisted one more shovel full of dirt into the wheelbarrow, which would be taken by another prisoner and sifted through for the gravel it contained.

When six o'clock finally came, the S.S. guards blew their whistles. Time for evening roll call had come. Karl crawled out of the hole he was digging and laid his shovel on the tool cart. Then he fell in line with the other prisoners and marched to the north end of the camp, taking his place in roll call formation. If all went well during roll call, a luke warm bowl of watery turnip soup awaited the starving prisoners. Perhaps even a chunk of stale bread or a piece of moldy cheese.

By now Karl's black and white striped uniform hung on his body like a death shroud. His ankles and calves were no longer big enough to hold up his socks, and his shoes had holes in the soles. His hair had thinned enough that his scalp could be seen, and the hair that remained had turned completely white. He was so thin that even his gums were receding. They could no longer support his teeth. Karl could feel the loose ones as he ran his tongue over their bases. He had seen too many of his fellow prisoners grow thin and die. He knew he was not going to last much longer. If the malnutrition and exhaustion didn't kill him first, he knew the new typhus epidemic would.

After the hour it took to call roll the prisoners would run for their barracks to get their bowls, and then they would line up to receive their evening meal. Later they would have the chance to wash the dirt from their bodies and rinse out their bowls. The barracks lights would go out at eight-thirty and the flood lights would then come on. If he was lucky, Karl would fall asleep before he had to listen to the death breath of someone around him. He had heard the death breath, that deep rattle of inconsistent inhaling and exhaling, enough to know who was about to die and who would live through the night. Sleeping next to a corpse was perhaps the greatest horror in Dachau.

The morning roll call came at six o'clock. When the S.S. blew their whistles and banged on the barracks doors the prisoners would take their place in formation again, and go through the same process they had the night before, with the exception that there would be several dead prisoners who would not report for roll call. It was not unusual for five to ten men to die each night, including those who chose to cross the wire and step into the forbidden zone.

Mornings also brought a fresh supply of prisoners to take the places of the dead. When the train arrived the new prisoners would be stripped and marched through the disinfecting hut, where they were deloused. Then their hair would be shaved off and they would be issued their black and white striped uniform, along with their bowl, a bar of soap, and a towel. The bar of soap was supposed to last six months. Failure to present a bar of soap during an inspection could result in the prisoner being punished. Also, failure to present a clean, shining soup bowl could bring the same punishment.

Punishments varied by the type of prisoner and their particular offense. Prisoners with the green triangle of

363

career criminal, thieves and burglars, might be sentenced straight away to the penal barracks. These men were earmarked for severe treatment. "The Tree," a post that was erected in the bunker yard was perhaps the most feared. The post had a hook at the top. The condemned man was shackled with his hands behind his back. Then the executioner would lift the man's shackles up onto the hook so that the prisoner's heels could not touch the ground. There he would hang, with his arms stretch out behind him, for a minimum of one hour. This punishment often led to the shoulders being dislocated as arms were twisted out of their sockets.

Other punishments included "The Trestle." This was a rack that was used for beating the prisoner. His hands would be shackled to the top of the trestle and his bare body would be bent in half, with his ankles shackled at the bottom. The executioner would have soaked his leather whip in water to ensure maximum flexibility. Then he would administer a minimum of twenty-five strokes. The prisoner was forced to count each stroke of the whip, and if he lost count, the executioner would start all over again.

"The Standing Cell" was another feared punishment. Condemned prisoners were forced to stand in a cell no larger than a telephone booth for three days and three nights. On the fourth day the prisoner would be transferred to a regular cell and eat regular prisoner fare for one day and one night. Then he would be returned to the standing cell for another three days. This form of punishment could continue for up to forty-two days.

Then there was "The Wall." This was the fastest form of punishment. Death by firing squad was quick and efficient. Many of the green triangle prisoners, especially if they were second time offenders, were marched straight from the train to the wall to receive their punishment.

For the general camp population, hunger, disease, and harsh labor served as their daily punishment. They were also tortured every minute of every day by the smell of the burning bodies in the crematorium, and the screams of those who were being punished by more vigorous means. But the screams of those being punished were not the only one's they had to endure. They could hear the screams from the infirmary, of those being medically experimented on by S.S. doctors.

Yes, Dachau was filled with endless forms of torture and horror, but no less than any other Nazi concentration camp. Sachsenhausen, Buchenwald, Bergen-Belsen, and Ravensbruck all held the same tortures, along with countless others. No one could escape them, even if they happened to be transferred to another facility.

"I can't eat this, Professor," Karl whispered as he slid his bowl of turnip soup to the middle of the table.

Professor Otto Wolfe was an elderly man near eighty, who had just arrived two weeks before. The professor had been on his way to Paris for a conference when the Gestapo pulled him off the train in Munich for having contraband material in his possession. Something to do with literature that was banned in Germany.

"Karl, you must," the professor whispered back. "You won't survive if you don't eat."

"I'm not going to survive much longer anyway," Karl sighed.

"You don't know that."

"Yes, I do. I have watched how strong men come in here and waste away to nothing. Most don't last a year. I have been living on borrowed time for over six months now. What difference is a bowl of putrefied turnip soup going to make?"

"It could mean the difference between life and death," the professor coughed, as he tried to argue the merits of a bowl of soup.

"Don't try to talk, Professor. Your cough is growing worse." Karl reached out and laid the back of his hand

365

against the professor's forehead. "Your fever is getting worse too."

Professor Wolfe smiled calmly. "It's the typhus. It won't be long now."

Karl coughed. "For either of us."

"It's really not so bad to die," the professor wheezed. "Soon I will join my mother and my father, my brothers, and all the other Wolfe's who have gone before me." He smiled weakly at Karl. "Maybe your Wolfe's are a kin to my Wolfe's, ja?"

"No, I don't think so, Professor. My name is not really Wolfe," Karl sighed. "It's von Rauthenau. The S.S. registered me under a false name."

The wrinkled skin on Professor Wolfe's head crinkled up even more. "Why would they do that?" he asked.

Karl shrugged his shoulders. "I don't know. Perhaps they have confiscated my factory and my family fortune. Perhaps it is so that my family will not know where I am. I have no idea what motivates the Nazis to do the things they do."

Professor Wolfe nodded his head. "Your factory, I'm sure."

"At least Leeza is safe. That's all I really care about now. I will die knowing that she is safe and well cared for. I made sure of it."

"How did you do that?" the professor asked.

Karl smiled. "I transferred over a million marks into a Swiss account for her, and I bought her an American passport. I'm sure she is playing with the New York symphony by now."

"Ah, your Leeza is a musician?"

"Yes! A violinist," Karl exclaimed, and then began to cough again.

"Come, Herr von Rauthenau, drink your soup." The professor pushed Karl's bowl back in front of him. "Drink up and tell me of your Leeza. Tell me how she makes her violin sing. Describe the music to me. And let us dream that we are there, watching her perform. What would they play in New York?"

———

Klaus's right eye was swollen shut, making it very difficult to read the morning paper. However, he could clearly make out Heinrich Mueller's picture, there on the front page, as he was being forced into a police wagon. Klaus took little satisfaction in seeing the picture. *He's in a nice comfortable Austrian jail cell when he should be rotting in a concentration camp like I did.* The article told that eight Nazi agitators had been arrested during the riot in the Judenplatz. It also listed the seventeen names of Jews who had been killed during the riot. *They should have lined the Nazi bastards up against a wall and shot them then and there.*

Julius began to stir on the couch. He moaned as he tried to sit up. Klaus flung the newspaper down on his desk and rushed to his side. Julius opened his eyes and saw Klaus looking down at him. He blinked, and then blinked again as if to clear the sleep from his eyes. "I must look horrible, I know," Klaus groaned. Julius just stared at him. Klaus' face was black and blue, and his nose was obviously broken. There was a bandage across his forehead, and another one around his chest.

Julius pointed to Klaus' bandages and scrunched up his face as if to ask "What in the world happened to you?"

Klaus tried to explain as he helped Julius into a sitting position. "There was a riot in the Judenplatz yesterday. I went to check on some friends. I guess I was in the right place at the wrong time."

Julius touched Klaus's bandaged ribs and then he touched his own. Klaus knew he was asking if his ribs were broken.

"Not broken. Just cracked, I think. I'll be all right. It looks worse than it really is," Klaus smiled reassuringly. "Nothing compared to your injuries. How are you feeling this morning? You have been asleep almost forty-eight hours."

Julius put his hand to his crotch.

"Oh!" Klaus grinned knowingly. "Yes, I'm sure you do need to use the WC. Do you think you can stand?"

Julius shrugged his shoulders and winced from the pain.

"Shall we try?"

He nodded his head.

Klaus put his arm under Julius' and helped him up with a groan. But as soon as Julius stood, the room started spinning and he collapsed back onto the couch. Klaus collapsed beside him. "What a fine pair we are?" he chuckled. "How about a bedpan?"

Julius blinked once.

After the necessities were taken care of Klaus asked, "Are you in much pain?"

Julius blinked once.

"Where?" Klaus asked.

Julius pointed to his back.

"Let me see." He removed the bandage on Julius' lower back. Two of the stitches had torn out. "I'm going to have to close them, and you're going to have to stay down from now on. Do you understand? No more trying to get up. At least not for a week or so."

Julius blinked his eyes once and then pointed to his head.

"Yes, I'm sure you have a hell of a headache."

Julius blinked once again.

"Do you hurt anywhere else?"

Julius pointed to his ribs and hand.

Klaus understood. "They are going to be sore for a while. I can give you something for the pain, but I want you to eat something first. Are you hungry?"

Julius blinked once and then twice.

"Ah, yes and no. Well you obviously won't be able to eat much anyway. How about trying some chicken broth?"

Julius blinked once.

Klaus poured him a cup of soup from a small kettle on the hot plate in his office. "I'm not much of a cook, but I don't think it's too bad."

Julius held the cup awkwardly in his left hand and balanced it with his bandaged right hand as he brought it up to his lips. Carefully, he sipped a few drops and scrunched up his face.

"What's the matter?" Klaus asked.

Julius held the cup out for Klaus.

"You want me to taste it?"

Julius nodded his head.

Klaus sipped the soup. "It tastes fine to me."

Julius shook his head slightly and scrunched up his face again.

"Does it taste like...like metal?"

Julius nodded.

"It's the blood in your mouth," Klaus remarked. "I'm sorry. I tried to rinse you out as best I could, but...Well, I couldn't get it all. I'll get you a glass of water to rinse with." By the time Julius rinsed his mouth out, and had a few sips of broth, he was exhausted.

"That's to be expected. You are very weak. You lost a lot of blood. I'll give you a shot for the pain, but it's going to take a long time to get your strength back. I'll stitch up your back after you fall asleep."

Julius nodded and closed his eyes. Then suddenly he thought about the Stradivarius. He raised his bandaged hand and pretended to play.

"Your violin?" Klaus asked.

369

Julius nodded.

"Fraulein Trevor took it to Leeza in Berlin."

Julius nodded and fell off to sleep.

Klaus returned to the newspaper and waited for the shot of morphine to take effect. Under the picture of Heinrich a smaller headline read, *"Hitler Threatens Retaliation if Austrian Nazis are not Released at Once!"* "Fuck Hitler," Klaus grumbled. "I hope the Chancellor has enough balls to tell Hitler to go straight to hell. I hope his little Nazi demons rot in the worst Austrian jail possible. Really, they should be shot."

---

Leeza opened her eyes as the bright morning light filled her bedroom. *What? How did I get here?* Then she turned over and saw Amy sleeping next to her in the bed. Quickly, she looked under the big fluffy comforter. She was still wearing her teddy and silk panties. Relieved, she looked at Amy. She was still dressed in the khaki pants and green sweater that she had on the afternoon before. Leeza smiled. *She must have carried me. But how…*

Suddenly, Amy's breathing changed and Leeza knew she was about to wake up. Quietly, she slipped out of bed and got dressed. Then she slipped out and ran down stairs to make some coffee. She didn't know weather to be embarrassed or grateful that Amy had taken her to bed. It had been a long time since she slept so soundly.

When Leeza returned to her bedroom carrying a tray of coffee and croissants, Amy was just coming out of the bathroom. "Good morning," she smiled.

Leeza blushed. "Good morning. Would you like some coffee?"

"Ah, breakfast in bed. What a lovely way to start the day. Did you sleep well?"

370

Leeza blushed even brighter. "Yes, I slept very well. Thank you for putting me to bed."

"You are very welcome," Amy beamed. "You needed it."

Leeza put the tray on her dresser and asked, "Would you like to listen to the radio while we have breakfast?"

"Sure."

Leeza switched on the set and poured the coffee. Schubert's *Impromptu in E flat major* crackled through the speakers. "I still like to listen even though I don't get to play anymore."

"Why don't you play anymore?" Amy asked softly.

Leeza handed her a cup and they sat on the bed. "I just don't have the heart for it anymore. Not since Uncle Karl..."

"You should, you know," Amy interjected before Leeza started dwelling on Karl.

She smiled shyly. "Maybe."

Suddenly the music was interrupted by a news bulletin. The radio announcer said that the arrest of Austrian Nazis during the Judenplatz riot had prompted the Führer to propose a prisoner exchange with the Austrian government. Chancellor Schuschnigg was said to be considering the proposal and would hold a press conference later in the afternoon to announce his decision.

Amy stared at the radio on Leeza's dresser. "Riot? What riot?"

The radio announcer soon answered Amy's question as he began to give the details of the riot. "Yesterday, after the arrest and execution of convicted murderer Julius Barkowski, Jews in Vienna took to the streets in revolt."

"Julius!" Leeza cried.

Amy put her coffee cup on the night stand and said, "Shhh. It's just Hitler's propaganda, I'm sure. Julius is safe with Doctor Gessler."

The radio announcer droned on. "Nazi party members tried to assist the Vienna police as they worked to put down the revolt, but were arrested along with the riot instigators. The Führer is now negotiating with Austrian officials for the release of the Germans being held in jail."

"I've got to get back," Amy exclaimed. "Newman is probably wondering where in the hell I am. I'll bet the INS office is going crazy right about now."

"Do you have to go?" Leeza cried.

Amy looked at her. She saw the fear and pain in her eyes. She reached over and took Leeza's cup and put it on the night stand beside her own. Then she stood up, pulling Leeza up with her. Stroking her hair, she whispered, "I have to. But I'll be back as soon as I can."

Leeza hung onto Amy tightly, but didn't say anymore. She couldn't bare the thought of her going away and leaving her alone again, but she knew it was her job to be at the press conference.

Amy brushed her hand up and down Leeza's back, trying to calm her, to reassure her that everything would be all right. Then she held Leeza's face in her hands. "I will be back," she insisted as she stared into Leeza's eyes. Leaning in close, she kissed her ever so gently. "I'll be back. Just as soon as I can."

---

It was cold inside Notre Dame when Wilhelm knelt beside Ernst von Rath in front of the crucifixion alter. Wilhelm had come this morning expecting news that the high command was ready to act and arrest Hitler. Even though Generals Bloomburg and von Fritsch were no longer in command, the plot to assassinate German Ambassador von Papen had been uncovered in Austria, and he was sure that it was a sign that France and England had done their part. The Paris newspapers headlined the story and screamed about Hitler's diabolical plot to assassinate his own ambassador. Of course Hitler had staunchly denied that there was ever a plot, but the cat was out of the bag, and the world knew it. Surely the other German generals would still carry out their plans to take over the government in Germany.

After seeing the story in the papers Wilhelm had felt such relief. His heart beat wildly with the thought of returning to Germany in triumph over the madman. He had been right to go to Churchill and Eden. They had gotten to Schuschnigg in time to save von Papen. Now Britain and France were sure to stand with the generals when they arrested Hitler. Admiral Canaris had been wise to send him with the information.

Wilhelm crossed himself and glanced at von Rath with anticipation. "You have good news for me?"

"On the contrary," von Rath whispered.

Wilhelm's heart sank into the pit of his stomach. "What do you mean?"

"The Italian Embassy held a goodwill dinner party last night. Count Grandi and Anthony Eden were there. Eden tried to talk to Grandi about the situation in Austria. He wanted to know if Mussolini would stand with Austria and guard her independence as promised."

"What did he say?" Wilhelm choked.

"Prime Minister Chamberlain was there too. He kept cutting Eden off. Every time Eden broached the subject, Chamberlain would change it. He kept talking about how much his friendship with Mussolini meant to him. How much Britain valued its friendships with both Italy and Germany."

"What?" Wilhelm barked.

"Shhh!" von Rath hissed.

373

Wilhelm couldn't believe what he was hearing. "We ask for a show of strength from the British and they continue to offer their devotion and friendship to Hitler?"

"Shhh!" von Rath insisted. "Yes. Exactly."

"Didn't Hitler's plot to kill von Papen show them anything?" Wilhelm groaned, trying to contain himself.

"Yes! But neither Churchill nor Anthony Eden are the Prime Minister of England. They have no real power or authority. Only Chamberlain can stop the madness. And he is too weak to stand up to Hitler. He only thinks of appeasement."

"Then he is a fool!" Wilhelm barked.

"Yes, he is. This morning Mussolini spoke with Hitler on the telephone. They laughed at Chamberlain's weakness. He is a laughing stock to them."

"What about Eden? What did he have to say during all this?"

"He asked Grandi straight out, what Mussolini and Hitler had planned for Austria. Grandi looked like he had swallowed a toad, but didn't answer before Chamberlain called for a toast to the British-Italian friendship. Eden didn't drink the toast."

"I'm surprised he was invited to the party at all. The Italians hate him. He was one of the few in the British government to insist that Italy pull their troops out of Spain."

"You should have seen it. Eden was humiliated. Chamberlain cut his legs out from under him, right in front of Count Grandi. Chamberlain might as well have cut his balls off while he was at it."

"So, that's it. Austria's fate is sealed? What about the other generals? Surely they won't march their troops into Vienna."

Ernst von Rath hung his head. Anyone looking would have thought he was deep in prayer. "You haven't heard?"

"Heard what?" Wilhelm whispered in dread.

"Fifteen other generals have been arrested. Our cause is lost."

# Chapter Twenty-Six

## Special Of The Day

After Amy left, Leeza stood in the study staring at Julius' violin case. *It's so much like the one Uncle Karl gave me.* Then the thought finally occurred to her. *Uncle Karl! He had our cases made. He must have known about the secret compartment. Was he working with Julius? Why didn't he tell me? Why didn't Julius tell me? Is that why he's in Dachau? Did the Gestapo know he was working with the Jewish underground?*

Suddenly Leeza felt a rush of pride surge through her. *Uncle Karl must have been working with Albert, just like I am.* Leeza remembered the day that Albert had first come to her about his grandchildren. "He said, 'Herr Karl offered his help.' Was Julius somehow getting passports for Albert's grandchildren?" Leeza shook her head in amazement. "Probably." Then she thought about the passports in Julius' case. *I've got to get them to Eddi as soon as possible.*

"Where did you get them?" Eddi asked.

"From a friend, but it's too much to explain now." Leeza was in a hurry to get to work. "I'll come by tonight," she blurted. "Will Elizabeth be here? I need to show her something."

"I'll call her and ask her to come by for dinner," Eddi frowned. "What do you want to show her?"

"Later!" Leeza called over her shoulder as she ran out the door. "I'm very late!"

When she got to the factory, Albert was waiting in her office. She smiled and said, "I'm sorry I'm so late. Just give me a few minutes to get into my coveralls and I'll be out."

376

"Fraulein Leeza," Albert sighed. "That is not why I have come to your office."

Leeza paused and looked at Albert. He obviously had something on his mind. "What is it then?"

Albert hesitated. "I need your help."

Leeza took a seat on the couch and motioned for Albert to join her. "How can I help?"

"There are more children," Albert sighed.

"Well bring them in for goodness sake!" Albert played nervously with his hat, but didn't say anything right away. "What's wrong?" Leeza asked.

Albert hung his head. "They are not in Berlin, Fraulein. They are in Munich."

"Munich?" Leeza exclaimed.

"Ja, in Munich. I have a friend of a friend, if you know what I mean. My friend has sent me a message. He says that he is hiding three children and needs help to get them out of the country. I was hoping that you might know a way."

Leeza leaned back on the couch and heave in a deep breath. "I don't know, Albert," she sighed.

"I understand, Fraulein Leeza. I thought it might be too much to ask."

"No! It's not that. I just don't know how to do it. We don't have anyone in Munich that I know of. Anneliese and Margo are there right now trying to recruit...Wait a minute! That's it. Margo and Anneliese can take the children into Austria. They are already there!"

Albert smiled. "I knew you would think of something, Fraulein Leeza."

"Yes, but how can they contact your friend?" Leeza wondered out loud.

Albert rubbed his balding head. "If you can get a message to them, I can get a message to my friend. We can have them meet in Marienplatz in front of the glockenspiel."

377

Leeza smiled. "Perfect. Say tomorrow afternoon at five o'clock?"

"Ja, I think that would work," Albert smiled.

"Tell your friend to carry a single white rose. When two women approach him, have him give the rose to the women and say that 'Albert sends his regards.' Margo and Anneliese will reply with 'Leeza sends her regards.' That's how they will identify each other. Now the only question is how do we get the children new passports?"

Albert's face went blank. "I don't know."

"I'll take them on the midnight train to Munich!" Hanna barked from her desk. She had obviously been eavesdropping on their conversation. Leeza and Albert just looked at each other and smiled.

---

The telegram Leeza sent arrived at the Beck Hotel in Munich late that afternoon. Margo tipped the delivery boy and closed the door. "It's from Leeza," she exclaimed.

Anxiously, Anneliese asked, "What does it say?"

Margo cleared her throat and began to read aloud.

*"DEAR FRIENDS - STOP - HANNA WILL ARRIVE ON THE MORNING TRAIN FROM BERLIN - STOP - YOUR HOSPITALITY IS APPRECIATED - STOP - LOVE LEEZA."*

"That's all it says!" Anneliese cried.

"Ja," Margo replied. "What do you think it means?"

Anneliese shrugged her shoulders. "I can't imagine. Maybe we should send her a return wire with the news that Professor Jaeger is willing to form the Munich White Rose."

"No, that would be too dangerous. Lets just wait and see what news Hanna brings."

Hanna stepped off the train in Munich carrying three blank Austrian passports in Julius' violin case. Margo and Anneliese were there to greet her. They waited until they got back to the hotel room before they flooded her with questions. Hanna quickly gave them the run down on the Jewish children in Munich, and told them that Leeza wanted them to take the children to Jenbach. She also explained about Julius and his violin case.

"Sure! We'll take the children," Margo exclaimed, "but what about their passports?"

Hanna smiled and opened the violin case just the way Leeza had showed her. "All we have to do is take their pictures and type in their names. You are supposed to meet the gentleman at five o'clock in front of the glockenspiel in Marienplatz. He will be carrying a single white rose. He will greet you with 'Albert sends his regards.' You will reply, 'Leeza sends her regards.' Then you can find out the ages and sexes of the children, and make arrangement to take their pictures."

"But we don't have a camera," Anneliese cried.

"Yes we do," Margo smiled. "When I spoke with Professor Jaeger and explained how we did things, she said one of her students had a camera. She was sure the girl would help. Professor Jaeger also suggested using the university's dark room to develop the film."

Anneliese grinned from ear to ear. "That's wonderful, Margo. All you told me was that she was willing to help. You didn't say she had already set up half the operation."

Margo shrugged. "Now all he have to do is find a way to get the Austrian Seal over the pictures."

"What happens if we can't get it?" Hanna grumped as she lit a cigarette.

"We won't make it across the boarder."

379

"Well," Anneliese held up her hands in resignation, "we came here to set up the Munich White Rose. I guess we had better get to work and recruit someone at the Austrian consulate."

"Or bribe someone." Hanna tossed five gold coins onto the bed. "That should be enough to buy three stamps."

Margo and Anneliese stared at her in amazement. "Where did you get these?"

"Compliments of Master Barkowski, but if you ask me, I think they came from Karl von Rauthenau," Hanna said as a matter of fact.

"Karl?" Anneliese asked.

"Ja. I know he invested in gold coins before Hitler became chancellor. I was the one who told him to buy the coins. Several years ago gold was the only currency that had any value in Germany. I think these are Karl's coins. He probably sent them to his Swiss safe deposit box, via Julius. That's probably why he had this violin case made for him. He knew he was being watched and Julius was reasonably free to travel without notice, being in the orchestra and all."

"Why didn't he simply give Leeza the coins?" Margo asked.

"Good question," Hanna frowned. "He was probably trying to protect her."

---

Leeza curled up under her comforter remembering wonderful times with Julius. The scene of them standing on the Charles Bridge in Prague came into her mind. As if it was yesterday, she remembered their conversation.

"Don't worry, my darling," Julius had said. "When this holiday concert tour is over I shall purchase you a beautiful princess for Christmas."

"I don't want you to purchase anyone for me," she had replied. "I want to fall in love naturally. When it happens it happens."

"What ever you want, my darling. But don't wait too long. Should my prince show up, I wouldn't want to leave you all alone."

Then she remembered him twirling around with the Stradivarius dangling from his finger. She had chastised him for being so irresponsible, and wondered if he had ever been that childish with the new case Karl had given him. Then her mind focused on the case.

Suddenly Leeza remembered the letter from Karl that the Gestapo had delivered. She reached in her night stand and pulled the letter out of her Bible. At the time Leeza hadn't thought much about the lines that said, *"Should you have an hour of need, remember how your little violin case soothes your worries. Julius knows."* Then she thought about Julius' violin case. *Uncle Karl had mine made by the same craftsman. Lindheim! I wonder?*

She jumped out of bed and ran to her closet. There on the top shelf lay her Amati, safely tucked away in it's Lindheim case. Quickly, Leeza pulled it down and ran back to bed. Her heart beat wildly with anticipation. "Did you create another secret compartment, Herr Lindheim?" She hesitated for a moment before trying to turn the lock casings.

Then she heard Karl's voice on that Christmas morning in the Tyrol two years ago. *Go ahead, Leeza*, he had whispered softly. *Play something for us.* Holding her breath, Leeza twisted the casings. They moved. She pushed up twice and the top opened just as Julius' had. Inside there was a letter addressed to her.

"Oh, Uncle Karl. What have you done?" Her voice quivered as if Karl were in the room with her. Slowly, she opened the letter and read it.

*My dearest Leeza,*

*If you are reading this letter you know that I have lost my battle with the Gestapo and am no longer with you on this earth. Don't grieve for me, my dear sweet niece, for I am with your father in heaven, and we are watching over you even as you read these words. Know then that I have loved you as if you were my own child. Not even death can change that. Therefore, it is for this reason I have placed a considerable sum of money in a Swiss account for you. See Herr Meyer at the Zurich National Bank. Account number 11617611047.*

*I want you to take the money and leave Germany. By now, Julius should have secured an American visa or passport for you. Please, take the money and go to America. It pleases me to think of you playing with the New York symphony, or some other American orchestra. There is enough money for you to start a wonderful new life. Please take it with my blessings.*

> *Your loving uncle,*
> *Karl von Rauthenau*

Leeza's hands began to tremble, and her eyes filled with tears as she replaced the letter in the envelope. Then she looked into the bottom of the lid and saw a velvet bag. Putting the letter aside, she opened the bag and spilled the contents into the lid. Out came several gold coins and a new passport. Hesitantly, she opened it. Inside she saw her own face. *It's me. I can't believe it. How did he ever manage this? I don't remember having my picture taken, but it looks authentic. And who decided on my name. Lisa Trevor? I guess it sounds American enough. I wonder if Amy knew about this? No, probably not or she would have told me straight out. Uncle Karl, how did you know this name? Julius, you darling idiot, were you the one who picked the name? Were you trying to tell me something? Lisa Trevor? What made you think...?*

Now, somehow, Julius' words from so long ago seemed prophetic. He hadn't purchased Leeza a lover, but he had purchased the name of the one she loved. "How did he know how I felt about Amy?" she muttered to herself. "He couldn't have." The she remembered the time when she and Julius, and Karl had gone to the bar during the Olympics. How Julius had seen her watching Amy. He must have talked to her after I left. Amazing.

Then Leeza's thoughts turned to Karl. *He must have been working with Albert to get his grandchildren to America. I wonder if Uncle Karl told Julius he wanted me to go to America too? Maybe he asked Julius to find a way to get me to there. Maybe Julius just chose Trevor because it was the only American name he knew. But why didn't Uncle Karl tell me himself? He must have put it in the case when he and Mother came to Vienna after...*

# Chapter Twenty-Seven

## Desperate Measures

Admiral Canaris had recalled Wilhelm to Berlin just long enough to give him orders to go to Berchtesgaden, Hitler's mountaintop fortress overlooking the German-Austrian border. From this vantage point the dragon could drool over his anticipated prize. Austria was Hitler's homeland and he wanted it more than he wanted any other laurel. If he could take it without blood shed it would prove that he was not only a great statesman, but also a brilliant military strategist as well. It would gain him the respect and admiration of the military generals.

"Why Berchtesgaden?" Wilhelm asked anxiously.

"Hitler has called for Chancellor Schuschnigg to meet him there in three days," Admiral Canaris answered as he slid Wilhelm's orders across his desk.

"But why me? Why would you send me to this meeting?"

"The Führer," Canaris spoke the title with a sarcastic edge, "has called for each division to send representatives. This is his chance to strut like a horny peacock in front of the elite military officers. He will humiliate Schuschnigg in front of the officers and they will return to their units and tell how masterfully the Führer dealt with the Austrian chancellor."

"But I won't do that," Wilhelm said, half pleading with Canaris not to send him.

"That's exactly why I am sending you," the Admiral insisted. "You will see the little toad for what he is. A blustering, arrogant manipulator."

"Schuschnigg might not even come to the meeting," Wilhelm said hopefully.

384

"He will come." Admiral Canaris was confident. "He's an honorable man. Young and inexperienced, but honorable. He still hopes that things can be resolved peacefully. He wants peace above all else. What he doesn't know is that his country is only the first piece of real estate on Hitler's list."

"What do you mean, Admiral?"

"After Austria will come Czechoslovakia and then Poland."

"You've got to be kidding!" Wilhelm exclaimed.

Admiral Canaris walked over to his maps hanging in the corner of his office. He flipped over several to reveal a map of Europe with no borders between Germany, Austria, Czechoslovakia, and Poland. "Plan Otto!" he slapped the map with the back of his hand.

"Plan Otto?" Wilhelm whispered.

"The Führer screams continually for more living space for Aryans. This is how he plans to get it."

"But even if the Austrian Anschluss comes, Czechoslovakia and Poland will fight to the bitter end!"

Admiral Canaris returned to his desk. "The Führer believes that they will fall like dominos once Austria capitulates. He might be right."

"Surely England and France will not stand for such an advance! They have mutual defense agreements with Poland."

"So far, England and France have not shown any backbone. We tell them about Hitler's plan to assassinate von Papen and all they do is attend a party and talk of friendship. What makes you think they will fight for Poland or Czechoslovakia when they won't take a stand for Austria? No, Wilhelm, England and France won't make a move against Hitler because they are afraid of war. They will do anything to avoid it. As long as it never comes knocking at their doors, they will continue to look the other way."

Wilhelm felt the hopelessness of the situation in the pit of his stomach. "It is not their fault," he sighed. "It is ours. We let ourselves be seduced by his ravings. We let him get this far. We looked the other way when good people started disappearing. We could have spoken out, but we didn't. We just buried our heads in the sand and let him take over."

"Unfortunately, you are right. But now, with so many of the generals removed from power, we don't have much of a chance to stop him."

Wilhelm smiled a sarcastic smile. "We have empowered a bully and now he will crush us all. It is too late for us to speak out."

"That's all it would take, you know," Canaris laughed bitterly. "If France or England would only speak out against the take over of Austria, Hitler would back down. All it would take are words. At this point in time the military cannot sustain a war. We have not rearmed sufficiently. We would not last long in a fight. Hitler knows this and so do the generals."

"So what do we do now?" Wilhelm asked.

"You go to Berchtesgaden and report back to me. I need a reliable source of information in that meeting." Admiral Canaris heaved in a deep sigh. "Then we wait for our opportunity."

Wilhelm noticed the ominous tone in the Admiral's voice and could only guess what he meant. "I will leave right away, Sir."

---

Chancellor Schuschnigg refused the prisoner exchange that Hitler had offered. "Well at least he has a little backbone," Jim grumped.

"Yeah," Amy replied. "But I don't think Hitler's going to let the matter drop so easily."

"Naw, me neither."

Everyone sensed the tension, but didn't know what they could do about it. "I'm going to head back to the hotel," Amy sighed. "I haven't done my laundry since...since I can't remember when. If there's going to be an Anschluss, I'd at least like to face it in clean clothes."

Jim chuckled hopelessly. He could read the handwriting on the wall as well and the next person, and his hopelessness had defused his ongoing personality battle with Amy. "I know what ya mean, Trevor. I think we're all gonna need a clean pair of drawers to face what's coming."

The Sacher Hotel was abuzz with newspaper reporters from all over the world. It seemed that the eyes of the world were trained on little Austria, and what was going to happen there. The tension was so thick you could slice right through it, and the patriots of Austria were already sharpening their knives. Amy decided to have a drink before she went upstairs to gather her laundry.

"Bourbon, straight up," she called to the bartender as she slid onto a stool.

"Make that two!"

Amy spun around and saw Wilhelm standing behind her. "What are you doing here?" she exclaimed.

"Would you care to join me at my table?" Wilhelm grinned.

"We've got to stop meeting like this," Amy laughed. "People will begin to talk."

The bartender slid two bourbons down to them and Wilhelm laid a couple of bills on the bar. Then they retreated to a table in the corner. "I was hoping I would find you here," Wilhelm held up his glass in a salute.

Amy returned the salute and took a sip. "What are you doing in Vienna?"

"I am on my way to Berchtesgaden."

"Berchtesgaden? Why?"

"Hitler has called Chancellor Schuschnigg to a meeting there."

"Why?" Amy asked with a reporter's excitement.

Wilhelm pulled a piece of paper out of his pocket and handed it to her. She unfolded it and began to read. Amy glanced up at Wilhelm in shock. "This is an ultimatum! A list of demands." She began to read them out loud.

*"One - The ban against the Austrian Nazi Party will be lifted immediately. Two - All Nazis in jail will be granted amnesty and will be released immediately. Three - Dr. Seyss-Inquart will be appointed as the Minister of Interior of Austria and will be granted authority over the police and national security. Four - Glaise-Horstenau will be appointed Minister of War and the Austrian and German armies will establish closer relations with a program of officer exchange to begin shortly. Five - Assimilation of Austria's economic system will begin with the appointment of Dr. Fischboeck as Austria's new Minister of Finance."*

Amy was nearly speechless as she laid the document on the table. "Schuschnigg will never sign this."

Wilhelm downed his shot of bourbon. "We shall see."

"When is this meeting going to take place?"

"Day after tomorrow. I will be attending. Hitler wants his officers to see him crush Schuschnigg." Amy slid the piece of paper across the table. Wilhelm slid it back. "That is for you. I have my own copy. You should also be aware that Hitler will not stop with Austria."

Amy stared hard into Wilhelm's eyes. "What are you talking about?"

"Plan Otto."

"What's that?"

Wilhelm proceeded to tell Amy everything that he and Admiral Canaris had discussed. "I saw the map myself. No borders between Germany and any of its eastern neighbors."

Amy called for another round of bourbon. "Make them doubles!"

Wilhelm gave her a wry grin. "Have you seen Herr Churchill recently?"

"No," she replied. Then she looked at Wilhelm's smile. "Why?"

"I was just asking."

"You want me to take this document to him, don't you?"

"For all the good it will do. He and Anthony Eden are impotent in this situation."

"Damn!" Amy mumbled as the bartender brought their drinks to the table. "This whole situation is hopeless."

Wilhelm paid for the drinks and waited for the bartender to retreat. "Have you had the chance to talk with Leeza?"

"Yes. I saw her last week."

"What did she say when you told her that I had gone to Churchill?"

Amy suddenly remembered the Gestapo file on Karl. "I didn't have the chance to tell her. Things are really complicated with her right now."

"What are you talking about?" Wilhelm was obviously growing agitated.

"I'm talking about you lying to her," she snapped.

Wilhelm looked dejected. "I explained to you why I did that!"

"Well, it's coming back to haunt you. Leeza has a copy of the Gestapo's file on Karl. She knows he is alive!"

"What? How?" Wilhelm sputtered anxiously.

Amy thought better of telling Wilhelm the whole story. "I don't know. I only know that she knows he is alive."

"This can't be!" Wilhelm exclaimed. "He can't possibly still be alive!"

"Well according to the file he is! There's no recorded date of death! No release date. According to the file he is still alive."

"It must be an old copy!" Wilhelm exclaimed.

"That's what we have to find out!" Amy sniped. "Before Leeza goes off and does something stupid."

"You have to convince her, Fraulein Trevor. You have to make her understand that Karl cannot possibly still be alive." Wilhelm was pleading. "It will be her death if she tries anything foolish."

Amy sat back in her chair. "You know Leeza. She is determined. But I could hold her back if I could tell her that you were working on getting some more recent information."

"I can't!" Wilhelm exclaimed.

"Don't give me that, Captain Schroeder! If you can get your hands on this," she waved the ultimatum in front of his face, "you can certainly find out about a single prisoner in Dachau!"

Wilhelm was angry now. "I would be risking everything!"

Amy smiled calmly. "It's either you or Leeza. Which will it be?"

"You are blackmailing me!" Wilhelm stammered.

"You claim that you love Leeza like a daughter!" Amy spat. "Prove it!"

Wilhelm slammed his fist down on the table.

Amy slammed hers down beside his. "Prove it!"

They stared into each others eyes for several seconds. Then they each downed their shots. "Fine!" Wilhelm exclaimed. "But you had better keep her from doing anything stupid until I can get the information!"

"Fine!" Amy hissed through clenched teeth. "I'll go and tell her that you are working on it. In the meantime, I'll see if I can arrange a meeting with Churchill, to show him this!"

"Fine!"

"Fine!"

Wilhelm headed off for the meeting at Berchtesgaden and Amy glanced at her watch. "Great! Just enough time to do my laundry before the evening flight to Berlin."

---

Leeza was overjoyed to see Amy standing at her front door when she came home from the factory. "Come in! Come in!" she stammered as she fumbled to unlock the door. "I hope you haven't been waiting long."

"No, not long," Amy shivered. "I took the evening flight."

"Have you had dinner yet?"

"No."

"If you'll give me a few minutes to clean up and change, we can go to Bamberger Reiter," Leeza beamed.

*Hmm, Romantic.* "Yeah, sure."

"I know the maitre d'," Leeza called over her shoulder as she ran upstairs. "I'm sure he can get us a table. Make yourself at home. I'll be right back."

Amy browsed through Karl's library while she waited for Leeza to come down. *Dante, Shakespeare, Goethe, Schiller, Rousseau, Voltaire, Plato, Boccaccio, Chaucer, Pico della Mirandola, Erasmus, Machiavelli, Luther, Copernicus, John Locke, Hobbes, Gibbon, Shelley, Byron, Hegel, Kant, Poe, Marx, Melville, Thoreau, Hugo, Tolstoy, Dickenson, Dostoyevsky, Wilde, Freud, Yeats, Cocteau, Jung, Eliot, and of course Hirschfeld. What a fantastic library.* "Karl von Rauthenau, you must be an incredible man!" Amy mumbled to herself. "And look, you even have Mark Twain's *Adventures of Tom Sawyer*."

"He used to read that to me when I was little," Leeza sighed. "*The Adventures of Huckleberry Finn* is up there somewhere as well."

Amy spun around and saw Leeza standing in the doorway. Her breath caught in her throat. In just a few minutes Leeza had managed to wash the grease from her face, brush her hair, and change into a pretty sweater and black slacks. Tonight she wore the pearls. *God she is beautiful. As long as I live I'll never get used to looking at her.* "You look wonderful."

Leeza blushed. "Danke."

Amy caught herself staring. "Um...I...I was just admiring Karl's library."

Leeza smiled. "He loved to read. When I was a child he read all of Herr Twain's books to me. I was fascinated with your Miss-i-ssipp-ee," she struggled with the name. "I'm sorry. My English is not so..."

"It's wonderful," Amy grinned. "Yeah, the Mississippi is one big river."

"I would like to see it for myself one day."

"Really?" Amy was surprised.

"Oh yes!" Leeza beamed. "And the American West! I would love to see the Grand Canyon. Ride 'm cowboy! It all sounds very exciting!"

Amy laughed. "What do you know about cowboys?"

"When I was a little girl, Uncle Karl took me to the *Wild West Show* when it came to Berlin. It was great fun. I saw Buffalo Bill Cody and Annie Oakley and Chief Sitting Bull!"

"Really?" Amy laughed. "I would never have pegged you for a wild west type."

"It was thrilling! But I must admit the wild Indians scared me."

"Well," Amy sighed, "Hitler's not the only one who knows how to round people up and lock them away. I'm sorry to say my government did the same thing to the Indians that Hitler has done to the Jews."

"Oh no!" Leeza cried. "They were savages! They murdered innocent people!"

Amy shook her head. "No. They were not savages. The *Wild West Show* is like Hitler's propaganda against the Jews. The Indians were just people, like us. They were just trying to live their lives the only way they knew how. We were the ones who killed them!"

Leeza grew quiet, contemplating what Amy had just told her. "I see. Maybe I do not want to see the American West after all."

Amy's heart sank. "I didn't mean to discourage you. Colorado, Wyoming, even Arizona are all beautiful. It's just that you can't believe everything you read or see in the movies."

Leeza nodded her head. "Shall we go?"

"Yeah, I'm starved."

---

"Fraulein von Rauthenau!" the maitre d' greeted Leeza as she and Amy walked in. "How good it is to see you again."

Leeza smiled warmly. "Franz! It has been too long!"

"Yes, it has," he replied with a slight bow.

"I didn't have the chance to make a reservation," Leeza whispered coyly. "Do you have a table available?"

"For you, of course!" Franz winked. "This way." He led them to a table in the middle of the room, and as they took their seats he unfolded their napkins and placed them in their laps. "Tonight we have fresh Salmon, grilled to perfection with a lemon butter and white wine sauce, with a sprig of dill."

"That sounds lovely, Franz. I'll have that."

"And your wine?"

"Surprise me!" Leeza grinned.

"How about a nice glass of Bernkasteler Doktor?" Franz smiled.

"Wonderful, that would be lovely."

Then Franz looked at Amy, "And for you, Fraulein?"

"I'll have the same."

Franz gave a friendly bow. "Very good!"

Amy looked at Leeza after Franz left. "Bernkasteler Doktor?"

Leeza laughed. "It's a wine produced in Bernkastel-Kues, along the Mosel River. The legend is that in the castle, high above the village, the prince lay dying. After all traditional medical treatments had been administered with no results, a servant offered the prince a glass of the wine. Miraculously he was cured. Hence the name."

Amy smiled. "What a wonderful legend."

"And the wine is superb," Leeza grinned.

The wine was as good as Leeza said it would be. Clear and white, semi-sweet, with a nice bouquet. The salmon was also wonderful. Amy didn't want to spoil the mood by talking about something that might upset Leeza, so she decided to wait until after dinner before she broached the subject of Karl. When the waiter took away their empty plates and poured them another glass of wine she finally decided to ask.

"If you don't want to talk about it, I'll understand, but I was wondering if you have decided anything with regard to you uncle?"

Leeza frowned. "It is always on my mind, but unless Elizabeth can come up with something new, I don't quite know what to do."

Amy took a deep breath. "There is something I need to talk to you about."

"What is it?" Leeza eyed her suspiciously.

"It's about Captain Schroeder."

"Wilhelm? He is last person on earth I want to discuss."

"Yes, I can understand why you feel that way, but there is something about him I think you should know."

"I know everything I want to know about that traitor!" Leeza snapped.

"Not everything." Amy sighed as she pulled out the document that Wilhelm had given her. "I think there are many things you don't know about him. Take a look at this." She handed the paper to Leeza.

Leeza unfolded it and began to read. "Where did you get this?" she said in awe.

"From Wilhelm. He gave it to me in Vienna, just before I left. Leeza, he has been working with Winston Churchill and Anthony Eden. He has been giving them information. You're right about him being a traitor, but it's not what you imagine. He has been working with the German High Command. They were planning to arrest Hitler if England and France will show some backbone."

Leeza couldn't believe what she was hearing. "Wilhelm? Wilhelm is working against Hitler?"

"Yes," Amy answered pleadingly. "He's not what you think he is."

Leeza folded up the list of demands. "All I know is that he let my uncle go to Dachau without so much as lifting a finger to help him!"

"That's not true! Leeza, Admiral Canaris found out that Wilhelm helped Klaus escape. That's why he transferred him to Paris. So he couldn't help your uncle. Canaris wouldn't let Wilhelm jeopardize the general's plans. They needed him. Canaris has been sending Wilhelm to Churchill and Eden with information. Information that could have meant the end of Hitler's reign. That was the only way he was allowed to help Karl. By helping all of Germany!"

"So he knew Uncle Karl was alive and he lied to me! I will never forgive him for that! He betrayed me and he betrayed Uncle Karl. I hate him!"

Amy sighed in frustration. "He loves you, Leeza," she said softly. "And he loves Karl. He is haunted by the fact that he wasn't able to get Karl out! All this time he truly believed that Karl was dead. He believed he was being kind in telling you that he was dead. He didn't want you to suffer any longer than necessary. Now he's taking great risks to make up for it. He's at Berchtesgaden right now. He's gathering information for Admiral Canaris and the other generals."

"What good does gathering information do?" Leeza was angry. "If he is gathering so much information, why can't he get information about Uncle Karl?"

"He's going to!" Amy exclaimed impatiently. "We just have to give him a chance. As soon as he's done with his mission, he promised to look into it." Amy picked up the folded piece of paper. "In the meantime, he's asked me if I can get this to Churchill. He's trying to stop the Austrian Anschluss!"

"What good will getting that to Churchill do?" Leeza asked angrily.

Amy was more than a little frustrated. "If the British and the French don't take a strong stand on the Austrian problem, Hitler will take Czechoslovakia and Poland next!"

"What? That is crazy! Where did you hear that?"

"It is called Plan Otto!" Amy proceeded to tell Leeza the details that Wilhelm had told her.

"And you believe him?" Leeza exclaimed.

Amy leaned back in her chair and stared at Leeza with deadly seriousness. "Yes. I do. It makes sense. Hitler has been screaming about needing more living space for Germans. The Sudetenland in Czechoslovakia is filled with Germans. Germany lost Danzig and its port in the last war. It all makes perfect sense to me, and if England and France don't stop Hitler at the Austrian border, he will move on to take Czechoslovakia and Poland. This is the only way to stop him! Don't you see? Wilhelm is trying to save more than just one man. You know Karl would want that!"

Leeza sat back in her chair and thought about it. She thought about the violin cases and the Swiss account. She thought about Julius and Klaus, and how Wilhelm had been able to save Klaus. Then she thought about how long Karl had hid Klaus from the Gestapo. She remembered the American passport Karl had purchased for her. *Amy is right. Uncle Karl would not want Wilhelm to risk everything to save one man's life.* "But the English won't help the generals stop Hitler. Every day I read in the newspaper how France and England are such good friends with Mussolini and Hitler. They won't do anything. They have let him go this far haven't they?"

Amy took a deep breath. "I can't argue with you there. Things don't look good," she sighed. "Even after I spoke with Churchill about the map, and Wilhelm told him about the assassination plot against von Papen, still England did not act!"

Leeza was shocked. "Wilhelm was the one who exposed the assassination plot?"

Amy looked surprised. "Yes! That's what I've been trying to tell you. Wilhelm is doing everything he can to stop Hitler, short of assassinating him!"

Leeza couldn't believe it. Then she thought about the American West, and chuckled sarcastically. "He's trying to be another Buffalo Bill Cody."

Amy smiled sadly. "Too bad he's not more like Wild Bill Hickok. We could use a good law man right about now!"

The waiter came to the table and offered them dessert and coffee. "We have a nice cheesecake, or perhaps some Black Forest cake?"

"I'll have a piece of the cheesecake," Amy replied, "and coffee, bitte."

"I'll have the Black Forest cake," Leeza smiled, remembering how much Karl love it.

"Very good, Frauleins," the waiter bowed.

Amy sat back and thought about the American cavalry riding to the rescue in all of the wild west shows. "You know, maybe we have been going about this the wrong way."

"What do you mean?"

"I mean, we have been depending on England and France to come to the rescue."

"Yes?"

"Well, what if we looked to someone else for help?"

"But who?"

The waiter interrupted Amy's thought. "Danke," she said as he placed the cheesecake in front of her.

"Danke," Leeza smiled at the cake in front of her.

"I'll be right back with your coffee."

Amy took a bite of the cheese cake. "Umm, this is delicious."

"You were saying?" Leeza asked impatiently.

"Wait," Amy waved her fork as she swallowed another bite.

The waiter returned with a pot of coffee and then retreated to the kitchen.

"You were saying?" Leeza insisted.

Amy swallowed another bite and took a sip of coffee. "I was just thinking about what we were talking about earlier."

"And that was?"

"You said Wilhelm was acting like Bill Cody, and I said we needed a Bill Hickok."

Leeza scrunched up her face. "Bill Hickok?"

"Yeah, he was a U.S. cavalry scout and marshal. A law man. Anyway, the name jogged my memory. When I was

398

in college studying journalism, I did an internship under Hick."

"Who?"

"Lorena Hickok," Amy said as she took another bite. "Hick's one of us."

Leeza scrunched up her face again. "One of who?"

Amy leaned in close and whispered. "You know," she said with a wink. "A lesbian."

"Oh!" Leeza grinned. "No, I didn't know."

Amy leaned back. "She was the one who taught me how to drink bourbon. Anyway, that doesn't matter except that Hick's really close to the First Lady."

"The President's wife?" Leeza asked in amazement. "Frau Roosevelt?"

"Yeah. Word has it that they're really close, if you know what I mean." Amy winked again.

Leeza's mouth dropped open. "The First Lady is a..."

"All I know is that they're really close. Anyway, I was just thinking, Mrs. Roosevelt is very knowledgeable about foreign politics. Maybe if I went to see Hick, she could get me in to see the First Lady, being her personal press agent and all. If I showed her this," Amy waved the folded document, "I'd be willing to bet she'd talk to the President. She has a lot of pull with him."

"You're not serious," Leeza laughed.

"Why not?"

"Because, you can't just ring up and make an appointment with the First Lady of the United States of America!"

"The hell I can't," Amy exclaimed.

"You think this Hick person could arrange it?" Leeza asked in wonder.

"I don't know," Amy grinned. "Hick and I had some good times together."

Leeza frowned. "I'll bet!"

Amy saw right away that she had stepped in it. "No! Not like that! I mean during my internship, she really showed me the ropes. She took me under her wing and taught me how to be a good reporter. She showed me how to get along in a man's world."

"And so you think the First Lady will intervene on Austria's behalf," Leeza asked, finally taking Amy seriously.

"There's only one way to find out!"

"You have to go to America," Leeza sighed.

"Yup, and the sooner the better. The meeting at Berchtesgaden is taking place tomorrow. I should probably try to catch a flight out tonight."

"Tonight!" Leeza exclaimed. "But I was hoping…" Amy looked at her with a quizzical expression. Leeza caught herself. "I was hoping we could spend more time together."

"After I get back, I promise," Amy smiled warmly and touched Leeza's hand.

Leeza looked down at her cake. "Of course. What you are doing is very important."

"You've got that right. If I can get to the First Lady in time, she might be able to twist the President's arm and get him to take a stand on the Austrian problem."

Suddenly Leeza's heart was beating wildly. "You make it sound like it could happen tomorrow!"

"I don't know about that! But maybe the day after," Amy winked. "If all goes well!"

Amy reached into her pocket for some money to pay the bill. "In the meantime you have to promise me that you won't try to do anything about your uncle. No matter what happens, you must wait for Wilhelm to contact us with information."

"I will," Leeza sighed. "I wouldn't know what to do even if Elizabeth told me that he was alive."

Suddenly Amy felt the little sapphire ring in her pocket and froze. She looked up a Leeza longingly. *Not now, Trevor. Not when you are leaving her.*

"What is it?" Leeza asked.

"Oh, nothing."

"If it's about the check, I'll just put it on my bill," Leeza smiled.

"Uh, no," Amy hesitated while she fumbled in her pocket. "I've got it covered."

After Amy paid the bill she helped Leeza on with her coat. Pulling her hair up from beneath the coat, the fragrance filled Amy's senses. *You have got to be nuts, Trevor. Leaving her here tonight. She obviously wants you, you idiot.* "Well, I should be off to save the world," she sighed.

Leeza laughed. "Should I call you my American Wild Bill?"

Amy just grinned. *You can call me anything you want.*

# Chapter Twenty-Eight

## The First Lady

It was a cold morning in early February when Chancellor Schuschnigg was greeted by Hitler on the steps of his magnificent villa, Berghof. Schuschnigg was accompanied by his aide and Hitler was flanked by three generals. Wilhelm, along with various other officers watched from the second story windows as the Führer and generals Keitel, Reichenau, and Sperrle exchanged greetings with the mild-mannered chancellor and his aide.

After the initial pleasantries had been exchanged, Hitler and his generals led Schuschnigg up to the second story study. The room, with its great plate glass windows, took in sweeping views of the snow capped Alps, and of little Salzburg below. Chancellor Schuschnigg, yielding to his old world manner, complimented Hitler on the room's decor. Immediately Hitler burst into a tirade that didn't stop for two hours.

"We did not gather to speak of the fine view or of the weather. You have done everything to avoid a friendly policy. The whole history of Austria is just one uninterrupted act of high treason. That was so in the past and is no better today. This historical paradox must now reach its long overdue end. And I can tell you right now, Herr Schuschnigg, that I am absolutely determined to make an end of all this. The German Reich is one of the great powers, and no one will raise his voice if it settles its border problems here and now!"

Wilhelm and the other officers invited to Berchtesgaden were listening from an anterior room. *He just told Schuschnigg that no other country will stand with Austria,* Wilhelm thought.

Chancellor Schuschnigg was shocked by Hitler's outburst, but tried to remain congenial and diplomatic. "Austria's contribution in this respect is considerable."

"Absolutely zero!" Hitler shouted. "I am telling you, absolutely zero. Every national idea was sabotaged by Austria throughout history, and indeed all this sabotage was the chief activity of the Hapsburgs and the Catholic Church."

"All the same," Schuschnigg responded, "many an Austrian contribution cannot possibly be separated from the general picture of German culture. Take for instance a man like Beethoven..."

"Oh! Beethoven? Let me tell you that Beethoven came from the lower Rhineland," Hitler insisted.

"Yet," Schuschnigg said, trying to stress his point, "Austria was the country of his choice, as it was for so many others."

"Be that as it may! I am telling you once more that things cannot go on in this way. I have a historic mission, and this mission I will fulfill because providence has destined me to do so. Who is not with me will be crushed. I have chosen the most difficult road that any German ever took. I have made the greatest achievement in the history of Germany, greater than any other German. And not by force, mind you. I am carried along by the love of my people."

"I am quite willing to believe that," Schuschnigg responded, but he was already growing tired of this bantering.

Chancellor Schuschnigg was not the only one growing tired of Hitler's blustering. *Isn't he ever going to get to his list of demands?*

"We will do everything to remove obstacles to a better understanding, Herr Hitler, as far as it is possible."

"That is what you say now, Herr Schuschnigg. But I am telling you that I am going to solve the so-called

Austrian problem one way or the other! Listen, you don't really think you can move a single stone in Austria without my hearing about it the next day, do you? I have only to give an order, and in one single night all your ridiculous defense mechanisms will be blown to bits. You don't seriously believe that you can stop me for half an hour, do you? I would very much like to save Austria from such a fate, because such an action would mean blood. After the Army, my S.S. and Austrian Legion would move in, and nobody can stop their just revenge. Not even I."

Wilhelm listened intently. *So, he threatens war.*

"Don't think for one moment," Hitler continued, "that anybody on earth is going to thwart my decisions. Italy? I see eye to eye with Mussolini. England? England will not move one finger for Austria. And France? France could have stopped me in the Rhineland, but now it is too late for France."

A shiver went up Wilhelm spine. *Too late for France? My God! He can not possibly mean to take France as well?*

"I give you once more, and for the last time, the opportunity to come to terms, Herr Schuschnigg. Either we find a solution now or else these events will take their course. Think it over, Herr Schuschnigg, think it over well. I can only wait until this afternoon."

The Austrian Chancellor was obviously frustrated. "What exactly are Germany's terms, Herr Hitler?"

"We can discuss that this afternoon!" Hitler shouted as he stormed out of the room.

---

Although Amy had slept throughout the flight back to the states, she got off the plane in New York feeling cramped and drained. *I've got to call Hick before I jump on the train. God I hope she's in D.C. and not off on assignment somewhere. Damn, I should have called from Berlin.*

"Associated Press," the switchboard operator answered.

"Lorena Hickok, please."

"One moment."

Amy thought about Lorena Hickok as she waited. The last time Amy saw her, Hick was a five foot eight, two hundred pound, cigar smoking, bourbon drinking, poker playing, hard-boiled political reporter. In fact, she was the highest paid female reporter in America.

"Yeah!" Amy finally heard Hick's voice on the line.

"Hick! It's Amy Trevor!"

"Hey, Kid! How the hell are ya?"

"Great!" Amy answered. "And you?"

"Oh, can't complain. Hey, I read your piece about Hitler and the map. Good stuff! Who was your source?"

"Thanks, Hick. Actually, it was Winston Churchill."

"You're shitting me!"

"Nope."

"That's great, Kid. So, what can I do for ya?"

"Well, that piece about the map, that's what I want to talk to you about. I need your help with something."

"Me? What the hell for? I mean, I'd be happy to help, but I'm not a European expert."

"Listen Hick, I just flew in from Berlin. I'm still in New York. If I take the train down to Washington today, can we get together?"

"Yeah, sure Kid."

"How about six o'clock?"

"Great! But let's meet over in Baltimore, at the Coconut Club on Madison near Howard. Do you remember the place?"

"Of course," Amy grinned. "How could I forget a place like that?"

"Yup, filled with the most gorgeous dames in the tri-state area!"

That night Amy and Hick had a happy reunion at the lesbian bar in Baltimore. "What'll ya have, Kid?"

Amy grinned. "What else is there?"

Hick smile and then waved at the bartender. "Two bourbons, straight!" After they got their drinks, Amy and Hick headed for a table near the dance floor. "So, Kid, how that hell are ya?"

"Good!" Amy smiled.

"And how's old Jim Newman treating you?"

"He's as ornery as ever, but he keeps me on my toes," Amy laughed.

After they brought each other up to date, Hick asked about Amy's interview with Churchill. "How the hell did ya land him?"

"Actually, he asked to see me. I couldn't believe it. He wanted a female reporter. That way if anyone saw us together, they'd think we were having an affair!" Amy laughed.

"Hell, I can understand that! I wouldn't mind if people thought we were having an affair. It's good for the image!" Hick chuckled.

Amy grinned. "Rumor has it you're already having an affair." Then she leaned forward and whispered, "With the First Lady! Is it true?"

Hick just grinned. "You know I don't kiss and tell, Kid." Then she winked.

"What's she like?" Amy asked as she took a sip of her bourbon.

Hick beamed. "The dame has class, Kid. Tremendous dignity. She's a real person."

It was obvious to Amy that Hick was in love. "You really love her don't you?"

406

Hick nodded. "Did you know that back in '33 I quit the newspaper and took a New Deal post."

"Yeah, I heard!" Amy cried.

"Yeah, just so I could be near her. Now I'm a liaison between the press and the White House. You're lucky you caught me at the Associated office this morning. Most of the time I'm at the White House."

"That's amazing, Hick! Congratulations! But what about the President? I mean, doesn't he care that..."

"Naw. Hell, he's too busy with his mistress to give a damn what Eleanor and I do."

"But she still has a tremendous amount of influence, doesn't she?" Amy had a sinking feeling in the pit of her stomach. *What if Mrs. Roosevelt is on the outs with the President? What if she can't make him understand what's going on in Europe. Then what the hell am I going to do?*

"Kid, I'm gonna tell you what no one else in the country knows." Hick leaned forward and whispered. "The First Lady runs this country. Franky doesn't make a decision about anything unless he runs it by her first. Just because they have a sexual understanding doesn't mean that they don't respect and love each other. Franky knows that he wouldn't be President if it weren't for her. Believe me, she's the one runnin' the show!"

"Thank God!" Amy exclaimed, "Because I really need her help!"

Hick scrunched up her face. "What's goin' on, Kid?"

Amy spent the rest of the night recounting everything that had happened in Germany over the last couple of years. Together, she and Hick drank at least a bottle of bourbon and discussed everything from the early persecutions of gay men to the more recent arrests of lesbians. Amy told her about the horrors of the concentration camps and the underground movements she had encountered.

"I've personally helped over a dozen Jewish children escape from Germany, and there are so many more. If we don't do something to stop Hitler from entering Austria, he's gonna take over the whole continent. Churchill and Eden are willing to help, but Prime Minister Chamberlain is a wimp. And the English parliament is following Chamberlain's lead. Churchill and Eden have been hamstrung."

"So, you want Eleanor to pull some strings?"

"Yeah. If she's willing. I've brought a document to show her. Hell, she can have it if it will do any good."

"Let's see it."

Amy pulled Hitler's ultimatum out of her pocket. "Right about now, Chancellor Schuschnigg is reading this."

Hick looked it over. "My German's a little rusty, but I'm sure Eleanor would want to see this. I'll show it to her in the morning."

---

The next morning Amy was invited to have lunch with the First Lady at the White House. Hick had already explained the situation in Europe and Amy found the First Lady more than willing to help. Eleanor was familiar with the circumstances in Europe, after all, she had gone to school in England and had traveled widely throughout the continent. The President's wife was also a great human rights advocate. In the United States she had taken stands on women's issues and rights and had spoken on behalf of the poor and infirmed. *If anyone can do something, it's this woman!* Amy thought as she listened to Mrs. Roosevelt.

"I will speak with Franklin straight away. I'm sure he will want to see this document, Miss Trevor. May I keep it?"

"Of course, Mrs. Roosevelt."

"Thank you," the First Lady responded. "And you must call me Eleanor."

"And you must call me Amy," she beamed. Then she grew serious. "The German officer who gave me that document also told me that Hitler won't stop with Austria. If no one opposes him there, Hitler plans to move on to Czechoslovakia and Poland. He wants the Sudetenland and Danzig. If someone doesn't threaten him over Austria, he will take more. It's called Plan Otto."

"Well, Amy. Lets see what we can do to curtail Herr Hitler's ambitions, shall we?"

Amy smiled. "Thank you, Mrs. Roos...I mean, Eleanor. Thank you."

"I will speak to Franklin this afternoon. When are you planning on returning?"

"As soon as I know if the President is willing to help," Amy answered.

"I see. I will call you as soon as Franklin has made his decision," the First Lady smiled. "Hick, will Amy be staying with you?"

"Yeah," Hick answered. "We'll be waiting at my place."

"Well then, I suppose I should excuse myself to the oval office. Amy, it was lovely meeting you," the First Lady extended her hand.

Amy was surprised by the strength with which Mrs. Roosevelt shook her hand. "Thank you again, Eleanor. It was wonderful to meet you."

"Hick," the First Lady leaned over and kissed her on the cheek, "I'll see you later?"

"I'll be here just as soon as I see the Kid off on the train."

President Roosevelt was sitting in his wheelchair looking out the window when the First Lady entered the oval office. He held a secret dispatch from Anthony Eden in his hand. "Ah, Eleanor. I'm glad you're here. Take a look at this." The President handed her Eden's communiqué.

"I have something for you to look at too, Franklin. I just had the most interesting lunch with young Amy Trevor, the reporter from Europe. Let me know if you need help with the translation, Darling."

The President read Hitler's demands while the First Lady read the British Foreign Minister's communiqué. Eden was asking for an indication of Roosevelt's intentions toward Hitler. He asked if America would be willing to be part of the solution. When she finished reading, the President asked his wife for a few minor clarifications in Hitler's demands.

After she gave her interpretation, he asked, "What do you think? I have promised the American people that we would remain neutral in Europe's affairs."

"Franklin, I know that our own people are out of work and starving, and that the last thing they want is to go to war. But as human beings we can not just stand by and watch as others are run out of their homes and are butchered by the thousands. We have to be part of the solution."

The President hesitated. "But war? My God, we still haven't recovered from the last one. America is in the middle of a depression. What possible help can we offer?"

"I believe that Anthony Eden is simply asking for our voices. Franklin, we can't bury our heads any longer. England and France need us to stand united with them. If we raise our voices now, we might prevent the war from starting. We must help them, if only with our words."

The President ran his hand over his face. "I'll try to arrange a conference with England and France." Then the President punched the intercom button on his desk. "Secretary Wells, get me British Ambassador Lindsay on the line."

"Thank you," Eleanor smiled as she patted the President on the hand. "You're doing the right thing." After his wife left, President Roosevelt began drafting a letter to Anthony Eden:

*"The time has come for the great democracies of the world to come together in a conference. It is to our mutual advantage to discuss the situation with Germany and Italy. Offering to share equal parts of the world's resources might satisfy those nations."*

---

Later that afternoon the First Lady proofread the President's letter to Anthony Eden. "I think this is a very good start, Franklin. Now if you will excuse me, I have a telephone call I need to make."

Hick took the First Lady's call. "That's great, Eleanor. Yes...um...huh, yes, I'll tell her. Thanks, doll. I'll see ya after while."

"Was that her?" Amy asked anxiously.

"Yup."

"Well? What did she say?"

Hick smiled. "The President sent a secret communiqué to Anthony Eden. He's calling for a conference with France and England."

"You mean they're going to stand together against Hitler?" Amy asked enthusiastically.

"That's what it sounds like, but don't quote me!" Hick laughed.

"Thank God. Now maybe they can shut Hitler up once and for all. Leeza's going to be so excited when I tell her!"

"Leeza?" Hick grinned. "Who's Leeza?"

Amy blushed. "I don't kiss and tell," she grinned. "You taught me that, remember?"

Hick laughed boisterously. "Kid, you're all right. Let's have a drink before you hit the road."

"You got it!" Amy beamed.

---

Leeza called Albert and Hanna into her office and closed the door. "I need…" she hesitated, "I need you both to do something for me."

"Anything, Fraulein Leeza," Albert chirped. "You know that."

Hanna took a drag off her cigarette and eyed Leeza suspiciously. "What?"

"Recently," Leeza began, "I have been made aware that Hitler plans to take Austria by force, if necessary. Even now he is in negotiations with Chancellor Schuschnigg at Berchtesgaden."

"What?" Albert exclaimed. "But Austria is…That is to say, Austria will never capitulate to Hitler. Austria is Austria, and Germany is Germany!"

Hanna nodded her head and blew out a puff of smoke. "Albert's right. Schuschnigg and the Austrians will never surrender to Hitler, no matter what he threatens."

"I hope you're right," Leeza sighed. "But I have it on good authority that Schuschnigg will have to stand alone in his fight."

"So, what can we do about it?" Albert asked.

"Well, my sources tell me that if Hitler marches his troops into Austria, he won't stop in Vienna. He'll go right on to Prague and even Warsaw. That means that war is inevitable."

"What about the people we have been moving into Austria?" Hanna barked. "Margo and Anneliese just got things set up in Munich!"

"I know," Leeza sighed in frustration. "But we're going to have to start looking for alternatives, just in case. And that's what I want to talk to you about. Should Hitler move his troops into Austria, he won't stop there.

Hanna and Albert looked at her as if she were crazy. "What?" they cried. "Even he's not that crazy."

"Yes, he is. He calls it Plan Otto! Wilhelm has sent me this information. We have to trust that what he says is true. And if that is the case, I want to be ready. Hanna, I want you to start drawing cash out of the bank. A little at a time. I want to be able to give our employees some traveling cash."

"Traveling cash?" Hanna grumped. "What for?"

"Because they are going to have to move on," Leeza answered.

"But why? What about their jobs here at the factory?" Albert asked.

"Albert," Leeza groaned softly, "there won't be a factory if Hitler marches into Austria."

"What do you mean there won't be a factory? Of course there will be a factory!" he cried.

"No, Albert, there won't." Leeza gave Albert and Hanna a few seconds to absorb what she meant. "I want you to rig the furnace so that I can blow it up at a moment's notice."

"What?" Albert yelled. "Blow it up! Why?"

Leeza just gazed at Albert. "You know why," she said.

When Albert started to protest, Hanna jumped in. "She's right, Albert, and you know it. You know very well how Karl felt about producing steel for weapons of war. This is exactly what he would want. If he were here and Hitler took us to war, Karl would blow the factory up himself."

413

Albert just stared at them in disbelief. "But what about getting people out of Germany? If there's no more factory, there's no more hiding them."

Leeza hung her head. "I don't have all the answers, Albert. But we need to do this. We all have to try and stop Hitler any way we can."

"But this won't stop him. There are other steel manufacturers in Germany. He'll just get the steel from them!"

"Yes, he will. But if we can slow him down, even for a few weeks, that might buy England and France, and even America, enough time to stop him for good. All I am saying is that we need to prepare, that's all. Just in case."

Albert thought about what Leeza was asking him to do. He didn't like it, but he said, "Ja, I will do it. I think it is crazy, but I will do it."

Leeza looked at Hanna with a questioning stare. "Ja, I'm in," Hanna answered. "It's what Karl would want."

"Good! Then it is settled. I've heard from Olga in Hamburg. Things are going well there, but they haven't found a way to move people into Denmark. Luise is in Trier, and Eddi tells me that some of the women there are willing to help get our people into France. So let's start moving our employees and friends to Munich and Trier. When Olga makes a contact in Denmark, then we can start using that road as well."

"But what good is moving people through Munich into Austria, if Hitler is going there?" Hanna grumped.

"As long as the door is still open, I think we should use it. If they can get as far as Austria, then they have a chance at getting into Switzerland or even Czechoslovakia. We just have to stay one step ahead of Hitler, that's all. But hopefully, it won't come to that."

On the return flight to Berlin, Amy couldn't sleep. She was too excited that the nightmare might finally be over. *When America, Britain, and France speak out, Hitler will be forced to listen. Even if he moves into Austria, they will force him to withdraw and the German generals will have every excuse they need to get rid of him.*

Then she thought about all the lives that had been ruined by the little madman. Thousands of gay men had been carted off to the concentration camps. Thousands of lesbians and other strong women had been sentenced to Ravensbruck. Jewish children had lost their parents. Jewish families and communities had been destroyed. Priests and ministers had been accused of treason and homosexuality and then forced into slave labor. The mentally ill and physically disabled had been exterminated.

Amy thought of all the people she had known before Hitler came to power. *Helene Stocker, Lotte Hahm, and all the other beautiful women of the White Rose Ladies Society. I wonder if they're still alive? Karl, if you're still alive, hang on. Help is on its way. Leeza is going to be so excited. God, she'll be able to play again. In Vienna. She'll be so happy. I can't wait to give her the good news.*

---

When her plane finally landed in Berlin, Amy called Leeza to make sure she was home. "You're back!" Leeza cried. "Bitte, tell me everything went well!"

"Better than I could have imagined!" Amy exclaimed, "But I don't want to talk about it over the telephone."

"I understand," Leeza replied with excitement. "But, tell me, did you get to see her?"

"Yes," Amy whispered, "and she's going to help us. But I can't talk about it now. I'll tell you when I get there."

"I'll be waiting." Amy heard the smile in her voice. "I can't wait to see you."

She hung up the telephone and jumped in a cab. Leeza ran upstairs to change. When Amy knocked on the door, Leeza greeted her wearing a flowing silk robe. Amy's breath caught in her throat. *How does she expect me to talk politics when she's dressed like that!*

Leeza threw her arms around Amy and pulled her inside. Amy barely had time to drop her duffel bag by the front door before Leeza dragged her into the study and plopped her down on the couch. "So, tell me all about it! What did you say? What did she say? Are the Americans going to stand with Austria?"

Amy just laughed. "Slow down! I haven't slept in twenty-four hours!" Then she took a deep breath. "I talked to Mrs. Roosevelt and told her about Plan Otto. I also showed her the document Wilhelm gave me. Mrs. Roosevelt took it to the President. He's going to call a conference with England and France. He wants them to stand together for Austria."

Leeza couldn't believe her ears. Suddenly the ramification came crashing into her consciousness. "My God! Then it will soon be over!" she cried. "They will stop him!"

Amy nodded her head. "That's the plan," she grinned. "Soon you'll be playing that violin of yours. And I'll be there to hear it."

"You don't have to wait," Leeza exclaimed as she leaped from the couch. "I can't remember when I last felt like playing for anyone, but I want to play for you now!" Then she took her little Amati out of the case and held it up to her chin. Slowly she drew the bow over the strings and the violin sang to life.

Amy sat watching in amazement as Leeza played for her. The light and buoyant melody filled the room, making Amy feel warm inside. Leeza swayed to the music, gliding gracefully as she danced around the room. Amy felt like she was watching an angel. When the song ended Leeza lowered her violin and placed it back in its case.

Amy was speechless. "What was that?" she whispered in awe.

Leeza smiled and made a deep bow. "Beethoven's *Violin Romance Number 2*. It's my favorite!" When she stood up the tie on her robe slipped open, but she was too excited to notice.

Amy's breath caught in her throat again. Underneath the robe, Leeza was wearing the same black negligee she had seen in Paris. She stood up and walked over to her. "It was beautiful." she whispered. "And so are you." Then she slid her hands under Leeza's robe and around her waist. "Thank you for playing for me."

Leeza blushed. "You are welcome. I love the way that song makes me feel."

"I love the way you make me feel." Then Amy held Leeza's face in one hand and gently kissed her.

Leeza wrapped her arms around Amy and opened her mouth slightly. She felt a warm sensation flood her body and she began to tremble. Amy pulled back from her kiss. Leeza whispered, "Don't stop."

Amy smiled and brushed Leeza's face with her finger tips. "Are you sure?"

Leeza dropped her eyes. "No one has ever kissed me like that," she whispered.

"I have wanted to kiss you like that since the first time I saw you. Do you remember? The Saint Valentine's Day Ball? I fell in love with you that night. I wanted you so much it scared me. That's why I ran away."

Leeza stared into Amy's eyes. "I fell in love with you that night too. But then everything went so wrong. Hitler and the Gestapo. Uncle Karl and the…

"Shhh," Amy whispered, putting her finger to Leeza's lips. "That's all over now. President Roosevelt and

Anthony Eden are going to take care of Hitler. You don't have to worry anymore."

Leeza kissed Amy's finger. "I never dreamed things could be good again. It's been so long." Leeza took Amy's face in her hands. "Thank you."

Amy smiled and hugged her tightly. Then she twirled her around the room and they both began to laugh. Hope and joy filled their hearts. Hope for Germany, hope for Karl, hope for all their lost friends, and most of all, hope for each other. Their joy was insatiable as they held each other.

When they finally stopped twirling and laughing, Leeza gazed into Amy's eyes. She could see Amy's longing. Slowly, she slid her robe off her shoulders. Then she began unbuttoning Amy's blouse.

Amy gently took her hands and pulled them away. "Are you sure?"

Leeza responded by kissing Amy more passionately than she had ever kissed anyone. The news Amy brought had lifted the dark, fearful shadow from Leeza's face. She felt freer, and more in love than she had ever dreamed possible. "I have never been more sure of anyone in my life. I love you, Amy Trevor. Take me upstairs."

# Epilogue

## July 2000

The Pride Parade was in full swing as Kate and Ann made their way through the crowd. That was the first time Kate had seen the pink triangle. She hadn't been out very long and was curious about everything. "What's up with the pink triangle bit?"

"It's our symbol," Ann shouted over the din of the crowd.

"Why's that?" Kate yelled.

"Because of the Nazi persecution during World War II. Gays and lesbians wore the pink triangle in the concentration camps."

A woman in the crowd overheard their conversation. "Not lesbians," she said.

Ann knit her eyebrows in confusion. "What d' ya mean?"

The woman motioned for them to follow her to a booth across the side walk. "Lesbians wore the black triangle. Only gay men wore the pink triangle." Kate looked at all the jewelry in the booth. Almost all of it had some kind of black triangle incorporated into the design in one form or another. "You should know your own history," the big dyke barked. "It's important for us to remember."

While Ann listened to what the woman had to say, Kate looked over the jewelry. There, at the corner of the table she spotted a pendant. It was a white rose with a black ribbon around it, pressed into a triangle. She picked it up. "What's this one mean?"

The big woman smiled. "Ah. That one commemorates the lesbians of the White Rose resistance group. They did a hell of a lot during the war."

"How do you know all this?" Ann asked suspiciously. "I've never heard anything like this."

The big dyke shrugged her shoulders. "Unfortunately, not much has been written about lesbian history. Most of us don't know. But through my art I'm trying to get the word out."

Kate was intrigued with the pendant, and more with the idea of it. "How much is it?"

"Twenty dollars."

Kate looked at Ann. Ann grinned and pulled her wallet out of her back pocket. "So, how do we find out more about the White Rose and the black triangle?" she asked as she paid for the pendant.

"Well, you can always visit the Holocaust Museum, or you can take some classes at the university."

"Classes?" Ann asked. "What classes?"

The big dyke smiled. "You can get a degree in Gay and Lesbian Studies now."

Ann's eyes flew open. "What?"

"Yup. You can major in Queer Theory or Women's Studies, or you can do Gay and Lesbian Studies. Most universities are developing programs right now."

Kate and Ann looked at each other blankly. "Huh, ya learn something new every day."

That day was back in June of 1996. By September of that same year, Kate and Ann had registered at the university. Kate was fascinated with history and wanted to learn all she could about lesbian and gay history in particular. Ann already had her bachelor's degree so she went for her master's in gay and lesbian studies. Unfortunately, their small town university in northern Arizona did not offer much in the way of queer subjects, but that didn't stop them from pursuing the study. Ann registered in the Master's of Liberal Studies program, which allowed her to work on developing a lesbian and gay studies program as her master's thesis. Kate had to follow the traditional curriculum for her undergraduate degree, but was able to take many of the classes Ann had gotten started at the relatively conservative university.

Now that graduation day was finally approaching, Kate had time to sit back and mull over all that she had learned in the last four years. "You know, it's amazing how much our people don't know about their own history," she mentioned to Ann.

"Yeah, and what's even more astonishing is how much has happened since World War II. God, when you think about how far we've come it really makes you think."

"I know what you mean," Kate smiled. "I just wish I had the opportunity to talk to one of those women in the White Rose. I wish I could tell them about the legacy of resistance they passed on, and how much good it has done. Can you imagine what they would have been like at the Stonewall riots back in 1969 when gay men and lesbians began fighting for their civil rights?"

Ann grinned. "They'd have kicked some ass, I'll tell you that much. And they'd be so proud of everything that's happened since Stonewall."

Kate smiled to herself as she ran down the list of changes in her mind. *What would all of the soldiers that were booted out of the Army and Navy think about England's recent decision to allow homosexuals to serve in Britain's Armed Forces? And what about Vermont's legislation to recognize gay and lesbian couples in the same way they recognize straight couples? And just like Berlin in the 20s and 30s, we have our own capital cities now; San Francisco and New York, Rio and Amsterdam.*

Kate sighed as she pinned on her graduation cap. She was thinking about the women of the White Rose. "I wish I could tell all of you about the laws that are changing. Just this year Texas, of all states, repealed its sodomy law. Can you believe it? And you'd be amazed at all the books and videos that are coming out. Even the Holocaust Museum in Washington D.C. has a gay and lesbian section."

Then Kate frowned at a thought that occurred to her. "Unfortunately, not many of our people even know about the museum, let alone go to see it. Not many know that you ever existed, or how hard you fought."

Ann came in their bedroom. "Who are you talking to?"

Kate was a little embarrassed. "Myself."

"Did you have anything interesting to say?" she grinned.

Kate blushed at first, but then she thought about the question. "Yes. As a matter of fact, I have a lot of interesting things to say!"

Ann laughed. "Oh?"

Kate brushed her bangs up under her cap and zipped up her gown. "Let's stop by the florist shop on our way. I want to wear a white rose to graduation." Ann smiled. She knew what Kate was thinking before she said it. "I think it's appropriate. Those women were the reason I started college, and I think they should be there when I get my diploma. We should remember them, and the sacrifices they made."

"Amen!" Ann smiled. "I agree whole heartedly. Let's get two. I'm graduating as well, ya know." Then she handed Kate a fluted glass of champagne.

"What's this?"

"Just a little pre-graduation celebration." Ann raised her glass. "Here's to you and me, and to the women of the White Rose!"

"Here, here!" Kate smiled as she clinked her glass against Ann's. "May they be remembered one day."

# About the Author

Laurie J. Kendall resides in Baltimore, Maryland, with her life long partner Bobbie DeVoll, their family of four legged friends, and her adopted gay father. She holds degrees in History and Women's Studies, and is currently pursuing her Ph. D. in American Studies. As an ethnographer, she specializes in religious culture, as well as gay and lesbian cultures in the United States. As a historian, her interests include mytho-historical cultures and history reconstruction projects.

Printed in the United States
23917LVS00001B/28-54